JUNK

GENERATION

Junk Generation

Richard Vokey

Two Minds Publishing

twomindspublishing.com

junkgen.com

Two Minds Publishing

Published in 2011 by Two Minds Publishing.
1 3 5 7 9 10 8 6 4 2
First Edition
Printed in the United States of America.
Set in Palatino Linotype.

International Standard Book Number (ISBN): 978-0-9810468-0-8

Library and Archives Canada Cataloguing in Publication

Vokey, Richard, 1948-

Junk generation / Richard Vokey.

ISBN 978-0-9810468-0-8

I. Title.

PS8643.O42J85 2010   C813'.6   C2009-906731-5

To Arlene, my wife and partner in life and writing, who has endured my stubborn flaws for a quarter century and has made me a better man.

To our son Dylan, for choosing the better parts of two imperfect parents.

To my late father-in-law Chester Babst, for his honest hard work, generosity, and his love of straight talk and a good book.

What if?

What if 9/11 never happened?

What if the year 2001 was remembered for something completely different?

For a series of man-made catastrophes that may seem unthinkable—like the A-bomb once did—and yet will almost certainly come to pass.
Here is how Volume Two of the history of the human race may begin.

What if . . .

Meet the Kitchen Sink Killer

Kevin Dougherty

Pity Carmine Santini. Hizhonor's troubles have only just begun.

Homicide sources tell me that our soon-to-be-former law-and-order mayor, not to mention you, me, the wife and the kiddies, have a serial killer on our hands.

We're talking Major League Maniac.

Yet it took New York's Finest, budget boosts and all, more than a year to put two and two—and two plus two plus two or three more—together and to figure out, whoops, we've got a problem here.

And a tricky one at that.

"It's like that old game," says my homicide guy. "The one with the butler doing it in the living room with the carving knife. This guy does one with a hammer and the next with a garrote. A stripper in Queens, followed by a gynecologist on the East Side. One month, there's only one. Next week, there are three! We haven't seen the kitchen sink yet, but if we don't get moving, it'll show up. You know, the Ballerina, on the Empire State Building, killed with the Kitchen Sink!"

No suspects yet but we do have a body count. Wait for it . . . four "certains" and . . . SEVENTEEN probables!

Hear that creaking sound? It's the roof about to cave in on the last national GOP star whose name isn't already dirt.

The sky's fallen for every other Republican in the country, of course. All that's left is a few feeble cries beneath the rubble.

The Vanishing Billions boondoggle and President John Mason's pitiful insistence on pleading National Security to save his neck have condemned the GOP to decimation in the 2004 election.

It was stonewall time again at yesterday's White House news conference. Sure, said Mason, I'll reveal where you can find the $72.5 billion secretly diverted from Defense, State, and Health and Welfare budgets. But "only at a time that serves the security interests and fundamental well-being of all of the people of the United States."

Time's running out.

Fewer than fifteen hundred more lying days till elections.

The National Security defense must be employed judiciously. It can be a silver bullet but to take the nation for a ride you first need to have some real fear going—war, an attack on the homeland. Pearl Harbor, for instance. Right now, Americans aren't scared or angry. They're just bored and not in the mood to hold their noses each time the President opens his pie hole. There's a smell about the Mason's claims that just won't go away—like that stuff you pick on your shoe.

Americans like politicians to do their horse stealing out in the open where we can see them. Corporate kickbacks, defense contract junkets, pardon payoffs, that sort of thing. It may be abusive, degrading, dysfunctional, but, hey, that's who we are!

But steal big bucks on the sly and wrap it in the Flag and you insult our intelligence.

Santini's own cornball integrity has inoculated him so far from Masongate but it won't make up for incompetence.

Not on crimes of violence.

If the cops have been inhaling doughnuts for 16 months while a serial killer litters our streets, the mayor's chances of surviving the Mason debacle may be just about done.

Even a mugging might seal the deal.

A tourist, say.

In Times Square.

With the kitchen sink.

Prologue

Near Oneida, New York
August 21, 1973

On a sunny summer afternoon, five children stand silent on an upstate New York hilltop, their play interrupted by an ominous discovery.

At their feet in knee-high grass is an untended grave with a toppled headstone.

Here lies Billy Stricks.
God gave him a Curious Nature
But Billy went Too Far

The dates, 1924–1935, make Billy about their age when he died. This demands pause. Four boys and a pretty girl think about—what? God? Nature? Just how far is "Too Far?"

Tom Daluskov breaks the spell by bouncing his fist off a smaller companion's shoulder bone. Tom is a natural born spell-breaker. One of those boys whose man-like frames and raw strength arrive early and have a mind of their own.

Leon Shivkovski's hand flies to his arm. "Ouch!"

"Shots!" Tom shouts. He lands a punch on Leon's other shoulder. "Shots," in Tom's view, is what separates men from the lesser species known as wimps. Boys take turns. Whoever "gives" first loses. The wimp's humiliation is inversely related to the pain endured before surrender. Tom never loses except occasionally to his best friend, Will Jefferson, who stands to his right.

"Okay, Leon," Tom says, offering his left shoulder. "I owe you two shots and you get three freebies because you're such a wimp "

Tom's insult is interrupted by a short shout and a blur of gangly limbs. Rachel Arianna charges, grabs him by the wrist and launches him off the crest of the hill.

Tom goes willingly and embellishes Rachel's triumph with a tumble. Big Francis Boyd, the fifth in the group, laughs and claps. Tom lies sprawled in the grass for several seconds before trudging back up the slope. His smile is crooked, his eyes bright with feeling. Rachel does that to him these days. When she's being bossy, Francis calls her "Mommy Rachel." But she's no mom to Tom. He's glad she's touched him.

The group comes together and looks west again.

"Why'd they drag us way out here?" Tom asks.

The five turn to gaze down into the nearby hollow. Their parents sprawl on big blankets in the shade of two trees. Lunch is over but there's still plenty of vodka. The talk will be brilliant and increasingly rowdy.

"Some stupid Russian thing," Tom continues. He sneaks a look at Rachel. She looks over and past him from her two-inch height advantage, arms crossed, unimpressed. Tom turns to Will. "Why are they way down there? Americans would have picked the top of the hill."

"Up here?" asks Will. "Up here with Billy Stricks' stinking body?" He snorts at Tom's stupidity. Tall, black, big-handed Will picks up a rock and tosses it in a high arc out into nowhere. "Oneida's thataway," he says.

"So what?" Tom sneers but with no real rancor. It's as if rudeness is bred in their bones.

"They built some kind of perfect society there. In the 19th century," Will says, unfazed. "Or tried, anyway." He launches another rock high into the sky. The others scatter. It comes straight back down.

"Will's been studying again," Leon says dryly when they drift back together. "Pretending he knows as much as the rest of us." In fact, none of them has done much homework ever, including Francis, although, in his case, the reason is his mental challenge rather than exceptional intelligence.

"Their Utopia crashed and burned," Will says with a smile.

"Built with inferior material," jokes Leon. "Human beings."

Francis comes closer to Leon, giggling, as if he's understood what was said. Taller than Rachel and broader than Tom or Will, Francis is the ward of Dr. Sigurd Shivkovski, Leon's father. Francis adores Leon, who treats him with kindness and cruelty in almost equal parts.

Laughter rolls up the hill. Rachel nods towards the adults. "They want to get out of the city," she says. "They're tired of Central Park and Coney Island. They work hard. Seven days and nights a week sometimes. They need rest and a change." The boys listen because Rachel is herself a listener, always in the know. 'Tom's dad and Dr. Shivkovski even talked about buying some farmland."

"Great," Tom grumbles, "I get to become a hick."

"On top of being a nerd, a Russki, and a lab rat." Will's smirk is half-hearted. There is quiet as the five offer silent thanks that this humiliating pet name has not leaked to the outside world. It emerged from the bottom of a vodka bottle many years before when their monstrously uncool parents celebrated the first arrival of the American-born generation.

Rachel finds it cute. In Tom it evokes angry claustrophobia. He and Will belong to the Science-Sucks Club. Will's thinking law. Tom would relish the combat of a courtroom but also wants to be a cop. "Going to paint his mean streak blue," says Leon.

"That's vodka talk," Will says of the farmland dream. "Once a year's plenty. They come out here, get drunk and badmouth Crick and Watson."

The badmouthing comes mostly from Tom's dad, and Leon's. Dr. Mikhail "Mike" Daluskov and Dr. Sigurd Shivkovski have a thing about James Watson and Francis Crick, the codiscovers of DNA, a.k.a. deoxyribonucleic acid, the Double Helix, the Book of Life, the twisting ladder-like material in every living cell that carries the complete instructions for building a living plant, insect or human being.

"Sour grapes," Tom calls it. The old man's shuduv-cuduv talk rankles because Watson's an American. "It's like they're dumping on the U S of A. They're lucky they got in the door."

"They're thankful, Tom," Rachel says gently. "But our parents lived hard lives. Watson and Crick didn't have Stalin to deal with. They could think and do whatever they liked at Cambridge. Your dad and Dr. Shivkovski were banned from genetic study even before the war. It contravened fundamental myths of communism. The Reds went with the voodoo brand."

Tom's heard it all before. The old men supposedly had breakthrough ideas that came at the genetic puzzle from an entirely new direction. Brilliant, at least the way they remember it. But they could do nothing but play with these concepts inside their heads for years while their bodies were starved and beaten half to death in the Gulag. Yes, it was tough, Tom reckons, but he didn't like the winks, nods and snide remarks when the two watched a TV program about the discovery of DNA recently. It looked a lot like envy and, though in Russian that was unintelligible to him, sounded much like the kind of loser talk his father liked to warn him against. The attitude irritates Tom even more now that they are getting rich—thanks to America. The Shivkovski–Daluskov partnership, with the grand name of GreenGene, Inc., has been landing one lucrative research contract after another lately, mostly in agribusiness. With biotechnology's rapid rise, Will's parents, and Rachel's, and most of the other lab-rat moms and dads have also landed good jobs or started their own small firms. Tom says: "Time to stop whining."

Rachel, defender of the faith, looks at him angrily. Her irritation would once have seemed irrelevant, or welcome. Now, it bothers him.

Rachel shouts: "Shots!" Tom's heart turns cold. He thinks she wants to slug it out with him herself. But she has more subtle tortures in mind. Rachel pushes Will forward, and speaks softly into her champion's ear: "I'm rooting for you, Will."

Will shrugs. "Big deal."

Tom's insides are in his throat. Will doesn't get it. He's growing as fast as or faster than Tom but doesn't seem to notice just how much Rachel has changed. Tom's tried to explain it— how she talks differently now; it's almost as if she can hypnotize people. "You know, like when she says, 'he's obsessed with baseball,' or 'it's an obsession of mine.' She's always saying it." Tom can't keep his eyes off her lips, or the rest of her, for that matter. Will gives Tom a look. "You're weirding me out. So she never stops talking. What else is new?"

Tom and Will start trading shots. They've studied the martial arts for more than four years now under Shanghai-born geneticist Dr. Bill Lee, another refugee from communism. They start with a rhythmic, rapid-fire strike-and-block exercise that's a little like patty-cake but with real contact. Soon they are tossing rights of middling strength against each other's left shoulder. Next they're throwing roundhouses like drunken sailors. Their taunts are loud and brave but their eyes begin to dull with pain.

Rachel laughs nervously. "You're both crazy!" she says, cheeks reddening. By provoking Tom's jealousy, she sees she has made this violent game even uglier. She also sees that everyone is in character. Tom is a bully but may grow out of it; Will is all boy but with a gentle inner calm; Leon, smiling and sucking on a blade of grass, is innately cruel and will always be dangerous.

Poor, uncomprehending Francis looks like he's going to cry. "You're both boring," Rachel shouts. "Just playing out a genetic script." When she turns and walks away, the two boys stop and follow, each happy to have been saved the potential embarrassment of giving in.

After a short silence, Rachel stops part way down the hill. She turns and says to Tom: "Look at your mom."

"What about her?"

"She's so beautiful. And so sad."

Tom is wary. He's heard Rachel on this subject—the subject of so-called "survivor guilt." Leon snidely and typically puts it another way: "Survivor guilt with complications." The brilliant young student in molecular biology, an Italian Jew, who in the 1930s was briefly infatuated by German genetic research. She'd gotten out, but never away. "Ancient history," Tom always says. That his mother may be a prisoner of unrelenting unhappiness is one of the things he refuses to think about.

But Rachel wants to talk. She's playing grown-up. "Yes, they do have their ancient histories, don't they? It can be difficult having older parents. You'd think they'd be wiser and more relaxed but, instead, they are totally and absolutely obsessed."

Rachel pauses and bends forward to look at Tom's averted face. "Why are you smiling?" she says a second or two later. Her own smile flickers and her pretty face begins to fall and coarsen. "Are you laughing at me?" Her voice is unsure, even a little fearful.

"Of course not, Rachel. Never. Never!" *Whoa*! Tom thinks. That came out way less cool than he would have liked.

Rachel laughs, surprised, and is immediately sunny again. Her fingers give his arm a "thank-you" touch. Tom feels like it's Christmas morning.

Will catches up. "Who's that?" He contorts himself as he walks, examining the emerging bruise on his left shoulder and pointing with his free hand at two strangers standing with Leon's and Tom's dads.

Farmers, they guess. An old man, small and wiry, and a much younger and bigger bearded adult. Mike Daluskov is moving his extended hand in a wide arc over the landscape. When the big man with the beard replies, he touches his chest and points to the west in the direction of Oneida.

"Mr. Hunter and his son Jason," know-it-all Rachel says

dreamily. "They own some of the land we may buy one day."

Snatches of the conversation float toward the youngsters as they pass. Mike Daluskov is looking down at the big farmer's boots. ". . . Ia Drang Valley . . . Mekong Delta . . . . "So they're telling war stories, Tom thinks. His dad throws his bear arm over Sigurd Shivkovski's shoulders and Tom knows that he's bragging about the two of them at Stalingrad. The younger Hunter is nodding towards his own father, who seems not to be talking. ". . . the Ardennes . . . but threw his boots away." They hear: "Belsen-Belsen . . . "—it's the voice of the older Hunter. "Auschwitz—." That would be Shivkovski.

They catch up with Francis and Leon who has stationed himself at some distance from the adults but close enough for safety. Tom feints towards Leon's shoulder anyway and Leon flinches. "Hit me again, and I'll tell my father," he tells Tom.

"What's your dad going to do? He likes me and, besides, my dad can kick his butt with one hand tied behind his back." Tom wants to please Rachel but his mouth is on autopilot. "You name it, Leon, I've got you beat. Chess, or arm wrestling, IQ—WISC or Stanford-Binet—RBIs, ERA, TDs, KOs, everything from A to Z."

Leon's calm. "When I decide to kick your butt, your swelled head won't even know it's happening."

"The ultimate loser's scorecard. So what will be the point?"

Will laughs. So does Francis but Rachel looks glum.

Leon tries another tack. "Shots won't cut it in science. Let's see who gets the Nobel." Ignoring Tom's shrug, he points back toward their fathers. The farmers are gone now. Mike Daluskov and Sigurd Shivkovski seem to be arguing. Tom's dad, far the bigger man, is circling his slender friend, who looks elegant even in his picnic clothes, gesturing with his big paws. These quarrels have become frequent lately. Work, the kids believe.

Leon grunts in disgust. "Take a good look at him, Tom!" he says. He is nodding at "Mad Mike," as Tom's father is sometimes called, not always with affection. "There's your future. That's you in forty years."

Tom loves his dad but sometimes wishes he could control himself better, be calm, be cool, like Leon's father. "They're both warriors," he heard his mother say to someone on the phone last week. "Mikhail leads from the front; Sigurd's a sniper."

"And that's not your future, Leon," Tom replies. "*You* take a good look. Everything your dad is—smart, tall, good-looking, funny, battle-tested, you know, a winner, a guy with actual friends—you definitely are not."

Leon takes a swing at Tom. Tom twists easily out of the way and at the same time gives the smaller boy a light but insulting smack on the cheek.

"You're pitiful!" Rachel says coldly. "So tough, so mean, so scared to death inside." She raises her chin and continues: "A mass of insecurities and contradictions. A pitiful borsch of biochemical reactions you mistake for deep feelings and wonderful thoughts."

"Rachel's been eavesdropping on the old folks again," Leon sneers. "Sounds like Tom's dad when he's liquored up." Rachel lunges and Leon scurries away. "See!" Rachel's laugh is brittle. She looks from Leon to Francis to Will to Tom, who is alarmed. Rachel never loses it but now her lower lip is quivering. Her voice cracks as she says: "The rest of you are little liars. Hung up inside over just about everything! It's big talk all day and scared sh . . . stiff of the dark at night," Rachel stares at Tom. "Ever wondered why that is?"

"Billy Stricks may know," he replies cockily, worried by her behavior but always ready for a scrap. He motions back towards the hilltop grave. "Let's dig him up and ask." Tom can't stop himself from pushing Rachel's buttons. "Sounds like a job for Science Woman," he says, pressing an index finger to his temple and crossing his eyes. He adds, coldly: "Why don't you take it to the lab, Rachel. Maybe when you're old and fat, you'll have it half figured out."

"If only you knew!" Rachel says, shaking her head. She is weeping softly now. "But you're nothing much more than a pile of junk. Dumb slaves to your genes. A chemical mess of anxieties and obsessions."

Tom and Will exchange a glance at the "O" word but Rachel's tears prevent them from laughing. She runs off towards their parents. Tom's mother stands and waits with open arms and a tender smile, as if she already knows what has happened and understands why.

"Let's get out of here," Tom says to Will. "Hang out a bit with Billy, the kid who went Too Far."

"Must be having her period," Leon shouts up after them.

"See?" Tom says sarcastically. "There's a scientific explanation for everything!"

Part One

1

New York City
May 25, 2001

They were adult lab rats now, grown up, even overgrown in Francis's case, but still an odd couple, even for Times Square. A bit Laurel and Hardy, Leon's father, Sigurd Shivkovski, had once called them. A bit Homer and Mr. Burns, joked Rachel Arianna. which is what Francis, an ardent fan of *The Simpsons*, would have preferred. Today they would be part of an experiment and Times Square would be their lab. As dusk settled on the city, Leon Shivkovski and Francis Boyd fought through the throngs to watch what would happen when nurture, nature, and a set of synthetic circumstances interacted at a predetermined flashpoint.

The subject to be observed was one Matthew Agneau, another lab rat and an unknowing participant in their fun. He should arrive any time now. "We'll bet one hundred dollars on it, Francis," Leon told his perpetually childlike companion when they reached the observation point. He nodded toward the NASDAQ ticker across the street where the closing price of GreenGene Inc., the gigantic Shivkovski-controlled biotech corporation, was completing another triumphal lap. "Looks like it's a risk I can afford."

"Okay," said Francis but he sounded petulant. Although the Shivkovskis had always fed, clothed and cared for him, he had recently learned to count up to 20 and it likely seemed a lot of money when it took you five goes to get through a pile of bills. "Anyway, I can't lose because Matthew is a wimp."

When not at "the Farm," Francis followed Leon everywhere — or at least tried to. At six foot seven and 350 pounds, he was hard to miss. His heft and height were normally accented by a startling thatch of unkempt red hair and a bumpkin's wardrobe of scuffed work boots and cavernous denims. But Leon had put them in disguises this evening and had towed Francis to the barber earlier, where the hulk had watched horrified as his sheared locks were trampled underfoot. His eyebrows were gone too and he wore a large black tuque down over his ears. Instead of his usual farmer's duds, he sported a Fubu 05 T-shirt.

As for Leon, dress and demeanor usually declared him Made in Manhattan. But he had not shaved for a week — likely for the first time in his adult life — and had dressed his slight yet strangely ominous lupine form in jeans, sneakers, a credible fake moustache, and a stained Yankees cap. These were major concessions for the sartorially correct geneticist billionaire, although even the Everyman outfit could not contain his potent aura of self-election and ill will.

"There he is," Francis shouted, pointing across the street.

Leon consulted his wristwatch and nodded approvingly. So like Mathew Agneau to be right on time! And Mathew would rise to the occasion — of that Leon was sure!. "I'll tell you what. Let's make it five hundred! If Matthew hesitates more than five seconds, you win and I will pay you 500 smackers!"

Francis hung his big head. "Why are you making me bet?" he whined. "You know I don't got money."

"Don't *have* money," Leon snapped. "I do not have the money." He regarded the bigger man irritably. He'd made his first mistake by blabbing about this little game to Francis one day when he tailed him around the GreenGene executive suite like a lovesick puppy. His second error was to let him come along. The big lout often wore him down. He just wouldn't take no for an answer! And now Leon would have to babysit and maybe miss some of the fun. "Okay, forget the bet, Francis," he said. "You're tired. Hold on to my sleeve. We'll get a little closer."

Matthew Agneau waited patiently in front of the NASDAQ façade. He had dressed with the same care and precision that distinguished his work as an internal auditor at Citibank. If he looked uncomfortable at all, it was because he'd left his briefcase at the office and felt a little lopsided.

Matthew smiled and nodded once or twice at puzzled passing pedestrians, as if their mere existence was a source of great joy. Matthew had a heart of gold. The one person in his office who could be counted on to go out of his way for folks suffering illness, grief or a run of bad luck. A good banker not only kept good books, he liked to say, but also took good care of friends and community. Matthew had not learned this in a book or a church, either. It was quite simply bred in his bones.

Francis pointed toward a large African-American man approaching Mathew. He tugged at Leon's sleeve. "Is that the bad man? Are you sure Mathew will be okay?"

Leon checked his watch. "No, can't be this guy. It won't happen for another three or four minutes." He turned toward a sudden cacophony of car horns behind them, up near 50th Street There was shouting and angry screams and then the crunch of metal on metal. The police officers in the patrol car parked on tourist duty nearby got out and lumbered toward the sound of the disturbance. A bunch of sailors in town for Fleet Week were headed that way too—much to Leon's relief. An unwelcome intervention by the Navy could wreck his experiment.

Now Leon caught sight of a striking blonde striding down Seventh Avenue towards the NASDAQ building. He checked the time. Early! Too early! But still the woman came, weaving swiftly through the slow-moving crowd. Her beauty was evident even at this distance and the short fire-engine red raincoat and the matching shoes accented her long legs and confident gait.

She passed behind Mathew Agneau who was facing the street as he awaited an old lab-rat acquaintance seeking help and comfort who would never show. No more than 10 seconds later came her shout, both angry and fearful. And then a scream.

People nearby, startled and wide-eyed, scampered instinctively for safety. This opened a clear vista for Leon and Francis. They could see the woman in red playing tug of war with a mugger. Heels dug in, she hung grimly to her large color-matched handbag while a very tall, heavily built African-American man—the man Francis had spotted—pulled angrily at the strap.

"Give it up, lady," he shouted. Then, pulling harder, he roared: "Give it up, BITCH!"

Francis's eyes grew large. Leon glanced at the Times Square police post nearby but it was empty.

The mugger pulled with both hands one more time but the blonde would not let go. He paused, hung his head an instant, and then launched a ferocious overhand right. As if in slow motion, Leon saw the woman's fingers uncurl from the bag. Her finely formed features turned skywards as she fell back in expectation of the blow. Her legs gave way, twisting obscenely at knees and ankles. The black man's fist seemed to catch her on the eye and forehead. The force twisted her body in midair. When she hit the sidewalk, her shoulder absorbed some impact before her head collided with the concrete.

Francis's left hand shot out and fastened on Leon's arm. "That's not how it was supposed to happen!" he gasped.

Stunned as well, Leon took one step off of the curb, as if preparing to cross the street, but stepped back and up again.

The mugger reached meaningfully inside his black bubble jacket. He roared at bystanders to get out of the way and any would-be Galahads seemed adequately deterred. He broke from the circle with a couple of quick shoves at the backs of fleeing New Yorkers and when he looked around to see if anyone was following, Leon had had a good look at him.

This was not the man he had hired. This man was older, bigger, and tougher looking and had a deep pinkish scar as wide as a pencil cleaving his chin.

Up at 50th, the honkfest and the yelling had become louder. They drowned out the initial calls of "Help" and "Police." More thrilled and fascinated now than alarmed, Leon watched the mugger pull up the hood of a sweatshirt and move through a stream of people who knew nothing of what had happened. His escape route seemed absolutely clear.

Except for Matthew Agneau.

Matthew wasn't one to ignore a woman's scream. When he heard the cry, he'd stepped out on to the street to get a better view. He'd seen enough to guess what was happening and now he saw a man leaving the area and shoving a bright red woman's handbag inside his jacket. Behind him, a few agitated witnesses pointed in this man's direction.

"Watch this, Francis," said Leon, focused again. "Here is a man whose altruism is innate. He just can't help himself."

As an auditor, Matthew Agneau had a bit of the sheriff in him and he now placed all of his five feet seven inches and one hundred and forty pounds into the path of the oncoming suspect. When he held up his hand like a pint-sized traffic cop, Leon could not suppress a sneer. The mugger didn't even slow. Leon half hoped that he would run right over the officious little twit rather than dodge him halfback style, as planned. Mathew in the meantime was proving himself human and conceding a tad to instincts older and stronger than the do-good impulse. He had backed off half a step and his traffic cop's pose was withering into a jittery palms-up plea that said, okay, maybe we should just talk about it.

"Oh boy, Matthew," Francis said breathlessly, "Oh boy oh boy oh boy!"

The mugger neither dodged Mathew, nor ran him over, nor punched him as he'd done the woman. Instead, he pulled a ten-inch carving knife from his puffy jacket and plunged it deeply into Matthew Agneau. Matthew's jaw dropped, his eyes widened and his two arms flew apart as he jackknifed at the midriff and received the blade.

Francis made a croaking sound. There were screams and shouting all around.

"What the hell . . . ?" Leon rasped.

After that, no one saw where the assailant went, least of all Francis. All he could see was the great spurt of blood. It was bright, bright red. Redder than the lady's raincoat. Redder than anything Francis had ever seen before.

Matthew Agneau lay unconscious, his head cradled in the lap of an ad executive already wondering why he had become involved. Someone had bundled Matthew's coat to apply pressure to the wound. As the blood pool grew, onlookers enlarged their circle to avoid staining their shoes.

"Thank God," someone shouted as Francis and Leon pushed their way into the inner circle around the wounded man. "There's an ambulance just up the street."

Across the circle, Francis saw the woman who had been mugged! Blood dribbled from one of her nostrils but she looked angry, not frightened. Right beside her, two more people appeared on the inside of the circle. They clung to each other in obvious distress. One, a pretty, well-dressed platinum blonde, was sobbing into a handkerchief. Around the shoulders of her bright red jacket was slung the arm of a tough-looking, powerfully built black man in a baggy jacket and toque.

The man glanced angrily at Leon, as if he knew him. He threw his shoulders back in a sign of vexation. He directed a silent opened-mouth query towards Leon. "*Whathafug. . .?*"

Leon warned him off with a scowl and quickly pulled the weeping Francis out of the circle, leading him back across the street to their pick-up spot. From the corner of his eye, Francis thought he saw the woman who had been mugged watching them. Her eye was already almost swollen shut.

When their car pulled up and the back door popped open, Leon pushed Francis in.

As they drove off, Francis looked out the back window. "You know what, Leon? That girl is just as pretty as Rachel!"

Leon took hold of Francis's earlobe and turned his head back towards the front.

"You know what else, Leon?" Francis continued, ignoring the abuse. "I'm not paying you! All bets are off."

Leon smiled weakly at Francis's use of this idiom.

"Yes, you're right, Francis," he said, patting the big man's trembling hand. "Someone rewrote the script."

2

All eyes were on Dr. Rachel Arianna. For the fifth straight year, her guest introductory lecture to Genetics 101 at Columbia University was packed. Along the back wall and in the doorways and aisles, seniors, graduate students and professors who had crashed the event rubbernecked for a better view. She was a rare creature these days—the scientific celebrity—and usually put on a good show.

Rachel Arianna adored props. And of the many theatrical devices in her bag of tricks, she knew that she herself was the most effective. That's why a Columbia science department honcho had first invited her, half jokingly, ten years back to "show them that genetics and brilliance can be sexy"

Rachel was touching down at the time from two weeks of evanescent celebrity. A month before, she had achieved a landmark breakthrough in plant genetics. It would have escaped all public attention had she not run into a CBS news producer at a Tribeca party. Even in a roomful of models, the Arianna look caught the producer's eye. Rachel had luxuriant chestnut hair, classic high cheekbones, huge amber-flecked brown eyes and plump sensuous lips that served to soften the effect of her intimidating intellect. *60 Minutes* used her to sex up a piece on sperm-bank babies they had languishing in the can. *Dateline* loved her. So did *20/20* and PBS.

Once she'd done Oprah, Rachel had begun to recognize a fatal flaw in public attitudes. People were paranoid about science but perfectly comfortable with the thing that left them so vulnerable to its growing power—appalling ignorance. She tried addressing this contradiction with humor. "What do you think will come first," she asked Oprah, "a genetic cure for cancer or one for fat thighs? And remember, I said *think*, not *hope!*" People giggled but reached for the potato chips rather than a book that might have enlightened them about the fateful role genes played in their lives and would play in the future of their children and of their children's children.

"Stop bitching and do something about it," the Columbia administrator had told her when she complained about it all at a social gathering of lab rats at the Upper East Side apartment of fellow biotech millionaire Leon Shivkovski. "Teach. Put on a show!" "Yes," Leon had added with his trademark smirk, "be yourself—the smart tart. Madonna does Madame Curie."

As the lecture hall quieted, Rachel introduced herself. The audience erupted in cheers and applause. There were loud whoops from the young men jammed into the front rows. An appropriate response, Rachel thought, since the tight cut of her pant suit had been designed precisely for them, although she had observed over the years that for very fundamental evolutionary reasons the merest glance at her adult body's profiles was likely to earn approval, obvious or covert, and instant attention, in one form or another, from most males in the 12–95 age category. A seedy, serious-looking, thatch-topped lad just behind the freshmen yahoos was somewhat less moved. But then he looked a little stoned.

"Nothing wrong with a little enthusiasm," Rachel said softly to restore silence. "It shows we want to be here. And we *do* want to be here. We want to stay here. Forever, if we can. *To be!* This is the goal of all Life. Life with a capital L, of which we humans are just one of myriad ephemeral manifestations. The *not to be* option is a purely human hang-up, a product of human consciousness, which itself, while astonishing, is just one of countless embellishments and peculiarities that have turned up over the past three billion plus years since somewhere in the primordial soup the first cell of Life was ignited."

Rachel paused to take in the beauty of the students before her—the perfectly imperfect end product of a process that had begun in a swamp. "You've come a long way, babies," she told them, "even though it's well established statistically that freshmen classes have a higher than average incidence of genetic mutation."

When the laugher died down, Rachel talked about the soup. Back in 1953, two University of Chicago scientists had tried to recreate that three-billion-year old inanimate broth from which life had sprung somehow by combining methane, ammonia, hydrogen and water. They zapped it with a bolt of ersatz lightning—from a wall socket, possibly. Lo and behold, amino acids! The very chemicals from which, under the direction of human genes, are constructed the proteins that build and operate the people in this room.

"DNA can mean immortality," Rachel declared. "That first

single cell bacteria, that first quickening molecule of life, lives on today in you, you and you. And if you follow the urges that nature so generously bestows upon us, then you will more likely than not pass that ancient descendent on to your children along with all the other good and bad ideas that have been tried out as we evolved." Rachel paused for her by now infamous Genetics 101 lecture not-a-virgin pose and to say "allow me to thank our sensual Mother Nature now for my personal favorite among those urges, which would be the flush of and appetite for love and the *ecstasy* with which it rewards us for doing what is good, right, natural and fun with the opposite sex."

When the howls and yelling had died down at the front, she continued in straight mode. "So we're all sisters and brothers, begat of the same infinitesimal mama-papa in the same primordial goo. But it took a while to work up some stream. First came the Big Gulp. After a billion boring years of single cell existence, a big cell swallowed a smaller cell and, as they say in corporate takeovers, synergy was achieved. Not always a smooth road, of course: in the Canadian Rockies are found 570-million-year-old fossils of many, many life forms that have not survived. Only two hundred million years ago, ninety-six per cent of all the life forms on Earth were wiped out by a huge natural calamity. The dinosaurs got their comeuppance around 65 million years back, making way for domination by mammals and, so far anyway, humans. That's why one famous Japanese geneticist calls evolution the survival of the luckiest. But lucky or not, every twist and turn, every change, everything that been added along the way—including a lot that didn't work – is recorded there in our DNA."

Rachel held up two tiny pieces of bone. "Nothing's erased. Sometimes ancient genes, or even the actual material they expressed—that is, directed the body to create—were recycled for different uses. There's a bone in many fish that supports the gills; when we were fish that bone used to support our gills too. Those fish bones are incredibly similar to these. Our bodies use them now for a different purpose. They vibrate with the ear drum and send signals to the listening centers in our brains."

Rachel liked to pursue one goal from her own agenda in each year's lecture. Last year it had been the need to push back against the religious right's benighting assault on the science of evolution. But today, for deeply personal reasons and based on troubling private knowledge, she felt it was more urgent than ever to take on the left and an area of political correctness she believed to be terribly misguided.

Despite progress, it still remained far too difficult in America and elsewhere to discuss all the implications for life, society, and even for civilization and future generations of genetics and genetic science in full, widely, and out in the open. This was mainly a hangover of the decades-long dark age that had followed the abuse and twisting of genetic knowledge by the Nazis, which had been reinforced by the perverting influence in academia of the other totalitarian ideologists in the Soviet Union. But it was not genetics or the discussion of genetics, however distorted, that had led to the Holocaust and the other great crimes of the first half of the Twentieth Century. It was manipulation and misdirection in some groups of people of universal predictions that were built into the genes of every man, woman and child on earth who lived during that period and in every other time over tens of thousands of years of human history. These included the compulsion toward tribalism, the otherwise beneficial and essential ability to categorize, and dozens of other human traits and predispositions shared by the wrongdoers, the victims, and the bystanders alike. And not talking and knowing about genetics now, and not being able to understand and to demand to be informed and to approve of what genetic science was up to was becoming as dangerous to the well-being of nations and humankind as ignoring the antics of the totalitarians in the Thirties had turned out to be.

So, given that it was her job here anyway, she'd found a new way to stir things up today. It would require a "volunteer." Looking up from her notes, she said: "We now know from DNA that man first rose in Africa, although these days, due to tiny differences in DNA, that is more obvious in some than in others." She scanned the audience silently for a moment before finally gesturing towards the very top of the hall. "Excuse me, Sir," she said. "Yes, you Sir, in the pink shirt, please step down here."

If anyone doubted that Will Jefferson would do virtually anything for Rachel Arianna, here was incontrovertible proof. Will stepped forward from the spot where he'd been planted, did his best *who-me?* imitation and bounded down the steps to the stage.

"The genetic story is a story of oneness and of wonderful

variety at the same time," Rachel said as her fellow lab rat approached her. "There are probably fewer genetic differences between people of what are regarded as different races than there are between two strangers from the same ancestral village in Ireland or Iraq. But while we are all remarkably alike, let's not forget that it's the broad range of little differences that give human relations much of their dynamism and spice."

"You might say *vive les differences*," said Will bending towards the microphone.

"Yes, handsome, I second that emotion," Rachel responded, giving him her campiest up and down and winking at the audience, "and I thank Momma Nature again for these wonderfully exciting urges." Still ogling him, Rachel maneuvered Will with the tip of a finger to where she wanted him on the stage. "Stand back a bit. Chin up. Shoulders back. Wow! Good, that's perfect."

"One of the things we've discovered from DNA analysis," Rachel said when she turned back to her audience, "is that there is far less genetic variety among the billions who live outside of Africa today than among those who remained on that continent and their more recent descendants." Rachel turned back to Will, who watched her with an indulgent smile. "Now, I think we can agree that this gentleman is extremely good looking." She waited for the applause, although it far less enthusiastic than before and tending toward the nervous. "But we will focus today not on his face but on his body. I am willing to bet that his ancestors came from West Africa. And, yes, I know that this is a pretty safe wager, given the historical record. But I am judging by his build."

Rachel sensed politically correct death rays burning into her back but felt she needed to ramp up the umbrage a good deal farther.

"This build is one of my favorites and is indicative of, though not limited to, West African genetic origins." She looked at the audience. "Would you call him chiseled, ladies? Ripped? Buff?" she asked. There were giggles, happy shouts—but also boos. "Low body fat content—it's hot in that part of the world, and has been for most of the past million years. Studies have shown that West African males—and females, for that matter—have a higher fast-twitch muscles content than, let's say, your average German. Power out of the blocks. Their bone structure and the dynamics of their build favor the explosive short run. As a result, a statistically exceptional large number of athletes of West African origin have won gold in the various sprint events at recent Olympics. But little or nothing in long distance."

"Hey, stop that talk!" someone shouted. "That's racism!"

"As it happens," Rachel continued blithely, "many of the long-distance titles have gone to men probably related to a single Northeast African tribe—the Kalenjin. Just as men from a wide stretch of Eurasia, with their thick powerful torsos and short limbs, often dominate the lower weightlifting golds. And the Japanese sumo champions are in a panic because, no matter how much they work and eat, Samoan-Americans just seem to get bigger than they can. And the world's strongest man contests often seem dominated by huge blonde northern European men." She approached Will. "Those men have muscles with marbleized fat—evolution's answer to long millennia of cold winters" She took hold with both hands of one of Will's biceps. "But I prefer the look—and the feel—of West Africa."

An African-African student leapt to her feet. "I'm very uncomfortable with this," she said in a clear firm voice. "This has to stop."

Rachel looked up: "May I ask why?"

"You are objectifying that man, treating him like a piece of meat, a sex toy, a slave on an auction block."

"Excuse me," Rachel said softly, "but while I may have suggested a degree of sexual interest I believe there is nothing in my words or actions that indicates I regard this man as chattel."

"Don't you get it, lady? *He's black*!" The student was seething. "If you want to make a point about genetics and physique and whatever, you darn well pick someone else!"

"So, we establish that the problem is that he is black," Rachel said pleasantly. "I will assume that the objection, beyond the obvious poor taste and impropriety of some of my script here today, is not about miscegenation. Instead I have entered treacherous territory by simply discussing the role of genetics in human attributes while using an ostensible member of a long down-trodden minority group as an example of how muscle and bone structure can indicate a genetic pathway through time and space."

"You are a racist and a bigot!" someone shouted through the silence from the back.

Rachel smiled. "Let's think about it for a moment. If I had

chosen one of the young pink-skinned hunks from the front rows here as an example instead, would we be having this conversation? It's not me, it's you who are seeing black, so to speak. It is not me, it is the young woman who spoke up who has reacted to the powerful subconscious cultural taboo against discussing genetics within a million miles of anyone representative of a group that has been persecuted in the past on the false basis of inferiority or unacceptable fundamental difference. I never even mentioned the infinitesimal divergence in DNA that makes one person's skin pigmentation better suited to greater exposure to the sun than another's. You *saw black* and that made my lifelong friend Will Jefferson here *nothing more* to you in the moment. The furor would also have occurred happened had I asked a Jewish student to come up and we had discussed the possible mish-mash of evolutionary and cultural reasons that the average IQ scores for Jews are slightly higher than the average for other ethnic groups. Yet had my volunteer been Chinese or Korean and we'd debated whether higher math scores were completely cultural outcomes or partly genetic, nary an eyebrow would have been raised. No relevant traumatic historic context to muddy the waters of what should be regarded as purely healthy scientific inquiry."

Will stepped forward and took hold of a mike. "Ladies and gentlemen, I apologize for my part in this subterfuge but I agree with Dr. Arianna that it does illustrate an important point. I have no doubt that some of you experienced a pang of anxiety today. You saw an outspoken geneticist on the stage and a man with black skin, which equated in your minds to a toxic mixing of genetics and race, which to you must alway leads to racist claims related to lower test scores or higher crime statistics." He smiled at Rachel. "You also saw an over-the-top attempt to focus attention on my physical type and build, which I am afraid led to thinking in some of you that may have been bigoted against my racial group and against the genetic science. You thought, 'she's saying that African-Americans are bigger and strong than other men,' which she wasn't, 'so the next thing she's going to say is that they aren't as smart,' which she wasn't and didn't."

Rachel moved up beside him. "I think Mr. Jefferson is saying that he forgives you for stereotyping him and for confusing all the hateful twisting and perversion of genetic information with the honorable and absolutely essential science of genetics itself. By the way, if you wish to avail of the fruits of Will's stratospheric IQ and summa cum laude performance at Yale law, you may do so for a thousand dollars an hour."

Will moved back and took a seat as Rachel continued. "I too apologize for deliberately provoking you today." She bowed in the direction of the young woman who had complained. "And I applaud the person who stood up and spoke out. It's groupthink, timidity, toeing the line and the great silences that have made much of history's worst damage possible. Which is why I appeal to you to get interested, get smart, and when the need is there, get angry! We worry about what people are doing to our air and our atmosphere. We worry about what's happening to our water and our seas and our forests and our food. And yet we don't know a thing or seem to care a whit about what may be happening to the very blueprints and building blocks of every single living thing on the planet."

Rachel reached out for an imaginary doorknob, turned it and stepped up and through an imaginary portal on the stage. "We are passing through a previously impassable barrier into the new world of the Genetic Age. Man can now reach in and manipulate the life code of any plant, animal, bacteria or virus on earth. We are entering a world of endless possibilities. It is exciting—but it is dangerous. That is why we cannot *not* talk about genetics, no matter how painful, divisive, open to misinterpretation and misuse such discussions become. It is simply not an option. And that is why you, the citizens and future leaders of this country and this world, must not only learn the basics of genetics but learn to pay attention to what is happening in that arena and make sure it is all in the open for the rest of your lives."

Rachel preferred never to end on a heavy note. So she was thankful when the slightly disheveled youth who'd looked stoned earlier rose hesitantly to his feet and raised his hand.

"Aha!" said Rachel. "What do we have here? Will you identify yourself please?"

"My name's Wally Anderson," the man said rather more confidently than Rachel had expected. "I have a question."

"Hmmm." She observed him carefully for a moment, raising an eyebrow. "See what I mean about freshmen classes?" When the laughter subsided, she invited Wally with a nod to speak.

The firm voice again. "I've enjoyed the lecture but there are important matters you've ignored. I'd like to know your position on Frankenfoods, you know, genetically modified foods."

"I take them sitting down, Mr. Anderson." Rachel replied, crossing her arms. "With my mouth open, generally, at least to start with. I let nature and Miss Manners be my guide." After some further laughter, she continued: "It's a topic that your classes will discuss. Once you've spent a few months covering the bare basics. A little knowledge is said to be dangerous but in my experience it beats the heck out of dumb slug ignorance."

Wally Anderson's smile was his best feature. "Do you think it's helpful to insult slugs?" he asked without a hint of malice or humor. "A slug is God's creature. God's creatures, or, if you will, Mother Nature's, are becoming extinct at a vastly greater rate than ever before. Big corporations are playing genetic roulette with the genes of plants and animals. Doing exactly what you just warned against. Remember what E=mc^2 brought us? Well, get ready for the genetic bomb. We are being fed some of these Frankenfoods, at incalculable risk. Corporations may accidentally produce a super weed that destroys all of our food crops. Or a synthetic version of the Black Death."

Rachel's reply was serious. "You are right to be concerned, Mr. Anderson. There is indeed the possibility that GMOs — genetically modified organisms — in plants and animals will do us and the environment damage. It's our job to act responsibly. Start by reading this course and taking another one. You will also learn, of course, that besides raising the specter of accidental famine or pandemic, the Genetic Age will likely bring cures for some of our most terrible diseases. A new age with endless possibilities, and not all of them good. It's enough to make your brain hurt."

Rachel raised her gaze to the rest of the audience. Wally seemed about to speak again but sat down instead.

"Mr. Anderson here has brought God into the picture," Rachel continued. "Whatever your beliefs, however, there's little doubt that genetic research will one day lead us into the human soul and that day may come sooner than we think. Until then, your assignment is to read chapter one. And to be ready for the next class, when you will face a real professor."

With her childhood friend and lecture prop Will Jefferson at her side, Rachel walked off the stage.

3

A calf's hide executive chair in the Manhattan headquarters of a giant multinational biotech corporation was a peculiar place in which to find a rumpled, unemployed tree hugger like Wally Anderson—especially at 3:35 in the morning. But Wally got around.

He didn't care who loved him or who hated him or who, like the hot Columbia lecturer today, had a laugh at his expense. The task of saving the world for future generations demanded long hours and a thick skin.

Without great forests to maintain Earth's ecological balance, Wally believed, we would all gradually die of asphyxiation. That's if we didn't starve to death first. And Wally wasn't going without a fight. He had protested old growth logging in the Northwest by stringing himself from douglas fir branches 100 feet off the ground. To protest their nuclear power plants, he had buzzed aircraft carriers like the USS Enterprise in rubber protest dinghies.

Wally was a *what-if* kind of guy. He believed in pre-emptive action. For example, what if we'd simply stopped science from splitting the atom? No Chernobyl. No Hiroshima or Nagasaki. Problem solved.

Education through political action was another pet cause to which he had donated much time and energy. He'd been in Britain and France last month, seeing the sights and tossing bricks through fast food restaurant windows. Nothing personal, but when greedy corporations started poisoning humankind with genetically altered snacks, folks needed to know.

The enemy in this case was Frankenfoods. Named after Frankenstein, Mary Shelley's fictional physician, who'd cobbled a human from assorted graveyard leavings and kick-started his creature with electricity (the much-feared little understood marvel of Ms. Shelley's age.) But Frankenstein was a harmless clown compared with the monsters that mad and greedy lunatic geneticists would soon loose upon the earth. They were using viruses to mess with animal and human DNA. They were rolling the dice with humankind's future. Next thing it would be, like, *whoops! The Black Death, Final Episode!* And every city, town and village from Nanking to Newark would be left a howling wilderness.

This is why Wally now sat before a computer screen in GreenGene Corp.'s inner sanctum. He was striking at the enemy's heart. He'd felt this thrill only once before. In a tiny Greenpeace boat on a heaving sea, he'd seen a humpback whale and heard its mournful call. A different ocean had engulfed him in that moment. He'd become an infinitesimal part of this majestic yet vulnerable life force, ready to serve all things great and small. A Knight of Nature upon whose valor the survival of the kingdom might depend.

Wally checked his watch. It had taken some doing but his trap was set. Device installed and double-checked; trigger set. The Movement had frequently benefited from the fact that in Wally's handy family you never called a plumber, you borrowed a wrench.

Yet Wally was reluctant to leave. Down on the New York streets, he'd be just another night bird, a raw-boned geek with a thick mat of Viking-straw hair. Up here, snug in the enemy's throne and clacking through the enemy's vault, he was helping to save the world.

Wally maneuvered the mouse and clicked on a folder called "Labyrinth." He reached into his pocket for the remnants of a joint he'd used to warm up for the break-in.

A long index appeared on the screen. He scanned the list as he lit his smoke. He clicked the top folder, titled "Minotaur," and was greeted with the request for a password.

Wally breathed deeply and in quick succession tried every genetic term he could think of. Followed by names from the ancient Cretan myth. Next came the genetics Pantheon—the Cricks, Watsons etc., the groundbreakers whose John Hancock might fulfill a DNA-splicer's need for a readily remembered code. None worked.

Why not Mendel? he thought, the Austrian monk who'd sorted out the laws of hereditary genetics while breeding peas in the monastery garden.

Mendel. Gregormendel. Greenpeas. Mendel's peas. Mendel's garden. No, no, no, no and no.

Wally had no expectation of stumbling on a password. But he was feeling a buzz and his fingers just kept moving: Peagarden. Genegarden. Gregor'sgarden. Gardenofeden, thesecretgarden,

Mendel'ssecretgarden.

Wally typed and looked around the darkened room at the same time. Maybe I should go, he thought. Grass always made him paranoid. Gregorssecretgarden. As he hit the Enter key, he thought he heard a movement in the deep shadows beyond the plate glass doors. His heart jumped. But when he peered harder, holding his breath and straining his eyes, there was nothing there.

Now came the surprise. The Minotaur file was open. The subfolders were simply titled "Level One," "Level Two," etc.—up to "Level Thirteen."

Wally flicked the burning ash off the joint and ground it into the carpet. There could be some real dirt here!

Level One opened its myriad subdirectories. Wally hacked in and out of them randomly. Mostly indecipherable text files, some illustrated by equally complex schematic drawings of DNA and RNA regions. This was an unexpected challenge. He gave his head a shake, trying to clear his mind.

Wally clicked his way into a file titled "Candidates," and into a subdirectory named "Retired." He hit one of several hundred numbered files in the directory. On the screen appeared a picture of a mouse. It seemed ordinary enough, although the photo was grainy and had likely been taken with film many years earlier and scanned some time later. Below the picture were a few paragraphs of genetic gobbledygook. Wally supposed that GreenGene was using the mice in testing for new cancer and heart disease therapies, although, with mice genes now showing up in tomatoes, you could never really be sure what the biotech giant was up to.

After rolling down through another few hundred six-digit-number files, he double-clicked again. Another mouse. More gibberish. There were two photos this time. Mug shots, really. Frontals and profiles. Why was that? he wondered. A mouse was a mouse was a mouse.

Wally sat bolt upright. Had he heard something? The scuffing of a shoe. His ears were ringing from the weed. He peered for a long time at the empty desks and the darkened offices beyond. Just in case, he put his remote-control trigger on the floor between his legs and pushed it gently under the desk. It was hidden but he could push the button with his foot.

The bud had been a huge mistake. Wally felt sloppy. Without noticing, he had scrolled down through pages and pages of file names. He tried a final random click.

Yet another lab rodent. A centerfold candidate, it seemed. Twelve pictures, many of them close-ups! It looked bigger than your average mouse. Still, oversized transgenic mice—mice that had been modified with a human growth hormone gene—were old hat (as, for instance, were transgenic Coho salmon, which grew to up to 37 times the size of their natural siblings.) It was the larger head, Wally began to realize, that set this specimen apart. The distinctly more prominent skull had pushed the cute pink ears down the side of the head.

Wally's finger wavered above the mouse button, but something held him back.

He leaned towards the screen, his nose just inches from a close-in shot. The surge of emotion was deep and visceral. It was that oceanic feeling again, a sensation that often seized him when he felt one with the world. He looked hard and long, trying to focus. Finally, it struck him.

It was the eye.

He'd never looked into the eye of a mouse before. And now he realized he'd seen that look before. Back in his Save-the-Whales days.

They had pulled their speedboat alongside a great humpback whale. It had surfaced. For an instant, Wally and the wise mammoth were eye to eye. It was the look of the Ages—and of an incredible knowing and intelligence.

Wally backtracked and clicked on "Level Three," planning to view a sampling of everything GreenGene was up to. This was getting interesting. Who could tell? Maybe this mouse had suffered deformities from ingesting GreenGene's genetically altered low-fat potato chips. Or some other kind of Frankenfoods.

He roared down the list and clicked on page 47.

The screen showed what appeared to be the face of a monkey. A dead monkey, Wally guessed, its eyes rolled back up into its oddly shaped head and its mouth seized by a grisly rictus. The brow seemed less pronounced . . . .

The overhead office light switched on.

Wally knew what was coming.

Behind him, he heard a man's yell, angry and frightened at the same time: "Freeze. Put your hands on your head." Now another man, a young security guard, moved into view with an automatic aimed at Wally's face. "Slowly. Lift the hands slowly," he said, "or I'll blow your head off."

"Relax man," Wally drawled. "I'm not the one who's dangerous. It's your boss, GreenGene, that's going to wipe out mankind."

"Sure," said a voice off the side. "The boys at Rikers will want to hear all about it."

Wally raised his hands with deliberate care, entwined his fingers behind his head, and stretched.

It took only a moment for his foot to locate the trigger box beneath the desk.

Now Wally saw a beefy middle-aged NYPD cop having a close look at the stepladder he had left by the rear emergency exit. Wally had intended to return it to the janitor's storeroom on the way out.

"What have you been up to here, son?" the cop asked. "Anything you want to tell us about?" He spoke into his radio.

With their suspicions aroused, Wally figured, the cops would carry out a thorough search, at the very least. More than likely, they would also bring in the bomb squad.

That settled it. He'd sacrifice a lot of the impact if the device was activated now, but it was better than aborting altogether.

"Smells like someone's been genetically altering weed," the second security guard said with a smile.

Wally now wore his own small grin. He looked at his three captors one by one. "Back in the Fifties," he said, "they taught the kids at school what to do in the event of a nuclear attack. You bend over, put your head between your knees, and kiss your ass goodbye."

"Gee, we learned a different saying in the Marines," said the guard with the gun. He sneered at Wally. "Nuke the whales."

Wally's foot pressed the button.

The fire sprinklers whirled and spat. It was amazing to Wally just how much liquid they could dispense. For a few seconds the system pumped water, eliciting angry shouts and cursing. The viscous blood-red liquid Wally had put pumped into the system quickly followed and produced even greater excitement.

Wally heard furniture crashing behind him. There were more cops and security guards in the room and they were all scrambling to escape the deluge. Only the dutiful guard who was covering from the front didn't move. Soon his hair, face and uniform were stained a deep red. Wally licked at the liquid streaming down his own face and was pleased that it retained the sweetish, slightly metallic taste of blood.

Now the paunchy police officer made an appearance, looking like he'd been dipped into an oversized bottle of tomato sauce. "What the hell is this?" he roared. The cop charged forward, ripped Wally's hands off his head, and locked his wrists into cuffs. Almost on cue, the sprinklers shut off.

The office loudspeaker went into action. The voice was Wally's.

"Ladies and gentlemen," the announcement said. "Without your consent and/or prior knowledge or adequate warning, you have been exposed to a genetically modified organism."

All faces turned to the nearest speaker.

"There is no use wiping or washing the red liquid off. It has done its work already. You have been poisoned! Through your skin this liquid has introduced a retrovirus into your blood stream. It carries several newly manufactured genes, which, even as I speak, are burrowing into your cells and your DNA. It is likely that you yourselves will undergo no noticeable change in your lifetimes. Of course, I can no more promise the certainty of that than GreenGene can realistically pledge not to pollute the Book of Life or, indeed, the very Tree of Life, in some unforeseen but nonetheless catastrophic way.

"Be warned. The DNA changes that are even now occurring in your body will be passed on to any children you may have from this date, and through them, the mutations, and whatever strange effects they produce, will endure for generation after generation until your individual line comes to an end, or until the end of human history.

"We thought it only fair that those who through negligence, apathy and willful ignorance support the evil work of genetic experimentation should be among the first to suffer the consequences."

For a full ten seconds after Wally's speech ended, the room was silent. The middle-aged cop looked down at Wally before glancing at his own red-soaked hands and clothing.

"Too late, you dirty terrorist," he said with a smirk. "My kids are all grown up."

"Right," Wally replied politely, always on the lookout for a convert. "But what do you know about the food they eat?"

4

You would never think it, Jimmy Regan liked to tell his buddies, but in New York City the weirdoes even hang out at the hardware store. Jimmy had been tossing them out of his place in the Bronx for years. Weirdoes walking in off the street in a doped-up funk of one kind or another. They seemed to get a kick out of staggering around shitfaced, mumbling at the towering shelves of nuts and bolts. The worst of them were also looking to rip off a good Makika drill to pay for their next buy. Then Jimmy would be out a couple of hundred bucks.

The guy Jimmy had spotted this day was weird too but in a different way. Back in the plumbing section but no plumber, that's for sure. Dressed better than the usual streetlife in the neighborhood but again kind of weirdly too. A blue dress shirt, nice plain brown tie up top but matched with rumpled work jeans and a pair of Army boots. Blond hair but Jimmy was thinking it must be dyed or a wig. The guy's eyebrows were black over a youngish, good-looking face with a fairly tan coloring but a German or Slav face, not Mediterranean. Built, but more like an athlete than a tradesman.

Jimmy watched the new weird kind of weirdo from the end of the aisle for a moment before moving quietly up on him from behind.

"What's this for?" the guy said without even looking round. Jimmy was still six feet away and this spooked him for a second. But he couldn't let these creeps have the run of his store. You had to stand up for yourself. He would rather take a sledgehammer to someone's knees than hide behind the counter and hope for the best. So let whatever had to happen happen.

Jimmy kept coming, took the little plastic packet the guy was holding from his hand, and put on his best snarl.

"You buying this?"

"What is it for?" the guy, who's maybe 35, asks, a little bit like a kid who expects the world to be explained to him on demand. The dark eyes are as clear as a kid's too. Kind of unlived in but none of the I'm-empty-fill-me-up look of the crackheads who often spilled in through Jimmy's door like wind-blown garbage. Could be the guy was a little slow. Yet no, it wasn't that either.

So Jimmy checked out the package. A PVC cable saw, which was not your usual saw but maybe eighteen inches of thin stainless steel cable with a loop at each end covered with rubber to protect the fingers when you put them through to hold it. Really just a wire with little handles. The wire would be hot when you finished.

"Two twenty five," Jimmy said, adding a 50-cent consulting fee. "See that drawing?" He held the package up in front of the weird guy's face. The sketch showed the wire with two fingers through the loops thrown over the top of an upright drainpipe and already cutting two-thirds of the way through. "The wire will be hot when you finish. Just put it round the pipe and slide the wire back and forth."

"It cuts steel?"

"No! It's for PVC, or ABS—plastic stuff." Jimmy held the tool up and away from the dopey yet undoped guy like maybe he was too stupid to be allowed to buy the thing. "Listen, I'm willing to sell you what we got around here but this ain't no Home Depot. I'm not going to hold your hand or tell you how to use a wrench or wipe your . . . you know, that kinda stuff."

"Why not?"

Someone else Jimmy might have given the bum's rush. But this guy was big and powerful. And his eyes were kinda innocent. Another kid's question.

"Well, there's the time it takes," Jimmy began, more patiently, but with no one else in the store right now that line didn't work so well. He tried another tack. "I tell you how to do something and I take work away from real plumbers—my bread and butter. I start running a plumbing kindergarten here and they're gonna take their business elsewhere. Same with real carpenters and real electricians. Besides I also lose all my friends."

Jimmy made a *got-it?* gesture with his two hands and crooked his head.

The clear-eyed gooney guy seemed to think about it for a minute.

"So what's your—?" Jimmy was intending to ask if this guy's mammoth two bucks and change purchase was indeed going through when the goof interrupted.

"I don't think you should be driving the do-it-yourselfers

away." Very serious now, very grownup. "And you don't have to worry about your plumber friends either."

"Oh yeah," said Jimmy dryly. "Why don't you tell me about it? Anyway, I got all day."

"There must be a lot of plumbing projects that don't get done because the plumbers are too expensive. That's business that your friends the plumbers won't get anyway. But if a do-it-yourselfer learns how to put in a new sink or change a tap or a kitchen faucet, he can probably do that and you end up selling material you never would have sold."

"What are you, one of those marketers or economists or something?"

"No, I'm nothing like that." The guy just kept on going, hardly taking a breath, like he had to get it all out at once. "Do-it-yourselfers make mistakes. They don't measure twice, cut once. They waste a lot of material. That's good business for you. More volume."

"Money isn't everything," Jimmy said. Business was dead this morning and he had to admit this guy's thinking was as clear as his gaze in some ways.

"Sometimes do-it-yourselfers make mistakes too big to fix. Or they do it wrong. They mess it up, which means they have to call a professional. Maybe one of your plumber friends." In one quick darting motion, while he spoke, the guy snatched the cable saw bag lightly from Jimmy's hands and hung it back on a display hook with the others.

"You're not taking that?" Jimmy asked softly. He'd been startled by the speed and deftness of the move. The weird guy was full of surprises.

"I don't need it right now." He walked toward the front of the store, checking out the shelves. He stopped at the paint-stained front counter and looked at his watch. "I don't know when I'll be around here again."

"Oh, you some sort of salesman, or something," Jimmy asked, a little curious now. "Around the city?"

"No." Blunt, no explanation, just on to more gooney talk. "If I do buy it some time, I promise you I will use the PVC cable saw not for plumbing. So your friends don't have to worry about losing business."

"Whatever you say, pal," Jimmy said, thinking *gimme a break!* "Kind of you, I'm sure."

But something about the looney-toon still made Jimmy a little nervous. Maybe a little gesture was in order in case he was dangerous. Jimmy moved behind the counter and began rummaging in a messy drawer for something he'd just remembered. But when he looked up, the guy was gone. So he pulled up his tall stool and began looking round the store, thinking.

About a minute later, the strange guy poked his head back in the door. "Is what I just told you, to help your business, like a good deed, do you think?" he asked.

"You bet, pal," Jimmy said, getting to his feet quickly and opening the drawer.

"Good, because today is a good-deed day and this is a good-deed district."

"Whatever," thought Jimmy, rummaging through the rejects and returns in the drawer again. Must be some church thing or one of those radio station contests, he thought. "Here," Jimmy said loudly, finding what he was looking for. "A small reward for your good deed. It's only been used once."

The quick hands again. The super weird gooney guy took hold of the used PVC cable saw, fit his fingers through the loops, and snapped to straighten the wire. "Thank you," he said with the crystal-clear thousand-yard stare. Jimmy thought he could feel the cold burn through his face and straight out the back of his skull. The eyes held Jimmy's for a while this time but still going right through like he was looking at Jimmy's past, or his future. "I promise I will not use it for plumbing."

Jimmy gave him the *whatever* wave again and turned and pointed to a large patch of wall bare except for Miss Nuts and Bolts December from a torn 2000 calendar.

"Whadya think?" he asked the goof. "I'll put a big sign up there, saying: "Ask Jimmy . . . ?"

But when he looked back for an answer, the weirdo was gone.

5

Oneida, New York

Carrie Hemmingford had just finished explaining the James Fenmore Cooper connection to the term Leatherstocking Country to a stout German couple when she spotted three of her favorite people in all of Oneida County. Over by the $24.95 o.b.o wrought-iron hat rack, the Hunters—Dwight and his son Jason—looked on patiently while Jason's wife, the lovely Chelsea Hunter, fussed over an only slightly battered lampshade that might prove an attractive accent to their parlor on a farm about six miles west of Route 12B.

"Excuse me," Carrie told her guests. "I sense a sale."

Saturday morning yard sales were chaotic and Carrie had to run back and forth constantly between prospective customers on the lawn near the outbuilding and guests coming down for the 7–11 am farmer's breakfast in her Utopia B&B dining room. She always met the challenge, however, and still managed to keep up with all the new gossip—the little there was, at least, of which she was not the original source.

"So, how are the neighbors?" Carrie asked Jason Hunter when Chelsea, who'd been a real hippie back in the Sixties, wandered off to check for new items in this week's pickings.

"No more devil worship, as close as I can tell," Jason replied. "No doubt the orgies continue. But behind closed doors."

He was joking, of course, because the Hunters' neighbors had ceased to be good grist for Carrie's mill many years ago. Over the past three decades, they had erected a sprawling nationally respected institution for research and the care of orphans and ill and mentally challenged children on four abandoned farms purchased from the Oneida National Bank. There had been missteps, however, especially at the start.

No one could properly complain about the design. Jason himself said it should have won an architectural award. From a distance, the scattered old red brick edifices and traditional farm-like outbuildings could be easily mistaken for any number of the 18th and 19th Century industrial towns that helped give Leatherstocking country its charm. In fact, the main building bore a passing resemblance to The Mansion, the house around which the historic Christian Perfectionist community had been founded in Oneida back in 1848 by the charismatic utopian John Humphrey Noyes.

"Reminds you of Disney, doesn't it?" Jason would say back then. "But I guess we can't complain. People show up in Oneida all the time to build heaven on earth. Must be a big underground nut magnet in one of the caves around here."

While the Noyes' utopian followers ordered their spiritual and physical worlds as a communal people living and working in one large, extended family, however, the Oneida Foundation for Child and Human Care and Development was a mite standoffish. The institute wanted to be left alone so much that it kept buying out its neighbors. The Hunters were the only ones who resisted the stream of fast-talking New York City lawyers who'd been knocking at farmers' doors with fat checkbooks for many years. The Hunters weren't going anywhere. Old Dwight had left the farm only once for any stretch of time—long enough to win the Silver Star in France and Germany during the Second World War. Jason's own Silver Star, earned in Vietnam, kept him away no more than three years. Pressure, moreover, was unlikely to put folks like the Hunters in a cooperative frame of mind.

"Still after you to sell?" Carrie asked Jason now.

"Pretty well gave up after we did the road deal," he said. By paying the ludicrously enormous sum the Hunters demanded for a small parcel required for its expanding road system about 15 years back, the Institute had ensured that the family would never need to farm again—or sell. This was the cause of great local hilarity. Dwight started calling his dairy cows "decoration."

Jason's and Dwight's stubbornness had been rooted in what they considered un-neighborly conduct. Instead of hiring locally for its construction, the Foundation had brought in outside workers for all but the roadwork and a bit of landscaping. Jason was a part-time carpenter himself at the time and there was always a local need for extra jobs and plenty of hard working skilled people to fill them.

Ignoring this was an affront yet the practice had continued once the Institute opened. Not only doctors and researchers but even nurses, orderlies and teachers were brought in from afar.

One of the extremely able community liaison types the Foundation kept on hand to soothe Leatherstocking tempers told local councils that only specialists could handle the sensitive cutting edge work the Institute had undertaken. The intensity of the care and research demands also required that the staff live on site, rather than in the surrounding towns and villages. A lot of businesses loved the Institute, of course. It was one of the biggest and most dependable customers in the Oneida and Utica regions. Jason guessed that the Institute played good citizen in other ways too—like when the local pols put their hands out.

Jason himself was as neighborly as the Foundation would let him be. He'd been curious from the start about the construction methods. They had produced enormous amounts of fill, for instance, far more than normal excavation would generate. To a Vietnam vet that signaled extensive underground diggings—not only gigantic basements but also other subterranean spaces and perhaps tunnels between buildings to protect the children from the central New York State winters. The huge mounds of soil and rock were a feature of all subsequent building programs as well, and the Institute steadily expanded.

But he never spied on the interlopers. He was no Carrie Hemmingford. And so he had been irritated by some terraforming early on in the project. One hill had been greatly heightened simply to obstruct the view of the new community's central sector from the Hunters' hilltop home. That was as good as calling him nosy. The Foundation flacks insisted that the landscaping was purely aesthetic; an attempt to touch up the institution's natural profile as seen from Route 12, though that was a heck of a distance away.

On the plus side, Jason, Chelsea and his father had always enjoyed the sight, albeit from afar, of several hundred children—seemingly quite healthy and normal—playing happily in the fields when the weather was good.

"No point belaboring things, is there, Carrie?" Jason said as Chelsea returned, lampshade in hand. "No one's perfect, though we do tend to work harder at it here in Oneida. And look at the way the Foundation protects the environment. Special run-off controls. All their sewerage treated on site. Every furnace stack, every roof vent fitted with an emission device. Doing good work too. It's not like the casino or the track over at Vernon Downs, where men and women ruin their lives and those of their families too. Taking care of children who are challenged, or whatever. Even those little infants they fly in on the chopper every once in a while."

Jason's eyes gave nothing away but a small smile formed above the lantern jaw. "How can you complain about that?"

Carrie shrugged, and straightened her colonial lace cap. She had always wondered whether Jason's "thing" with the Foundation—his once oft-expressed and still barely hidden discomfort and distrust—did not really have something to do with his father's mental problems.

The first signs that something was seriously wrong with Dwight had come after the Institute opened. Of course, Dwight had never been quite right since his time in the service. Apt to drift out of conversations, spend too much time alone. "He had a hard war," his son often said. Jason would talk about some place called Belsen-Belsen that his father had helped liberate, one of those Nazi concentration camps Carrie knew from TV movies would have been horrible to behold. Still, his father's serious descent—and, in effect, the end of normal happiness in the Hunter family—had begun only a few years after the Foundation's arrival and had accelerated as the Institute grew. Subconsciously, it would have been easy for Jason to seek a link between his dad's dementia and the strange neighbors and to tend to blame them for the family's suffering.

"How's your father these days," Carrie asked gently. She'd always had a soft spot for the Hunters, especially Jason, though she'd not posed much competition to flower child Chelsea.

"Enjoying his rocking chair," replied Jason stolidly.

"No worse than normal," Chelsea added brightly as she walked up. They all cast a compassionate glance at the old man who had wandered over to inspect a wooden wheel barrel planter. "He's still for the longest times. Whole days, in fact. And then the poor man gets down to that awful whimpering of his, and there's no stopping or helping him."

Neither woman looked at Jason for a moment. To see his face harden and his eyes search the horizon for an answer that wasn't there was too much for them to bear.

6

Assistant District Attorney Tom Daluskov thought he had left the felons, wise guys and wannabes back at the courthouse but his first step into O'Reilly's told him otherwise.

The specimen was not indigenous to this Upper West Side watering hole, as Tom, who was first hoisted onto a wobbly O'Reilly bar stool when he was five years old, would know. This had been his father's local. Tom had spent many a childhood evening sipping Cokes beside his dad and watching the Rangers on a 20-inch black and white up on the shelf beside the Tullamore Dew, the Jameson and the Connemara Peated Malt. He still took in some of the big Rangers games here but never had more than a couple of beers before *wham*, like someone tripped the off switch, he didn't want any more. His dad, Mad Mike Daluskov, had been the very opposite. All accelerator, no brake.

The interloper stood out right away. The expensive suit, to start with. O'Reilly's was frayed collar country. And the knuckle-loads of bling, hardly in sync with O'Reilly taste or culture. Body language was off too. The broad flabby back was humped forward over a female bar stool occupant in aggressive big bear huffing mode. The thick fingers grasped the back of a barstool and pressed into the slender occupant's back in an intrusive and predatory way. Huffing and puffing were not unknown activities in O'Reilly's but physical aggression in the course of unwelcome advances on customers of the fairer sex was frowned upon and had led to the odd donnybrook. Tom couldn't see much of her but it was obvious from the skewed stitch line in the tailored suit jacket and the awkward tilt of her neck that the woman on the stool—rather well-dressed for O'Reilly's herself and, come to think of it, sort of familiar—was not inviting or enjoying Big Bear's attention.

Ancient barkeep Patrick O'Reilly saw Tom coming and sent a resident tippler off to a booth. That freed the stool beside the lady and, before the big man could make his own move, Tom slid on to it.

"Rachel!" he said, forgetting the behemoth for an instant. "What are you doing here?"

"Figured you'd be here tonight," Rachel Arianna replied.

"Rangers—Bruins, right?" Hunched to one side in her seat, she winked and nodded to the hulk hovering over her. "Speaking of which, meet Marco."

"You the husband?" Marco, who roared this question, had a good voice, bass-baritone, and a bad case of vermouth breath. At about six four, not much taller than Tom, he was a good 50 pounds heavier, maybe 280. Marco Porco, Tom decided, or maybe just Fat Marcos for short.

"An old friend," Tom replied pleasantly. He would like very much to hurt Fat Marco but had to behave. Rachel would demand it and whatever Rachel wanted Tom deeply wished her to get. "Nice to meet you, Marco," he continued in a hilariously polite tone, "but you'll excuse us please. Lots of catching up to do."

Marco smelled submission and, sure enough, smiled knowingly, patted Tom disdainfully on the shoulder, and roared again: "Wait a minute, pal!"—really, the guy had a future in opera! "You are insulting me and insulting me is not a safe thing to do." One of his bear paws gave Rachel's stool a good shake. "First *she* thinks she's too good to talk to me. Now *you* think you can tell me to get lost!"

"Calm down, Marco," old man O'Reilly said quietly from the far side of the bar before explaining to Tom with mock sympathy: "Poor Marco here's got a girlfriend in the neighborhood but when he comes round today she ain't there. So, he's outta sorts."

More opera. "You shaddup, O'Reilly. You show some respect or I'll have to do something about you and your . . . ." Marco's voice trailed off—a momentary gas attack perhaps or maybe gradual recognition that reaction to his aria so far was distinctly underwhelming. O'Reilly, toweling out the Guinness glasses, regarded him with the tiniest of smiles and the rest of the room seemed either uninterested or mildly amused too.

Rachel, steadying herself with a hand on the bar after the stool rattling, concentrated on Tom's face, shook her head slowly, and mouthed the word "no."

Although he knew he shouldn't, Tom treated himself to some visualization. There were a dozen ways to get it done but what flashed in his mind was an image of Marco's two hands pressed to his face and fresh bright oxygenated blood from his newly broken nose spilling liberally out between and over his stubby bejeweled fingers, pooling between his lips, dripping off his chubby chin, trickling down his wrists to stain his white cuffs, and soaking his beautiful shirt until it stuck in little ridges over his round protuberant belly.

This had proved helpful to him in the past, especially since he'd begun real work on impulse control back in university. So he was now able to say to lovelorn Marco, "look, we all have a bad day once in a while, big guy, but why take it out on this lovely lady here? Let me send a drink over to you at that booth over there and maybe you can have something to eat and watch the Rangers kick Boston's ass and think everything out a bit."

And Tom almost wanted Marco to do just that—be nice, go sit in the corner—but only almost. The guy had borderline assaulted Rachel and she had even looked a little frightened a moment ago. A few years back—and maybe a few minutes from now—Fat Marco would face serious risk of painful bodily harm and possibly worse. So Tom felt that, so far so good, he was keeping everything under control, although, let's face it, he was also thinking that it couldn't really be over until the fat man sang his favorite tune once more and could justifiably be served his just desserts.

"How about this?" Marco now asked in his forceful basso cantante. "How about I fuck you up right now, kick *your* ass over to the booth, and then straighten out miss fucking stuck up here?"

"I'm sorry you feel that way, Fat Marco, because now I'm going to have to call your momma and tell her what an asshole Lardbutt her son is making of himself down at O'Reilly's."

Marco took a swing but ended up prone on the floor with his face squished into the scuffed tile and his left arm rising somewhat grotesquely up into the air, the thumb, palm and wrist locked in Tom's hold. "Listen to the pain, Marco; go with it," Tom told him as he maneuvered himself back on to his stool and reached with his free hand for the beer O'Reilly was pouring for him.

Rachel bowed her head for a moment, straightened herself on the stool and, quickly recovering her stunning smile, said, "sort of like Shots, right, Tom, or playing the righteous prosecutor? Triumph for you and punishment and humiliation for the other guy?"

"Be reasonable, Rachel. This guy attacked me!" Tom tried hard to keep the defensiveness out of his voice. Why, he wondered, after decades of obviously unhealthy and unrequited infatuation—of getting nowhere beyond perversely intense sibling-like lab-rat affection—did he still so desperately need to please this woman? The thought moved him to consider levering a bolt of pain into Marco Porco's shoulder assembly.

Rachel wagged a finger unobtrusively low over her lap. "No." she said quietly, her smile now a plea," "don't you dare hurt him!" She leaned forward to whisper. "You played him Tom. Led him exactly where you wanted him to go. After all these years, still the Itzhak Perlman of bullies. Punked him, I believe the term might be down in the holding cells. But we both know you're much angrier at me than at Marco. And we both know that you simply have to let it go."

When Rachel was around it was Tom who felt like a Stradivarius. He jumped a bit at the proximity of those lips to his ear.

"I think you can help the gentleman up now, Tom," Rachel announced in her bright lecture hall voice. "He seems to be feeling better."

Tom looked down at the defeated man. Marco was mouth-breathing and pale. "We'll let him rest for another minute," Tom told Rachel in a low voice without looking her in the eye. He knew he needed to slow down himself and was measuring his own breathing to bring his chemistry back into line. He felt like he had taken the first small bite of a large delicious meal only to be told that he couldn't have any more.

"Don't you and Will teach your students at WHUPASS to avoid violence at all costs? What about all your preaching? Western civilization, etcetera? The key turning point, yadayadayada, the assumption by the state of coercive power to enforce laws and met out revenge and restitution. You know, taking it away from clan and kin and tough guys in bars?"

Tom was cooling down but still impelled to lash out a bit. "But violence has been avoided, dear Rachel," he said quietly, meeting her sad eyes, which, incongruously, signaled capitulation rather than victory. "With the exception of poor big little Marco's feelings, no injury has been done. And spare me your plant doctor's read on the legalities, please. He assaulted you, he attempted to harm me, I subdued him, all in front of witnesses. I could have him dragged off to Rikkers and convicted of assault. We'll see what that does for his love life." He was calmer but Rachel had plucked another string and he was providing his usual vibrations. Although Will had been his best friend since childhood, whenever Tom heard his name come off of Rachel's lips he was likely to palpitate at least briefly with envy, fear and aggression.

"Don't turn nasty with me, Tom," Rachel said, lowering her own voice again. "Don't indulge that mean streak Leon says you have instead of a spine."

"If I was truly mean, rather than kind, I wouldn't continue fulfilling Leon's sick need to be thrashed repeatedly at chess."

"You can discuss it with him on Saturday."

Tom feigned surprise. He had planned to dodge Saturday's informal lab rat get-together, which was to mark the 25th anniversary of a scholarship fund "for deserving youth" their parents had established when years of ill-rewarded genetic lab work had transformed into sudden and almost boundless wealth.

"Forgot on purpose again? Leon's apartment. Noon. Be there. Your mom called me, which is the only reason I've subjected myself to . . . all this." Rachel had been extremely close with Tom's scientist mother since her early teens, when her own parents had died in a plane crash. "She wonders, as I do, why you often do not have the courtesy to answer our telephone calls."

Tom thought, because I'd rather suck razor blades than sit through another lab rat luncheon. Rachel was watching him closely. She glanced meaningfully down at beached and crumpled Marco. Tom knew she would go cold-assed on him for months now. She had always been utterly without forgiveness when it came to incidents like this even though she claimed to know how hard it was for him to subdue his temper and athletic impulses. "Don't whine," she once told him. "You're weak! If you had real balls, you'd show some control."

Tom released his lock on Marco's finger and wrist. Marco sighed and closed his eyes for a moment before sitting up and cradling his swollen hand in his lap. "Better clear out before O'Reilly calls the uniforms," Tom told him. The big man said nothing but Tom felt his eyes burning into his back as he left. There was an "attaboy Tom" and a little half-hearted clapping. It sounded more like relief than approbation. Some of the old-timers might remember a similar incident when Tom was younger that ended far more brutally in the alley around the corner. And there was the famous and far more serious affair at Manny's Café a few years back, of course.

Rachel's M.O. now was to cut and run. "I have mellowed,"

Tom told her as she made motions to go.

"That's actually very true," she said with a regretful smile as she got to her feet. "See you Saturday. It will do you good." Rachel hesitated before giving him a peck on the cheek.

O'Reilly paused from wiping the bar to toss a peanut at Tom's pensive head. "Cheer up, boyo!" the old man said with his tight little grin. "And just to let you know, I too have noticed the kinder, gentler you. Keep it up and Rachel will actually kiss you smack on the lips one day—in about hundred years!"

Tom managed a laugh and raised his eyes again to Rangers–Bruins. O'Reilly drew closer with his bar rag and stopped to watch the action for a moment. "Mind if I ask you something?"

"Sure, what?" Tom was pretty sure he couldn't finish his second beer and pushed it away.

"Did you dad ever knock you around?"

"No. Why?"

"Just wondering." "Mr. O'Reilly," as the younger Tom had called him until invited to use Sean when Daluskov Jr. reached legal drinking age, leaned on the bar and kept his eyes on the screen. "I still remember what you did to that guy in the alley. Figured maybe that was where all that anger came from."

What anger? Tom thought. He had just overshot a bit while straightening the guy out. But he'd indulge O'Reilly's attempt at fatherly psychobabble. "Genetic maybe—from my dad."

"Well, Tom, your old man was definitely a Mad Mike and could get very lively but he never swung on anyone in this place over those many years, despite plenty of good reason and lots of heavy drinking. In fact, he was pretty good at breaking them up with those big paws and that gift of the gab."

"Could have come down through either parent through recessive genes."

"Whatever! Anyway I know he was a war hero and what you showed at Manny's Café you probably got from him."

Tom didn't want to think about it—not his Dad, not the long-ago beating in the alley, not what had gone down at Manny's Café, not Rachel.

"Watch out for Marco," O'Reilly said as Tom stood to leave. "He's a wannabe but he has some real wiseguy friends."

But for Tom, like the rest of it, it was already ancient history.

7

FLASHBACK

New York City
June, 1997

ADA Tom Daluskov sat in the back seat, watching the headlights bob on Lexington Avenue. Officer T.G. Mancini, riding shotgun, was five minutes into the usual ode to the greatness and glory of the Anti-Crime Unit.

This was part of just about every ride-along and nowadays Tom and Detective Ray Franklin were hitching up with ACU every six weeks or so, sometimes once a month. It was their boys' night out. Ray set them up. He was homicide now but as a legendary alumnus he could ask pretty well anything from ACU and be sure of getting it. Besides, the younger ACU guys considered it something of an honor to have Ray Franklin in their decoy vehicle for a night shift, even if the experience was tainted by the presence of the ADA. Although ride-alongs were supposed to help the DA's office sell ACU collars in court, a lot of cops blamed prosecutors for the large numbers of perps who regularly walked, just as they knew that the same prosecutors often blamed acquittals and dismissals on sloppy or questionable police work. There was also always the risk that an ADA was a member of the Society for the Prevention of Cruelty to Dirtbags, which would cramp their style when things went down on the street.

Because these rides were off the books and basically for fun, Ray often tried to whip this latent animosity up as the evening began. Ray would let the blue collar cops know that Tom didn't really have to work, given his parents' rise from penniless refugees to biotech millionaires (or billionaires, depending on the detective's mood.) Tom was also "one of those marshmellows who took kung-fu." Ray would also sometimes claim, untruthfully, that Tom had political ambitions. Because why else would a spoiled-brat, rich-kid, smarty pants, pretty boy summa cum laude

Harvard Law School law grad be slumming in the DA's office and want to add an ACU ride-along to his resume?

After a couple of years, Tom wondered why Ray still bothered. Most of these cops were already aware of Tom's reputation not only for a near record criminal case winning streak but for winning mean and ugly when he had to, and anyone who'd seen him recklessly piss off and push around the courthouse step media knew he'd be instant dead meat if he ever entered politics in New York City. Word had also got around that the friendship between the prickly hard-to-love fifty-plus homicide policeman and the chippy prosecutor maybe 15 years younger had started when Tom and the nonprofit downtown martial arts club he and a buddy ran had somehow managed to get Ray's son off crack. Their matching sandpaper personalities had taken things from there. Sure, their ride-along hobby was a little strange but Ray was welcome in any ACU squad room anytime and Tom had proved himself useful — and discreet — more than once. The fact that Daluskov had been involved in upgrading the unarmed combat course at the police academy and could bring down its chief instructor in open competition also helped.

As Mancini's ode to ACU continued, Tom slunk lower in the lumpy back seat of their decoy cab and muttered: "I am the slayer and the slain."

"Say again, Counselor?" Mancini looked back sharply, before glaring at Ray Franklin, who was driving. "He's shittin' me, right, Detective? He's not saying poetry, right?"

Though it was from Pope — *A mighty hunter, and his prey was man* — Tom grinned and said, "Relax, Mancini, I heard it on *Law and Order*." Tom liked cops like Mancini but for some reason he also liked to wind them up — and Ray's spiel hadn't done a very good job of that tonight.

"Okay, okay." Mancini rolled his massive shoulders to shake off the interruption and continued Anti-Crime 101. "Like I said, it's nature. The hunter, he's just into it, but he's not looking out for other hunters — and that's how we grab his ass." Officer Jimmy Banks, who sat beside Tom and had hands the size of a catcher's mitt, also chimed in, although somewhat more laconically. "Nature works for us."

Tom recalled Pope again—*Nature's laws hiding in the night*—but kept his mouth shut. Lesson over, he hoped.

Not quite, however, because some of Banks' comments on the passing parade—"there you go, see? lowdown pimp, those are hookers but sure like those red boots, boosters over there, and bunch of mopes, going to swarm some Mom and Pop grocery tonight, for sure—cued Ray's request that Tom "tell them about the crime gene." For some bizarre reason, the detective was suddenly in danger of becoming a genetic determinist. Out of friendship Tom usually did his little number—sang for his supper, so to speak—at least till something more interesting came up but it worried him that the same cops who looked upon his lawyerly knowledge with barely concealed disdain seemed awed by a few scraps of genetic basics they should have picked up in Grade 10 biology.

Tom, as usual, began by noting that the "blank slate" concept, which argued that everyone was born as an empty canvas upon which environment and experience sketch personality and behavior, was back out of fashion now. It had held sway for many decades after the Nazis and racists have given genetic studies a bad name.

"Yeah," Mancini said. "If you were just a clean slate, all the poor people would be perps, and Wall Street and the Upper East Side as honest as the day's long. Instead, we've got scumbags from sea to sea."

"Right. It's not easy to discover why people act the way they do," Tom said. "Like disease, even the bio-chemical, non-environmental side of it is complex stuff. But now that scientists can read the code in our DNA, they can try to make connections between what is written in our genes and what happens in our lives. Example: Take the DNA of healthy people and compare it with the codes of people suffering from a certain disease. If you find that the same specific gene or genes in all the sick people differ in the same way from the same genes in the healthy subjects, you may have a lead on a possible genetic predisposition to that disease."

"Is that what they did with the crime gene?" Banks asked. "Matched the DNA of perps against the DNA of honest citizens?"

"In Holland, they identified a specific genetic defect that predisposes people to aggressive behavior that's often criminal. They watched a particular Dutch family for many generations.

Decade after decade, the males of this family have included a huge number of street fighters, rapists, arsonists, killers."

"Isn't that what the Nazis said?" Banks asked. "Some folks got better genes than others?"

Tom was about to tell them that a scientist he knew believed this so-called "warrior gene" also had benefits—making carriers more focused, for example—when he noticed three figures striding up an alleyway at the periphery of his vision. Something struck him about the way they moved, the set to their shoulders but they were gone from sight in an instant. Ray then nodded towards a small circle of three bubble jackets on the sidewalk in front of a greasy spoon called Manny's Cafe and said they'd come round the block again for another look. All three mopes had their hoods up on this summer night. Two had their hands plunged deep into their pockets. The third was consulting his wristwatch.

"So how these genes work Tom?" Banks asked.

Reluctantly, Tom continued. "Okay, refresher course: inside every cell of every living thing, there's that particular thing's design code, an overall blueprint with the detailed plans for its every single attribute, from the teeniest fat cell in Ray's sorry butt to the shape of your big toe to the gap between Mancini's front teeth. It's made from deoxyribonucleic acid, a.k.a. DNA. Forget the fancy name and think of a very simple code of only four basic variables here. They are usually represented by the first letters of the four chemicals involved but it can A,B,C,D, 1,2,3,4, or square, rectangle, circle, triangle, or, *do, re, mi, fa,* or four differently colored stones. This code is simply the combinations and the order in which those four variables line up. We're talking very small stuff here, molecular, because the stones have to line up in two lines about three billion letters long. And those lines have to be tightly folded up into long twisted ropy bunches called chromosomes in every single human cell. In humans, that's twenty-three pairs of bundles, half from mom and half from dad."

"It's that spiral ladder," Professor Ray offered helpfully. "That double helix thing you've seen all over TV the last few years."

"Right," Tom continued. "The four chemical molecules that comprise the code are locked into two lines and in sequence by a physical chemical structure that looks like a ladder. It's ludicrously simple in some ways but is the essence of the wild and amazing thing that is human life on earth."

Tom pulled out his notebook and started scribbling. "Part of the ladder's side is made from phosphate and sugar molecules stacked on top of one another. Ignore them—they just help hold things together. It's the steps of the ladder that compose the code. Each rung is made up of just two molecules from the four code chemicals. They stick pretty strongly to the phosphate-sugar side rails but the hydrogen atom that holds them together in the middle is kind of weak."

"Adenine, cytosine, guanine and thymine," Ray said, glancing into the rearview mirror.

"Right, those are the code's chemicals but we'll just call them A, B, C and D. Chemicals often attract or repel one another. In this case, A and B will stick only to each other. Same with C and D. So the ladder rungs have only four possible combinations." He showed his notepad to Banks:

$$A - B$$
$$B - A$$
$$C - D$$
$$D - C$$

"In between the A's and B's and D's and C's are non-code Hydrogen atoms," Tom said before running two lines down the outside of the rows of letters. "As noted, phosphate and sugar molecules attach to the A,B,C,D's on the outside and stack up on each other to make the ladder's sides. Three billion steps, a full 360-degree twist every ten and a half rungs, and you have human DNA, identical in each and every one of an individual's cells."

"Saywhaaaat!" Tom and Banks turned towards the high-pitched voice outside. On the sidewalk next to the cab, which had been stationary in the traffic for a minute or two, a beaten up old black man in a soiled coat was staring at them. He held an empty Forty in one hand, and wobbled slightly. "The man can dance," Banks said, "but butt ugly!"

The drunk stumbled, bent down and peered in the open window. "Wha you lookin at?" he asked Banks hoarsely "You wan everyone to be jus like you? Ever think what a miser . . . miser . . . ble world that would be?"

Banks winced at a blast of fetid breath and turned away. "Aaaaargh. This guy's part skunk!"

The drunk was at least six feet six inches tall, with a face rich in furrows. The eyes, Tom noticed, seemed remarkably clear. "Hey, you there," he said more quietly, pointing at Tom. "You there. I see it. I see that you understand. You know all bout them cells, am I right? I heard ya just now. You tell your big black-ass friend here, the world's got all sorts of people and some times just ain't their time, but other times just are."

"Be careful what you say," growled Mancini. "That's the future President of the United States you're talking to."

"Sure! Why not?" the old geezer said. "Maybe he's got the stuff and maybe it'll be his time. Not me yet, though. I've got the stuff but it ain't my time."

"Please step back on to the sidewalk," Ray asked.

"Oh I know you's poh-lice! I know that cause I'm a one-man neighborhood watch." He pointed his bottle hand toward Tom. "You take care, Mr. President. You got my vote."

The traffic began to move. Banks pointed at Tom's notepad.

Tom continued with little enthusiasm. He explained that what counted was the order of the chemical steps, especially on stretches of the ladder that contain the instructions to make proteins and design structures.

Ray piped in. "Genes are packets of instructions. And there are some differences in the pattern and order of those As and Bs and Cs and Ds in each person. Now that we can read that pattern, we can nab folks from the DNA in their hair, spit, blood, sperm."

Tom held the notepad up and slashed a line right down through the middle of the rungs of the ladder. "And the reason we've got zillions of bugs, plants, animals and people around," he said, "is that every living cell regularly runs a chemical chainsaw down the steps of the ladder, knocking out the hydrogen in the middle that holds the two sides together."

He quickly scrawled two half ladders, with their half rungs— the As, Bs, Cs and Ds—sticking out into nowhere from single sides. "But there are also A, B, C, D molecules floating freely in the cell. Being sticky they attach themselves in the natural pairings to the recently divorced As, Bs, Cs and Ds whose asses are hanging out off the two half ladders. The A with the Bs, and the Cs with the Ds. Hydrogen atoms jump in to glue things together in the middle of the stairs. The phosphates and sugars stack up and glob on to make new side rails. Presto! You have two identical ladders, instead of one. The whole blueprint has been copied—only takes about half an hour in a human cell.

Replication. You get a new cell."

They were heading downtown again, a block over from Lexington. Tom watched the street carefully to see if the three men he'd noticed in the alleyway had made their way to Third.

Mancini said: "So those DNA ladder copies go in your sperm and into your old lady's egg and that's how the blueprint gets passed along to your kids, and their kids?"

"Something like that. It's why there was probably someone who looked a lot like you mixing it up with the Greeks and Carthaginians in Sicily two thousand plus years ago."

He drew another ladder and again ran the pen-chainsaw right down the middle. "Half a ladder can also run off a special photocopy of its other half. Similar process. If there's an A hanging out, the other side has to be a B. Or a B produces an A, a C a D, a D a C. This new working copy—this half a ladder—is called Messenger RNA. It's able to move part of the DNA code from the information headquarters in the center of the cell—say a locked room in Manhattan—to a factory area on the outskirts in Queens. It's an exact transcription of the DNA code in a gene, a half ladder of half rungs—the As, Bs, Cs and Ds stacked in the precise order determined by the DNA's matching ABCDs."

"I get the picture," said Banks. "I see this long piece of wood with all the short ABCD half-rungs sticking out."

"That's pretty well it," Tom continued. "There's one more chemical step now. This is how the DNA code – information – is turned into our flesh, blood, hormones, everything from our physical appearance to the brain chemistry that helps make our personalities."

Mancini and Banks watched him carefully.

"Out in Queens," he said, "depending on what kind of cell it is, a particular stretch of this long Xeroxed half ladder is put to work on an assembly line. The sequence of ABCDs along the rail of the ladder is the coded recipe, the instructions. Imagine a stretch of the ladder written on a long piece of paper. You have BDACDBDCABBBDCA and on and on. Every three letters makes a distinct chemical code. They call them codons."

Tom scribbled a line of letters and divided the line by threes. "You can make 64 different three-letter codons from the four letters available. But you only need twenty to build and keep a human alive. It's a chemical attraction thing again. There are twenty amino acids floating around in the cell factory. Each one will line up only beside a specific three-letter codon. ABC, or DAB, DCA, etcetera. Remember Lego from when you were a kid? Okay. You can think of each amino acid as a different colored Lego piece. Or, if you played with toy trains, you can think of the amino acids as different train cars—you know, cattle cars beside BDC, oil tankers next to CCA, caboose, etc. Once they're lined up beside the code chemicals, the pieces join together end to end and pull out of the factory."

"Nitty-gritty now," said Ray. "This is us."

"Those trains are proteins. Depending on the sequence of cars, or Lego pieces—the combination and sequence of amino acids—they are hair, or muscle or testosterone. The info copied from the ladder code in Manhattan has directed and decided just what kind of train, or protein, has been made in that cell."

"Protein, like in a good steak, right counselor?" Banks said.

"We are proteins—top to bottom—muscle, bone, not only the color of our eyes but the glint in them. Proteins are also what make us tick, from Officer Mancini's testosterone to the neurotransmitters—the brain chemicals—that make Ray such a pain in the courtroom some mornings."

"But whadabout this crime gene, this warriors' gene?"

"What is often called a genetic defect," Tom said. His mind's eye flashed again to the first of the two trios he'd seen on the street. "There are and have always been genetic mutations—small mix-ups in DNA lettering."

"That's how everything evolved," Ray said knowingly. "The species of plants or animals whose random changes made them procreate and survive better hung on. The ones with the lousy changes flunked out and didn't have any or many offspring. Those changes never stuck or didn't last through tough times."

"I don't know about that," said Mancini. "In NYC anyway looks like every mutant that ever lived survived."

Tom resumed the lecture. "Something, whether it's radiation, or even some gene that itself is there to periodically provoke mutation, causes an error in the reproduction of DNA. Often, it makes no difference because the change occurs in the old code that makes up most of our DNA and which most scientists believe we don't use anymore. They call these long stretches of ladder that don't seem to do anything now 'junk genes.' " Tom knew that Shivkovski and apparently his father had long thought very differently about this, as had the great American Nobel laureate geneticist laureate Barbara McClintock back in the 1950s. But he'd stick with the current otherwise universal opinion in the genetic trade. "But if an A becomes a B at the wrong place on the DNA ladder outside of the vast stretches that are junk and within the stretches that actively code, it's a huge problem. All you need is for one codon to be messed up. It might read AAD instead of AAC, and you may not be able to produce a specific protein that your body or mind needs. In a lot of us, that tiny spelling mistake is a little like a death warrant already written up and waiting inside to kill us. Wild guess is that there are forty thousand disease genes in us. Cystic fibrosis is only one of many diseases we know for sure is predisposed by this kind of genetic glitch. Missing three letters. On the other hand, my father's associate claims that the dropping of just two ladder step base pairs of As and Bs or Cs and Ds that encode for the muscle protein myosin sparked the mutation of humans from apes by making their jaw muscles smaller and weaker and leading to the growth of bigger brains."

"And those Dutch perps?"

"The men in this Dutch family have a genetic glitch that is passed on through generations in their family. When the Lego or the little train cars line up to make a certain protein—the enzyme MAOA—something is wrong with the code and it doesn't work. MAOA is needed to make proper use of neurotransmitters. Those are brain chemicals, like dopamine, epinephrine, norepinephrine and serotonin."

"The stuff that makes you nice and peaceful, right, Tom?" Ray hung the last right and pulled over to the curb.

"Put it this way—you don't want folks with the warrior gene and an imbalance in these chemicals watching *Pulp Fiction* too often." Tom peered up the road. "Serotonin imbalance has been linked to all sorts of emotional problems—depression especially, which is why they invented Prozac. Aggression in men, alcoholism, suicide. If you doubt that brain chemistry affects the way you feel, take a few belts of whiskey and wait for the chemical buzz. So the general theory is: your overall personality— whether you are John Q. Good Citizen or one of those Palestinian teenagers who volunteer to be human bombs in the Middle East— is partly determined from birth by the chemical balance your inherited genes maintain in your brain. Lately, they've done brain scans and spinal taps to show that many convicted murderers use different parts of their brains from the rest of us when they get angry—all accelerator, no brake—and have a different chemical cocktail running their brain and central nervous system."

But Tom's lecture was over now because they had circled back to Manny's Café and it was coming up on the right.

Tom got his action that night but it ended badly. Only one of the three possible perps was still outside Manny's when they arrived. He was pacing back and forth, hands deep in his pockets, even jumpier than before. Mancini and Banks got out about 60 feet before the café to cut off one escape route. As Ray and Tom rolled slowly past the restaurant, they saw a dozen diners inside, including a terrified young girl with a broken doll in one hand and her fork in the other, focusing on someone in a hidden corner of the room.

Ray called in a possible holdup in progress. He double-parked and ordered Tom to stay in the cab. Tom obeyed at first, but when the lookout seemed to make Mancini and Banks, and bolted in Ray's direction, Tom jumped out of the car, tackled the kid and held him in a wristlock against a dumpster in the alley Then he heard the first shots from inside the restaurant.

As Ray moved to take a firing position out on the street, he grinned crookedly at Tom. "Hold him here. Tom, I'm telling you, you mix in this and I won't friggin speak to you again." Tom adjusted his hold on the frightened suspect, so he could peek around the corner and know what was going on. He felt a little for the perp and even knew his name now. Darryl. He worked with youngsters not much younger or different a few nights every week at WHUPASS.

Things went well, at first. Daryl's two friends emerged from the café with a plastic takeout bag. Their automatics were in their belts. They barely noticed that Daryl was gone, before Ray, Banks and Mancini had lined them up at gunpoint, disarmed and cuffed them.

The strange thing was Daryl was now shaking even more than before. Tom wondered why. Perhaps adrenalin aftershocks. Tom doubted that his own pulse was far above its resting normal. He felt sadness over what they might now find inside Manny's, some disappointment at having been restricted to the periphery of the game, and a slight elation at the victory. Just as Daryl's physical reaction was imprinted by millions of years of evolution, if somewhat tainted by the ingestion of drugs, Tom's was a genetic reward passed down from the first hominids who had hunted well and successfully. But he also felt himself filling again with the stillness that so often took him before a trial or full-contact competition. Could it be that he and Daryl knew in their separate ways that there was still more to come?

The image of three men disappearing up a back alley flashed in Tom's mind just as shouts and another gunshot sent curious onlookers scrambling for cover. He almost knew what to expect when he peeked around the corner.

Ray, Mancini and Banks were down on their knees. Behind each stood a hooded figure with a gun held to the police officer's head. They were agitated.

"Mothafuka," one yelled.

"Down, bitch," screamed a second. "Down on your bitch knees."

The tallest man, the one in the middle, was screaming: "Yo fuckin gonna watch, bitch. You watch, bitch!"

Tom winded Daryl with a blow to the midriff, and let him slide slowly to the concrete. Back hugging the wall, he slipped round the corner and edged towards Manny's. The three gunmen had their backs to him, their attention focused on Officer Bill Mancini.

"Do the bitch!" the tallest man screamed. Unbelievably, people gathered at a distance to watch. One of them was the drunk with the empty Forty! He looked straight at Tom, who was still 10 yards from the nearest perp.

Ready for betrayal, Tom dropped his head. His thigh muscles exploded as he sprinted forward, but as his feet left the ground, Tom saw Officer Mancini's head whip back into a halo of blood and flesh. The policeman's body pitched forward on to the sidewalk with a thud. So stunned were the onlookers that Mancini died without a sound from anyone, no shouts, no screams, no oral acknowledgment at all, even from the wobbly-kneed gunman, who looked down at the shattered skull as if someone else had done the work.

Only the tall man talked. "I'm raggin you, bitch," he screamed at Ray, as Tom's leg lifted for his flying kick. Tom had to go through the nearest gunman to get to Ray's would-be executioner, who now pressed the gun barrel into the nape of Ray's neck. Tom's body was horizontal now and high off the ground. The heel of his cross trainer struck behind the nearest gunman's right ear. Tom caught sight of a small gold earring as the assailant was propelled unconscious out on to Lexington. Tom had held back, probably sparing the man's life, because he needed momentum for an awkward midair spinning kick and a punch that he hoped would knock both the crazy tall man and Mancini's killer off balance. He made contact. But it was messy. More like a fullback's end zone dive than any move recognizable from the martial arts. Tom's elbow connected with a skull. The other perp got Tom's butt in the ear.

The three of them clumped to the sidewalk together. Tom landed hard on his hip but was first to his feet. The man who had just murdered Bill Mancini reached out for his fallen gun. Tom kicked him in the throat, and spun hard on his heel towards the tall man. As he did, the mad face of Ray's tormentor came into view. So did the barrel of a gun. Tom saw a flash and felt his mouth fill instantly with warm thick liquid. His gurgled shout propelled a plume of red droplets out into the glow of a street light.

Tom kept going for the simple reason that his body showed no inclination to stop. Eyes wild with drugs and bloodlust, the tall man flicked his head back in confusion and aimed again at Tom's obviously wounded yet strangely still oncoming face. The propensity of opponents to assume that a target was immovable had always amazed Tom. He ducked and twisted just as the man squeezed the trigger. The muzzle did drop but only enough to deliver a bullet over Tom's shoulder and into the bowels of Mancini's killer who had been likely choking to death behind him.

The tall man had one last chance. He hesitated and dropped the barrel for a safer shot—to the body. But before he could pull the trigger, an empty 40-ounze beer bottle shattered across his wrist. The gun clattered to the pavement. The belligerent neighborhood watch drunk had disarmed the tall man and some witnesses would later claim had actually kicked the gun away. Tom was in an instant face to face with Mancini's killer. Perhaps the gunman saw something in Tom eyes because his own filled with fear and when he began to step back and to speak his voice skidded up the register as he uttered his last words. "Aw right, bitch . . . . "

Tom struck him with the first punch he'd ever learned, a straight right. He aimed for the heart with all the hand speed he could muster. At the instant of contact, he pulled his fist back.

The tall man dropped like a stone. Tom knew he had killed him.

"Goddam animal," growled the old drunk, walking the few steps to Tom. "Good work, son. Like I told you, your time and your stuff." Tom reached out as the old man who'd saved his life began to stumble off. He stopped when he saw Jimmy Banks kneeling on the sidewalk, weeping and holding Bill Mancini's shattered head in his huge blood-soaked hands. Next thing Tom knew, Ray was there, making him sit down. "Where're you hit?" he asked. Ten seconds later, the first backup car fishtailed on to the scene.

The events at Manny's Café left Tom a hero to most, although a few civil libertarians, human rights advocates, and political opportunists questioned whether the DA's office staff benefited from the services of a man who had arguably carried out a public execution. The media orgasm was prolonged by graphic visuals captured by one of New York's gypsy cameramen only seconds after the first patrol car arrived. It showed Tom running his hands over his blood soaked head and face, checking for wounds, and eventually sticking a finger out through his cheek from inside his mouth where the bullet had exited. He wiggled it and said something incomprehensible that drew a half smile from Detective Franklin. Inside Manny's Cafe, Tom shoved paper napkins into his mouth as he headed to the back room where five known drug gangbangers lay face down in a neat row and very much beyond repair.

The cameraman later caught long-range footage of Tom and Dr. Gail Haggerty, a New York medical examiner, conversing over the gunman's body. The media made much of the fact that the two had apparently dated briefly some years ago. It was that kind of story. Tom ignored his week of fame. He and the department and the media tried but failed to find the hero with the 40 and it would be many years and far away in more ways than one before Tom saw him again.

8

Tom dragged himself to Leon Shivkovski's apartment on Saturday because he couldn't say no to his mother or Rachel. They eyed him occasionally from across the room and seemed satisfied that he was fulfilling his social and clan duty for a change.

Lunch ended and most of the celebrants were gone. That left the lab rat children of the scholarship's founders and their scientist parents alone together in Leon's capacious living room. This wasn't a Saturday of fun and games at Brighton Beach anymore, or a picnic in upstate New York. For one thing, of the eight scientists who'd shared vodka and laughs in the farmer's field so many years before, five were dead. Rachel's mother and father and the parents of Tom's best friend, Will, had died in a plane crash when the two were teenagers. Mad Mike Daluskov was gone too.

Much blood had been spilled in other ways too and wounds had been left to fester, forcing the old folks to retreat behind the quaint armor of polite reserve. As in the wider lab rat community, where bickering over competing business interests and professional reputations was constant, resentment was rife. So were hints of tawdry behavior, betrayal, and dirty secrets. None of it much interested Tom and he avoided the core lab clan although he did find it amusing that, like so many real blood-related families, half of the members hated one other's guts.

"Okay, Tom," said Rachel to break a long silence, "give us the dope on the Frankenfoods fellow who painted GreenGene headquarters red."

"Yes, Tom!" Leon drawled. "Lucky you! The deserter's chance finally to do his tribal duty."

"I don't know who'll catch the case, Leon," Tom said politely, in deference to his mother's presence and wishes. "I can't talk about it anyway. Especially to GreenGene. Your company is the complainant here. My friendship with you could be seen as a conflict of interest."

Tom underlined "friendship" with a slight smirk. Leon's distaste for humankind in general was known to all but so was his much deeper hatred for Tom. Tom, for his part, was no longer sure of how he felt about Leon. He disliked the viciousness but admired the intelligence and drive. And lately he'd begun to realize just how hard a time he'd given the much smaller Leon as a child. Part of his mellowing, perhaps? So he now tried to humor him, particularly through their marathon series of chess games. These were conducted almost exclusively by email and voice message but when they did come together, they tended to bring out the worst in each other.

Leon's lip curled at the mention of friendship too. "We spoke with the police, of course," he continued. "A single-cell conversation, as you would know, Tom, being a practicing partner with them in the garbage disposal trade."

Tom could guess what cops like Banks and Mancini had made of Leon, who was GreenGene's chief of research. To spite the son, he turned to Leon's father and boss. "My advice," Tom told the GreenGene chairman and CEO directly, "is to cooperate fully with NYPD. Don't make yourselves unloved. There will be a hundred new cases tomorrow and a thousand in a week. Things can slide at the best of times and you need a conviction to scare other protestors off."

Dr. Sigurd Shivkovski, tall, frail, twinkly-eyed yet formidable, stood off a bit behind a couch. He wore his usual look of mild amusement, as if there were no end to life's follies even though his own had often been witness to unspeakable horrors and despair. Tom was not invulnerable to the old man's charm. Ever the performer, Shivkovski was a favorite of the girls and boys on the business channels. He was open about his own faults and foibles and generous in his praise of others. He called Tom's late father, who had been GreenGene's co-founder and Shivkovski's lifelong friend, a "pure genius." It was when the old man mentioned Mike Daluskov, however, that Tom's blood tended to boil.

Shivkovski Sr. listened now and made a little bow. "We will do precisely that, Tom. Thank you for the sage advice. As for the perils posed by the ignorant mob, well, some of us here have lived through the kind of nightmares that can result."

Everyone knew what he meant. Shivkovski, a survivor of the Soviet Gulag and a liberator of Auschwitz, leaned forward on his walking stick and looked in the direction of Tom's mother, Dr. Sophia Parviati, who had been a near victim of Adolf Hitler. She did not return his gaze and merely nodded. Her husband and Tom's stepfather, Dr. Hank Adams, perched protectively on the arm of his wife's armchair. A World War II OSS officer, he might also have had something to say but chose not to.

The silence surprised no one. Only in lab rat society was it not considered odd that friends estranged for decades continued to attend the same social gatherings where they never spoke to one another but remained impeccably polite. "Communities are bound by both the good and the bad," Tom's mom once told him.

The split had come in the 1970s and was presumed to relate directly to Tom's father's suicide. This had followed frequent disagreements that were threatening Mike Daluskov's lifelong collaboration with Shivkovski. It was a friendship forged by fire, not only in the Soviet Union's camps but in the Battle of Stalingrad. Yet something had been destroying it. Jealousy, perhaps? The accumulated weight of scientific false starts, wrong turns, and wasted years? Tom sometimes wondered whether it had been disputes over the moral ambiguities that so often hide beneath science's shimmering surfaces.

The suicide had changed Tom's life and attitudes in a few awful minutes. Science owed him a father and he was someone who carried a grudge. His best friend Will had also later rejected the laboratory (also for law) but Will had remained at home in the lab rat community when it became his only family. Will often seemed downright reverential in the presence of the elders. While outspoken and sassy in the world beyond, Rachel could also seem passive and even defeated during lab rat gatherings although Tom knew she often jousted enthusiastically with Shivkovskis Senior and Junior when they were on their own.

Only Tom made it clear that but for friendship with Will, passion for Rachel, and deep love and respect for his mother and Hank Adams, he could walk away from the lab rats and never look back. Only Tom thought science required a good smack once in a while to keep it in line. Only Tom was always ready for a fight.

"Ah yes, the ignorant mob—the lab rat's burden," Tom said softly, turning to Leon again. "And the dumb flatfoots. But then who else is going to protect our creepy helpless little scientists and their stock options while they hide in their labs from the real world out there?"

"Not to mention the innately sadistic perverted prosecutor who gets off on tormenting whoever's within reach, guilty or innocent." Leon's voice was rising. "Here's the difference between you and me. You wrestle in the gutter each day with a few carriers of genetic sub-strains that have been around for thousands of generations. But you can do nothing—nada—to help civilization or improve humankind. You can't lock up your perps most of the time, never mind tame them. And yet we helpless geeks, so ignorant of such great human advances as the plea bargain and the choke hold, can help lift millions from poverty and transform global culture in a single good day at the office. That, of course, is in addition to coming alterations in the human condition that will last not a thousand but millions of years."

"No paeans to science today, please, Leon," said Rachel, who appeared bored. "And no attacks on protectors. We have a couple of former soldiers here, including your father."

"Yes, and we are all aware of your camp following proclivities, Rachel. I regret to inform you that arousing young men in a university lecture hall may fulfill your fantasies but does not qualify as help or protection. Your application for sainthood is denied."

"I'm no Mother Teresa but I'm wise enough to see why Wally Anderson is concerned. We're moving on genetic manipulation at lightning speed. If we alter the DNA of a human germ line cell— which, as I need not tell you but will, is a cell destined by its code to become an egg or a sperm—then that change will be passed on through all time."

Tom was surprised to hear Rachel join in the dissent and so, apparently, was Leon, who whispered, "my, my! I suggest the lady doth protest too much."

"I am simply taking human nature into account. It is in us, and more so in some of us than in others, to go where others fear to tread. Our young Wally is right. The world needs to keep its guard up."

Shivkovski Sr. apparently deemed it time to interrupt. "But science is careful, my dear Rachel, as you most certainly know. We go perhaps where others have not thought to go but we go on their behalf and we tread very carefully. We may judge the care we take by the results. The only reason that human life flourishes so incontrovertibly today and, indeed, seems on occasion alarmingly fecund, is that some of us—most of the best of us, actually—are scientists. Only a few generations ago, even the most materially privileged lived in hygienic squalor and ignorance far worse than the poorest of the poor endure today.

People died like fleas. Died en masse in actual fact, that is — not just in the ill-informed, self-induced nightmares of the bedwetters from Greenpeace. As for lifestyle, well, yesterday's idea of heaven is life on earth for billions today! Again, thanks to scientists. Indeed, we must now invent new maladies and pains so that Oprah Winfrey and Jane Fonda may cure us."

Rachel raised her hand to cover a fake yawn, said nothing and looked away.

Shivkovski, warming up, raised a slender finger. "And what new paths will we explore? What about childbearing? The awful physical ordeal for women! The colossal waste of time! Do you wish to be rid of it Rachel? Consider it done! Virtually. Another gift from science!"

"We'll let us girls decide that, I think, good Doctor." Rachel had redonned her you-bore-me mask. "Unless you boy scientists get into a peeing contest and things get out of control."

Shivkovski finally looked irritated. "Let's be clear," he said. "It is science that has provided the great options and choices upon which our modern freedom rests. Scientists empower, ennoble and liberate humankind. It is not science that has oppressed women through history, as you have implied, my dear. Quite the opposite. It has been the lack of science. It has been and continues to be ignorance and the cultural mumbo-jumbo of the tribe, clan, religion and the ideological sects."

As he continued, Shivkovski turned again toward Tom's mother. She was listening but had her eyes on Rachel. "We hear them in every age, the witch-burners and scaremongers, the righteous thugs. They hate freedom. And knowledge. And science. 'We know best!' they chant. All others must be punished. 'Do it our way! Or else!' These Frankenfoods terrorists have the cultural genes of the Inquisition, Hitler, Stalin and Pol Pot. And, yes, of course, I had almost forgotten! The genes of the louts with the torches who terrified poor Mary Shelley's Frankenstein!'"

Tom took advantage of the ensuing silence to begin an exit. Will, who had remained a silent spectator throughout, gave him a "later" sign before whispering something apparently funny into Rachel's ear. Tom felt a brief pang of his chronic jealousy. Rachel called out to him. "Will forgot to tell you but I actually ran into Wally Anderson before he trashed GreenGene. I realized it after I saw his picture in the papers. He was the same young man who spoke up at my Columbia lecture this week."

Tom stopped in his tracks, suddenly tense. "Did he give you any trouble? What happened exactly?"

"He was sweet. A gentleman." She spoke hurriedly before adding, "I know that look, Tom. Calm down. " She turned to Tom's mother. "Auntie Sophia, please tell Tom to be fair—and gentle—with this young man."

Tom decided to get the details later by phone. He kissed his mother on the cheek, high-fived his stepfather, and shook hands with the elder Shivkovski, who held on. "Tom, it's a blessing you are there for us. To defend all that we love—all that your father loved."

Tom's grip tightened on the frail hand. He thought, *don't mention my father, you old prick*, but said, "as I've told you Doctor, there is no chance I'll be handling this case. It can't happen. Not with my family's links to GreenGene and you."

He was almost out the door when Leon caught up and steered him toward a large window seat. Sunlight streamed down on to a beautiful chessboard and the latest in a series of games that, at Leon's insistence, had gone on for many years. "Your turn," the perennial loser said eagerly. Tom normally emailed his move once a week. Leon, who seldom won a match, had suddenly requested this ludicrously slow schedule the previous year. To make things more competitive, Tom gave himself only ten seconds after learning of Leon's move to decide on his own.

"This is new," Tom said, admiring the swirling patterns of the board's blues, greens and browns. The game's grid was superimposed in white. Tom touched the board. Acrylic.

"The design looks vaguely familiar."

"Fractal. Computer-generated."

Bullshit, Tom thought. But he was in no mood for more jousting. He moved a pawn and set off for WHUPASS.

9

"I don't want it," Tom said as he strode through the door. He'd known what was up the moment he was summoned to District Attorney Allen Rubenstein's digs. The tabloids had been feasting for days on the so-called "Ketchup Terrorist" and Wally Anderson's redecoration of GreenGene's offices with a ruddy vinaigrette. Rubenstein didn't like this kind of attention.

"Just for that, you can handle the NASDAQ mugging, too!" That would be the killing in Times Square on Friday, another headline the DA didn't need.

"You mean we have an arrest?" Tom took a seat.

Rubenstein finally looked up from his paperwork. The sparkle was gone from his once lively eyes. "I mean you're going to help your cronies in homicide and anti-crime get one. Talk to your pals."

"Will do."

"Nice of you to accept the work," the DA growled. "And I don't want you begging for anything! What the police department owes you can never be paid back. Never!" Rubenstein's irritation over Tom's refusal to cash in politically on his Manny's Café 'heroics' seldom faded for long. "For Pete's sake, if I'd had a break like that at your age, I'd be president now."

Tom laughed. "People still want to be president?" The DA, a Republican, still clung to the hopes that President John Mason would snatch vindication from the jaws of seemingly inevitable impeachment. If he didn't, Rubenstein would likely go down eventually with the Mason ship.

Rubenstein ignored the low blow. "Once you've made sure NYPD is moving hard on the NASDAQ killing, whip the Frankenfoods thing into shape."

"I have major-league conflicts. My father was a GreenGene founder. My mother was once a corporate star and major shareholder. I know the CEO and half the scientists personally."

"Past tense. Once. Founded. Owned. You let me worry about the optics. We need someone special up front on this one. With a scientific background. Didn't your father have a cousin who sharpened Einstein's pencils?"

"It will be a colossal waste of time. They'll want a trial, and turn it into a morality play, starring a genetic apocalypse they've dreamt up on reefer."

"No they won't, because you won't let them." Rubenstein tossed a folder onto his Out stack. "I don't get you! There are ten people in this office who'd kill for either of these cases. Besides, people are asking for you specifically—on both."

"The mayor?" Another Republican on death watch. "Why? Didn't think Shivkovski was that big a donor."

"This town is not fond of terrorism. And these Frankenfoods protesters are on crazy pills these days. They think they can trample all over the law and it cannot be allowed to happen. The other one's self-explanatory. New York City is safe for tourists, especially places like Times Square. We have to get that message out to the muggers. Would go for the death penalty on this one if we could." The DA looked up and changed the subject. "What are these Frankenfreaks upset about, precisely?"

"Well, Al, genetic science is exploring unknown territory." Tom was inching his way to the door. "Folks worry they're going to fall off the edge of the earth and take the rest of us with them."

"Must make you wish your father's pal Einstein hadn't discovered genetics, right Tom?"

"As you well know, Sir, it was Mendel who posited the first laws of hereditary genetics."

"Right, Mendel, Hitler's evil doctor!"

"Mendel. Not Mengele. Gregory Mendel. A German monk."

Rubenstein was smiling widely now. "What the heck could a monk know about sex? On second thought, I don't want to hear!"

"He figured it out in his garden, playing with his peas."

"See? That's why we need you. If this thing goes to trial, we can't afford to look stupid in the courtroom." Rubenstein went back to the papers on his desk. "Throw the book at this Franken character. No deals. Here's something old Mendel the pea gardener would know: you've got to nip it in the bud."

10

Hurling rocks at an anti-globalism demo was one thing. a weekend locked up on Riker's Island quite another. Wally Anderson looked a little worse for wear.

"How we doing, Wallace?" Tom asked, showing the young protestor to his seat. "I asked them to bring you here because I figured you'd like a break. After all, you're going to be inside for a long, long time and probably in place a lot worse than Riker's."

"Nonsense," said Ryan Tilley, a generally incompetent attorney with loose ties to the green movement. "He'll make bail tomorrow

"Don't count on that, Wally," Tom said. He sat on the front edge of his desk, squeezing his WHUPASS handball and occupying the young man's space. "We could go to town on you — all the way from burglary and resisting arrest to assaulting police officers and attempted murder. But it's the Feds I'd worry about. Counter-terrorism is a crusade for them. They're looking hard at locking you up and melting the key down to make dumdum bullets."

"Is this what's happening to American justice?" Wally asked His voice wobbled slightly but he looked Tom straight in the eye "You show me the 'Horror'" — he made the quotation marks himself — "and tell me afterwards how you're going to frame me."

"Listen," Tom said gently. "You are not the victim of a conspiracy. The guy responsible for your present woes is sitting in your chair. Besides, framing you would be redundant. You were caught red-handed, quite literally. Loved the ketchup, by the way."

Wally's lawyer now tried to earn his keep. "When a jury hears how Wally was trying to save their children's children from the horrors of GNOs —."

"That's G M Os, Mr. Tilley," said Tom. If Wally wanted to justify his acts, he'd have to go to trial and take the stand. Tom would butcher him even under normal circumstances. With the inept Tilley on his side, it would be even worse. Tom wondered where all the legal talent was on this case. The big ecological groups like Greenpeace had money and dedicated top-flight lawyers at their beck and call. Was someone cutting Wally loose, or had he been a loose cannon from the start?

When Tilley remained silent, Tom continued. "You don't want a jury listening to you, Wally. At the very least, they'll learn what a confused, dangerous loony tune you are. You will also bore them—usually a fatal move. Worst case, you'll make them feel stupid, or morally deficient, and they'll punish you for it. Go to trial, and you will get the max."

Tom had skimmed the 5s and other police reports, and had watched the video of Wally's initial interrogation, looking for signs that the man's presence at Rachel's lecture had been anything other than coincidence. On paper, at least, the kid's movements in the days before the GreenGene break-in had loner written all over them. The young Viking seemed earnest but not violent and perhaps open to some logic.

"I know a little about struggle tactics, Wally. You're no Nelson Mandela or Che. You can't do your cause any good from the inside of a prison and I don't see your face on a poster. Why not let one of those self-righteous types who call the shots play the martyr this time? Cooperate a bit, and we'll see if we can keep you out of Attica. Consider it a tactical maneuver."

"Don't let him scare you," Wally's lawyer advised before lapsing again into silence.

"I'm scared *for* you, Wally," Tom said, "scared for a decent, largely law-abiding man who got carried away. What you have done is serious but I don't want you subjected to prison life when there's a way to prevent it that won't damage your cause at all."

Wally leaned forward to whisper. "Can we talk without my lawyer here?" Tilley objected but Wally signed a waiver.

"What if I can give you a huge case?" Wally asked excitedly after Tilley left and slammed the door behind him. "A case that will make you famous?"

"Famous is good, but first you have to tell me who helped you plan the GreenGene action." Wally's guilelessness could be an act. Tom needed to be sure that neither he nor any of his associates posed a threat to Rachel. "Any other targets we should know about," he asked softly. "Besides GreenGene, I mean."

"No. As I told you, I'm a one-man band. I make it up as I go along." Wally sounded more relaxed now, and ready to cooperate. "It took me a month to plan this gig. I spent my last dime."

Tom pretended to check the investigation report. "Let's see. The Metropolitan Museum. You say you were there the afternoon of the GreenGene operation." He peeked over the folder at Wally. "Any beef with the arts? Do old paintings pose a threat to the humpback whale or the purple-nosed puffin? Planning a dye job on a Van Dyke?"

"You're kidding, right?" Wally looked shaken. "I'm an artist myself, man! Take a better look at the file! I could have majored in Fine Arts. It's just that my mom and dad wanted me to make the most of my sciences and math—you know, because I'm, like, gifted. I was at the Metropolitan to relax. I love that place!"

Tom folded his hands behind his head, waiting for more. Still part schoolboy, Wally straightened up in his seat.

"This wasn't an operation, Mr. Daluskov, it was a performance! Think about it. All I wanted was for people to experience for themselves the alarm and dread they'd feel if they learned the facts about GMOs. It was theater! The dye comes down, and everyone in the GreenGene office thinks they've been contaminated with a substance that can scramble their genes. Imagine the sheer terror of those first few moments, or hours, actually, because no one will know it's mostly ketchup until the lab process is finished. That's what I counted on. Especially the women. They'd have to think about what GreenGene is doing. They'd have to begin to realize that as employees, they bear responsibility. Just think of how much these people know, how many dirty little secrets they've collected over the years! Some of them would quit. And some would start blowing the whistle!"

Tom inched toward the information that bothered him most. "You demonstrated technical ingenuity and skills in GreenGene headquarters," he said, "so you can see why we're concerned about public places. Before the museum, you were up at Columbia. Any targets there? University research labs, for example? Or an individual?"

"Columbia?" Wally's eyes unlocked from Tom's for a moment, wandering to the WHUPASS class pictures on the wall. "Columbia? Oh, yeah. Of course. The babe. I couldn't just sit in my room. I was nervous, you know? And someone told me about this babe professor who gives this great lecture every year on genetics. So I went up there and took it in."

"You sure you weren't reconnoitering the campus?"

"Nope." Wally's eyes held steady. "Why would I? Our greatest support comes from academe, man!"

"What about this professor, what's the interest?"

Wally's laugh seemed quite natural. "I told you. She's super-hot." He continued more seriously. "But brilliant too. Dr. Rachel Arianna. Published many times in *Nature*. She puts on a show. She understands theater."

"So you and your friends sat through her lectures?"

"I went alone," Wally said firmly. "This whole thing, remember, is a one-man play."

"You went alone and—what?"

"I listened. Enjoyed. I asked a few questions to stir things up. It was a good chance to introduce our concerns to hundreds of bright students. Look, Mr. Daluskov, no one much cares about individual scientists. They're mostly foot soldiers."

"So are the GreenGene office workers, aren't they?"

"Yes, but that's just it. The real enemy is the corporation, which brings me to—"

"To what?"

"To what I have to tell you! I saw things at GreenGene, Mr. Daluskov. Secret records. Absolutely weird. You want a case? There is stuff going on in that corporation that would blow the roof off the GMO debate."

"Right, I forget. The horror." Tom did not believe that Wally had pulled his stunt off entirely alone but it would take time and some nastiness to drag it all out of him.

"So, what's the next trick?" Tom asked. "You going to grab a couple of secretaries from the GreenGene office and lock them in a dark basement, maybe tell them they're about to die, put an automatic to their heads, and pull the trigger? Anyway, you'll use blanks. What's the harm in that, right?"

"No, we would never do that. It's not the same."

"The end effect on the victims is, in fact, the same. As it happened, the only folks you terrorized were cops and security guards. But what if your plan had worked? How would the Big Green Man feel now, if you'd put scores of women, some of them pregnant, into emotional shock? A great victory for Wally Anderson, do-gooding tree-hugger?"

Wally was about to object, but slouched in his seat instead. This was a good sign. Tom continued in preacher mode.

"Greed's just one of the deadly sins. Human nature has a whole shitload of other hidden motives and dark subconscious impulses. Perhaps on the inside, your frothy-lipped eco-guerrilla pals are just the Nazi Brown Shirts all over again, but with new slogans and different tastes in clothes."

"Nonsense!" Wally said. "We have the right to demonstrate, and we have a duty to get the truth about Frankenfoods out there. He added, more hesitantly: "Sometimes more radical steps are necessary."

"That's the problem. If we allow your 'urgent action' on behalf of your belief, everyone else can get in on the act, too. What if GreenGene decided to play by your rules? Or worse. Maybe beat you up, or bomb your house, or find a way to turn you into a juicier tomato? The other side of the argument can have its radicals, too. Perhaps they snatch your sisters or children off the streets, and stick sharp sticks in their eyes. That's how it all starts in the many shithole countries around the world. That's why we have the laws and set rules of governance of a democratic society. In the world you're heading for, where everyone gets to cut throats to get what they want, it's the maniacs and cutthroats who end up in charge."

Tom watched as Wally digested this bit of conventional piety. "Okay, Wally," he said, sitting back in his own chair. "I'm all ears now. What's this weird stuff you saw at GreenGene?"

11

After a workout and sparring tonight, Tom had treated his favorite students to rehydration, protein and carbs at the greasy spoon across the street from WHUPASS. The Rialto's food hadn't improved in the 12 years since he and Will Jefferson set the nonprofit martial arts school up but the kids liked it just fine.

Two of the three were black belts and apprentice instructors — Detective Ray Franklin's son Billy, who had beaten a crack habit and now trained as a physiotherapist, and his girlfriend Mary, who was studying to become a teacher. As Tom tucked into the rest of his steak, he watched the two lovebirds chat on the sidewalk outside where they were waiting for Ray to pick them up. Beside them was a much smaller Latino boy barely able to fill his baggy white WHUPASS uniform, which was complemented by a Yankees ball cap worn back to front and a seemingly huge pair of sunglasses. He was twirling a white cane at tremendous speed when it suddenly separated into two shorter pieces that then flashed ferociously in the neon light through rapid attack and defensive forms of Arnis, the Filipino art of stick fighting. When Billy apparently asked him to stop, the boy pretended to conk himself on the head and fell down in a heap.

Tom had known Carlos Chavez's mother since before the boy was born blind nine years earlier. They were next-door neighbors. He'd chatted with her on their landing less than a week before — the same landing where Carlos had been swinging a baseball bat or bouncing or kicking a ball of some kind almost perpetually since he could walk. Angela was an assistant head ER nurse and had chuckled as she told him about "the seven street tough grown men we had in last night soaked in ketchup and vinegar who thought their genes were mutating." They had been only nodding neighbors until Angela knocked on his door one day long ago when media criticism was rising over his actions at Manny's Café. She had thanked him for putting up with Carlos's playtime noise, the collateral damage to a potted plant, and for standing as goaltender during the boy's numerous soccer shootouts. Then she said the ER had long been dealing with men on Angel Dust. "I know those men were on the Dust and so I know that you had no other choice."

Already impressed by Carlos' stubborn high spirits and remarkable athletic potential, Tom offered to enroll him at WHUPASS and to make sure he got there and back safely every day. Angela had hesitated but Carlos had prospered, just as Tom knew he would. Not that his mother stopped worrying, of course. The GreenGene prank had its funny side, she'd said last week, but "so many things seem to be going south—the stories about the President and corruption and, my goodness, this Kitchen Sink maniac! Just about cut some poor man's head off last night in Queens. It's like he's randomly picking cherries. I'm scared to let Carlos out on to the landing alone."

That Tom had taken on a little responsibility for another human being surprised some, although Will and he had been helping bent, broken and struggling kids and their parents on the QT at WHUPASS for many years. "Even Daluskov," said Will, "can't be a badass all of the time." Rachel offered a cheek buss and congratulations that Tom was "finally doing something *for* rather than *to* somebody else." "You're the one who's getting a good deal," his stepfather Hank told him. "You'll teach Carlos a few things but he'll teach you a lot more."

Tom watched Billy answer his cell. After the call and some discussion, the three came running in. "Sir, Dad says he's bringing a nice surprise for you," Billy said. "A hot vic, he said, for an interview. Then he told me to tell you, the woman mugged in the Times Square homicide." Carlos moved forward. "Sir! Then he said to tell you, wipe the mustard off you face and get your elbows off the table. Sir." He bowed and the three of them laughed.

Ray's unmarked police car pulled up outside and the two older students headed back out. Carlos bowed again, waited, and then reached up and gave Tom a hug around the neck. The younger students were required to thank and/or hug the parent who had brought them after each WHUPASS class. Since Carlos was fatherless and Angela was generally at work or asleep between shifts, Tom, Will, Ray or Billy or Mary were the usual stand-ins for this ritual of respect and appreciation. Carlos was twirling his cane again as he breezed past the "hot vic" on his way to Ray's vehicle.

Eva Martin did not look the victim type, nor, for that matter, like a tourist. In fact, as she moved toward him, Tom had an odd premonition. Maybe, after thousands of dates, short stands and false starts, there might be life beyond Rachel after all.

"Mr. Daluskov," the blonde woman said as he stood and she held out her hand. "I'll sit down, if you don't mind?" She touched his shoulder as she invited him to retake his seat. "I can pass the salt and pepper."

Eva Martin's lightly powdered once black eye remained a yellowish purple. It was still half-closed and highlighted her otherwise delicate features. Tom was glad that the mugger had apparently landed only a glancing blow.

The veteran waitress Lucille smiled broadly at Eva. Tom hadn't been in the Rialto with a date-type girl in eons. Eva ordered a breakfast pack of Special K with skim milk and any reasonably fresh piece of fruit that might reside in an eatery like the Rialto.

"I like this place," she said brightly. "No one gives a darn what you have for dinner." She leaned towards him. The eyes were less brown than green. "I suppose the waitress is cheerful anytime the customers aren't shooting up."

"Careful, Ms. Martin," Tom said quietly. "I know New York's given you a rough ride. But this is a good neighborhood. Good people. The Rialto's a family restaurant."

Eva's glance took in the floor. "Well, someone in the family should swab the decks."

"Father in the Navy?" Tom asked, chuckling.

"No. I was. Tried it for a couple of years. Didn't like the atmosphere. Something to do with confined spaces and men on a diet like yours."

"I'm sure their senses were tested, too, but in a nicer way."

"My goodness!" Eva's smile was more country than maritime. "In New York just one week, mugged once, and flirting with an ADA."

"Plus witnessed a killing—busy woman, but you seem to be handling it pretty well."

"I've found it unwise to dwell on traumatic events." The body language remained relaxed but the manner turned businesslike. "Still, let me walk you through it, which is why I asked Detective Franklin to bring me here."

Eva told the story with swift precision. It differed not at all from what Tom had read and heard. No tension in her voice, even through the rough parts—including the skewering of the fallen

Mathew Agneau. "Poor brave man," she called him. Solemn enough but maybe a little cool—as if perhaps she'd think more of Mathew if he had got the job done.

"I wonder why you didn't cut your visit short?" What was her story? Washington official, knockout, on vacation in the Big Apple—alone! Doing what? Shopping? Cruising?

"Adrenaline, anger," Eva said, looking up over a spoonful of cereal. "I'd love to be around when you get that guy." More ice there. She softened up a bit. "It could be I'm still in shock. It's hard to believe, I guess, but I actually come to New York to slow down." A small laugh. "I'm with the State Department. Trade negotiations. Perpetual jet lag. I'm back and forth to Asia and Europe, three, four times a month, sometimes more. Phone calls, emails, faxes all times of the day and night. I'm dotting the tees and crossing the eyes even in my sleep. So when I get a couple of days off, I come to New York just to be alone, walk the sidewalks, see a play, catch up on my Zs."

Tom thought, *and get laid*? But his mind rolled quickly past that possibility for now and on to the info Ray had passed on earlier. Mathew Agneau was supposedly in Times Square to meet someone but that someone had not contacted police afterwards and no one at work or among Agneau's friends had any idea who it might have been. Ray found this strange. So were the facts that the killer had mugged someone in such a heavily policed area and had wielded a gigantic carving knife to murder a man in plain view whom he "could have blown over with a deep breath" and who posed no real threat to him at all. The autopsy had shown that the blade had "practically come out the poor guy's back." Tom was thinking that Eva here could be of no help on these matters when he recalled Ray's parting reference to "dopplesomethingorothers." He made a guess and asked the woman: "So what about these doppelgangers Detective Franklin told me about?"

"Yes. Strange. The doubles." She arranged her spoon in the empty bowl. "I'm trying to keep some of Mathew's blood in his body. I look up and what do I see? Me! Not an identical twin, of course, but the same color, length and cut of hair. An almost identical jacket with an identical red. Virtually identical shoes. She's weeping profusely, staring at the dying Mathew. And around her shoulder is the arm of a man who's a fairly close copy of the murderer. Big and powerful. Same hoodie. Everything the same, except he has no big scar on his chin, and he looks upset too. Could have been sent on down by central casting to replace the mugger."

"Did you talk to them?"

"The Navy medics arrived. I needed to keep the pressure on Mathew's wound, and give them a fill on what happened. We were lucky it was Fleet Week but not lucky enough, I guess. When I looked again, the doppel gang was gone." She watched Tom for a moment. "On the other hand, they could've just been two people out on a Friday night date and upset by what they'd seen."

"Lots of New Yorkers dress alike." Tom smiled. He paused. "Beauty like yours, on the other hand, stands out in any crowd, matching coats or not."

"You're very sweet," Eva said quietly.

Tom was out of order here. Eva would be a witness in this case if it ever came to that but he was a little bored tonight and the premonition had made him curious.

Eva asked: "Who was that little boy, the blind child? He was leaving when I came in?"

"Carlos. Neighbor and buddy. He studies at the martial arts school a bunch of us run—right there across the street." Tom pointed through the Rialto's front window.

Eva peered through the grime and laughed. "I'm sure the children love the name." She watched him with a small smile. "When little Carlos said goodbye to you tonight," she said after a moment, "I realized I hadn't sensed that kind of trust in a child in years. Not since my little brother still considered our dad his one and only hero."

"What can I say?" Tom replied, grinning and, he feared, blushing a little. "Beats getting your head handed to you by judges all day." He was about to try to extend their evening together, but had one more question before he made his move. "A couple of witnesses mentioned seeing a huge white man in a 05 jersey and a smaller guy with him after the attack. Said they were acting suspiciously although the police couldn't pin anyone down on why they stood out."

"No," replied Eva, after appearing to run through her memory. "There was a lot going on that night, but nothing like that stands out."

12

Dr. Sigurd Shivkovski and Dr. Rachel Arianna watched Shivkovski's ancient housekeeper Katya hobble across the living room towards them against the spectacular nighttime backdrop of Central Park and the Upper West Side.

"You and I may be the most fortunate people on earth, Rachel," Shivkovski said as they accepted their glasses of champagne. "If that were true," Rachel replied, "I would not have to spend my evening alone with Leon."

Shivkovski's eyes sparkled at this jibe. Leon and Rachel had been as oil and water since he had begun these once-a-month mentoring and ersatz family evenings after Rachel was orphaned. He saw the sniping as natural. And Shivkovski had had a good day. Rachel had watched him earlier spinning the GreenGene headquarters break-in on CNBC. The bright young business news things had soon been eating out of the old man's hand. His old world urbanity usually de-thorned most ethical issues — and there was nothing not to like about GreenGene's balance sheet. Profits and the stock price seemed destined to rise forever.

Shivkovski rose and put his glass on the mantelpiece. "Yes. I apologize for having to leave you two this evening. A minor emergency but it must be tended to." The glint remained in the old man's eye. "Do you really find Leon so deficient?"

"Please!" Rachel laughed, going along with the joke. "We all know there are predispositions. Matches, even. He ain't my type."

"We cannot all be beautiful people. There are more important things than setting hearts aflutter and inspiring the urge to rut."

"Oh, I don't know. I manage to fit it all in."

Shivkovski raised his glass to her. "Well, Leon is what he is. If he cannot find a mate, perhaps evolution has decided he should leave no genes behind."

"Why do I suspect that's not going to happen?"

The old man frowned but otherwise ignored the sarcasm. "What do we hear from Tom these days?"

Rachel eyebrows rose. "My goodness, pumping me for information! The Frankenfoods protest case, am I right? Is Shivkovski of Stalingrad unnerved by a hayseed's prank?"

"I have my employees' safety to consider." He made to leave.

"Tom will tell you anything. Do anything for you, in fact." He smiled faintly. "Please find out what you can from him. We're interested to know what abhorrent practices this Anderson fellow imagines GreenGene is up to."

"To be fair, perhaps I should tell Tom a secret or two about you in return? I do know a few after all."

"As you wish, my dear. Tell him anything you like."

That got Rachel's attention.

"Oh yes, young lady, I mean it!" Shivkovski's eyes were bright. "I'm feeling complete these days—and tiring of the niceties, if only a little." He watched her face. "On the other hand, I love Tom like a son and timing is everything. None of us wants to cause the others pain, do we? Unless or until we can't avoid it."

Bluff called, Rachel reached for her champagne.

Leon Shivkovski's lips were pursed and a squint encased his close-set eyes.

Rachel's fork stopped halfway to her mouth.

"Are you looking at my ear?" She returned her utensil to the plate. "You are! You're looking at my ear! Please assure me you have not become interested in my body either as a whole or in its constituent parts. I'd like to keep this meal down."

Leon took a swig of overpriced wine, courtesy of the GreenGene corporate account. "You have a certain frosty allure, Rachel," he said dismissively. "Some of you might even be nice to touch. But you're not smart enough for me. I can't get it up for dumb chicks."

"It would be unkind of me to weep with joy but consider me relieved." She returned to her duck.

"Why be kind to me when you're so mean to Tom?"

"Tom seems to be on the Shivkovski brain today. Your father was just after me to spy on him."

"Wow! And pile betrayal on top of rejection! But since your life's work is to make Tom miserable, why not?"

"Puppy love isn't terminal," Rachel said sharply. "The right girl will come along for Tom. Why the concern, anyway? You envy and resent him. I sometimes think you would like to see him dead. Because he is so much smarter than you."

"Smarter than me?" Leon sneered. "The guy's a lawyer!"

"He's not only smarter, he would have made a more perceptive scientist than either of us. He doesn't accept that we're merely, as Edward Wilson put it, 'the summed activity of a finite number of chemical and electrical reactions.' He doesn't see everyone as a pile of nucleic acids. He respects our essence. He believes in a human spirit."

Leon rolled his eyes, faked a yawn and pretended to consult his watch.

"Okay Mr. Smart Guy," Rachel said with a murderous smile. "Those chess games you two play—who always wins?"

"He does, but only at his primitive level."

"I see. So every time he checkmates, you chalk your defeat up as a victory in another upside-down dimension, which you alone inhabit, no doubt? I suppose you get your sex there too."

Leon appeared untouched by these taunts. "Tom cut and run from science because his father killed himself. Mad Mike couldn't handle the stress and neither could the son. They were afraid. Afraid of riding on the cutting edge of man's journey into the unknown. They didn't dare look upon the centers of mankind's—"

"Save it for the investors, Leon."

"You want to talk about human dysfunction?" Leon said. "Tell me why you've allowed poor god-like Tom suffer so pitifully in his unrequitement the last twenty-five years? Why not stay away and spare him the agony of your presence? Or put him out of his misery—never heard of a mercy fuck?"

Rachel dabbed at her lips with a napkin. "To exist is sometimes to suffer. In your case, for example, to burn with envy. Tom can handle it. And, yes, I would consider giving him some relief but for the fact that I don't get off on men who don't get off on science."

"I don't believe you, Rachel." Leon's smile was cool. "But for a low-down liar, you do have beautiful ears."

13

Tom found Ray at the new Kitchen Sink killings task force office. The techs were still running cable for computers so a uniformed cop was doing it the old way and sticking red, white and blue pins into a big wall map of the five boroughs. The reds, Tom guessed, were for confirmed Kitchen Sink killings. The whites would be for possible attacks and sightings. The blues? Stakeouts?

Ray stood in front of a TV set on an 8 p.m. dinner break. From the mournful audio, Tom could tell it was more on the presidential crisis. Endgame, Tom thought. The normally strident notes of American politics had been replaced in recent days with graver tones. Even party hacks now believed something more crucial than partisanship was at stake.

Someone turned the TV off. "I could use some of those billions for overtime," Ray said after swallowing the last of his sandwich.

"Got a minute for my mugging?"

"Your mugging's old news, Tom. Can't compete with this." He did a double take and laughed. "Oh, I get it. It's *personal* now, is it? You and Eva, huh? I knew you two would hit it off."

"You were right—for once." Tom moved towards the big map. "Guess I better solve this thing for you so you can pitch in on mine."

There were a lot of red pins, 15 or 16. All kills. Most of them in Queens. "He was all over the map for the first few," Tom said. "Wonder what the attraction is in Queens."

"No idea. Couple of those pins are new. Including that one near JFK. At first we thought some drunk had made a mistake. We took another look. Our boy somehow got this poor jerk to drink battery acid."

"Prosaic. Way down the ingenuity scale right? Next to the one where he just brained the guy with the brick."

"He has his bad days, like the rest of us. On the other hand, the one with the meat thermometer showed a certain *je ne sais quoi*. And the ME reckons the guy hung around for a couple of hours, as the body cooled down. Taking its temperature. Like it was a class project, or something."

"What's the latest?"

Ray pointed out the pin. "Real ugly. The old guy, retired from the Postal Service. His head was just about cut off. Our friend got behind him and threw this thin wire over his neck. He put his boot in the small of the old guy's back, and rather leisurely worked the wire back and forth so it cut its way into the flesh of the neck, throat, etc."

Tom's hand touched his throat. "Guess the cutting of the carotid artery would have knocked the vic out fairly quickly at least."

"Yeah but the killer still kept cutting away. Then the wire snagged and started to fray. Apparently happens sometimes when plumbers use them too. That's what he used — a wire-saw that cuts through plastic plumbing in spots where you can't use a regular saw."

"Drain pipe, huh? We're getting pretty close to the kitchen sink."

"The perp seemed quite upset that things didn't go as planned. He made what was already a hell of a mess even worse by trying to free the wire. It broke and he had to leave half of it behind."

"Maybe he's not as handy as he thinks." Tom stepped back and looked at the map again. Something looked familiar but he couldn't figure out what. He'd come back for a longer look, if he ever found the time.

14

Tom smelled the marijuana the moment he left the elevator. No staircase run tonight. His knee, banged up by Billy Franklin in sparring the day before, needed ice not work. He could have used the anger release, however. Rubenstein had been all over him today. How the hell had Tom let Wally Anderson make bail? Blame the judge, not me, Tom told him: Free Speech Leach, the rowdy protester's best friend.

It hadn't helped that the lab had pronounced Wally's genetic plague juice harmless and indeed, if the reported benefits of a Mediterranean diet were to be believed, healthy and nutritious: ketchup, tomato sauce, balsamic vinegar, thickened with olive oil. Wally posed no threat. He was bailed out by two rich kids—the kind that picket the same corporations that populate their trust funds.

"I want to show these enviroterrorists we're serious!" Rubenstein had shouted. "We go for the max. Anderson does time!"

Since hanging hippies from lampposts was not normally Rubenstein style, Tom reckoned Shivkovski was putting pressure on him via the mayor. The Republicans couldn't raise a nickel these days and so the billionaire was calling the shots.

None of this put Tom in the mood to tolerate dope in his apartment building. It was full of kids, for one thing—and if it was some of those same kids doing the pot, they were in need of a good scare.

Tom opened his front door and shut it without entering. He waited until he heard telltale scuffing on the stairs not far below. He tiptoed back into the elevator, descended three floors, and started quietly up the stairway.

Stealth was hardly necessary. The offender was too absorbed relighting his roach to hear Tom coming.

"Made bail, I see!"

Wally Anderson jumped a foot in the air and did a full half-twist before dog-paddling halfway up to the next landing.

"Thank God it's you," he gasped, hand clutching at his pounding heart.

"You're right, Wally! There are law-and-order-types on this

floor. So if it wasn't, you'd be chewing baseball bat by now.'""

Wally sat for a moment, then reached for his fumbled roach. Tom's foot beat him to it. "Not jumpy enough yet? Or in enough trouble? What the hell are you doing here?"

"I'm being followed."

"Really? And coincidentally you seek refuge in the one building in New York City where I happen to live?"

"No, of course not. Mr. Daluskov." Wally tried to switch on the woodsy charm. "I was coming here to talk to you when I noticed this big, blonde guy following me."

"We can't talk without your lawyer present."

"We got rid of my lawyer, remember?"

"No, *you* got rid of him. So now you'll need a new one. I don't see why some big outfit like Greenpeace isn't stepping forward for you."

Wally stood up and brushed the dirt off his hands. "I don't do well in a big organization. Problem with authority, I guess. Or bureaucracy. I have plenty of, you know, friends and, uh, contacts, but I . . . we like to do our own thing, you know? Contribute in our own way. I'm sorry if this looks bad. I wanted another off-the-record talk, that's all. Never been followed before. When you didn't answer your door, I guess I was a little afraid to go back outside."

A door opened on the landing below. Tom decided to move the meeting upstairs but warned Wally again that without a lawyer along they couldn't discuss his case. Newly washed sheets billowed in the breeze on the roof. Tom waved at Carlos, Billy and Mary who were preparing for a belt presentation on the far side of a clothesline.

"It's not about my case," Wally said. "It's about GreenGene and the stuff we talked about before."

Tom reckoned that would be Wally's stories of unholy experiments on mice. "My responsibilities don't include the genetic rights of rodents."

Wally dropped into a squat. "You know, Mr Daluskov, I checked you out." Tom grunted. "There are plenty of greens among the Harvard alumni. There's obviously an impression among your law school classmates that you're a big- and great-things guy. One woman remembers you very well—and she's still hot, by the way. Says you've got the Cromwell or Cincinnati—no, Cincinnatus—gene. The man who's born ready but not necessarily eager. The call might never come, but if it does, it will be a special call, and you'll be the obvious one to answer it."

"Besides being ridiculous, that is irrelevant. I told you Wally: I'm a people person. Try the SPCA."

"Killer bees affect people, right?"

Tom knew a bit about the so-called killer bees. Apparently, the result of a breeding experiment gone bad in the 1980s, their genetically altered swarm, sting and pursuit instincts had indeed killed a number of people as they spread north from Brazil through South and Central America and finally into the United States.

"And what about transgenic fish," Wally asked.

"Mouse fish, are they? They eat cheese and swim from cats?"

"No, fish that have been given the gene for human growth hormone. They grow and mature sexually faster, are bigger overall and probably because of that attract more mates. Trouble is their survival rate is only two-thirds that of your normal wild fish. Darwin's turned upside. A so-called Trojan gene is introduced into nature. After forty generations, one transgenic fish can reduce the potential fish population by sixty thousand."

"Stung to death and deprived of sushi!"

"What about killer rats!" Wally would not be made light of. "It's not funny when you understand that these possibilities are real." He pointed toward Carlos, Mary and Billy. "You want killer rats infesting this neighborhood, massing and attacking those kids over there? Farfetched? Maybe. But once you create your genetic mutant and you let it out into nature, you can never get it back into the box again."

"You don't cook up killer rats or any other substantially altered life in a few days at the lab," Tom said, head back, enjoying the sunlight. "Even a slight genetic alteration usually makes an animal cell unviable. Besides, science knows where the money is. Killer rats don't sell."

"It could happen by mistake. All it takes is a couple of breakdowns or breakthroughs. Smart rats would kill off or otherwise outsmart and eventually outlive dumb rats the way we did the other hominids. Like the Neanderthals, who never developed throwing weapons and ate the same dumb diet for 100,000 years. These rats would put a lot of other species out of business, too. They might be smart enough to mate for intelligence. That means they'd get smarter faster than we did, even. Might end up doing some genetic engineering of their own!"

"You want to see laws written, and regulation introduced?" Tom asked Wally. "Go for it. You have a chance to make a difference." On reflection, Tom figured Wally's guerrilla theater at GreenGene had had most of the makings for successfully launching this kind of propaganda campaign. "Instead of breaking the law, take your rat story to the media. They'd love it. Shine a light on these things. The killer rats will run but you'll attract other kinds of vermin, including politicians."

"Exactly!" said Wally. "And that's why my trial will help!"

Tom turned from him as his students approached. "Carlos, this fellow intends to waste many weeks of my valuable time in a useless trial. Kindly kick his butt over the side."

"Okay, okay," Wally said, feigning fright. "I'll plead. But you guarantee you'll look at any stuff I dig up on GreenGene."

"We can't talk about that now," Tom said, mostly as a formality. "But here's a promise: you bring me anything that indicates public endangerment and I'll look into it. But you do anything illegal again and this is the last time we speak."

Wally nodded his agreement. He walked to the edge of the roof and leaned over to peek down into the street, then stepped quickly back. "Can you protect me?" Wally whispered when Tom approached. "The guy who followed me is down there, the blonde guy by the mailbox."

Tom saw a tall broadly built blonde man leaning against a wall, his eyes fixed on the building's front entrance. The man looked up and saw them watching him. He folded his newspaper and walked around the corner and out of sight.

One more thing that Tom would raise with Shivkovski.

15

Gerald hadn't heard from the boss for five days. It was 6:45 a.m. and he had already done three 400-rep sets of pushups, sit-ups and knee-bends. He'd prepared breakfast, consumed it and finished the dishes. After days of make-work activities, his room was so clean it practically squeaked.

Fortunately, Gerald knew that restlessness was natural.

The boss had told him that nature impels all living things to seek and pursue what they and their species need to survive. Short-term, these things were often no more than nutrition, water and relatively clean air. But there were other drives too. Sex, for instance, and the nurturing of the young. Geese flew south in the autumn. Many billions of other compulsions ruled the lives of many millions of other animals, insects and plants. Mosquitoes came into the world and demonstrated immediately that one of the only important things in life was to lay some eggs before they died.

Gerald could recite every word of every one of the boss's lessons. But all he really needed to remember were the facts about "the Big A"—the boss's name for the horrible anxiety that took hold of Gerald when things didn't go the way they should, and which made him work so darn hard to get things right.

The boss said the Big A was integral to the way humans work. Some wished to lead, some to follow, some to join, some to go their own way. Power, wealth, triumph, service, approval, comfort, safety and love and knowledge were, in varying degrees, sometimes together, sometimes independently, merely great antidotes to the Big A. It all depended on the apportioning of genetic traits and needs—the chemistry of character.

Some kept the Big A at bay with great striving. The long and difficult struggle to decipher nature's puzzles, for example. Or to recreate or interpret the essences of existence in literature, music, paintings and sculpture. Some people kept the house extra neat and tidy. Others bought shiny SUVs. "Take the Big A away," the boss once said, "and life has no meaning."

Gerald was a striver and a neat nut who had to get it right. Like the chain on the chainsaw last night. He spent three hours picking debris from the little hollows and washing out the blood and the shreds of various tissues. He re-oiled it before returning the saw to its proper place on his shelves. It felt good to see it there, immaculate, like all the other tools and tokens.

He was still jumpy, though. He peered out his window at the crackheads on the corner. When the boss didn't call, when there was no task to attend to, Gerald guessed he got as strung out and twitchy as they did without their drugs. It began as unease and grew into distress. He often pumped iron for hours to fight the mounting tension. Eventually his whole day went dark. The drip-drip of self-doubt became an ocean of self-disgust. "Why am I like this?" he once found himself shouting. "What the hell am I good for?"

The boss had told him: "Next time this happens, remember how lucky you are. You know you will get new jobs. You know they will always be there. And you know you can complete them and find serenity for a time. A lot of people do not have that blessing. They have no way out—no way to beat the Big A. It never goes away."

The boss was right. When the calls came in, Gerald calmed right down. A few butterflies, perhaps, but he was in the groove. Determined, content, talented, trained and ready. And when the thing was done, and done right, well . . . . Gerald not only walked on air, he became one with the Universe! He experienced an orgasmic lightness of being. He was stardust for a while, afloat in a Milky Way of pure contentment.

That's why he did the freebie. It had not been assigned; it was on his own time. In fact, he wasn't even sure it was allowed. But it had to be done, or else the sloppy work in Queen's would bug him for weeks—and affect his performance at other tasks.

He told that hardware store owner Jimmy to his face: "I don't care if I got the plumber's cutting wire for free. It is a tool. It is supposed to work correctly. I had a job. I take pride in that. Maybe you don't but I do! Your cheap substandard rotten tool made me mess up. Do you know how much that hurts me?"

Jimmy had looked angry and scared at the same time.

"It's a poor workman who blames his tools," he said.

That was a little more than Gerald could take. And his eyes must have shown it.

Jimmy suddenly offered to pay for the damage–even provide a plumber for free. Gerald had seen Jimmy's trembling hand reaching for his crowbar, which he kept handy below the counter beside the cash. So he gave Jimmy a casual swat across the jaw with the flat of a big framing hammer, the kind with the nice blue rubber grip.

He looked up and saw the chainsaw. Gerald had admired the machine the last time he'd been in. He felt creative today. So he drew all the blinds and hung Jimmy's GO AWAY, I'M CLOSED FOR THE DAY sign on the front door. He remembered the big yellow rubber rain overalls and hoods he'd seen up Aisle 3. The first one he tried fit pretty well, as did the gumboots. Gerald was working freehand here–no instructions, rules or guidance. But back at the school, he remembered other kids talking and laughing about chainsaw massacres.

After he'd dissected Jimmy a bit, he wondered what was so hot about chain saws, at least when it came to human flesh. The tool slipped and skipped all over the place and, overall, cut pretty badly, except for bones. For applications involving soft tissue, you could see why people had stuck with simple sharpened single-edge implements for so many millennia.

Gerald brought the chain saw home, compensation for the lousy pipe-cutting wire Jimmy had given him, which had become snagged in the cartilage of that client's neck up in Queens.

He had tidied up before he left the store, however, and left a message. He had secured Jimmy's severed head using the vise mounted by the cash register for small adjustments and repairs. He'd put the newly painted sign beside it. The sign said: "Need Help? Ask Jimmy!" With a felt pen, Gerald added: "But don't expect a good answer."

Now, back home by the window, he saw a crackhead down on the street leap to his feet and scurry round the corner. Gerald jumped too. The telephone was beeping.

His fingers trembled slightly as he began to punch in the code.

There was a message.

Gerald listened carefully and allowed himself one sigh of relief. There was a job to do, thank goodness. No more waiting and half going crazy. His eyes scanned the uppermost shelves. He was sure he had a good wrench around here somewhere.

16

It was his turn to host and he knew it would be a downer but Tom brought up Sigurd Shivkovski and the GreenGene break-in at the biweekly family dinner. As silence crackled round his kitchen table, he also asked how upset his mother and Hank thought Shivkovski might be about Wally Anderson's fishing expedition. His mother stiffened when he said that Anderson was being followed and recounted the activist's claim to have found evidence of over-the-top genetic manipulation at GreenGene.

"Cooked this yourself, did you?" Hank asked with a small smile, holding up a piece of the freshly delivered pizza.

"Oh, come on!" Tom said after a moment. "Don't clam up! Isn't it time you let me in on the clan's dirty secrets?"

Tom's mother took a sip of her wine. "If I told you the subject is private and painful, would that suffice?"

"I suppose it has to." She had not said "unimportant," Tom noted, but consideration outweighed his irritation, if only barely.

Hank crossed his sturdy forearms on the table. "The surveillance—you sure it's not NYPD? Or the Feds?"

"I'm pretty sure it's neither." He told them more about Wally's claims. His mother's eyes widened and sought out Hank's.

"Could they be watching you?" Hank asked.

"Me? Well, maybe, I guess. If they are, it had to look strange—this perp coming to meet with me at my apartment building. Wally is like a puppy. One kind word and you can't get rid of him."

Dr. Parviati laid her small hand on his shoulder. "Instinct draws them to integrity and strength." Her fingers seemed to tremble.

"Are you going after GreenGene?" Hank asked.

"For what? They're the complainants. Our Wallyworld character can't seem to grasp that. He's too excited about this mighty mouse he thinks he saw. He was smoking weed at the time, by the way."

"For safety's sake," Hank said, "check to see if you're under surveillance yourself. Remember the elevator double-back trick I told you about? I'll also get someone to check your place for bugs.

But they might have had someone with a directional mike on the next roof."

"Who'd follow me?" Tom was genuinely surprised. Hank hadn't talked tradecraft with him since he was a teenager. His mother's overreaction was also puzzling. He thought for a moment. "It's Leon, right? You think loony Leon has someone watching me because I won't do his bidding on this case?"

Hank shrugged and raised his beer to his mouth. Tom turned to his mother.

Dr. Parviati spoke slowly. "If someone was shooting at you, that would be Leon. This sounds more like Sigurd, bold yet cautious. It is not necessarily illegal, after all."

Tom felt the familiar anger blossoming in his gut. He understood the old-brain limbic logic even as it gripped him: my father is dead; old Shivkovski may be partly to blame; he should not be messing with me; time to rip his throat out.

"Legal?" Tom said. "Depends who he's tailing and how far he's gone. Leave out the ancient history if you want but I still need an honest assessment. Would he willfully interfere in the process of justice? Would he be stupid enough to stalk an ADA? For that matter, is he capable of reckless scientific experiments — maybe not this mighty mouse thing but something crazier?"

Hank did the talking. "Sigurd is the end product of vast innate talent and extreme life experiences. His view of the world and his fellow man has been shaped by what he and your father saw, endured and perhaps did in the Gulag and the war, things that we perhaps can't imagine. There may little he is not willing to do in the name of science. His already extraordinary attitudes and resources are greatly leveraged each year by new theory and technologies. What may be going too far for us may be for him not nearly far enough."

Tom recalled Billy Stricks' gravestone.

"So I should keep a close eye on old man Shivkovski."

Hank nodded. "It would be a good idea even in the best of times."

The next morning, Tom voicemailed his next move to Leon. "Kd2," he said after the beep. He smiled. On the chessboard at least, if not in one of Leon's hallucinatory alternate dimensions,

Shivkovski the Son was about to go down hard yet again.

Tom then managed a friendly tone in a message for Shivkovski Sr. "Consider this a courtesy call. The accused in the break-in case believes he has been placed under surveillance. Indications are that this may be true. Any such activity, especially by GreenGene and/or its agents and associates, would damage chances for a successful prosecution. This is not the old country, Doctor. We can't shoot them in the basement. You claim to know me well and so you will agree that there is more than a little of the Mad Mike in me. I will take any attempt by you to interfere in the operation of the justice system personally. The gloves will come off. And who knows? Perhaps I'll join you in throwing away the rule book."

17

Jason Hunter had learned about the cave system only four years earlier.

On nights when his father's moans and grieving ruled out sleep, Jason rummaged through stacks of family papers in the silent attic. The correspondence, children's journals, even a few love letters, had been wrapped in oilcloth with the farm accounts and notes about crops and weather. One of these ledgers gave up the secret of what lay beneath the Hunter farm.

Jason's granddad had come upon the cavern systems by accident almost 75 years earlier while digging foundations for a bridge over a small stream. He had inadvertently emulated cave explorers who seek out hidden entrances by digging into sinkholes and other geological formations that indicate that water is seeping into the earth. As Jason learned from subsequent reading, underground caves often have no surface opening.

The discovery was a call to adventure for the Hunter men at the time and for their neighbors and close friends, the Stricks. They'd expanded the entrance, equipped themselves with miner's lamps, and learned that the three interlocking caves were for the most part passable, if greatly challenging and fraught with many dangers.

Library books taught them that underground caves are formed by the flow of water that has seeped through the chemical byproducts of decaying vegetation. The weak carbonic acid can dissolve huge amounts of limestone and dolomite over many millions of years. It seeks routes along cracks, fissures and in the joints between large rocks, and carves out the passages, shafts, chimneys and rooms. When water works down from widely scattered points on the surface, it is not unusual for one of a cave's many underground tributaries to accidentally intersect with the tributaries of another. This had happened eons ago beneath what was now the Hunter and Stricks properties.

Jason's grandfather mapped much of the system. He named prominent landmarks and features after family, relations and friends: Sarah's Stalagmite, for instance, and Dick's Dead End. They rechristened the system the Hunter-Stricks Cave after months of expeditions showed that it ranged many hundreds of yards on both sides of the boundary between their two farms.

Children were barred. Sheer underground rock faces and crevasses that were hundreds of feet deep made the cave a perilous place even for grown men. But Jason's dad and his best friend Billy Stricks, then both 10, were happy to risk a licking. They had been underground a dozen times before the day Billy died. He was smothered when rock and earth that was nurturing the Stricks' own cornfield a few feet above him gave way. The cave logbook asked: "Did poor Billy know he was just a stone's throw from his barn?" Rather than carry the boy's small body many hours along the tortuous route back to the entrance, the Stricks and the Hunters dug a narrow shaft at the collapse site and lifted Billy out by rope. They buried him atop the farm's highest hill. Jason's grandfather confided to this journal that he didn't care for the tombstone's suggestion that Billy "went too far." "Died too young was more like it," he wrote, but the Stricks had always "been immoderately fond of moderation." This was not the story that the Stricks and Jason's parents had told him about the grave on the top of the hill. They said Billy Stricks drowned. The logbooks showed that both families believed that the cave would always be a fatal attraction for children. They resealed the entrance at the Hunter end and never spoke of it again.

For the adult Jason, however, the story was a gift. The cave not only offered a distraction but also presented an opportunity to decipher the puzzle of his unneighborly neighbors, who in his view had long ago lost their right to privacy. His grandfather's maps showed that the system penetrated well past the perimeter security fences of the Oneida Foundation but fell short of the massive excavations for the main buildings. He was sure that the Institute did not know about the cave or how it compromised their massive effort to ensure security and secrecy. The VC themselves could not have done a better job.

Jason uncovered the cave mouth the first time he tried digging. He cleared it and built a sturdy locked entrance with old timbers and a rusty hinged iron gate he picked up at the dump. No field-wandering children would see it once his sod-topped construction palette camouflage was in place. Then he picked the brain of an old tunnel rat during a Vietnam vet reunion and dropped in on cavers' meetings around the state. He even did some "vertical training" on an old railroad bridge, all the time picking up the tips he needed from experienced cavers but keeping the existence of the Hunter-Stricks Cave secret.

On days off and during some of his father's worst nights, Jason went underground to dig, crawl, slither, slide, skid, climb, and trudge through a dark world that in some ways seemed more carefree than the one he was escaping above. It took him 12 tries to find the spot where Billy Stricks died. From the logbook, he knew it would be marked by the boy's baseball glove. A water trickle nearby showed where the chute up which Billy had been lifted had been dug, refilled, and buttressed. Now, if needed, it could provide covert entry to the Oneida Foundation's complex.

Jason marked the 1.5-mile route back to the entrance with florescent paint. He cut hand and footholds in smooth limestone rock faces for difficult climbs and descents. Where ceilings were high enough, he drove bolts into the walls for hand guides made of chain. At the steepest points, he secured cable ladders with aircraft wire and steel rungs. He mounted battery-powered floodlights at many dangerous stretches and stockpiled second-hand caving gear, including helmets with headlights, carbide lamps, and warm clothing, gloves and boots. If someone besides Chelsea had come to know, he would have lied about his motive. He was preparing to bring tourists into the cave. He was preparing for a North Korean nuclear strike!

He worked in the cold and the damp for a year, then two, then three. When his father's anguish spiked to increasingly new heights, the colder, the damper, the darker it was, the greater the tranquility Jason was able to find. His wife teased him. "All you need now is your army." She considered it therapeutic yet somehow serious too. It was Jason himself who sometimes wondered whether he was losing his grip. Like his old man.

18

Tom was pleased but not surprised. At least not at first. He and Eva were unattached, fit, and drawn one to the other. They ended up in Eva's hotel room that first evening. He'd spent most of the night. As he'd suspected, there had been an edginess to her that stirred him but also a coolness and distance that allowed him to hit the sidewalks afterwards feeling invigorated but free.

Freedom was crucial in these matters. Tom could not deal with encumbrances, much less entanglements. The good thing was that Eva seemed unlikely to be interested in strings either. She lived in Washington and spent most of her time working abroad. As the next day wore on, however, he amazed himself. Rather than hoping that the woman would not call, he was hoping she would. By 5:30 p.m., he'd telephoned Eva himself. She asked to visit WHUPASS.

When Eva arrived, Tom and a handsome black man Tom later introduced as his best friend Will faced each other on a sparring mat. Three dozen students ranging from white belt toddlers to black belt teens were gathered round them in their uniforms and gear. Will's fists were loosely clenched and slung a little low, his feet in fighting position and his eyes did not leave Tom's until he was well into a leftward spinning motion that turned his back, with its black and red WHUPASS logo, to his opponent.

Eva told Tom later that she reckoned few people would have been able to react before they saw his eyes again—and by then it would be too late. Will would have pivoted 360 degrees, his right foot would be head height, and the explosive power of his legs and gluts and three decades of relentless training would have propelled the callused ball of his foot into the opponent's head, wreaking serious or perhaps fatal damage.

Tom, of course, knew what was coming and pulled back his head just enough for the demonstration to leave no injury. After a few words to the assembled students on the technique, Detective Franklin's son Billy and girlfriend Mary jumped in for some sparring first with Tom and then with Will. The two older men held the youngsters at bay with blocks, punches, and jumping and spinning kicks. The school remained silent except for the thudding of bare feet on the mat and plywood flooring and the sounds of motion, breathing, the combatants' sharp yells and contact but when the four finished and bowed to one another, the young audience erupted in whoops, whistling and applause.

"The kids like to see the old geezers perform," Tom told Eva when he joined her. "Gives them a nice low bar to shoot for." Eva continued to watch as Carlos Chavez, minus shades and baseball cap, moved to the middle of the floor. Billy and Mary, standing on chairs, held a square piece of wood at least two feet over the boy's head. After a bow in Tom's direction, Carlos leapt up and whipped his right leg into the air. The board split and splinters flew.

Eva joined in the cheers. She leaned closer. "You seem happy right now so where is all this violence that seems to seep from your pores coming from?"

"This isn't violence. It's determination, self-discipline. Overcoming obstacles brings people peace."

"I'm not talking about this, I'm talking about you. I'm a Navy brat. I grew up with Marines and Seals. I know the smell of surplus testosterone."

"Turn off, is it?"

"You already know that it's not." Eva laughed. She cupped his arm in her hands, pulled him towards her, and was about to whisper in his ear when something across the room caught her eye. "Who's that?" she asked in a low voice. "A girlfriend? She's awfully beautiful but right now she looks like she's about to cry — or commit murder."

Tom followed her gaze. It was Rachel, standing beside Will. She was here to see Carlos awarded his brown belt but wore a look of hurt or disappointment Tom had never seen before. It disappeared the moment she saw Tom watching. She smiled and waved and turned to catch Carlos as he rushed into her opening arms.

"That's Rachel," Tom said. "I think I've mentioned her. One of my closest lab rat buddies. Looked for a moment there like she'd had a sudden unpleasant insight on the dark side of rhododendron sex. Always the deep thinker."

But Tom felt a surge of triumph. Rachel had indeed been upset and had tried to hide it. The tables, for once, had been turned. Carlos had broken a board today but perhaps he was the one who was busting through a wall.

At dinner, Tom talked mostly about Carlos. He told Eva how other handicapped students had benefited from time at WHUPASS and how much he and Will regretted having been unable to have their mentally challenged childhood friend Francis join the school. Tom had not seen Francis for years but had asked the people responsible for the man's care — "the Shivkovskis, once close family friends" — whether it was possible. Another lab rat, Leon Shivkovski, had given the idea the thumbs down. Leon was "a very strange and difficult guy" but also very attached to Francis. So at least Will and Tom knew that he would provide Francis with the most advanced care money could buy.

Eva listened but said nothing.

After a short walk, they kissed somewhat chastely and went their separate ways, although Tom was still thinking about Eva when he powered up the stairs to his apartment.

The call came around 2:10 a.m. Tom wasn't asleep. Eva wanted to come over. The request would have normally set off alarm bells but Tom felt no hesitation whatsoever. She would be there in an hour. "Go back to sleep; get your rest; I just want to be next to you."

He did sleep. Or perhaps he only thought he did. Because he suddenly found himself standing at the window, hands spread against the frame.

Tom knew he merely had to wait a while before this rare yet familiar sensation would pass. He'd had these small seizures all his life. Some came abruptly, interrupting a moment of stress, anger or fear. Others showed up out of the blue. Still others seemed premonitory and were often followed by a minor or middling crisis in his life, or a sharp change in direction. A gentle tingling ran up his back and through his neck and shoulders. He felt an elevation in his body temperature, heard a rushing noise in his ear, and experienced sensations of brightening light and passing shadows.

When it was over, he always felt more finely tuned. Calm, resolute, sharp, fluid. Ideas, all cleanly chiseled, stood up in neat lines for his consideration. He mind saw — without actually seeing — the broad strokes and fine weaves of life laid out before him, informing his next moves. At least that's how it seemed

Tom reckoned it was a neurological tic, perhaps brought on by training. He'd had time for some pretty good workouts in the past week. Time did sometimes seem to slow when he fought or sparred.

But that didn't explain the oceanic feeling, a sense of belonging and goodwill towards man that bordered on the sappy. He had started experiencing the episodes as a young child. They had alarmed him and so he had done some reading.

"No, my darling," his mother had told him, "you're not an epileptic. Neither do you have a brain tumor, or a direct link to aliens or to God." She had taken his face between her hands. "These are merely the feelings of life. The feelings of being human."

19

"Leon," Francis asked, "why doesn't Tom like us?"

"Because he's a son of a bitch."

The childlike Francis had needed calming after the Times Square incident. Leon had been spending more time with him. They were in Leon's private "playhouse" tonight a floor beneath the senior executive offices at GreenGene's headquarters, surrounded by genetic sequencers and other shiny lab equipment. Few people knew the room was there. Leon had a secret entrance from his executive suite one floor up—the stairway descended from his private bathroom. Francis loved coming in that way.

Francis was shocked at first by Leon's harsh words but a surprising small new voice had been encroaching on his consciousness in recent weeks. An image darted through his mind's eye of Tom's mom, Dr. Sophia Parviati, and he heard the voice again. A sly smile crept to his lips and he heard himself say: "That's not a nice thing to call Auntie Sophia."

Leon sat bolt upright in front of his computer screen. He made an exaggerated face of surprise—the kind a parent might produce to please a child. "Way to go, Francis! You're quicker on the uptake every day." He patted Francis on one massive shoulder. "See? I told you I'd help you get smarter. But Dr. Parviati isn't your aunt, or mine, so let's not use that term. It confers a certain grace and dignity—" He paused. "—Something that *bitch* does not deserve."

Francis laughed again, though his eyes darted around to make sure they were still alone. You could never tell whether Leon was joking or just being mean.

"She's so bloody smug and yet she actually worked with the Germans for a while in the 30s." Leon was adjusting his instruments. "Nazis, some of them! I'd say that that's taking scientific objectivity way too far! Of course, she beat it when she saw which way the whirlwind was blowing."

Leon looked up at Francis, as if this giant child understood who the Nazis were. "It's funny. They always say Darwin and genetics and eugenics led to Hitler but it was as much the result of hundreds of years of virulent Christian anti-Semitism. Why blame genetics? Why not ban religion instead?"

"Is that why you hate Tom's mom—because of the *nasties*?"

"Nazis! Not nasties! I don't hate her. She fell into my sights tonight by accident." Leon was absorbed in his work but looked up after a moment. "Keep talking and listening, Francis. It's good for you. Especially right now. You're a growing boy again and you need all the mental exercise you can get."

Leon began lecturing on atavism, working as he spoke. Atavism was the accidental reappearance of normally dormant traits. Dormant meant sleeping. Inside of us, Leon said, were the genes that "expressed" the traits and stages humans had gone through on the long road from the start of our existence as a single living cell, possibly three million years ago. At one point, for instance, we weren't much more than scum on a pond. But the genes that made that goo from the nutrients around us still existed in our bodies. Some were doing something else now.

"Making the goo in our noses?" Francis said, eliciting a grudging smile from Leon, who continued: "Some genes never learned how to do anything except make goo. Since we weren't goo anymore, they now did nothing. Just slept and were dormant. Just like our genes for fishy scales and monkey tails. And lots of fur, except—!" Leon shouted. "Except that occasionally, through a mutation, an old gene gets kick-started again."

"You mean people grow tails?" Francis asked.

"Sure. It could happen. In Mexico there was a family with hair all over their bodies, even on their eyelids, because a 25-million-year-old gene—one of the sleeping beauties—had accidently woken up."

"Are you looking for that one, Leon?" Francis asked. He knew that Leon and Dr. Shivkovski not only looked for genes but also manipulated them. Manipulate. M-a-n-i-p-u-l-a-t-e. Francis even knew what it meant. Lately, he could pick up an idea, hold on to it, and pick up some more. It was still there if he needed it later. He used to pity other people, especially men, when they couldn't lift a log or a stone that he found light. They must have looked at him in the same way when he could not understand something simple. That's what they called him. S-i-m-p-l-e.

"Sleeping beauties. Another name for dormant traits," Leon said. "Sometimes whales are born with the vestigial hind limbs they grew out of when they returned to the sea forty million years back. Vestigial. V-e-s-t-i-g-i-a-l. Sometimes, vestigial traits show up in embryos but disappear as the fetus matures."

Francis was looking at the top of Leon's head. Between the thinning strands of hair, his scalp reflected the neon glare.

"Are you sure you don't want to find the fur gene, Leon?" he asked, though he was too shy to take the matter any further.

"We leave that Mickey Mouse stuff to corporate profiteers. Those greedy capitalist jerks won't leave as much as a skid mark on history and civilization." Without looking up, Leon patted his pate and wagged a finger at Francis. "And don't think I don't know what you're referring to! You're a barrel of laughs today. But baldness genes and obesity genes? Forget it! Same with the Big-Dick gene. We're after the big heart, the big mind, the big soul, the way-the-fuck-over-the-top-no-one's-gonna-stop-us-now genes!"

Francis laughed and danced along with Leon, who was flailing his arms and twirling around on the wheels of his chair.

"As our friend Will is wont to say, we're going to open a big can of whoop-ass on these greedy, pea-brained corporate scientist freaks. Those oinkers will still be dreaming about identifying the gene for suppressing farts when we calmly achieve the transcendent moments, one after the other."

Leon stood and winked at Francis. He held up a small container. "Francis, maybe you should turn your back," he said with mock solemnity. "This is a rather intimate moment."

Francis knew not to take him seriously. "What is it?" he asked.

"Skin. I have skinned a beautiful beast." Leon held the slide up. "You know, from these cells, I could grow an entire person—a clone. Scrape some tissue from the ear of a bull, for example, take the nucleus from the cell and pop it into an unfertilized egg that's been emptied of its own nucleus. Implant it in momma."

"You're not going to clone a beast, are you?" Francis didn't want to get that crazy.

"Of course not," said the scientist, moving toward some equipment at the back of the lab. "I'm just going to have a peek at some DNA for a little project I have in mind."

"DNA from the beast?"

"From the beauty, actually," he said. "A woman. Brilliant. Quite phenomenal. She fell asleep—too much to drink." Leon smirked, appearing mildly embarrassed "Well, okay, I slipped her a little Mickey. Some flunitrazepam in her wine. A roofie."

"What's that?"

"Nothing harmful. It's a date-friendly drug. She goes to sleep; she doesn't remember what happens. Sweets for the sweet."

"So you skinned her?"

"Yeah, I skinned her." He held up a stainless steel scraper. "I ran this lightly over her rather exquisite ear lobe."

"Tonight? When you went out at dinner time?"

"Even crazy people have to eat."

"But wasn't tonight the night when you have dinner with Rachel at your father's house?"

Leon smiled blithely. "He had to leave before dessert and Rachel needed a little nap afterwards."

"This is one of the things I'm not supposed to tell about, right?"

"Don't worry. You won't. Even under torture."

"Why not?"

"Because you've got the pain resistance of elephant dung. And I'm smartening you up so that no one can trick an answer out of you."

The phone rang. Leon looked at the display but didn't answer.

After the fourth ring, the lab message prompt sounded, and after the beep, a man's voice said: "Qc2." Tom's next chess move. "Hey, Leon, you're doing pretty well this game. I might even break a sweat." Another pause, followed by: "When you see your dad, tell him I'll have good news soon on the break-in. And you can thank him for being such a model American citizen and not abusing his position of power and influence. As well as taking his place in line." This last bit carried an edge of sarcasm.

"Is that Tom?" Francis asked nervously. Tom scared him somehow. He was angry a lot, even when they were kids. And Tom was never, never afraid of Leon or even of Leon's father.

Ignoring him, Leon picked up the receiver and punched out a number. After a moment, he said: "Qc2" and hung up.

Francis wondered why Leon called the other person and told them Tom's move but he suspected this was not something he should ask about. So he said instead: "Why do you and Tom always play chess like that?"

"The poor guy's delusional. Thinks he's smarter than me." Leon looked off into the middle distance. "But the day of reckoning when he finds out he isn't is fast approaching."

20

"I've got it!" Wally Anderson shouted when Tom answered the phone. The radio clock said 4:13 am.

"You've got what, Wally?" Tom asked groggily. "Besides a death wish."

"Sorry, Tom but I had to tell you! We've got GreenGene by the short and curlies!"

Eva opened her eyes and smiled. Just about nothing could spoil Tom's mood right now but Wally was sounding manic again and might be about to do something stupid. Such stupidity could in turn wreck Tom's careful plan to wrap up the GreenGene case for good.

"Look, Wally," he said. "Come in this morning at nine. Bring a lawyer and we'll get this done." Tom intended to devise a plea bargain that Rubenstein would find hard to overrule. Even if he did, the aggravation would drive the DA and Sigurd Shivkovski up the wall.

"Can't," Wally replied. "I need more time. A week. Let's make it a week from today—first thing next Monday morning. I've got things to do before I can deliver the whole package."

"What package?"

"You'll see, man! We'll blow the roof off this GMO thing. As long as I can make a full statement before sentencing."

"A few words, not the state of the union," Tom growled. "And I need the names of your confederates."

"I hunt alone—I've told you that already."

"OK, we'll work it out." Tom brushed a strand of hair from Eva's cheek. "A week from Monday, nine am, bring a lawyer. Meantime, stay out of trouble. Even a letter to the editor and the deal is off. Any more surveillance?"

"No." Wally sounded relieved. "I'm home free."

Six days later, on Sunday morning, Tom and Eva awoke at noon, ravenous. They passed by the deli and headed for a picnic in Central Park.

"Only child, right?" Eva said after they'd eaten mostly in

silence.

"Right. Lucky to be born period." Tom laughed. "Took some scientific shortcut to trump the fact my mom should have been too old for child-bearing. And my parents spent every waking hour in the lab, at least when dad wasn't closing down O'Reilly's bar."

"But you don't throw off those unhappy family vibes." Eva sat a little ways off, her chin on her knees, arms wrapped around tan athletic legs.

"No. Rowdy but funny and happy and interesting almost all of the time. I ignored the melodrama and, let's face it, I was their little prince. I had nothing in the world to complain about." Tom wouldn't tell Eva about the suicide—what a downer that would be on this perfect Sunday, not to mention irrelevant as far as he was concerned. "They were in love but carried a lot of stuff around inside, which would spill out in different ways. My mother barely escaped the Nazis and the old man was in and out of the Soviet Gulag for most of his adult life. He lost a lot of friends there and alongside him in the war." A clutch of teenage girls giggled past. A couple looked back and gave Tom the eye. Eva laughed. It was one of those days. "He died when I was pretty young but I'm still very close to my mother and to the very nice guy she later married."

"So when your father died, is that when you broke loose from this lab rat trap you told me about?"

"I guess so but it wasn't as if I was being groomed to be a scientist and rebelled. My mother was always the doting teacher but put no emphasis on science in particular. And from what I remember, the old man was trying to feed a whole new and different education into me every second week—might be options trading one time—options trading when I was nine!—then the basics of winning a hockey punch-up on skates, then Adam Smith versus Karl Marx, or process of the decades-long British political debate than brought about their abolition of and active campaign against slavery. But I think we have a suspicion right from the start of who and what we are meant to be. Maybe it's partly genetic, like personality. What about you? Born to serve?"

"I have two sisters—one an unmarried teacher, the other a housewife and mother of five. But my father was a Navy lifer, former Seal." Eva leaned back on to her elbows, losing the little-girl look. "I saw value in that, I suppose. I tried the Navy. But diplomacy also gives you the chance to fight for your country, so to speak, and, hopefully, for what's right, most of the time."

"War by other means, huh?"

"Maybe. Sometimes a girl's gotta do what a girl's gotta do."

They walked over to the Metropolitan Museum. Eva suggested they check each other's favorite exhibits.

Eva liked the Spanish painters and Matisse. Tom had been drawn since childhood to the temple of Dendur, the sandstone edifice that now resided in its entirety in the Sackler Wing. It was a wonderful symbol of human illusion, Tom reckoned—the illusion of constancy in particular. What once had clearly been forever was now patently part of the nevermore. It touched and amused him somehow.

The Dendur temple had mocked the idea of permanence even in its own time. It was adorned with the ancient Egyptian gods but built when the Romans ruled the Land of the Nile. Now, two thousand years later, the whole thing had been plunked down in Manhattan, literally under glass in a small corner of a giant complex erected by an entirely new and different civilization.

"Makes you wonder," he said, "how long it might be before everything we are, the way we do things, will be become a curiosity from the past."

But Eva wasn't listening and now her eyes lit up. She pointed up through the massive glass ceiling. In the sky above the museum, a brilliantly colored hot air balloon floated toward the park. Eva tugged at Tom's hand. "Let's see where it's going!"

Outside, the balloon cruised along the western edge of the Park, an exuberant blossom of reds, yellows, greens and blues against the green foliage and the stone, steel, concrete and glass of the sunlit Westside canyon wall.

"What a wonderful surprise," Eva said as the balloon turned lazily toward the Great Lawn, where a sizeable crowd was converging to watch its gradual descent.

"What a bummer," Eva said now as it came lower and the protest banners that streamed out behind the passenger basket became legible. "Save Yourselves," said one. "Frankenfoods Will Destroy Life," read a second. The third warned that "Thalidomide Was a Walk in the Park: Stop the GMO Plague."

"That's a little sick," Eva murmured, mirroring the uneasy feeling that now put a damper on Tom's wonderful afternoon. He hoped that Wally had nothing to do with this but the odds weren't good.

A final banner appeared to have been added at the last moment, an urgent afterthought or a late bulletin on drift toward environmental Armageddon. In rough handwritten lettering on a long piece of brown wrapping paper was an enigmatic call, written twice, as if the author was unsure of the spelling or was making the word up. In the first attempt, the capital R was italicized. In the second, there was a hyphen. "Stop R-evolution."

"An evolution revolution?" Eva said. "That what it means?" The balloon was low enough now for Tom to see that its one and only occupant was Wally Anderson. There went Tom's plea bargain hopes. One last banner became visible as the balloon's descent slowed. "Exterminate GreenGene Before It Exterminates Us." Then the balloon and Wally were skyward again as he fired up the heaters. Two policemen were charging towards him hoping to grab a rope that was trailing from the basket on the ground.

"Something's wrong," Tom said. "Look at Wally. He's crying like a baby!"

Tears streamed down Wally's face as he frantically shoveled pamphlets over the side and shouted into a handheld megaphone that he had obviously failed to turn on. A heavy cardboard box, full of leaflets apparently, plummeted to the grass. The cops began to push the crowd back out of the way. One of a clutch of young toughs shouted up at the balloon. "Commie litterbug!"

"Think he's having a bad trip?" Eva asked.

"In more ways than one," Tom said as two patrol cars rolled up. Tom flashed his ID, borrowed a loudspeaker and called his name out three or four times before Wally looked down and finally recognized him. He seemed to be trying to turn on his megaphone but was apparently blinded by tears. "Come on down, Wally," one of the onlookers yelled. "Hey, Wally!" another shouted, "Make like a bird!"

The balloon kept rising, taking Wally with it. He wore a look of bottomless despair. When he got the megaphone turned on, his voice was flat and mournful. "It's too late, Tom. It's all over."

A low murmur drifted across the lawn. Eva drew closer. Something ugly was at hand. People started walking away. A few ran.

Wally climbed up on to the side of the basket. He wavered, there, one hand on the rigging.

"Wally, I promise you that our deal still holds," Tom said evenly. "You will make your statement in court. Don't waste that chance! After this show today, everyone will listen to you. Now get back into the basket, sit down and wait. We'll bring you down safely."

"Don't do it, Wally!" Eva said quietly but Wally let go of the rigging. He put his hands over his ears, as if trying to block out some horrible sound. Miraculously, he seemed to balance on the basket's edge for a second or two before toppling forward. Gathering speed, he headed for the ground.

The screams from below shut off almost as suddenly as they had begun. Half way down, Wally seemed to stop for an instant, jerking upwards, before continuing his descent. He landed with a dead thud 30 feet in front of Tom and Eva.

"Goddamnit, Wally!" Tom muttered. Eva said nothing, just squeezed his hand. "Can you get back to the hotel all right?" Tom asked her. "I'm going to have to go to work."

"No. I'll hang around here with you." Her face was drawn, but determined. "I'll keep out the way."

They'd moved only a few steps towards Wally's body when fresh screaming began. A woman pointed into the air and bent to cover her small son's eyes.

Tom looked up at the abandoned basket. Wally had attempted to hang himself by tying the balloon's anchor rope around his neck. The drop had ripped him in two and now his Viking blonde head, wedged in the noose, floated casually above the horrified throngs in Central Park.

Part Two

21

Bent over this paper work, the old man looked tired and beaten. "What happened?" Allen Rubenstein asked without looking up.

"To what Camus called life's only important question," Tom replied, "Wally Anderson provided an emphatic response."

"Forget Camus and to be or not to be and answer *my* question: why are the papers saying you hounded him to death?" Rubenstein looked up and removed his reading glasses. "Were you actually in the park screaming at the kid when he did it?"

"If he was hounded at all, it was by GreenGene and the mayor's billionaire boyfriend Shivkovski."

"Leave the mayor out of it! For god's sake, Tom, Shivkovski's the victim in a criminal case. You were supposed to deal with this hard and fast *in court*! Instead, you become ringmaster for Suicide in the Park, the city's next big tourist attraction! And we get a disembodied head bumping against the windows up on Fifth Avenue."

"I told you. I even warned Shivkovski off but I think they got to him somehow." Tom helped himself to a seat. "He was going to come in today, in fact, and plea." Tom was growing tired of Rubenstein's theatrics, even if he generally liked and admired the man. This hissy fit was less about the suicide and the ways things looked than about the way things were. The DA, the mayor and their esteemed leader and president were about to self-destruct in one of the grotesquely humiliating ways so favored by politicians. The range of human behaviors and events seemed to orbit in only a partly random fashion around the dense black hole of immutable human nature. In politics, you could almost set your watch by it.

"If you want me to resign, I will." Tom meant it. In fact, he knew the instant that he said it that he was as good as gone. He'd had enough. And he was bored. But he would wait. He knew that Rubenstein would not want him to go — at least not yet. And Tom would need the powers and resources of the office a little while longer to find and punish those responsible for Wally's death.

"You're not going anywhere." Rubenstein was lowering the temperature. "Anyway, the young man saved us a lot of time and irritation. The GreenGene case is closed."

"Not quite. Wally Anderson was helping me in an investigation and I intend to follow it up." Rubenstein would be in partial retreat now and Tom was no longer willing to play nice anyway. So he would lay down the law. "Anyone who contributed to or caused his suicide has obstructed justice. Wally was bringing in evidence of possibly criminal acts by GreenGene Inc. and its agents."

Rubenstein bowed and shook his head. "You're not telling me anything I didn't already know. I understand that you have been in regular contact with the dope-head and even talked to him without his attorney present at your apartment building. You acted against this complainant's interests and ours as prosecutors and so in a way not compatible with the responsibilities of this office."

Rubenstein could only have heard about the meet on the roof from Shivkovski, who had obtained the information during a possibly illegal surveillance of an assistant district attorney.

"The kid came to me at my place of residence. I refused to discuss his case. He offered to provide this office with information of possible criminal wrongdoing. I am free and, indeed, required to pursue such an investigation. The only person who could have known about that rooftop meeting was the tail the Shivkovskis put on Anderson. Which brings up the question, Al, of how the hell you learned about it."

Rubenstein returned Tom's hard angry stare. "My business. Why didn't you tell me you had a family feud with Uncle Sigurd?"

"I told you not to give it to me, precisely because of the family connections. So the real question is, why didn't you listen to me?"

"I had my instructions," snapped Rubenstein, "and, unlike you, I followed them. What about the accomplices?"

"No leads. Instructions from who, exactly?"

"Never mind."

Tom leaned over the DA's desk, getting into the old man's face. "Out of admiration for your legitimate achievements, I won't make trouble for you on this, Al. But I am wondering why you've suddenly become a puppet on a string. Is Shivkovski helping finance your retirement? Or maybe you're like the president and saving the world in a secret way that's paying you billions?"

"You know damn well that I'm clean," Rubenstein spoke evenly, looking him in the eye, the anger gone.

Tom regretted his words. He also knew this GreenGene thing must have political dimensions he wasn't seeing yet. He took a step back to ease the tension. No point getting sacked before he could do what needed doing. "Okay. I'm going to treat the GreenGene case with professionalism. But I'll need to satisfy myself that neither GreenGene nor Shivkovski interfered with Wally Anderson in any illegal way. I will also look at any information Wally might have tracked down to see whether GreenGene is in contravention of local, state or federal laws and regulations."

"Did this Wally have something hard on GreenGene?"

"I intend to find out."

Rubenstein said nothing. He opened a drawer and brought out a bottle of whiskey. "Why is there never any in-between with you. It's always the moon landing or a giant fireball." He poured two drinks. "I could fire you right now for what you've done already."

Tom waved off his shot. Alcohol had no effect on him so why waste it? "I'd come after you. After all, that's what you used to like about me." He watched the old man take his shot. The hand was steady but the eyes were dead. "It would be my word against yours and Santini's but you two are soon to be fallen dark knights of an evil empire. I'm the hero."

"Maybe you *are* the hero," the DA mumbled. "You're a killer for sure and you're even finally getting the politics right. But nobody's going to remember Wally Anderson in a few days. Too much else going on. Even some kind of revolution in China — though people will wonder whether Mason isn't cooking it all up somehow to take the heat off."

Tom felt bad about seeing a good man down. "Old Shivkovski should have kept out of it," he said but Rubenstein seemed no longer interested in Shivkovski. He downed the second shot of whiskey. "I used to think the law would always save us," he said quietly, still avoiding Tom's eyes. "But this time it won't be enough."

"One last thing," Rubenstein said as Tom headed for the door. "And you can take this to the bank. Not everything is about you."

Rubenstein sat motionless after Tom left, and then punched a button on speed dial.

"You got what you wanted," he told the mayor. "He went away mad."

"What you and I want doesn't matter anymore," Santini replied. "It's way beyond that."

"Easy for you to say. If he blows a gasket, we ruin a brilliant career. Tom is one of the best I've ever had."

"It's beyond individual careers, too. Trust me."

"The well's run dry, Carmine. I intend to reserve what trust I have left for people who deserve it."

Rubenstein put down the receiver, cussed silently, and ran his hands, trembling now, through his wispy Grecian Formula locks. He snatched the next file off a tall pile beside him. The rest of the world could fall apart but not him. So what if the facades and ornaments of American government were soiled and tarnished. He still believed it was the Al Rubensteins of the nation who would make sure the internal, eternal American structures—democratic government and the rule of law—remained strong. He had a job to do, and he'd get it done, come hell, high water, or impeachment.

That reminded him. What with the gruesome circus in the park, and playing Santini's mysterious game, he had not asked Tom about the NASDAQ mugging.

The good thing was that the mayor appeared to have forgotten about it too.

22

"Welcome to Utopia," Carrie Hemmingford told her two young guests with as much enthusiasm as she could muster. She feared some of her disappointment might peak through. Her B&B visitors were generally a genteel lot but these two looked tired and unsteady and came bearing only backpacks. Not always a good sign. It could mean drugs, drink and a sexual extravagance that rivaled the honeymoon set.

Still, Stephanie was a polite, pretty little thing, if somewhat distracted. She and Sean demonstrated unusual discretion by asking for two rooms, not one. One was the large, pricey Hamilton bedroom with a canopied king, in which, Carrie was sure, the two would spend the night. They paid cash but the Visa platinum card was briefly and reassuringly visible. Drawn, troubled faces yet polished manners. Ratty backpacks, yet designer jeans. Camping gear, but stuffed into exquisite silver BMW. A puzzle all round.

Carrie was a born softie, however. She recognized the tremendous stresses and strains on the young these days—just look at that poor boy who had hanged himself last week from a balloon over Central Park! So, by the third breakfast, her unease had given way to concern. Stephanie eyes were frequently red and Carrie had heard her crying. Sean, though a healthy, outdoorsy sort, occasionally appeared not far from tears himself. They were in and out all day but never said where they'd been. They avoided the other guests. By nightfall, they were up in the Hamilton room. Carrie heard their mournful mumbling as they worried at their problems.

What was the story? Carrie wondered. Forbidden love? Unwelcome pregnancy?

So Carrie was surprised at the girl's question during their fourth breakfast: "What do you know about the Oneida Foundation? The big orphanage or whatever it is?"

"We saw it when we were driving around yesterday," Sean explained quickly. "It's huge! People around here can't have been too happy to have it plop down in this beautiful countryside."

"Well, finally!" Carrie was exultant. "I get to wear my other hat. Oneida's chief know-it-all!"

No one ever got farther than the Foundation's front gates, of course, but she gave them the lowdown anyway, or at least what she and the rest of Oneida knew, most of which had been churned out by the Institute's slick public relations machine. The Foundation took care of all kinds of needy children. Orphans, of course, but also children stricken by disease, or recovering from emotional trauma, or afflicted by "special factors" that made it hard or impossible for them to function well in the outside world.

Carrie did her best to respond to the couple's rather intensive questioning. Yes, she had met a few doctors, nurses and staff over the years. They were almost all from other places and lived on site. No, they did not say much about their work, come to think of it. But, like folks everywhere, some liked to get away from it all. The Utopia was perfect for a weekend, was it not? So she had heard a bit.

From what she'd gathered, the Foundation's work with children was extensive, expensive and, except for a few of the world's great hospitals, without equal in terms of its ambition and excellence. It included a wide range of advanced medical research.

Yes, she'd heard a few odd things. Some staff called the place "The Farm" but they were mostly city folk. There was grumbling on occasion about the enforced seclusion. One pediatrician in her cups said the Institute gave her "the creeps." The Foundation was paranoid about security and secrecy, in the view of some employees. "Doctors don't like to be put out of bounds," she explained. "They were asked to use security codes to move within the institution's areas and told they didn't need to know what's happening in Building X or Annex Z. That sort of thing."

"On the other hand," Carrie said, wishing not to sound negative, "it has been an ideal citizen." She had taken note of the Greenpeace patches on their knapsacks and told them about the careful tree and stream preservation efforts she'd read about and the state-of-the-art emission controls.

Sean interrupted, rudely Carrie Hemmingford thought. "So you don't know anyone working on the research side?"

She did not, Carrie replied with a tight smile. Research? Who were these young people? Industrial spies?

But later, after they'd talked some more—about the Eastern forest regrowth and the funny way the water in Oneida made everyone want to make the world perfect—Carrie wondered whether these anxious, caring young people perhaps knew something about the Institute that folks around here didn't but should. "What the heck!" she said to herself, removing her colonial bonnet to start the dishes. She would give Jason Hunter a call.

23

Will sat on the WHUPASS school floor, his legs positioned in a wide V in front of him for a hard stretch. "Man," he told Tom, who sat in a similar position a few feet away, "you wouldn't believe the bath I've taken the past two days. Everything's down twenty, thirty per cent this year."

Tom smiled wryly. "Crazy how a presidential impeachment vote can still spook the markets." Tom doubted that Will cared too deeply about the declines. For a hired corporate gun, he was perversely non-materialistic. The Armani suits were camouflage. There were no fancy cars, no lavish parties, no power palace. Instead, Tom knew, Will spent a lot of his nights poring over obscure Supreme Court decisions on civil rights. He suspected — with pleasure — that his friend was secretly at work on a book on the subject. Tom had even caught him hanging with a bunch of ACLU activists at the Rialto across the street.

"So," Will asked, watching him from his stretch, "what's up?"

"My nest egg's safe. The job? Not so much." Tom laughed. "Been acting out a bit. Wally suicide got to me. Getting fed up with my illustrious career." He hadn't told Will yet of his decision to quit the DA's office but Jefferson was a bit of a mind reader.

Tom's cell phone interrupted them. It was his mother. Tom had not called her since the incident in the park. The suicide and his role as a witness would have troubled her.

"We're concerned about you," Dr. Parviati began. "Sunday will stir old memories. The emotions may surprise you."

"Ancient history, Mom," Tom said a little sharply but he quickly added: "Why? Are you feeling —."

"Not really. I was inured to life's shocks by the time of your father's death. Numbed. You on the other hand were a child. And to see a suicide . . . a father . . . like that . . . . "

"I'm fine, Mom," Tom said reassuringly. He winked at Will, who, ever respectful of the old folks, did not return his smile.

"Good! Merely by deciding to be fine, one often is." She moved on in a vigorous tone. "Nonetheless, it helps to understand your anger and grief. There is also fear, of course."

"Fear of old man Shivkovski? Give me a break!" Tom checked his impatience. "We're talking a clown with a hat and cane here,

Mom, not a Kalashnikov."

"Fear of the unknown, my dear," she continued brusquely. "Believe me, you can ignore trauma but it works on your thinking and sensibility. I expect you will deal with the stress in your usual way, through action. In this case, as it happens, action is fine, even timely."

"Gotcha, Mom." He rolled his eyes for Will's benefit.

Dr. Parviati laughed softly, as if she could see him. After a pause, she continued: "Hank and I can't be of much practical help in this situation. So we may send someone to you who has appropriate skills."

"Shrink or hitman? What skills? Help how?" Tom was amused. "I'm an ADA with the coercive resources of government behind me, including tens of thousands of NYPD cops." Tom tried to imagine this "someone." Probably some creaky old spook Hank had rustled up from the old OSS days.

"I suspect things will move more quickly from here on," his mother continued, ignoring these comments. "Lines will be crossed. The boundaries themselves will also move. Procedure and the law are important, of course. But the closed system within which they and our government and civil societies operate has quite possibly been breached." There was a beep on the line. "This call is important," she said. "Please telephone tomorrow. First thing. You know I do not sleep long."

Tom tossed his cell on to a chest protector. Was she showing her age? "My mom's going Godfather on me."

Will still wasn't smiling. "Good for her! I'm fed up with that Russian fuck too. If you're going vigilante, count me in."

Everyone was at battle stations all of a sudden! Everyone wanted a piece of the Shivkovskis. What was up? Tom wondered. There wouldn't be enough of father and son to go around.

"It's my beef, Will, and personal. Which is why you and the rest of my family and friends should stay out of it. I plan to straighten the old dude out with little or no collateral damage and I don't want anyone else to get hurt."

"But you'll do what it takes, no matter what, right?"

Tom said nothing.

"I'm in. All the way. Period. Old man Shivkovski has broken the code and I want my licks."

"The Lab Rat Code—surely, you jest!" Tom, stretching, groaned at the melodrama.

Will finally broke a smile. "Let's put it this way, then. Stand in my way and I'll run you over." With a tone of finality, he added: "Like all good reasons, mine will be made manifest at the proper time. I'm working on a plan. Might even let you in on it."

On a purely selfish level, Tom welcomed the idea of the two original lab rat rebels teaching Shivkovski and Son some manners but what about Will's professional future if things went wrong?

As if reading his mind, Will said. "Besides, you're not the only one who's thinking career change."

24

Tom heard the voice twice. Once from a great distance, and again more clearly from just inches away. It was Eva. "Wake up, you're having a bad dream."

He laughed, opened his eyes, and lifted himself on to his elbows. His heart was thumping. It was a ridiculous feeling.

"You're sure about that?" he said, a little breathless. "Maybe you just want to have your way with me again."

Looking concerned, Eva touched his cheek. Her blackened eye, the only flaw on a body that now held him in thrall, was fading fast. So were the chances to nab her mugger.

"Nightmares on three straight nights," Eva said. "And they seem to be getting wilder. Is it Wally you dream about?"

"Don't know," Tom replied, lying. He admired her for a moment. "Don't worry about Wally. First we've got to get that mope who robbed you and killed Agneau."

"I'm upset about Wally too and I know how much it is troubling you. Shivkovski's on my shit list as well."

"Why not? Seems to be the new thing."

"What do you mean?"

"Will's gung-ho to nail Shivkovski, too, all of a sudden. My mother's talking like CK Corral is right around the corner. Wants to hire a gunslinger. We're working up to a good sized posse here."

Eva thought for a moment then said: "Yes, I can understand how your mother must feel about Shivkovski."

She caught Tom's look of surprise because she quickly added: "Tom, I should have mentioned it but Ray told me about your dad's death and the disagreements with Shivkovski in the Park that day. He wanted to warn me that suicide was particularly sensitive territory for you." She took his hand. "I'm so very sorry."

"Don't be. It was a long time ago."

After a moment, Eva said: "Look, I can make myself useful in this thing. People in Washington owe me. They must have something on an old Soviet exile like Shivkovski. It could help."

"See if they have something on my Dad as well."

It was Eva's turn to be surprised. "Are you sure?"

"Yeah. It's time for the whole story."

Later, with Eva asleep again beside him, Tom studied the shadows on the ceiling. He had been awakened not by a nightmare but by the reliving of a reality.

What he remembered was his father lying sprawled in his lab at the shore of a vast red lake. As if he had crawled up in search of a drink. Even in death, Mike Daluskov's thick powerful right hand, which protruded vertically towards the ceiling, had seemed ready for action. It still held the large jagged shard of glass that he had used to end his life. Rivulets of blood continued to drip onto the floor.

Tom had later heard his mother weeping on the phone. She said her husband had died in a rage, apparently at himself. The ferocity of the assault became part of New York medical examiner office lore.

Dr. Mike Daluskov had put his fist through a cubicle window, torn the piece of glass from the frame and set furiously about his body with it. The savage fissures in his abdomen had astonished the ME, who had seen Japanese soldiers commit hara-kiri during the war. Nothing he witnessed in the Philippines matched the frenzy into which Tom's father had descended. The willfulness and control of the final act was equally astonishing. Still standing, although ribboned with several mortal wounds, the suicide had neatly severed his jugular. He had never even noticed Tom standing there, watching him.

And now the death of Wally Anderson was bringing it all back to Mikhail Daluskov's son.

25

"Ground rules?" Tom asked the police officer once he was admitted to the cavernous Fifth Avenue apartment.

"That's the family lawyer over there." The uniform gestured towards a gray-haired man who stood on the far end of what looked to be a mile of marble floor. "We can examine this Wally Anderson kid's things here till 2 p.m. But not the daughter's stuff. You can bet your opera tickets they didn't approve of Wally."

The daughter, Stephanie, had been missing since the suicide, along with her boyfriend Sean, another Upper East Side Frankenfoods activist. Her parents had caught CNN's depiction of Wally's death and recognized the hot-air balloon. They had bought it a year earlier in an attempt to divert their daughter from eco-hysteria and impending class betrayal.

Tom needed to find the two kids now while a harassment case against Shivkovski was still feasible. He had called in another NYPD favor because normally they wouldn't have looked at the case, given that suicides lacked both a perp and a complainant.

The vic had spent his last night in the guestroom. It was as un-Wally-like as the rest of the home, with a spectacular view from which, had he been so empowered, Wally could have watched himself add a gruesome footnote to the history of Central Park.

The paraphernalia of protest was all around. It included spray paint and stencils. What appeared to be a huge cloth banner lay partly unfolded along one end of the room: "STOP FRANKENF . . . ," it read in large black letters.

From what the building doorman said, Wally had acted alone last Sunday, probably jumping the gun on a planned public display of some sort—hanging this banner, for example, from a suitably high-profile building in Manhattan. He had left the apartment early Sunday morning, picked up the large rented van in which the balloon kit was stored, and paid some passing teens in a Meadowlands field to help him set up and get airborne. "He was, like, all messed up, but happy," one kid told *The World*. "Like my little brother when he's smiling through his tears."

Tom found nothing in the drawers, backpack, or in a bag full of laundry. The silk sheets on the bed were twisted and sweat-stained. On a hunch, he removed a crumpled pillowcase. The uniform would bag and receipt it, along with an empty Pepsi can.

The small sleeping bag also caught his eye. It was neatly packed in a most un-Wally-like fashion. Tom pulled at the knot and, holding one end high in the air, unrolled it. A baggie of what was probably marijuana fell on to the hardwood floor, followed by a grease-stained notebook.

Wally's small focused scrawl covered every page even though the first entry was barely a month ago. GMO stuff, reflections on the "militant life," and even some catty gossip about Stephanie, whom Wally obviously liked, and her boyfriend, Sean, whom he did not. Flipping further, Tom came to a page on which in large capital letters was written: "In: 1:58. Out: 3:15." Below, in smaller text: "Uneventful. GreenGene changed all passwords (but not all the crummy door locks!) No computer access but . . . BINGO! Sloppy unsecured tape backups of secret hard drive files!!!"

Tom turned to the previous page. It was black with doodles all around a large scrolled red-felt pen heading: Operation Red Rain II.

So Wally had broken into GreenGene's offices again, which is where his "new information" was coming from.

Not a complete surprise, Tom had to admit. Maybe he'd subconsciously counted on it, or even encouraged it in some subtle way. He had certainly made it clear to Wally that they would need more evidence to proceed. That meant Tom might be partly to blame for Wally's demise, which in turn made it all the more urgent that he find the truth about why he died.

The diary might help and Tom began to skim it from the beginning. On one of the middle pages, Wally had written: "Misjudged Daluskov," apparently after their rooftop meeting. "Falls generally into the tough-but-fair category but there's the outline of a man-of-history inside busting to get out. Needs crisis, challenge, cause. Trick is to makes ours his. Friendly for a hard man."

Flattery from beyond the grave. But Wally had also been discreet. He had revealed no details of their discussions or deal. Unfortunately, this reticence extended to what he thought he had learned about GreenGene irregularities. No details. Just cryptic hints: "Tell Tom about smart mice—later." "MH—beyond belief!" Finally: "Next Monday, 9 a.m. Daluskov will get full briefing!"

Over the following pages, however, which covered the days

immediately before Wally's death and Stephanie's disappearance, everything changed. The scrawl became large and sloppy. Sentiment replaced reflection. Instead of GreenGene and GMOs, the subject became Stephanie and himself. "Pizzaface," he wrote on one page, underlined twice. "That's what they called me behind my back. She laughed. Demurely, of course." Tom struggled unsuccessfully to recall the extent of Wally's acne. On another page: "I was their pet hick. Still am." And: "They looked at me weird tonight. I DISGUST her."

"Dear Granny," he began on another page, "you were right. I am wasting my life. I have thrown it all away. All that you worked for, all that was given to me through the generosity of others. Think where I could be right now if I'd gone to MIT or Cal Tech. Your words: ingrate and fool. Correct. I'm ruined."

On the next: "Granny, you are lucky you lived in the last of the centuries Made by God."

Tom flipped back and forth through the notebook looking to learn when this despondency set in. A couple of pages before the handwriting began to fall apart, he saw a small cockeyed footnote he'd skipped reading earlier.

In tiny letters, Wally had written: "GreenGene mole good on MH last night. Stephanie & Co. out being rich somewhere, so brought him here. Security. He's being watched and no wonder. MH stuff is MIND-BLOWING! Mole doesn't do weed so agreed to several beers—loosen him up. Big mistake: I passed out on the couch. (Stephanie suitably impressed; only a matter of time now till she comes seeking my bod.) Can't remember mole leaving."

An arrow directed Tom to the next page, where the entry concluded: "Must penetrate MH BEFORE deal with Tom. Can't operate from prison. Up to me. These are the times that try men's souls."

A mole? It was possible, Tom supposed. After all, Wally's first break-in had been staged partly in the hope of stirring the consciences of potential GreenGene whistle-blowers. They'd have to pay the doorman downstairs another visit to try for a description.

Wally had taken his emotional nosedive only a day or two after this meeting. Why? Had he made his move on Stephanie and been rejected? From his work with teenage kids at WHUPASS over the years, Tom knew the lovelorn young could be astonishingly fragile. He knew from personal experience with

Rachel too.

Tom leafed through the final entries, including one in huge limp letters that said: "Stephanie? – GONE!" Wally was evidently a Sixties fan (Granny's influence?) and had Doors and Stones and Beatles CDs in his pack, along with an eclectic cache of current music. By now he was leaving whole pages blank but showed sufficient energy at one point to write on one: "It's not not evolution—it's R-evolution!!! <u>NO SOLUTION</u>!!!!" A few blank pages later, he'd written: "My soul = Howling Wilderness," before crossing out the "my" and substituting "Human." Another few pages on: "The End." The arrow pointed to a somewhat more substantial entry on the back of the page. The word "evolution" had been printed in large letters with a thick black felt pen. It had been repeated with an R and hyphen preceding it. "R-evolution." The last entry began with "R" in italics, placed in front of the root "evolution," perhaps as an afterthought: "*R*evolution."

That was it: nothing more except blank pages that, like many at the end of the notebook, were crinkled and stained, as if something had been spilled on them.

Tom moved back through the pages one by one to ensure he hadn't missed anything. The one new notation he found said: "MH. The Truth is in the Monkey House."

And somehow, in his wilderness of despair, Wally had found the way to leave a sign.

At the bottom of the page was an address.

26

To see Tom come through Dr. Sigurd Shivkovski's door nearly broke Rachel's heart. He wore the look of a man about to behave badly. And her dearest Will was hunting with him. They had even brought that woman, the mugging victim, who, come to think of it, had a predatory look about her too.

It's over, Rachel thought. She had hoped they might make it through their lifespans, or at least a decade or two more, without the trauma an open schism would produce. She ached for Tom because he did not know the kind of chaos he might be about to unleash, or the pain.

Ever the contrarian, Shivkovski Sr. seemed pleased to have his gathering crashed. "Brilliant timing," he said once the uninvited guests were seated in the living room. "Boredom and monotony have deprived our little get-togethers of verve but now the valiant Jefferson and the dauntless Daluskov ride to our rescue."

"Yes," Leon added dryly, "Tom is in character as always, though missing his jackboots. You do The Knock at the Door very well."

Rachel's unease grew when Will poked a finger hard into Leon's chest and said, " shut up until we invite you to speak. '

Leon response was more predictable. His sneer was insolence incarnate and he pushed the finger away "Well, well, who switched Will on?" he asked. "So Tom, do you think you and your testosterone soaked buddy can push us around the way you did that Wally Anderson? What next? Are well supposed to do headers off the balcony one by one? It is so like you to impose the death penalty for minor infractions—a little break-in, for instance, or a failure to invite you to dinner."

Tom ignored Leon, who then stood up and walked to the far side of the room where he appeared to make a call on his cell. Tom watched him for a moment then turned to the elder Shivkovski. "Will and I want to know whether you or GreenGene continued your surveillance of Anderson after I asked you to call it off."

Shivkovski smiled broadly at Eva, as if sharing a private joke and welcomed her warmly. "It is a great pleasure to meet you this evening, my dear. You have now met my son Leon, after a fashion, over there on the phone, and this is our dear colleague, Rachel Arianna."

Rachel faked her smile and she supposed that Eva was doing the same. After confirming that his guests needed no refreshments, the old man got back to the question. "Tom, I am sure that Eva will agree that it's no more fair for you to suggest that I had something to do with young Wally's passing than for the papers to accuse you of badgering him to death. Mr. Anderson intruded suddenly and out of nowhere upon all of our lives, not the other way around. When a man jumps in front of a subway train, do you blame the driver? GreenGene is the subway train in this case, acting responsibly in a controlled, transparent, and highly regulated way, going about its business of serving the greater good. Wally Anderson, meantime, was doing his job too, which was to be Wally Anderson. This task apparently required him to find his way to New York City and compel us to pay minor roles in the tragic twilight of a wasted life."

"Did you call your goons off or not, Doc?" Will asked. Rachel had never seen him behave so rudely before—at least not as an adult.

But Shivkovski raised a finger to signal he had not quite finished. "A more pertinent question is what made Wally what he was and do the things he did? Environmental factors always play a part. Poverty in a fatherless home, for instance. But so did nature. His IQ was in the top half percentile. The intelligence was mostly inherited, of course, as were several very important predispositions towards risk-taking and rootlessness, which led him to waste his genetic endowment, refuse scholarships and run from formal disciplines."

Eva surprised Rachel by speaking up. "And work for what *he* saw as 'the greater good?'"

The old man beamed. "Yes, another key factor! His psychological availability, as Robert Conquest put it, to absolutist ideas and zealotries. This was genetic. He hungered to commit to a cause he considered worthy. This is an endemic human tendency that nonetheless varies widely in intensity and direction. It has helped produce great and numerous good works in the name of Jesus Christ, as well as century upon century of Christian persecution of the Jews Recent downside outcomes include the tribal and utopian holocausts inflicted by the Nazi and various Communist parties."

"Is that why you hated him?" Eva asked. "Did this harmless tree-hugger become responsible somehow for your years in the Gulag?"

"Hate him? My goodness no! Wally was a peaceable man! I am merely stating that he did it his way, as Paul Anka famously put it. He rebelled, protested, proselytized, committed burglary and vandalism, engaged in dangerous acrobatic political theater, and apportioned to himself the right to impose his own view of the world on everyone else. All this and his suicide itself were in perfect harmony with the chorus he heard from his genes." Shivkovski continued to address Eva: "Were you aware that perhaps only two out of five Americans are able to conceive of a counter-argument to their own beliefs?"

"You're stereotyping him."

"But broad types do exist, madam, and the human ability to organize the elements of our environment into groups is central to our ability to function and survive." He turned finally to Will and Tom. "And now, to answer your question, it was precisely because Wally was what he was that we *continued* our perfectly legal surveillance. It was an entirely legitimate precaution. He was planning more assaults on GreenGene property, perhaps again putting the safety and emotional well-being of our staff at risk. We employed no 'goons,' as Will so unkindly put it. In fact, the 'tails' you speak of were not only non-violent and but grossly inept. We lost track of Mr. Anderson several days before his death."

Tom moved on. "Wally Anderson believed you have been conducting genetic experiments with mice in an attempt to increase their intelligence?"

"Mice!" Leon had finished his call and returned to his seat. He bent forward and put his head in his hands. "You've got to be kidding! You've come here to talk about mice!"

Tom's face said nothing but Rachel now realized he didn't know as much as she feared he might.

"Mice and labs?" Shivkovski said. "Horse and carriage. They go together. But, yes, we did explore rodent intelligence. Many, many years ago, however."

"What about monk—?"Tom cut himself off. "What about

cloning — cloning of humans?"

Monkeys? Was that what Tom was about to ask, Rachel wondered. Still off course but relatively more recent.

Leon sat back and sneered. "Wally would not approve, Tom, because this ain't a fishing expedition, it's a whale hunt!"

"I must agree, I'm afraid, Tom," the old man said. "Your lack of imagination disappoints. Cloning is an everyday tool in our labs but cloning a human? Whatever for? Was Michelangelo a copycat? Did Einstein retread old theories? Cloning's for sissies or the high school science club."

Rachel once again noticed Shivkovski glancing expectantly at Eva. What does he know about her that I don't, she wondered. Eva clearly made Leon jumpy too. But Eva herself was busy watching Tom. Rachel could see there was genuine caring and affection in her gaze. But a certain caution too, and — what? Coolness? Calculation? Was something actually off with this woman or were Rachel's own complex emotions twisting her judgment? To begrudge Tom his happiness after all his pain would be horribly unfair. Yet she felt a crushing sense of loss because it was obvious that Eva would not be here had not the relationship advanced to a stage that for Tom was unprecedented.

"If cloning's not your bag, Doctor," Eva now asked, "what is?"

"My job is to be Sigurd Shivkovski, workaday scientist. I do what scientists have always done. Do my smart part to chip away at the great marble challenges."

"Pardon my father's modesty," Leon interjected. "We work on the big-time greater goods that only science can deliver. You know, liking making it possible that the four of every five children who used to die by the age of five now live full lives. Itty-bitty things like that. And all the while trying to dodge the dim-witted peasants with their flaming torches."

Eva asked: "Not a fan of the precautionary principle, Doctor?"

"Mob-speak," Leon said quietly. His eyes remained locked on Tom's. "A cynical Greens' perversion of the do-no-harm instruction to doctors in the Hippocratic Oath. Do nothing in science until the outcome is certain. Nothing is certain in advance. Ergo, do nothing, period. Ergo: no cures or treatment for thousands of diseases and ailments from which science has rescued us. Ergo: back for humanity to lives that are nasty, brutish and short."

He turned to Tom once more. "You appall me! You forget that your own father was among the first to conceive the idea of building a 24th chromosome. Genius! But, of course, he was also a self-hating, maniacal fuck-brained bully—like YOU!"

Time to calm things down, Rachel decided. "Oh, shush, you two," she said, standing and ruffling Leon's awful hair. She crossed to the sofa where Tom and Will had sat down side by side and dropped between them, wiggling her hips to make room. She balanced herself by placing one hand on Tom's upper thigh. He jumped and, if the past 30 years were any indication, would now be now wrestling with an intense physical reaction.

Rachel watched for Eva's reaction. The woman obviously noticed the provocative touch but her reaction was again highly controlled. Surprise, quickly contained, a flash of anger, also swiftly subdued, followed by what Rachel guessed was a rapid appreciation of the situation and an equally deft return to a state of alert calm. Rachel didn't bother looking at Will. She already knew how upset he would be, even despite the somewhat special circumstances.

Tom got up to go. "We are awed by your scientific wonderfulness, Leon but try this on for size: Kd7. Checkmate." When the elder Shivkovski approached and offered his hand, Tom said: "I plan to wind up our little chess game pretty soon, too, Doctor. The result will be the same, I'm afraid."

Rachel marveled at the old man's cool. "Anything that keeps us in touch, my dear boy, is my pleasure entirely."

The expression of cruelty and pleasure that had crossed Leon's face, however, chilled Rachel to the bone. 'My congratulations, Tom," he said with a voice that sounded both agitated and drained. "That is a positively killer move."

27

The first thing Carlos heard was the squeak of a worn running shoe. The air bubble in the heel had sprung a leak. A second pair of shoes arrived on the landing outside his locked door. He heard a man whisper. "Let's get in and out fast."

Carlos could tell that the man was turning his head as he spoke, looking at the doorways on the landing one by one. Maybe choosing a target. Carlos went cold with fear.

His mother's shift didn't end for another three hours. And he was blind. He saw nothing but black foreboding shadows. He remembered the boys at WHUPASS kidding him about *Wait Until Dark*—if these men broke in, he would be as vulnerable as the blind woman in that scary old movie. Just this afternoon, he'd wondered if that Kitchen Sink murderer was crazy enough to kill a blind kid.

Now Carlos heard scratching—metal against metal. It was coming from Tom's front door. One man spoke to the other: "He said Daluskov'd be away for at least another hour." *Thank goodness!* Carlos thought. *They aren't coming in here!* He laid his forehead against the wall and tried to control his breathing.

Relief gave way to self-disgust. Tom, after all, was his teacher and friend. He couldn't cower and do nothing while these men burgled his home. In the corner by Carlos's door was his special WHUPASS white cane. It was a gift from Mary and Billy and could be broken down into two weapons to emulate the bamboo sticks used in tandem in Arnis, a Filipino martial art in which WHUPASS had made Carlos particularly adept.

As Carlos reached for the sticks, he heard one of the men outside say: "I'm almost in." He picked up the phone and dialed. The 9-1-1 operator was attentive but deadpan. As the son of a nurse, Carlos knew he must move this call up the triage list. "The apartment belongs to Assistant District Attorney Tom Daluskov," he whispered.

"*The* Tom Daluskov?" the operator asked, her tone rising. "You sure about that, honey?"

"Yeah, and my friends who might come up the stairs any

second now and bump into these criminals? One of their fathers is Detective Ray Franklin, NYPD."

Carlos put the receiver down on its side. He heard the 911 operator speaking urgently behind him as he walked towards the door. "Now, Carlos, I want you to stay on the line. Don't move. Just keep listening. The policemen are on the way and they will want you to help walk them up the stairs—."

But that would take too long. The men would get into Tom's apartment. They might also get away. He had to act. He *owed* Tom in so many ways. In four years at WHUPASS, he had grown from a timorous shut away to a blind kid who could hang—and scrap, if he had to—with "the light-dependent," as Tom sometimes called the sighted.

Carlos left the phone and the 911 operator dangling.

"Hi!" he said amiably, his white Arnis cane in hand, as he stepped out on to the landing. "What are you guys doing? That's my friend Tom's place. He's an assistant DA." Maybe they didn't know they were burgling an ADA's apartment.

The metal scratching stopped. So did the shuffling. The deeper, tougher sounding voice said: "Hi there, kid. Mr. Daluskov hired us. We're from Fontana Door and Key. Gotta fix his locks."

"Why don't you wait until he gets home?"

The second man spoke. He sounded to Carlos like the sidekick. "Because your friend Daluskov can't get in anyway until we fix the lock, dummy!" Then: "Hey, are you're blind?"

"Better watch how you talk to me." Carlos put on his biggest smile. "I could kick both your asses."

The taller man's growl was cut off by a softer noise—the tumbling of the lock chambers in Tom's front door.

Carlos could hear that the tough man was standing up and facing Carlos now. "Why don't you come in with us, kid, and we can wait for Tom together."

Carlos felt the fear spike again. And from up the stairwell came the voices of Mary and Billy, calling his name.

"Grab him," the tough guy said. But Carlos knew the landing the way lifers know their prison cells. He heard the other man coming and could almost "see" him reach out with big beefy hands. He whipped the white cane and the blow shattered the bones in the man's wrist. Carlos spun and followed up with a downward strike to the head—holding back lest he strike a mortal blow.

"You little prick," the tough guy said from Tom's doorway. Carlos could not risk waiting for him to pull a knife or gun. He moved in three accelerating strides towards the voice, brandishing the Arnis cane high over his head as a diversion. He launched a low descending flying sidekick. He guessed that he missed the kneecap but he put the man down and did considerable damage, judging by his howls of pain.

"Go back, you guys! Burglars!" Carlos shouted down the staircase to Mary and Billy. He scrambled into his apartment and locked the door. Carlos heard the injured men enter the elevator, whimpering and cursing. Billy and Mary kept on charging up the stairs. One of the burglars fired a warning shot—into the ceiling, Carlos guessed from the sound.

"Did you hurt him?" Mary screamed from two landings below.

"Maybe next time. We'll send the guys with the L's!" the tough guy shouted as the elevator door closed.

A few seconds later Carlos heard the footsteps on the last flight of stairs. He opened the door and jumped into the arms of his oncoming friends. "Are you okay?" Mary kept shouting. She dislodged his grip on her, put his hands down at his sides, and turned him around twice, apparently looking for scratches and dents.

"No I'm good, I'm good," Carlos said, trembling now yet incredibly happy. "Except I might have peed my pants!"

"Join the club!" Billy said and the three collapsed in laughter on the landing floor.

28

Tom and Eva found the police on the landing with Carlos, Billy and Mary. Once he was sure the children were safe, Tom headed back to Shivkovski's apartment. Carlos had told him that the burglars knew he would not be home for a while. No one had expected them at Shivkovski's this evening. The tipoff could only have come from someone there. Tom remembered seeing Leon on his phone but when Ray Franklin arrived, he decided to wait to tell the detective who was already in a rage. "When I find out who endangered these kids, I'm leaving my badge at home."

Vigilantism was breaking out all over but Tom would keep that fact from Shivkovski for now and play the angry but hamstrung ADA that the old man felt well able to handle.

Tom hammered at Shivkovski's door for more than a minute before Katya's gnarled fingers undid the locks and latches.

"What's the hurry, Thomas," the housekeeper rasped. "He's not going anywhere. In fact, he's waiting for you."

"Where?" The vast living and dining space was empty.

"In his playhouse no doubt," Katya said. "That man grows more odd each day." She led him into a huge but empty galley kitchen where cable news babbled on about the coming impeachment trial and the latest violent demonstrations in Washington. When Tom pretended to look in the oven for the missing Shivkovski, Katya gave his scarred cheek a painful pinch. "Just wait! He's here! You are like your father—no patience! Don't worry. You will be rewarded by a strange but entertaining show!"

A door marked Pantry opened up and Shivkovski appeared. "Be careful Tom, she enjoys causing pain—it's the Lenin gene." Tom knew the story. Shivkovski's wife died while delivering Leon. He had never remarried but 20 years later had suddenly spent wildly from his newly earned wealth to track down his hard-nosed former Gulag jailer, buy her way out of the USSR, and engage her as his head housekeeper. Katya reminded him each day of a time when the life he led now was beyond imagining. Except for their verbal sparring, however, she did little actual work, leaving that to younger, more appropriately skilled staff and spending most days watching baseball and CNN. "Do not grow too cocky," she now told the two men while pointing at the

TV screen. "The proletariat is rising up. We are in the early innings in historical terms and there is plenty of time for a comeback."

"Come Tom," Shivkovski said, ignoring her and turning back into the "pantry." He led Tom down a hallway before stopping, turning again and taking Tom gently by the shoulders with his spindly hands. "I have just heard about the incident at your apartment. Someone has made a terrible mistake and we must talk about it. But first, if you do not mind, let me look at you!" Shivkovski's face was suddenly joyful. "So calm! So much in control of your anger. You are maturing so quickly now, Tom. No longer a slave to your inheritance of volcanic aggression." The face grew grim. "Stalingrad — we were there you know! I was a coward, of course. I am not even ashamed of it. But your father — fearless, ferocious — ."

"You know about the break-in?"

Shivkovski turned towards their destination up the hall. "Yes, I received a telephone call. Thank goodness that no one was hurt!" He stopped before a small steel door. "May I invite you into my inner sanctum?"

"Here, there, it doesn't matter. I require some answers. Do you admit that you sent two men to break into my apartment? Probably to look for what Wally Anderson stole from GreenGene the second time in. They're guilty of assault on my young neighbor. They fired a gun, endangering two of my students, including the son of a homicide detective. You are out of control, Doctor, and I'm afraid you may find yourself under lock and key for a second time in your life."

"I had absolutely nothing to do with this, Tom." Shivkovski smiled gently. "It was quite definitely someone else." He paused. "However, I will make it up to all three of the children involved and especially to young Carlos. A remarkable and valiant young lad."

"Was it Leon?" It seemed the only alternative. "Because someone — you or Leon, is my guess — will go to jail for this."

Shivkovski took Tom's elbow, urging him through the door. "Oh, I don't think so. No, there will be too much else to do in the coming days. Come in and let us talk. It may be our last chance. But please do not expect me to rat out my son. As you point out, I am after all an ex-con and therefore governed by our code of silence. Speaking of the Gulag — see?"

Tom bent, stepped through the door, and was momentarily stunned.

Here, secreted amid twenty rooms furnished in expensive but largely conventional billionaire taste, was an astonishing anomaly: walls of rough timber and mud, hewn wood bunk beds, holes in the roof patched with filthy rags, moss and old paper. It was, of course, a meticulous and starkly realistic replication of the world Shivkovski and Tom's father had survived in the prison camps of the former Soviet Union.

"These were the best of the accommodations your father and I ever enjoyed, a veritable Ritz Carlton of the Gulag." Shivkovski's feathery hand remained on Tom's elbow. "Most of the time we were in the large buildings with many others. But this was home for the two of us alone for two whole years." He made a wide scarecrow gesture with his arms, as if addressing a crowd from the center ring, and motioned for Tom to take a seat on the bunk opposite his.

Tom didn't know whether to laugh or to call for the men in the white coats.

"I am a great believer in hidden passageways and secret rooms," Shivkovski said. An open bottle of vodka sat on the plank table with two glasses, one half-full. "Is this not how the human mind is built? We are on a great adventure to locate its dark corners and scary basements. And there are monsters in the attic. They come out once in a while to feast on terror and bathe in the vast oceans of blood we so love to bring forth. It is no wonder that the public panics each time we peek through a new door."

"This is a little too Gothic for me, Doc, and overall I'd say human behavior is a known commodity. It produces some interesting and seemingly new hands sometimes but we've seen all 52 cards before."

"Ahah!" said Shivkovski, lowering himself gingerly on to a blackened straw mattress. "You see! We think alike!" He pointed to the vodka. "Come. Drink!" The old man's movements seemed more vigorous here on his Gulag set and less refined. "Like you, I find life's range of surprises far too limited. We're boxed in." He indicated the moldy timber walls. "By nature. Locked in by the narrow boundaries and puny repertoire imposed on us by evolution!"

Shivkovski tossed Tom a ragged piece of cloth that proved to be an old coat. "Put it on." Tom went along; it became suddenly colder.

While the temperature dropped, the stench rose. Tom thought he might gag. "Don't be concerned," Shivkovski laughed. "Peat, excrement, urine, the bacteria and essences of men and vermin in close contact. But the smell is synthetic. And harmless. I'm too soft and old now to risk what remains of my health. I seldom let the temperature drop near a realistic level nowadays. Rarely spend the night anymore. Still, it is a reality check, no? And yet there is more anxiety out there than in here!" He pointed, presumably to the penthouse beyond the timber walls.

The lights in the room dimmed and the audio kicked in. Sounds of mumbling male voices, snoring, and the metallic clinking and clatter of tools, perhaps "outside." Shivkovski bowed his head, revealing a freckled pate, and put his face in his hands. Tom suspected that this moment of solitary despair was not a pose.

Tom poured himself some vodka. "So what is the story here? All this reminds you of what you escaped? Where you came from?"

"Absolutely not!" said Shivkovski, snatching up his own glass and taking a healthy swallow. "No, this is not what I escaped. This is where I *am* and indeed where I always will be. I come here to remember *what and where we really are*. This is not another place or time but now and perhaps *forever*. This box keeps me focused. This box helps me laugh at the innate timidities that have so often hobbled human potential and endeavor."

As long as Shivkovski was eager to talk, Tom decided he would see where it led. "Okay Doc, I think I get that part. But once you are reinvigorated by your reality check in here what is it that you and GreenGene get up to that has Wally Anderson so excited? Growing human hearts on a vine, cooking up the sequel to the Black Death?"

Shivkovski sighed. "The only plague on humanity, my dear Tom, is humanity itself. And yet we also represent the only possible cure. As for GreenGene research, our stockholders are upset at how careful and conservative we are. In our more radical moments, we make your greens more crispy and better for your health. Even Wally's grandmother would approve."

Tom's eyes were watery from the smell of what seemed like real wood smoke. Shivkovski uttered a few words in Russian and a computer killed the prison camp sound track, substituting the optimistic strains of Tchaikovsky's violin concerto in D. "There!" the old man said. "Such magnificence! That is us too! That is mankind at its current best." He held out his hand. Tom took it and helped him back up into a full sitting position.

"I'm hurt that you believe I would harm your Wally," Shivkovski said, massaging a kink in his birdlike neck. "We watched him, yes, but obviously not very well. A second break-in! That security firm! What incompetence! But hurt him? No! I am not now nor have I ever been in the business of hurting people. This will all be forgotten soon, believe me. There will be so much to do, and to think about." Shivkovski leaned forward, somewhat precariously, to put his hand on Tom's shoulder. "I loved your father like a brother and I know that as his son you have also been deeply affected by the manner of Wally Anderson's death."

Tom flinched a bit inside and yet his usual gut reaction to Shivkovski's mention of Mike Daluskov was strangely muted.

"I believe that acts like Wally Anderson's are subconscious cries to the gods and to our fellow men. They ask, why is life like this? Why am *I* like this?"

"No doubt you're about to tell me."

"We are prisoners, Tom. Captives. All human emotions, the full range of our fears, joys and drives, are fundamentally chemical. And the basic hardware that greatly determines the range and variety of these fears, joys, and drives in an individual is inherited."

"Genes are destiny, Doc?"

"Think walls again, Tom." Shivkovski huddled protectively over his vodka glass. "In terms of our abilities and the range of our behaviors, we have been confined within a high and impenetrable wall throughout evolution. The gene pool contains no more surprises, except in its seemingly bottomless capacity to disappoint."

"No nurture? No environmental effects?"

"They are large, as I've already acknowledged," Shivkovski seemed briefly irritated. More gently, he added: "Take you, Tom. Bit of a rebel, an outsider. Some of this is your genetic inheritance, some the effects of what we call 'life' and the micro- and macro-cultures you grew up in."

"Your old pal Joe Stalin was beaten as a child by an alcoholic father, beaten just as hard by a mother who actually loved him, and grew up in a Georgian community when even three and four year-old children were encouraged to brawl like the adult men during annual festivals. He was a small kid whose thrashings and humiliation probably turned him into the scrapper, rebel, genius of terror and mass murderer you and my father grew to know so well. Where's the almighty gene in that picture? How do your omnipotent genes come into it?"

"Granted, it is true that the trait least determined by our genes is individual warmth and a loving nature, which seem dependent on environment and upbringing. But not every Caucasian with a rough upbringing like Stalin's turned into a monster. Far from it. Genes from both papa and momma likely inclined him not only towards merciless savagery but also a poetic sensibility—he forgave and spared Russian writers over and over again for sins that cost tens of millions of nonscribblers their lives. His lack of empathy, his for-us-or-against-us attitude to even imagined opponents? That's hardwired into every human, although the wiring is more heavy duty in some than in others."

Tom could not resist sending a message. "So would you say that I have inherited my father's high-voltage circuits for rash acts and, perhaps, violence?"

"Indeed you have." The Shivkovski chuckle. "But it is the complex mix that is the raw genetic material for the woman or man. The undeniable fact, however, established over decades of studies of identical twins separated at birth and raised in different environments, is this: the fundamental traits that differentiate one person from another, the rough drafts, so to speak, of our lives, are scribbled on our beings at conception and at birth. IQ tops the list of these inherited outlines but it goes on quite endlessly. Who is likely to be sociable, who traditional, who willing to submit to authority and who more or less vulnerable to stress. Who likely to be aggressive, who independent minded, who tending to alienation from society, who bent on seeking control, who hanging back avoiding potential harm, who ready to feel satisfaction and happiness in life. Were you aware that practical joking and unrelieved cheeriness are often inherited?"

"So in theory, you could mess with DNA to produce slaves, sadists or stand-up comics?"

"In theory, yes. One day humankind may rule its genes and redesign its nature and personalities." Shivkovski poured himself another shot. "There are monumental obstacles, of course. Boost an individual's appetite for risk, for instance, and you can bump your head on stupidity."

"Ever thought of having a go at it, Doc?" Perhaps a taunt would inspire indiscretion.

"No, no. We are decades away — or so it seems at the moment. But if the time ever came and I was still around, I know the first trait I would install would be stubbornness. It's most likely a loop behavior, with the impulse repeated until the goal is achieved. You are sent back by chemical stimuli like anxiety until your senses determine that the job's been done. Persistence is a far greater determinant of success than risk-taking or aggression. Crucial to surpassing achievement throughout history. From the brutal extroverted conqueror to the solitary introspective artist. Beethoven had it! A man with the same talents but without the stick-to-it genes would never have completed the immortal Ninth."

"Decades? Really? Sounds optimistic."

"Oh, it will happen. Perhaps much earlier than I think. A few breakthroughs in the right research and progress can become exponential. Like the computer revolution." The old man took Tom's hand and pulled himself slowly to his feet. "No, just as $E=mc^2$ led to the atomic bomb and the nuclear age, genetic and genomic research will lead to Wally Anderson's R-evolution."

Tom reached down and raised his vodka glass. "Here's to Wally, then. Guess he got it right after all."

29

Martha Jordan saw him twice before she noticed the wrench. Stuck in bed by the window for weeks with a broken hip, she knew every crack in the sidewalk and every crackhead in the neighborhood.

He was leaning against the wall outside the drugstore. Neatly dressed, good-looking, the kind of man you'd think would have something to do this time of day. He didn't look like a stick-up artist but he was giving the up and down to just about everyone who passed his way.

After watching a moment, Martha reached for *The World*. One glance at the front page and her hands began to shake. It was him! There he was! The very same man as in the composite drawings and darned if it didn't get him just right. No doubt about it. The neat-looking white man hanging around across the street was the Kitchen Sink Killer!

Martha's trembling hand reached for the telephone but it wasn't there. Her daughter had forgotten to move it back from the couch this morning. And Martha had learned the hard way what would happen if she tried to get off the bed. She would break her hip, or back, or neck. And her lovely Filipina caregiver wasn't due for another hour.

Martha was about to shout for help but then reached up and covered her mouth. Her neighbors were all at work. And what if he heard? Her breathing quickened and she fought back tears. She couldn't get to the phone—and she couldn't get away from the window! Had he seen her? Had he looked up at her window and seen the old woman displayed there slowly going out of her mind?

Martha turned slowly to peek at the street, and then she touched her breast in relief.

The killer was looking at someone else. He was leaning back against the wall and watching Mary-Jane Taylor return home from her daily forage at the corner grocery. She moved at a glacial pace, one wobbly step after the other, with her wheeled walker-cart positioned in front of her for balance. He fished something out of his back pocket—one of those adjustable wrenches. His fingers began playing with the little screw that opens and closes the jaws. The tool for today's kill! A small smile sprung on to the killer's handsome face.

Martha tried to open the window, forgetting it had been nailed shut since the last break-in. And, my gracious me, the killer was talking to Mary-Jane! And Mary-Jane, that silly goose, was talking right back. The killer was smiling sweetly. And now he was taking her arm!

Martha grabbed the green onyx egg from the window sill. She would hurl it through the glass and scream at Mary-Jane. She raised her arm—and could not do it. Great tears of surrender rolled down her face. If she broke the window and screamed at Mary-Jane, the Kitchen Sink Killer might laugh at Mary-Jane, like it was a joke, and let her go. Then wait a minute or two . . . and come across the street . . . and start up the stairs of this empty apartment building to inflict his unimaginable tortures on a helpless Martha with his bright, shiny, adjustable wrench.

Martha sobbed deeply as she watched Mary-Jane trundle off in slow motion towards a meeting with her Maker. The killer held her arm protectively. They were, in fact, almost a funny pair to watch, Mary-Jane's waddle coupled with the killer's exaggerated wide-kneed, bow-legged, John-Wayne-like gait. They stopped and chatted outside Mary-Jane's building. Martha was praying hard now. When Mary-Jane entered the building and the Kitchen Sink Killer went in after her, Martha began to wail.

Martha was still shaking violently when the killer emerged ten minutes later. Mary-Jane was dead now but it was Martha's duty to remain calm and observant. She noted the white sneakers, and the pressed blue jeans, the hair color, the upright posture, the wide friendly smile. She would do her best to see in which direction that cowboy walk of his would take him when he made his escape.

But the killer wasn't leaving. He was right back leaning against the wall of the drug store. And now he was talking to another woman—a younger woman, a mother with a stroller.

Dear God, Martha prayed, please don't make me go through this again.

The man bent beside the stroller.

Martha's hand gripped the onyx egg.

The killer produced the shiny wrench.

Martha raised her trembling arm.

The man slipped the wrench over the nut of the stroller wheel and appeared to tighten it. The happy toddler leaned out to watch.

Martha closed her eyes to pray for courage. This time she must give the warning. She could not let the baby or the mother die. But when she opened her eyes again, the Kitchen Sink Killer was going in one direction and the mother and her child were headed in the other.

"Hey, Stern," Ray Franklin asked the young detective running the tip line. "Any joy from the composite?" It was nearly midnight and Ray was ready to call it a day.

"More than a hundred and fifty calls but not the one I was waiting for."

"Which one was that?"

"The one turning in Tom Daluskov." Grinning, Stern held up the new composite. "See the likeness? Not the jaw, or the nose, but from there on up?"

"Sort of." Ray's voice was thick with exhaustion. "So any calls about people whose noses and chins actually fit?"

"Like I said, more than a hundred and fifty perfect matches. Usual screwballs, and no fresh scents. Anything promising has been farmed out for follow-up. Only one call was halfway interesting. Too bad the rest of the story doesn't fit because the witness won the jackpot. She provided one of the secret clues."

Ray started to wake up. They had kept a few details from the best of the known sightings quiet in the hope that good tipsters would authenticate themselves by providing one or two unprompted. "Which one?"

"Bow legs. Woman is called by hysterical shut-in mom who says Kitchen Sink Killer grabbed an old lady right in front of her window. Forced her home to kill her."

"Check it out?"

"I went up there myself. The witness was upset, but sharp. Had the cowboy walk right off the top. Her victim friend, on the other hand, was very far from dead."

"Did she actually see the guy?"

"Up close and personal. And Mary-Jane Taylor makes the composite a match too. Now, don't get your hopes up but although she didn't see the walk because he was beside her, I guess, she also hit entirely without my prompting on the teacher-preacher tone, the kid-like sincerity, and neat-nut clues, although that last one already seems to be out there as a general impression."

"You're kidding!" Ray felt a little weak at the knees.

"Don't get your hopes up. Mary-Jane's story just doesn't match. To start with, she's alive. She says this guy teased her about her walker-cart, and offered to help her home. Carried her groceries for her up in the elevator, tightened the wheels on this walker contraption of hers with a wrench, which I might add he did not use to brain her. He lectured her on increasing her intake of oatmeal, washed the dishes rather than drowning her in the kitchen sink, and even swept the dust bunnies out from under her bed."

Ray said nothing. Sometimes it was better just to let the facts wash over you.

"Our boy scout refuses a coffee for his good deed, and returns to the street where, according to Mary-Jane, he'd said he'd arrived early to get picked up for a job in Brooklyn."

"We know this how?"

"From Martha, the bed-bound lady in the window, whose daughter made the call."

"So she really got a good look at him."

"Sure she did, Ray. But you know how subjective matching these composites can be. In any case, our window watcher sees the suspect waiting beside the drug store again. He notices a woman's stroller has a loose wheel. Out comes the trusty wrench. Tells the woman—we found her easily enough from the clerk in the drug store—he tells the woman she's lucky he hasn't left the district yet because he's already done his good deed." Stern paused and shook his head. "Can you believe it? The mom doesn't really look at the guy's face. Says she was too interested enjoying her baby's 'skills and interaction?' "

Stern didn't have kids of his own yet. "So is the guy picked up?" Ray asked.

"Last seen walking toward the subway. Maybe his ride didn't show. But, hell, Ray, look at the killer's MO. The one today is a boy scout. He can't be our guy."

Ray already had his feeling, however. He said: "Why not?"

30

Tom and Will had picked the spot where they would cross the line. They had little to go on when it came to Wally Anderson's death and GreenGene's sub rosa activities. So they would follow the lead that Wally had left behind and had possibly died for. Their illegal entry into the so-called Monkey House would merely secure intelligence for informal use in part two of their scheme — the facilitation of an entirely legal investigation of and assault on Shivkovski by NYPD, New York County, and any number of state and federal agencies. This would be tricky. They could leave no fingerprints on evidence that would allow defense lawyers to trace it back later to the poisonous tree.

So Tom wasn't happy when he learned that Will had blabbed about the operation to Ray Franklin. And that Ray, incredibly, had somehow passed the word on to his son. "Billy's demanding that I let him go along," Ray told Tom over coffee. "That means Mary will want in too."

"No way! Billy and Mary are out of it and so are you. You want to throw his life and yours down the toilet? What about the task force? That's a huge responsibility. We need you there."

Tom and Will had agreed that, caught or not, they would never appear before the bar again. Not as lawyers, at least. It wouldn't feel right. But it would be a criminal waste for Ray to risk wrecking his career when it simply was not necessary.

"Shivkovski put my kid's life in danger. I'm bringing him down one way or the other." The detective was still angry about the attempted break-in and the gunshot, even if it had only been a warning.

"That's why you need to live to fight another day. With Will and I disbarred, we'll need you on the legal flank. We keep the kids out of it.

"They can help without doing anything illegal. You and Will can't work on foot. You need to be able to get out of the neighborhood fast. So Billy and Mary will drive, drop you off nearby, leave, pick you up later. They'll be well clear of the main thing. Deniability. They can say, our teachers asked us to give them a lift and pick them up. That's all we knew."

"I was going to ask Eva to drive."

The detective gave him a stony look and his voice turned icy. "Oh yeah, the enigmatic Eva. She's a babe but let's keep this in the family, OK? Why don't you let her stick with finding out what's what in Washington?"

"Family, huh? You're a primitive, Ray."

"You mean a member of the real world, don't you? Life's the shits where I make my living. Family's real. And friends and honor. So the kids drive. Will's with you. I monitor from a distance. See? That's how family takes care of its own."

Tom watched Ray a moment, curious about this change of heart on Eva. "Anything on the mugging?" he asked.

"Kitchen Sink has me tied up but what I hear is, Zip. One of our best Times Square snitches says he never saw this mugger guy before. Could have drifted in for the evening but it takes guts. We've got uniforms all over that place. He did it no more than fifty feet from the sub-station!"

"So where was everybody?"

"Funny. Turns out two uniforms were grabbing a coffee, right. The rest were trying to stop a riot up Broadway a bit. Road rage. Some guy jumps out of his car and punches a Japanese tourist. Someone else deliberately rams his car. All hell broke loose. "

"Too bad. We could use a happy ending on at least one of these cases."

Ray hesitated before continuing. "You know, we've got this other snitch in the Square. This one's what you might call shaky a lot of the time."

"And?"

"He says he noticed our perp, this mugger, even before the thing happened. Says he was talking to himself."

"The snitch or the perp?"

"The perp."

"Stoned?"

"The perp or the snitch?

"That's the problem. My guy wasn't exactly straight at the time. Says when he first saw the perp he thought that maybe he was on the job."

"A cop?"

"Well, sort of. He says the mugger stood up real straight, shoulders back, you know. Like 'in the military' is what the snitch says."

"Probably prison buff." Substance abusers made lousy snitches. They'd say anything for cash and lived in a dream world. Still, Tom wanted to bring something home for Eva. "Have they really worked the pawn shops?" he asked. "Eva says she lost that small keepsake, the little cameo."

"Give me a break. He'd be lucky to score a reefer on that thing. This isn't the Antiques Road Show." Ray was about to continue but shut up and latched on to his coffee.

"Spit it out, Ray."

"Okay," the cop said, sitting back. "You'd think that this mugger would have worked with the Visa card, right? Offload it right after the mugging—get someone to make a few quick scores. But nothing. All he got was the cash. Two hundred bucks, right? That's what she said she had?"

"Right."

"So, not a ping from the card. Nada."

"He may have panicked. Hadn't planned on killing a man that night."

"But it also turns out she wasn't the one who reported it stolen."

Tom was not surprised. "She wouldn't be. It was a State Department card." Tom knew what Ray was thinking: on holiday on the taxpayers' dime.

"A little birdie at Visa told me Department of Defense. They reported it almost instantly."

"She used to be in the Navy. Maybe she's on secondment." The trade talks in which Eva took part often involved complex weapons and diplomatic side deals, he recalled. "What do you hear on Wally Anderson? Talk to the medical examiner?"

Ray started to speak but was interrupted by a brief bout of hacking. "Frankenstein was clean," he said finally, "except for pot, of course. As green in death as he'd been in life."

"That's it?" Tom asked.

"Yep. Well, he also had a cold. In fact, I'm thinking I somehow managed to catch mine from Wally's corpse at the morgue. That even possible?"

"A cold, huh." Something twigged at the back of Tom's mind. Something from way back. "Which ME handled him?"

"Hottie herself, the lovely Haggerty."

Tom would give her a call.

When they stood to go, Ray had one last suggestion. If Eva

happened to ask about their "little operation" tomorrow, maybe Tom should leave out the details.

Tom told Eva almost nothing. He and Will were developing a plan. He could see she would like to hear more but she didn't ask.

She brought him up to date on her Shivkovski inquiries — and in a way that seemed to clear up some of the confusion over whether she worked for State or DND. Eva said she had a colleague at Defense Intelligence who was an expert in Soviet-era scientist-dissidents. He, in turn, was on to contacts at the CIA. She'd met him while they were working a "good cop, bad cop" diplomatic operation involving several federal departments, including State and Defense.

Tom wasn't going to ask who paid her Visa bills; he knew nothing about the accounting intricacies of federal bureaucracies.

Nor did he ask why she was using her government Visa while on holiday, purportedly, in New York City. The U.N. was here. Maybe she was working on trade deals that she couldn't talk about. Or perhaps she culled her personal expenditures out of her claims when she filed her expense reports. It nagged a little. But Tom decided that sometimes you had to trust your instincts and have a little faith.

"Where are we now?" asked her controller at the Washington end.

"Personally," Eva replied. "I've got one foot in hell." She hadn't checked in with joint-ops for two days. The brass was jumpy about the distraction her unexpected involvement with Tom Daluskov might pose. Love wasn't part of her New York mission, at least not without the quotation marks.

"Can you complete?" the case officer asked. More senior officials were certainly listening in.

"Makes it tougher but I'm closer to them than we thought I could be."

"What's the downside?"

"No downside, mission-wise. You know the feeling. You accept that you and others you care about may get hurt, one way or the other. I can tell you that things are moving very quickly but not precisely when we'll get a breakthrough. Just weeks, probably."

"The faster the better. We have to move now. On all fronts."

"Roger that."

"How's the eye?"

"Tell the guy who did it he'd better lock up the family jewels."

They both laughed. They had risen through the ranks together—Navy, the CIA, the National Security Council and now this secret cross-agency White House unit. Eva was a close friend of his wife and a favorite of his children.

"So how do I put this?" her controller asked. His tone changed, indicating that the other listeners had left the line. "Congratulations *on finding someone*? Despite the lies, deceit, and double-crosses? Who knows, maybe it will work! Get all that stuff out of the way up front before the relationship instead of when it usually shows up, at the end."

"You never know. It will have to rain miracles for this all to end well anyway. I might as well catch one for myself."

31

From lock picking to unauthorized entry, it took Tom and Will no longer than 90 seconds to kneecap their legal careers. Of course, they had spent considerably more time than that casing the GreenGene's Research and Storage Annex, subverting the alarm system, and establishing that the place was unstaffed and unguarded at night.

Billy and Mary were parked a few blocks away. They would wait for an all-clear for the pick-up.

Tom and Will used flashlights in the outer office but flicked on the neons in the windowless room they entered next. The dust-encrusted computer terminals were not an encouraging sign. If command and control for Shivkovski's underground operations did exist, this certainly was not it. Will pointed to a heavy steel door with a small mesh window. They peeped into the darkness then slipped through it into the next room and listened with their backs against the wall.

Tom felt in the dark for a light switch. No luck. Will turned on his flashlight and ran it quickly back and forth across the room. The beam reflected back off a large glass surface, then, for an instant, glanced across what looked like a man.

They dropped to the floor. Had they somehow missed the presence of a security guard?

Total stillness. Followed by heavy breathing. Followed by a high-pitched hoot.

"You smell that?" Will whispered.

"Well, Wally did call it the Monkey House."

Tom felt again for a light switch. He was unsuccessful but banks of blinding neon now powered on anyway. As their eyes adjusted, they saw that a large warehouse space lay behind a plate glass window that covered the entire end of the smaller 30-foot-wide room they had entered. It was clearly a command or monitoring center. Computer workstations, mostly grimy and disused, stood in a line facing the bizarre observation area.

Behind the plate glass was a farmhouse. It could have been dropped out of the sky by a Midwestern tornado or built from scratch by a Hollywood set crew. Except for the fact that five or six chimpanzees sat or stood in various poses on its whitewashed front steps and porch.

Tom knew something about chimps, and these ones were different. Although their long hairy arms hung by their sides in what he remembered as the normal fashion, they were more erect than the apes he'd visited so often as a kid at the Bronx zoo. Their total silence was strange too and unsettling. Five animals watched Will and Tom with fixed gazes but apparent cool. A sixth, the largest, stood off to the side.

One of its long fleshy fingers was still on the light switch.

"Planet of the Apes," said Will. "The Prequel."

The largest chimp now bounded in recognizable chimp fashion to the top of the porch steps. There, with somewhat less ease, he stood again on his hind legs. The monkey raised and turned his right palm towards the interlopers. The lips of his protuberant mouth pursed tightly together and the big brow lowered in the aggressive so-called "glare face." He looked very much like a traffic cop and the message was clear: Stop!

The glare then softened and his other rangy arm pointed rather delicately towards a half dozen TV monitors positioned high on the left-hand wall. They showed what were apparently live scenes from interior rooms. In two of the shots, young chimpanzees sprawled on bedlike platforms, asleep.

"Little House on the Prairie, with fur," Tom said. The alpha male was informing Will and Tom that he considered them a potential threat to his young. The nuance he had employed was far beyond any cognitive ability ever claimed for their hairy wards by even the most aggressive chimp researchers. Farmer John knew enough about human perceptions and reasoning to be confident that Tom and Will would get the message.

That these animals had been shoehorned into an ersatz human habitat and obviously taught to behave a little like humans was not unusual in itself. Science had always done silly things. The discoverers stood not only on the shoulders of predecessors who'd got things right, but also on an Everest of dead ends, wrong turns, colossal failures, loony beliefs and often hilarious long shots and wild guesses.

But this was Shivkovski's shop and Tom knew the old man would never waste his time training monkeys how to ape people. If he wanted a better monkey, he'd build one from the genes up.

"Shivkovski's been messing with DNA here," Will said softly out of the side of his mouth. "Look at the thigh bones and the musculature—gluts and calves. Real chimps don't stand up that way. These guys are just begging for lower back problems."

For the first time in his dealings with Shivkovski, Tom caught a faint whiff of evil. He still hoped they were wrong. "Maybe they trained the muscles from birth—bindings, casts and splints."

"Face masks, too? I don't think so. Look at the mouth and jaws. They're different somehow, smaller. And the skulls—don't they look larger to you?"

They did. Tom glanced up at the monitors, following the eyes of the head chimp. Things were happening inside. Large apes moved quickly from room to room.

"There you go," said Will, nodding towards the screen. "The latest models."

These apes, probably younger than the ones on the porch, walked on their back legs with relative ease. The young and the infants, meantime, were starting to stir. For the first time, familiar—or somewhat familiar—chimp cries filtered out from inside the house.

The lead chimp finally found voice. As the sound blasted through speakers in the observation room, Tom's hair stood on end.

In range, the pitch was similar to those of the excited whoops, hoots, screeches and barks for which the chimp was famous. But this chimpanzee was enunciating in clear syllables. Complex words. It was speaking, with the obvious expectation of being understood.

The chief chimp's eyes did not leave the screen. Its face displayed none of the usual chimp expressions—not submission, not excitement, not playfulness, not fear or aggression. Deadpan, he repeated the string of perhaps 25 sounds twice. He looked at Tom, turned and "spoke" again to the others inside of the house.

A young chimp emerged, lumbering in the improved, more erect posture Will had noted, a sort of cross between gorilla and Cro-Magnon man. It crossed the porch, jumped to the floor and walked to a wall off to the right where it pulled open a switch box and punched one of several buttons inside. The body still said dumb animal but the clear intention and swift execution declared something quite different.

The video monitors went blank.

"Mutant handyman," Will whispered. "Coming soon to your Home Depot."

The animal looked at his boss and retreated inside with nary a glance at the two dumbstruck humans on the far side of the glass.

The chief chimp was watching them, however, and slowly approaching. His features were subtly altered by what Tom prayed was not comprehension.

"There they go again," Tom said. "Conversation. The big chimp issued a verbal order, which your handyman promptly carried out? Not supposed to be on their resumes."

That Tom knew anything at all about chimps was due entirely to his father. Mike Daluskov had been crazy about the animals. Tom knew, for example, that real chimps don't have long enough vocal tracts to produce the distinctive sounds of human speech. In this they resembled the late evolutionary species known as homo erectus. And human infants, who, until they evolve, so to speak, into older children, have tongues that are isolated from the pharynx. All are syllabically challenged.

In front of a languorous yet terrifying gorilla at the Bronx zoo one day, Dr. Daluskov had quoted a line from the linguist Max Muller, who believed that if any one thing marked the frontier between the ape and humans it was the ability to communicate verbally. "Language is our Rubicon and no brute will dare cross it."

Scientists had repeatedly failed to prove Muller wrong. But were Shivkovski's animals still "brutes?" And, if not, who had ferried them across the evolutionary Rubicon? Did this affront against nature have something to do with his father's death? Or his dad's break-up with Shivkovski? From what he observed and remembered from his childhood instruction, the boss chimp here could be 10 or 15 years older than Tom himself.

Tom tried to catch the chief chimp's eye.

When he succeeded, his heart fell and his voice rose.

"Hello," he said with slow careful enunciation. "We are your friends. We're friends of Dr. Shivkovski."

The chimp raised a hand and by crooking a finger motioned for them to approach.

"Careful," said Tom. "They're clever hunters even without the upgrades."

Tom and Will moved slowly towards the glass. The chimp watched. He stepped skillfully backwards and up one step. He reverted to traffic cop routine. The two men came to a halt. The monkey wagged his finger back and forth, then touched it to the big lips of his large rubbery mouth.

"Another human touch," Will said. "Me talk. You listen."

Now, all of a sudden there was real monkey house activity. Chimps hooted and hollered, jumped up and down and gamboled back and forth, knocking over chairs. The din had a violent, menacing undertone.

Tom and Will turned instinctively to their only route of escape. But standing behind the small mesh window in the door through which they had entered was a chimp who looked a lot like the Handyman. When they rushed for the exit, he retreated, an almost guilty-child look in his eyes. A dead bolt had been engaged from the outside.

It was fight time, flight being no longer an option. Tom grabbed a push broom and unscrewed the handle. Will unplugged two heavy steel surge protectors—makeshift nun-chucks. Neither these weapons nor the martial arts skills would do them much good. Pound for pound the chimps were several times stronger than even the brawniest humans. If they attacked in these numbers, Tom realized, his jaw muscles tightening, Will and he would soon be ripped to shreds.

Will pulled out his cell. "We'll have to call Ray or 9-1-1. If the kids have to wait for us much longer I'm worried they'll come in and get hurt."

He nodded towards the chimps who were watching—and listening?—intently. "9-1-1, I'm thinking. We'll be busted but this is just a sideshow—look at the broken computer screens. They've moved on to something bigger, much bigger maybe, and I intend to live long enough to find it."

"You're right," Tom moved them back against the wall, where he could go for chimp eyes with a broomstick he'd just picked up. "Better disbarment than dismemberment. But try Ray first. My hunch is, he's right around the corner."

Before Will could dial, all hell broke loose.

A tall chimp came running out of the farmhouse front door carrying a rifle and headed for what Tom saw was a small slicing opening in the glass partition. Tom and Will dove for the floor. The rifle barrel poked through the slot and exploded.

Tom felt a shot whiz over him and heard something hit the wall. An instant later, a second shot was fired from an enfilade position along the wall on their left. The chimps are well drilled,

Tom thought, half smiling, but are these real bullets?

"I'm hit," Will said quietly.

"Bad?" Tom asked, reaching for his phone.

"This has to be Candid Camera. It's a dart! They're tranquilizing us."

"Look out!" Tom shouted. In the ceiling above them a panel had lifted. The hairy arm of a chimp emerged. In its fingers was an elongated gray canister, which began fizzing and smoking as it dropped towards the floor.

Tom scrambled to escape. He heard another shot. He felt a sharp pain in his back. Everything went red. Then black.

Ray was 15 minutes from the warehouse when he heard dispatch act on the emergency call for the GreenGene annex. He dialed Billy.

"Listen carefully! Start pounding on the car horn, as arranged. *But don't wait* for them more than two minutes. After that, you've got to go. And be careful. There's a call out. Two cars responding. And an ambulance."

"I know, Dad. We're the ones who called 9-1-1. Tom and Will are down."

"Down? Shot?" Ray's voice was running away on him. He was fearful for his friends but terrified for his son and future daughter-in-law.

"No, tear-gassed or something. They're out cold. But breathing. I couldn't call you first. They need an ambulance."

"Tell me you're not inside!"

Billy winced. There'd been a time when ignoring his father's wishes was a pleasure. Now he felt guilty. "We're inside. We're beside them."

"*GET OUT OF THERE*! Who put them down? — Billy, you get the hell out of there right now!"

"But what about them, Dad. These crazy monkeys might come back. You won't believe it, Dad. Monkeys did it–I've got pictures!"

"OK," Ray grappled to regain his self-control. His son was hysterical; the monkeys did it? "You've done good, Billy. But this is like a war. We've got to limit casualties. There may be some of that gas around. You may have inhaled it. It could impair your judgment."

"We didn't give our names to emergency, Dad. And this is that lost cell I found two weeks ago."

"Good thinking. You can't do anything more for the boys right now. The first car and the paramedics may be only ninety seconds away. You want Shivkovski to be laughing at us? You want him to think he beat all of us in one fell swoop?"

"No," said Billy. "Mary agrees. She says we should leave. That's what Tom and Will would want. Apply the lessons of Sun Tzu. Withdraw in the face of superior enemy strength."

"Exactly! Don't worry about Tom and Will. If they're breathing, it's probably some sort of knock-out gas." Ray's heart was racing: GreenGene couldn't be that crazy, given liability, but who knows? Could be cyanide or serin! "The paramedics will take good care of them. Are you running?"

"Yep."

"I want you both to go straight to Carlos's mom at Emergency. I'm calling her right now and Doc Rubin too. We'll get you two checked out."

"Dad?"

"Don't worry. We'll have every doc in town taking care of Will and Tom."

"I know, Dad," Billy continued.

Ray could actually hear their four feet pounding the pavement. "But, Dad, Tom told me that if thing blew up we had to tip off all the papers and radio and TV stations. He said we'd especially need video and still photos."

Ray had every police reporter and gypsy cameraman in the city on speed dial. As he heard the car's engine rev up, he told his son: "Consider it done."

32

Dr. Sigurd Shivkovski watched the talking heads parse the latest political pronouncements on the impending impeachment of President John Mason. He and Katya, now becoming a Fox News fan, so greatly enjoyed crisis TV that they often wrestled for the kitchen's remote control. The characters, the posturing, the bald-faced lies, the execrable behavior reminded them so much of inmates, guards and incidents from the Gulag. The result was often gales of laughter or even choked silence or a tear.

Katya answered the phone just as the White House press conference went live. "Please take it outside," she said, passing Shivkovski the cordless and ramping up the volume.

The old man was astonished. The chimp program, long outpaced by other developments, had been shut down years ago. At least that had been his order, which he now knew he had been foolish not to follow up. Researchers sometimes fell in love with their experiments—and, if the lab creatures were cute and personable, with their subjects. Shivkovski recalled the excitement when they had brought forth the first viable transgenic chimpanzee with its bits of human DNA. The talented and rather lovely team leader entered a room of applauding staff members cuddling the tiny chimp in soft linen against her breast. Had he actually been stupid enough to believe that they would put these families down?

Hiding two dozen animals had likely been easy. The plug was pulled on the monkey project but the people in charge moved on to run billions of dollars of more traditional GreenGene operations—the mundane matter of pest-sterilizing rice strains, for example. With full autonomy and hundreds of labs worldwide—and monkeys, like mice, a dime a dozen in many facilities—love-struck scientists could hide, feed, and play touchy-feely with their wards for, as it had turned out, decades. The support costs were chump change, easily found in petty cash. This was particularly true in the case of these animals, which for obvious reasons pretty well took care of themselves.

Shivkovski returned to the kitchen to tell Katya. She clicked angrily from station to station. It was all the news conference except for a New York channel that had video. There, at the scene, were Will Jefferson and Tom Daluskov—strapped to emergency stretchers. Katya glared at Shivkovski. He rolled his eyeballs. From complicity in Russia's and perhaps history's greatest mass murder to nervous mother hen in New York—what gall!

But Tom and Will would be fine. Shivkovski was pretty sure he knew what had put them under and the thought brought a smile to his lips. Still, questions would be raised and the media mob would turn its sights on GreenGene. This would require damage control. He'd make himself scarce and let his PR pros handle it. In a week or so, he'd make a video statement from somewhere in Asia, perhaps with the participation of some of GreenGene's less esoteric research monkeys.

For now, however, Shivkovski and Katya remained glued to the screen. Early reports had suggested a gas leak at a GreenGene facility. How an ADA and a corporate lawyer happened to be there was not yet known. Animal activists could be involved.

The station cut to an interview with a young man who said he was the son of a New York City police detective.

"Billy Franklin!" Shivkovski roared with pleasure. "This Tom! Backup from his little WHUPASS gang. What cheek!"

Billy claimed that the victims had called WHUPASS to say they were being "attacked" by "super-monkeys" who walked on their hind legs and fired dart guns. But the only piece of video, shot by a gypsy cameraman, showed chimpanzees that looked distinctly normal as they ran up an alley, especially from behind.

Shivkovski would tell Communications to drown the media in details about countless research programs involving chimps while inserting some levity. Say monkeys had been provided human growth hormone genes in a common experiment—then wink and suggest people keep an eye out for them on tall buildings in Midtown. They should also suggest that the intruders probably knocked over an ape anesthetizing gas canister in the dark.

The phone rang. It was Leon. "We've got to do something about Tom," his son said. "He's out of control. He'll mess up everything."

"My dear bumbling heir," Shivkovski said quietly. "Stick to your scientific responsibilities. You will do nothing about Tom, *absolutely nothing*. He is merely working things out in his mind— life outside of science is a messy affair, I can tell you. He has just put a bullet into his law career. New challenges await. But he may also have done us a favor. Who needs a red herring when you have tall tales of smelly super-apes?"

"As long as no one finds them again. They've turned up at the pier, got into the warehouse through the skylights — with a key to the locks! Fortunately we had the special security there for one reason or another."

The chimps had a pre-planned escape route, Shivkovski thought. "Better move them quickly. To the farm."

Shivkovski hung up. The station was rolling file video of Tom Daluskov's checkered past. The mayhem a few years ago outside Manny's Café. A gruesomely bloodied Tom making like a gladiator. The heroism medal. Fetchingly modest but with a chip on his shoulder. Wally Anderson and the ugly Sunday in the Park. And in between the dozens of victory marches down the courthouse steps. The punisher, the bruising unrelenting champion. Plus WHUPASS. Going down in a heap from a kick by the little blind boy. A fine fellow! Shivkovski thought. Rough at the edges, perhaps loser on points tonight, but still bound for great things. Mikhail Daluskov would have been proud of his scrappy son — but also rolling with laughter at the irony of this moment.

Shivkovski would head for Madurai and the mountain rest house. Work and lay low for a while in India, home to dozens of emerging Caltechs and MITs and some of his best people. He'd tell Katya to have the Challenger stand by. But first he must see Tom!

He must tell him how tonight's events had linked him to his father. He must tell him whatever he safely could. Because time was running out and so much more was left to be done.

33

The Philadelphia Flyer left-winger never saw it coming. Collision speed was 50 mph. Force transmitted to the brain by the impact of the bodycheck depolarized grey cells and disrupted neurotransmitter functions, blood flows, glucose metabolism and the exchange of potassium and calcium. The abrupt brain acceleration stretched, tangled or killed the tails of many of the hockey player's brain neurons. He was unconscious even before his head hit the rock hard ice.

A teammate picked up the loose puck and fired it at the New York Rangers net. It ricocheted off the iron crossbar and cut of bounds up into the roaring crowd. There in the 15th row, a dark-skinned young man snagged the frozen rock-hard rubber disc with a bare-hand catch. Still moving at 50–60 mph, the puck should have broken bones but he spun almost 270 degrees to absorb some of its impact.

The injured Flyer lay half-conscious on the playing surface below. Blood spouted from his nostrils and mouth on to ice made pearly white by the television lights. "Get up," the man who had caught the puck shouted.

"Yeah, stand him up," yelled one of his five companions "On your feet, you fucking trembler!"

The six stood out in several ways. Although one sported the home team's colors, in the form of an undersized Rangers jacket lifted from a parked car during routine scavenging earlier in the day, the rest made do with dirty denim jackets and tattered bubble coats. Each had a large "L," looking homemade, sewn to its breast. They were all big, heavily muscled men, none under 220 pounds. What stood out most were signs of past violence that could signal a future threat. The faces of all six—four whites, a South Asian and an African-American—were ribboned with scars. Scores of them, including some that were long and deep and indicated extreme trauma. Their heads and hands were also badly marked and misshapen by the calcification of broken knuckles, noses and orbital bones.

Aside from the fact that downed winger played for Philly, not New York, this likely explained why no New York fans reacted to their crass comments. The silence continued when the six laughed and jeered as the Flyer was lifted rockily to his skates by teammates and a trainer held a blood-soaked towel to his face.

Philadelphia was just down the road, however, and the fallen hero quickly found a visiting defender.

"Hey, you guys," shouted a bulky Flyer fan only a dozen seats away. "Yeah! You guys with the Ls." The six looked over instantly. Their ravaged faces lit up with smiles, while the Flyer fan's five much smaller and perhaps less intoxicated companions looked like they'd rather be back in Philadelphia.

"What's with the Ls?" Philly asked, pointing with his beer hand. "What's it stand for? Lamebrain? Loser? Hey! Limp dicks!"

"More inferiors," one of six members of the L team muttered disdainfully.

"No," said another, casually assessing the group. "One inferior and a bunch of tremblers." The big Flyer fan's friends were now engaged in some eyes-down "you're-gonna-get-us-killed" head shaking. They knew they were no match for the bigger men with the butcher board complexions.

"Hey, Lily Liver," the broad-shouldered Philadelphian shouted now. He pointed at the South Asian youth. "You *stole my puck*. Give it to me now and I won't be mean to you outside after the game."

"Can I kill him?" the puck-catcher whispered to a slightly older man with fewer scars but a commanding demeanor. He looked wistful. "No. But you can punish him. A little. The only man we will kill this week is Thomas Daluskov."

On the street outside, the six young L-Team men fished a tangle of gear from their ratty knapsacks. Soon they were wearing an eclectic variety of headphones, some with small plastic earplugs, others as big as ear muffs. Though mostly cheap knockoffs of the better brands, the headgear was connected wirelessly to first-class radio transceivers in their pockets, and small wireless mikes on their lapels.

They would use the communications to spread out and make sure the six Philly fans—or at the very least, the Big Mouth—got to the corner where they had told him he could go to get his puck after the game.

As expected, Loudmouth and his friends made a beeline away rather than toward the agreed rendezvous point. One of the L team had positioned himself in their path. "Don't worry," he told the big Philly fan. "No one will hurt these tremblers, your friends."

"I'm here for my puck," the Philly Alpha fan said when they got to 30th and Eighth.

It was hardly a fair fight.

Though effectively one-handed, the puck-catcher used his hard rubber prize first to crush his opponent's nose cartilage and next to spin and put him down with a stunning but half-speed blow to the temple.

The South Asian shook his head. "Your friends are worse than slaves," he said, bending, opening the fingers of the downed man's right hand, inserting the puck, and closing the fingers again. "I am happy to give you the puck. I know you will be honored to pay for it." He stood and slammed the heel of his running shoe on the puck and the fingers that held it.

The Philly man howled in pain. "What the hell did you do that for?" shouted one of his friends.

The puck catcher held up his own swollen hand. "Now he can really call it his own."

"You guys think you're tough?" the man on the ground said. "Maybe we'll tool up and blow you fuckers away."

"You have good rifles?" the L leader asked, suddenly interested. "All they let us have are those old-fashioned Garands."

"What the fuck is that, man?" And what does that fucking L stand for?"

"Laconia."

"Where's that? Jersey?"

"No, the past," replied the puck catcher, laughing He paused. The men with the Ls on their jackets were listening to their headsets. "Take him now," said the L Team leader after a moment. He nodded towards the new owner of the puck. "He really should go home on his shield but I'm guessing that is not what his mother is expecting."

34

Arrayed across the DA's desk were the New York dailies. *Daluskov Busts Monkey Business. Daluskov in Return of the Apes. Chimps Outsmart Chump DA.*

The *Times* led with the meltdown in Washington. But the Monkey House story rated a triple-deck, three-column front page headline: *Trained apes allegedly gassed, shot at intruders. Chimpanzees may be genetically modified to increase intelligence. Controversial ADA in illegal break-in?* Billy's still pictures of the chimps, couriered to the city editor, had not been used. Incredulous editors suspected they had been doctored.

"Your reviews," Al Rubenstein said, waving a hand over the papers. "They don't teach common sense at Harvard?"

Rubenstein seemed to be getting smaller, desiccated by months of strain.

"Are you placing charges, Al?" Tom asked politely.

"Why ever would I charge you?" Rubenstein asked sarcastically. "It's not as if the whole of New York is looking over my shoulder and waiting for it to happen. It's not as though you were caught red-handed or lacked any credible excuse for your actions!"

Tom tried not to smile.

"You and your pal happen to jog past a warehouse in the middle of the night. You hear screaming, and think someone, and I mean that in the usual sense—some *person*—is in imminent danger. You investigate and feel obliged to force entry to provide assistance. It turns out to be a bunch of smart-assed, gun-toting monkeys who, in apparent self-defense, exercise their right of simian arrest."

"If it's a problem—"

"It is not as everyone knows that you're hung up about the Anderson suicide and so have a special interest in learning what kind of monkey business GreenGene may be up to in that particular warehouse. Even though, last time I looked, East River warehouses are still protected under the Constitution and the rules of evidence."

"We can solve the problem—"

"Why would it be a problem?" Rubenstein said. The Mason

crisis was always on his mind. "It's not as if we want to distance ourselves from people in positions of trust who behave as if they are above the law."

"Will and I will plea," Tom said. "We're done with the bar."

The DA shook his head slowly. "Will's not the only friend you're dragging down, Tom. Internal Affairs is looking at Ray Franklin. Detective Franklin, not even on duty, shows up out of nowhere at the warehouse. Next thing a uniform gets the idea someone's messed with the crime scene. The back door lock looked undamaged when the kid cop arrived. Uniform looks again fifteen minutes later after Franklin shows up and it's all banged up to conveniently look like the door was forced by two men effecting an emergency entry."

Tom volunteered nothing. "The Blue Wall's descending." Rubenstein said. "Turns out the detective in charge of the crime scene is another old buddy of yours, Banks, whose life you happened to save at Manny's Café. Suddenly, after a little talk with Detective Banks, the young uniform's not so sure anymore that the door wasn't damaged right from the start."

Rubenstein watched him for a moment, curiosity and sadness on his face. "This time last year you wouldn't have touched tainted evidence with a ten-foot pole, never mind break the law."

This time *last month* was more like it, Tom thought. But something had shifted inside him. He felt differently. The anger—the anxiety—he'd once experienced when someone, for whatever reason, broke the rules was simply gone. He felt only determination now. He was cruising. He could almost see the bumps and tight turns in the road ahead, though he had no idea at all where the road would take him.

His only regrets were for his friends—even the rumpled Rubenstein.

"I'm sorry about this, Al. You sure you're OK? You seem to be off your game. I expected to walk out of here with my head in my hands."

Rubenstein looked to one side then the other, as if he could see his problems closing in. "The whole world's gone crazy. The grounds shifting under our feet. By the hour." He managed a small smile. "Makes it hard to get off those big roundhouses I like to throw." He took a deep breath. "So! You're suspended, obviously. Indefinitely."

"Are you going to keep looking into the Anderson

harassment?" Tom asked, unsurprised. "What about these freak monkeys? And GreenGene? Will and I could have been hurt. That's got to be negligence. Gross indifference."

"That's not happening. We'd look even more stupid than we do now. Besides the chimps are heroes. Bagged a couple of no-good burglars. Give them a shave and a haircut and they'd be doing the talk shows, at least based on what you two claim. That's if you could find them, of course. As for GreenGene's ape experiments, Feds of various persuasions and with indecipherable acronyms are already looking at them."

"You mean the federal government still goes in to work?"

Rubenstein snorted dismissively. "I've just told you the official part," he continued, his voice taking on a more officious tone. "But here's the real lowdown. The mayor has asked me to tell you this specifically. You won't be coming back. Ever."

Tom smiled, again unsurprised. "The same will soon be said of the mayor. And of you, Al. Nonetheless, I'll do you both a favor. I resign."

"Want two pieces of advice from an old man?" Rubenstein asked as Tom headed for the door.

"Sure."

"You've got nothing more to lose. That's a lot like freedom. You have your skills, your friends in the right places, and time on your hands. If you want to get Shivkovski and GreenGene, now's the time to do it. "

35

As always, Gerald's instructions came encoded. The latest assignment told him where to go. He knew, generally, what he was supposed to do. Sometimes the directions were explicit, including the tools and techniques to use. More often, however, the boss left a few details up to Gerald.

Intuition was important, the boss said, and creativity. How the work was done should in part express who Gerald was. his individuality and uniqueness. There would also be random elements of time and opportunity in the mix.

This time the boss sent the "tool" in the mail. Gerald removed the brown wrapping paper. A very long white cloth belt, the kind he'd see the little kids taking taekwondo wrap round their waists and tie at the front in a sort of bow.

There was also a piece of paper upon which were printed two words: "Kitten. Child."

The rest—the where and the what of the assignment—was clearly specified in the code Gerald knew so well that he need not refer to the key.

Later, of course, he would double-check it anyway.

Measure twice, cut once.

Good advice.

Where had he heard it?

Probably from that irritating hardware store person.

"Ask Jimmy," the sign had said.

Ha!

36

Tom was eager to see how Shivkovski would respond to being under direct attack—because that was what the Monkey House probe had signaled, an impending all-out assault on GreenGene's secrets. Shivkovski sat in one of the low bench seats on the enclosed observation deck of the World Trade Center, with only plate glass between him and eternity. From behind, he looked bent and shriveled against the vast panorama of Midtown but his fragile hand rested somewhat imperiously on the handle of his long black cane. So it was hard to know whether Manhattan humbled the old man or he thought he owned it.

"So good of you to come," he said as Tom took off his WHUPASS jacket. To have requested that they meet here was, of course, just more cornball Shivkovskian theatrics. Shivkovski winked and pointed toward the Empire State Building. "The big man-made giant ape should be here any minute." Tom smiled but did not rise to the bait.

Shivkovski tapped the Plexiglas with his cane and leaned forward to peer down. "Vertigo. Nature's way of keeping us from the cliff edge. But we are such strange creatures. We toy with our fears—horror movies, for example. We seek the thrill of the neurotransmitters we release in the same way that a horse in a pasture will suddenly snort loudly to generate the same kind of arousal. And yet we fear so many things that we have no need to be afraid of! Look at me! I cannot sleep properly without my daily shot of national alarm, my fix of gross indignation, my nightly snort of impending doom on CNN."

"Fear not the super-chimps—is that what you're saying?"

"A few tricks with a few monkeys? That's just science. Tom! A series of often ludicrous yet perhaps ultimately necessary steps. Like making sausage. Without experimentation, we'd have no medical cures, no global food security. And I can tell you a hundred things much scarier that are SOP in genetics today."

"One will do."

"You are familiar with vectors, of course."

"When you want to insert DNA to repair cells in a human

body — to combat cystic fibrosis, for instance–you have to build a delivery vehicle. You can take a virus cell that targets the affected area — the apical surface of the lung epithelium, for instance. You take out the virus nucleus, and insert your therapeutic DNA nucleus. Inject the altered virus cell and it will find its way to the target area, penetrate the target cells, and deliver your therapeutic DNA."

"Roughly correct. " Shivkovski said, tapping his cane again. "But here's the part that could be whipped into a public panic. Three or four years ago, researchers trying to develop better vectors pseudotyped cells of the human immunodeficiency virus, or HIV, by incorporating specific envelop proteins from the Zaire strain of Ebola into the cell's membranes. In vitro, at the time. But it worked! Can you imagine that the Jane and John Q. Public ever granting prior approval to that experiment — HIV meets Ebola? Can you see *The World's* headlines now, or hear Fox? They'd forget about this monkey business very quickly."

Shivkovski and GreenGene had taken some lumps over the Monkey House and he was clearly smarting. Both the green and the godly reckoned science had crossed the line. Great peril lay ahead. Slavery, colonialism, racist immigration policies, the Nazi death camps, uppity, apronless, job-snatching women — you could blame it all on science. It was time to shorten the leash!

"Don't worry, Doc," Tom said kindly. "Have faith in your spin doctors. Trust your lobbyists. Everyone will be back on the Mason deathwatch soon — except me."

Shivkovski nodded gravely out over Manhattan. "Yes, your pride must be bruised and I really must apologize for the unfortunate incident at the warehouse — although I had nothing to do with it."

"I might believe you but thousands wouldn't."

"Besides, you and Will wouldn't have missed it for the world! What's a dose of mild sensitive in return for a bit of acting out and little adventure?" Shivkovski placed a feathery hand on Tom's shoulder. "Don't worry, nothing to be ashamed about — the extended childhood has been a huge benefit to our species. And if you knew the genesis of this little joke, you'd be laughing right along with me."

"What makes you think I won't have the DA charge you? Reckless endangerment."

"To start with, your name is mud in that particular office.

from what I hear. More importantly I know and understand you, dear boy! You want to ride alone. You pursue total victory. You will always seek an epic battle that you see yourself ending mano-a-mano with a killer blow, not a puny legal skirmish that you would play no part in and from which your opponent would escape with a slap on the wrist." The old man paused, then winked. "Which I'm guessing is why you have resigned."

As Tom wondered who was providing Shivkovski with this inside information, his eyes met those of someone up on an observation walkway. The young man was hard not to notice, although Tom had not seen him before. Chances were this guy recognized him from the courthouse, because he certainly looked like someone who might have passed through the system at one time or another. Big, maybe six three, six-four, wearing a Rangers' jacket with a tatty L sewn onto the chest. What stood out, however, was his ravaged face, crisscrossed by dozens of scars, including a deep vertical wound from forehead to mid-bridge on his nose. A very bad car accident, Tom reckoned, or a whole ton of Shivkovski's epic battles, none of which it looked like he had won.

Shivkovski was smiling faintly now and eavesdropping on a young tourist addressing his wife and three children next to him. "This is why America is the greatest country on earth, Lil," the man said, a hand sweeping over the scene below. "There's nowhere else like it!"

"Touching, isn't it?" Shivkovski said when the family moved on. "One might speculate that an image of Manhattan has lurked forever in our primordial memory. A sort of final destination. But I see it differently. This skyline is to today's man what the first mud hut was to the first farmers. A big deal in its moment but small potatoes even in the medium run. This is *nothing* compared with what what is in our future."

"Chimps as CEOs?"

"Old news! Why build a better monkey? Evolution's done it already!"

"So what is Sigurd Shivkovski always humble contribution going to be?" Tom kept the tone friendly.

The old man showed his small imperfect teeth. "Everything that I *can* be up to I *am* up to. You know about our new breakthroughs in grains—outstanding! And ten—I repeat, *ten*, new pharmaceutical products likely to get FDA approval this year alone. Buy GreenGene stock. It's a bargain even at today's elevated price."

"That's business. What about weekends and hobby time?"

"You know my interests already!" The scientist's tone turned sharp again. "Are you a fan of Wells? The great British author, H.G. Wells? *Time Machine*, *War of the Worlds* . . . . "

"*The Island of Doctor Moreau*?"

"Not his best, but yes. It was in *The Man of the Year Million* that he wrote: 'It is not what man has been but what he will be, that should interest us.'"

"So you're conducting experiments into what man can become, are you?"

"I *think*, Tom. I do putter some, too, but mostly I think. The Gulag, remember? Constant thinking—thumbsucking, your father called it—rather than the hands-on lab work. The thing about thought is that, while useless so much of the time, it has on frequent occasions been the most powerful thing on earth! Well, one need merely look—." He gestured toward the Manhattan skyline. "Sir Henry Bessemer thinks up a way to mass produce steel—and *poof*, the skyscraper. Einstein's mind makes a happy turn – and *boom*, whole cities go *poof*."

"William Kelly came up with the steel process at just about the same time."

"Yes, of course. And American. We must not forget him." Shivkovski took hold of his cane, as if planning to leave. "Biologically, on the other hand, things have often remained the same for a very long time—until, suddenly, there's massive change. To make the great leap from a single cell organism to a multi-cell being with nutrients flowing between cells required only the simple device of clotting yet it took eons, until nature came up with fibrinogen. But that great leap forward one and a half *billion* years ago is why we're here! And the gene we use for the production of fibrinogen is identical to the one used by the lamprey fish and the sea cucumber, which are 500 million years old. We have inserted those genes into transgenic pigs whose milk provides fibrinogen to save the lives of people who will otherwise bleed to death after the tiniest cut."

"Very interesting, Doc," Tom said. "But what have you been doing that made Wally Anderson frightened of r-evolution, with the long e?'

"Nothing at all!" Shivkovski leaned on his cane and watched

Tom for a moment. Then the old man's face brightened. "But that reminds me! I have taken steps to compensate young Carlos Chavez for the unfortunate incident at your apartment. A scholarship. A new school for the blind, near Utica, absolutely world-class."

"What about Leon? Who or what wretched tricks does he have up his sleeve? And where the hell is he?"

"Calm yourself, my boy. Perhaps a turn around the observation deck is in order." Shivkovski pushed himself to his feet. "Leon is best used to refine work I've initiated. Provided with the foundation, he is extremely imaginative, even artistic. I will let him know you would like to talk." As they began to walk, Shivkovski said: "I just cannot see why you are so exercised about the possibility of so-called Revolution? What's the big deal? How do you think our species ended up where it happens to be right now? We, the sewer rat, the dung beetle and every other living thing are merely the current end products of a tremendously haphazard process. What evolution churns out is often unpleasant and certainly far from perfect."

Tom tried to keep the old man rolling. "Just wondering, but how could someone like you, a victim of a failed remake of humanity that killed tens of millions, even consider another crazy experiment? If you want to do mankind a favor, why not conquer disease and feed the hungry."

"Yes, why not!" Shivkovski smiled indulgently. "But is that all there is, as Peggy Lee once asked? What value do we add to the additional billions of numb and chubby lives that will result?"

"What about the unintended consequences? Evolution's had a billion years to shake out the mistakes."

"You sound like the people at this end of town who believe what 'Mr. Market' spits out is always right. Or that the cockroach and the cancer cell are the correct answer simply because they have conquered and survived. You say end heart disease but I suggest that if humanity could be spared some of its more damaging shortcomings, it would be as welcome and good as, for example, giving brave young Carlos Chavez his sight."

Tom laughed dryly. "Carlos is one of the happiest, most well-adjusted kids I know. He has dignity and a heart as big as a house. He's already more than fulfilling his huge potential."

Shivkovski stopped walking. "No matter, Tom. It will be a hundred years before we are even close to trying. And now, I will give up on you for today. Leave me here, if you don't mind." He gestured over his shoulder towards the Statue of Liberty below. "I will spend a few moments with my favorite lady."

Tom was disappointed. He had wanted real results rather than theoretical fencing.

"I shouldn't tell you this, but I will." Shivkovski stepped a little closer and his cane bumped against Tom's shoe. "The chimpanzees. That silly trick—the one where they shoot the dart guns. That was your father's idea." Shivkovski was chortling. It was a disturbing sight. "He loved the chimps and he thought it appropriate that they learn how to tranquilize humans."

Tom's felt a thrill shot through his spine. It was as if his father had reached from eternal midnight and across the empty years to touch him, lightly and tenderly and with a smile. So different from the savage madness of those final moments.

Shivkovski was still chortling. "If only you knew how much that show in the Monkey House had your father written all over it!" After a moment, he asked: "So, my boy, should I not leave town?"

"Go wherever you want, Doc. I'm going to forget about you for a while and find out where all your thumb-sucking may have led."

Tom called Angela Chavez. She confirmed what Shivkovski had told him. Carlos was on a three-week scholarship at a new if little-known institute for the blind near Utica. It was a wonderful opportunity, all expenses paid. The institute had told her that the scholarship had been underwritten by an anonymous donor on the recommendation of one Thomas Daluskov.

37

Of the attacks upon Tom in the days after the Monkey House fiasco, the most disconcerting were passive-aggressive and delivered via the cold shoulder and the frosty glare. Tom was a bumbler when it came to the women in his life.

His obsession with Rachel had led to periodic train wrecks in their friendship for going on three decades. Things had improved of late but it remained a mystery to him and many others why she had kept coming back for more.

Over the years, Tom's treatment of his mother had ranged from icy insensitivity and frequent disrespect during his teenage years to what Rachel had called "walking on eggs" as he grew more concerned in adulthood about her apparent battles with depression. Yet he and she had always been great talkers on matters external to their personal lives and, in the past 10 years, his mother had been more relaxed than he had ever known her to be. Tom credited honest, hard rock Hank, with his easy way and sure touch, for putting and keeping his mom's life on an even keel. He was sure she shared everything with him, including her demons. Tom himself had found in Hank a mentor and friend. He was happy to take his advice and particularly his hints on which doors in his mother's life should remain shut.

And now there was Eva. Two days after the Monkey House break-in, she had returned from Washington and torn a strip off Tom in front of his parents and Will for leaving her out and in the dark. She claimed that her military training could have mitigated their obvious incompetence but said that Tom's deceit had hurt her even more. "I love you," she shouted. "I didn't want to but I do. And I know you love me."

"You're right. I do." The words had surprised Tom almost as much as they had his mother and Will. But it was true. And this was not the only new trick in Tom's miraculously expanding emotional portmanteau. Where malign prosecutorial skepticism had once reigned, unqualified trust was making insidious inroads. Despite the holes and false notes in her story, Tom was perfectly content to suspend disbelief when it came to Eva. So when she demanded that she be consulted on all further "operations" against Shivkovski, he'd quickly agreed, inviting Ray's intense displeasure and brushing aside an obvious question—why so much interest in GreenGene when she never made a peep anymore about the mugger who'd almost knocked her block off? But Tom trusted his gut, which seemed to reinterpret her words, even as she spoke, into a plea for understanding. Something like, *I know the lying hurts you, Tom, but I beg you to trust me anyway.* Far from feeling suckered, Tom was intrigued. Finding out what was really going on would be dessert after the main course, which would come when they shut the Shivkovskis down.

"Do you think the animals are transgenic?" Tom had asked his mother the day of the Monkey House post-mortem. When Dr. Parviati and Hank failed to seek each other's prompts, he knew they'd prepped for this discussion, something that in itself delivered a subtle message of change.

"Let us say your observations raise that possibility," his mother began. "Genetic material from a human cell may have been added to chimp DNA. The donor cell is fused with an unfertilized chimp egg cell and once the embryo develops, it's transferred into the female chimp. Theoretically, if a billion things go right, it could survive and grow into a transgenic monkey—in this case a hybrid chimp-human. There are successful transgenic monkeys around already, of course—but mostly proof-of-concept experiments, to show, for example, you can get a transgenic rhesus monkey that expresses a particular fluorescent protein in its tissue."

Hank chimed in. "But remember, the more human DNA you try to transfer and use, the greater the probability that everything crashes and burns."

Tom's mother leaned forward in her chair. "We conclude that Shivkovski has indeed managed it. You and Will have described animals that have significant variations in their fundamental posture, appearance and motor abilities. That's crucial."

"So Shivkovski's experimented with different genetic combinations on different groups of chimps?" Will asked. "The Model A, the Model T, etcetera. And the range of differences is what proves something has been altered at the genetic level."

"Correct." Coming from his mother, this sounded like a certainty."

"It's the sci-fi horror classics coming true," Eva said. "H.G.

Wells. *The Island of Dr. Moreau* with the interbreeding of man and beast. *Sirius,* the story of the dog with human intelligence. But my own favorite's two hundred years old, good old Dr. Frankenstein's monster."

"It would be wonderful if that was the full extent of our concern." Tom had never heard his mother sound so grave. Something important was happening here. "Wells and Stapledon were brilliant men, of course. Knew their science. Even back then, they thought they lived in an age of dangerous runaway human knowledge and powers. But Stapledon supposed that it would take many thousands of years of horrible eugenics or freak evolution before the brightest humans would devise a way to manipulate hereditary factors in the germ, as he put it. Now, a mere hundred years later, we are there. And each day and each hour and minute, our learning accelerates."

"The man-beast thing has been a human fantasy for thousands of years," Eva said. " But—"

Tom squeezed her hand. The old folks were opening up, he thought, let's not lose momentum. Hank picked up the thread. "So what exactly is Sigurd doing? Transgenic mice have been used for years to study human diseases. At that level then, he's not trying anything entirely new. The chimps? Maybe he was attempting to develop test animals with human features. Monkeys with human hearts. You could subject those hearts to research and tests with far less restraint and compunction than if humans were involved—and get similar indications. But that's hardly startling, really—everyone knows GreenGene is deep into genetic medical research and, of course, GMO foods. Have you seen those ads they run saying people should waste no more time or energy on obtaining food each day than they do availing of air and water? Transgenic stuff may be old hat for him."

"Your Dr. Shivkovski likely has bigger fish to fry, so to speak," Dr. Parviati said with a wan smile. "Thinks out of the box. Your father was that way too. They loved to mix up tactics and theories the way we are mixing our metaphors."

Eva asked: "What's bigger than Frankenstein or your run-of-the mill-man-beast?"

"So far, science has been content to merely copy, or clone genetic code and move it around," Hank said. "You're still dealing with Nature's basic building blocks and its own designs."

"But what if you start writing code yourself and tossing it

into the mix?" All eyes turned to Dr. Parviati. She smiled in a sweet, almost shy way that touched Tom deeply. She looked relieved, as if she was freeing herself from a difficult weight. "That's really what Hank is getting at," she continued. "A mutation is brought about by a change in an organism's genetic code, the base pairs, the letters we all know about—the ABCDs of life in Tom's heretical simplified teaching manual. We don't know exactly why mutations happen. They appear random and accidental and yet have served a tremendous purpose, given the fabulous array of life we see and know of from the past, compared with our humble beginnings as bacteria. When the code changes work, or take, you have evolution."

Tom's mother moved closer to Tom, Eva and Will. "We may be near the point where we can try to write or amend that code ourselves. Once we're there, anything becomes possible, and I don't mean in a good way. We will remain hugely ignorant but still able to roll the genetic dice and take trillion-to-one shots in the hope that something, *anything*, takes and a new genotype becomes viable."

"The hijacking of Nature, right?" Eva asked.

"We'd be shooting blind," Hank said. Tom guessed he was keeping to the script. "It could be a century before we can count on getting steady results. But it is probably inevitable. The time is coming when man will usurp nature not only in manipulating plant and animal life but also in attempting to rebuild himself. It may come sooner than we think."

Will the lawyer tried to nail things down. "Sophia, Hank, let's see if I am reading you correctly. Are you saying that you suspect Shivkovski is heading in that direction?"

Eva spoke up. "And that you'd like us to find out?"

Dr. Parviati nodded her assent. "Yes, I think the time has come."

"The godmother has spoken." said Tom, " 'Sigurd Shivkovksi must sleep with the fishes.' "

"Be exposed is more like it," Hank said with a laugh. "Although we do have something of a Puzo twist for you."

"We are sending someone we can trust to help ensure your security," said his mother. "And to pick up your theme, it will be all in the family. Stephan is your half-brother, your father's son from the Soviet Union and, more recently, Brighton Beach."

"You'll know him right away," Hank said. "Looks like your

dad. Tattoos on his knuckles are somewhat distinctive."

"Wow!" Tom laughed softly. "The mobbed-up step-brother steps out from the closet. Let's be serious, though—we're afraid of Shivkovski?"

"Leon's instability will ramp up now that the wheels are starting to come off," said Hank. "We should be ready for absolutely anything from him, given that and his resources."

Tom's mother's tone turned businesslike. "It is likely to be messy. Sigurd is not in control of all forces that may come to bear. He believes in creative chaos." She approached and put her hands on Tom's shoulders. "Go along with me this one last time, please, Tom. Are you sleeping at home tonight?"

"Yes. Alone. Eva's dropping me off on the way to the Washington shuttle. Should I put a gun under my pillow?

"No, my dear. Tonight you'll be fine."

In the end, however, all hell did break loose, although not in a way that Tom could have predicted.

After he heard the knock and opened his front door, Rachel stood back a bit, smiling at his surprise. Her face was flushed.

"Are you familiar with the Last Days Syndrome, Tom?"

"Can't say I am." Tom stepped aside to invite her in. He still could not help himself completely and, with a twinge of guilt, felt glad that Eva had returned to Washington.

"That's understandable. I just invented it." She turned to him as he closed the door behind her. "In the last days and final hours when a great city is about to fall or the fear of death and things even worse take hold, the human tendency is often to drink, dance, or simply make love."

In an instant, Tom's feelings and respect for Eva, along with respect for himself were submerged in dark elation. When he spoke, his voice was thick with excitement "I guess I'd choose number three."

"It can only be this once." Rachel's hand began to unbuckle his belt. "Or should I say, one night." Her lips were against his ear. "I wanted to do this the other night." When his pants began to fall, she turned and backed them on to the couch, and said, "we've waited so long and I will not wait any longer."

Tom had neither the time nor the sense to wonder what

Rachel had meant by last days and final hours. But she wept often during their sleepless night.

By dawn, he wondered whether he'd dreamt it all. Yet there she was beside him, sleeping finally, all and more than he'd ever imagined she would be.

It astounded him that this life, still only partly lived, could have seemed, as it had only an hour earlier, virtually done. He had felt spent yet complete. Yet something else had begun to beckon, something as vague and opague as the rest of the day. And then he had realized that it was yesterday that was calling and tomorrow and that what Rachel had given him was liberation from the weight of his compulsion and the freedom to forget her and to be with Eva.

He was sure Rachel had sensed this new detachment even as she had made the offer that he had waited a lifetime to hear. If he would lay off Shivkovski, just live and forget, she could admit her love for him and they would make a life together.

He had told her no. He would always care for her but he was in love with Eva. Rachel, the mighty and once matchless second woman in his life, had wept quietly again but Tom realized this was not only about the two of them. All the signs and portents the three women in his life were giving up foreshadowed some great turning point. It would not be the end of days, of course, but probably something pretty big.

Before leaving quietly for his run, Tom left a note on Rachel's handbag: "Thank you, Rachel. You're like a goddess to me — and my first and longest-lasting love. But I've got to find my place among the mortals. Tom." He added a PS with a promise he could not be sure he could keep: "Don't worry. I won't hurt the old man."

He hoped she'd be gone when he got back.

Rachel had left when he returned but Eva was standing by the sink. He had not expected her today but this was hardly the time to say so.

"Oh! Hi." He nodded towards the coffee pot in her hand. "I was just going to brew some fresh."

"Your visitor left you a note." The keen hurt strained Eva's voice. She glanced at the tangled sheets visible in the bedroom. Two wine glasses, half full, sat on the living room floor. When Tom tried to speak, Eva said: "Do the right thing and read the note first."

It was on the bed, displayed beside his own. "It's my fault," Rachel had written "We should not have done this. *Please* be happy. And *PLEASE* stay away from the Shivkovskis. Nothing good can come of it."

Tom returned to the kitchen table and sat down in front of a mug and a spoon Eva had laid out. She leaned back against the counter. "Do you actually expect me to start this conversation?"

"It's the old line but it is true," Tom said a little belligerently before reminding himself that offense was not always the best defense. "This had nothing to do with *us*—with you and me," he continued, inanely, before pulling up for a second and then jumping way ahead. "I want to marry you."

They watched one another, both wary and surprised at the sudden turn.

"You will understand that I'm not ready at this particular moment to accept your proposal." She crossed her arms and turned to look out the window, still talking. "My mom would say you had to get it out of your system. I am definitely not my mother. But I did know that this thing between you and Rachel was like a force of nature. Nothing could really move ahead with us until you settled it in your head."

"What you and I have is infinitely more natural," Tom said. "With you, I'm in my own skin. With her, it's as if I'm not myself." He moved to stand and go over to her.

Eva held up her hand. Her voice trembled. "Don't interrupt. Stay there. As I said: nothing can be solid between us, or healthy, until you get it sorted out in your mind." Her voice hardened. "So if you had to sleep with her to do that, so be it."

Tom sensed she was ready to listen. "The last thing on earth I want to do is hurt you. You're the innocent in this mess. You've been mugged all over again."

Tom saw her stiffen. Eva didn't like being the victim. She swung round, fetched the coffee pot, and poured him a cup. "Don't talk about innocence. Not at our age. Not in this world. I'm a little screwed up too, Tom. And believe me, you'll find some of it hard to take. If and when we ever lay everything out on the table."

She sat down opposite him. "Meanwhile," she said briskly, "let's allow the other important things in our lives to distract us for now. I'm in no mood to fall into this shit ditch."

Tom waited a moment then asked cautiously. "Any joy in Washington?"

"Not in the way I expected." The Shivkovski material at the Pentagon had been thin and disappointing, Eva said. But her contact would continue trying to pry information loose from the CIA.

"But a very strange thing happened on the flight back. I was catnapping. I woke up. And while my eyes were still closed, I saw the license plate."

"Which license plate?"

"Remember I told you that when Matthew Agneau was bleeding on the sidewalk, someone said two men seemed to have recognized him and were running off? I realize now that I may have seen the two of them walk away—one a big guy in a Fubu jersey."

"And?" Tom was happy to finally pay some attention to the mugging.

"I saw them hop into a car?"

"And?"

"*That* license plate!"

Eva produced a pen and scribbled a number on a paper napkin. She stood to leave. "On the other thing, I get the feeling we'll be pretty busy so let's give it some time." She stopped before closing the door. "I'm getting a hotel room but if you ever want me back, you had better swab all traces of Rachel out of this place right now. And burn the sheets."

38

Tom called Ray Franklin, asked him to run the license plate number and hung up. The phone rang soon afterwards. He put it on speaker so he could talk with Ray and go through his email at the same time.

"You can run but you cannot hide." It was Leon Shivkovski.

"You're the one hiding, you little jerk. I'm tracking down those goons you sent to bust into my apartment and they're going to turn on you—"

"Bore me with your tough talk later. What's your next move?"

"Forget the chess, Leon. Play with one of your smart-assed monkeys. Humiliating you has lost its appeal."

Leon snickered again. "You truly believe you're winning! How pitiful. What a complete failure of imagination. It all means something completely different in another dimension—."

"Right. The one where you're dating Jennifer Lopez and chimps rule the world."

"Why is all right for you and Will to break into a GreenGene lab and frighten our poor animals but it's non-stop whining when someone tries to burgle your apartment?"

"You endangered my kids and you set your dogs on Wally Anderson—that's why." Tom was clicking through emails from fellow ADAs. Many were supportive of the Monkey House initiative—not a heartening sign, he felt.

Leon's voice softened. "If you're looking for the true mad scientist, leave my father and me alone and look at yours. We're amateurs. He's in a class by himself."

"What the hell does my dad have to do with all this?"

"My dad? My *dad*? What kind of baby talk is that? Where does the warm, fuzzy, false memory you have of the possibly martyred Dr. Mike Daluskov come from? Excuse me while I vomit."

"Spit it out, Leon. Do you good."

"Your old man was a maniac. Where do you think the chimp experiment came from?"

"I know. Your daddy told me."

"But that's all you know. Mad Mike would stick his home-made genes into anything that moved. In a good week at the lab, if he had it his way, there'd be more mutations forced on to life than the Jurassic period managed in 175 million years."

"Funny how no one else remembers him that way."

"How's Rachel?" Leon asked, apropos of nothing.

Tom smiled and allowed himself to gloat a little over his secret. "Seemed fine when I saw her last at your father's place."

"My, my, lying again. I happen to know that you two spent last night banging on each other's bones."

"Maybe you're omniscient after all." Leon must have someone watching the apartment.

"You go too far. But I may indeed know more about you two than you do yourselves. Which is why I tell you to refrain from further sexual contact with Rachel. Chances are good you were conceived in the same dirty test tube, which sort of makes her your sister."

"Nature frowns on such things, doesn't it?" Tom had never heard Leon so out of control.

"I'm not kidding you. It has long been my suspicion that your dad modified your germ-line cells. Ask around. They called him the vodka cowboy. I'm surprised you didn't come out with polka dots and a switch to make your nose glow in the dark—like his did in the pub. Who knows? Maybe he killed himself because he couldn't live with the things he'd done. Or maybe he looked down at you one grim day and was not pleased with his work. As for Rachel? Okay, we know her legal parents, Tony and Rebecca—dead with Will's paper parents in the Kentucky plane crash. But where did she *really* come from? And who's she to you? Genetically? You really believe that sperm of a Mr. Favaloro, a migrant Sicilian fisherman, and egg of an Irish waitress story? Gimme a break! That's where she got her brains?"

"Why not?" replied Tom. "The Favaloros could have been the savviest folks in the village for centuries and Miss Ryan's folks the sharpest peddlers in County Cork. Toss in some higher education and, presto. . . . science superstar!"

"Fine," said Leon lightly. "Don't believe me! I'd be in denial too if I suspected I was cooked up in a petri dish by a drunk. Your *dad* considered you a lab rat *quite literally*."

"Call your lawyer and drop by the DA's office tomorrow. Maybe you can plead to a couple of months in jail, followed by community service. You can teach multi-dimensional chess at the local psyche ward."

"That's not happening, Tom. But I'm willing to make another

kind of deal. You give me another game and I'll give you a clue in the Wally Anderson case."

"What kind of clue?"

"The kind you want. A clue that will further whet your appetite for conspiracy and I'll throw in some foreshadowing of the apocalypse as a bonus." Leon's tone turned friendly. "You know what I'd really like? One of those blind games we used to play as kids."

A blind game was a good teaching tool and helped break the monotony for impatient youngsters. They'd block the middle of the chessboard with a book or a large sheet of paper so that neither could see the other's pieces. Each would make a series of five or ten opening moves behind the screen. The book or sheet was taken away, and they played on from wherever they found themselves.

"Ready?" Tom asked. If Leon was to keep running off at the mouth, this was a small price to pay. Leon claimed to have made his 10 moves already so Tom quickly announced his own. He could hear the scribbling at the other end of the call. Leon read them back to double-check.

Tom asked: "So what's the clue?"

"I understand from my sources that poor Wally had a touch of the flu."

"You call that a clue?" Ray had said that it was a cold. But something stirred in Tom's memory and his mind began scanning for connections.

"Of course, it's a clue!" Leon sneered. "You could never be a scientist! No staying power. No taste for hard work and sacrifice. A scientist retreats from the dead ends and flings himself off a fucking cliff to see if that will work. He doesn't whine and whimper because, *daddy*, it's just too *hard*—"

Leon rattled on but Tom's attention was caught by an instant message on his laptop screen. It was Ray:

"You won't believe this."

"Try me," Tom typed back.

"The 'getaway' car Eva IDed at the NASDAQ mugging belongs to . . . ."

Tom was surprised. Something entirely unexpected. And, suitably, as it happened, bizarre.

Tom cut Leon off mid-rant. "What the hell were you doing in Times Square the night Matt Agneau was murdered?"

Finally, something put a sock in Leon's mouth. Tom would have liked to car. the silence.

The vehicle in which the two witnesses to the accountant's death had fled, Ray had written, was registered to the GreenGene Corp. A notation had been made in the file to send all correspondence, including several moving violations and a pile of parking tickets, to the office of the company's chief of research, no other than Leon.

Time for a tactical lie: "We've got you on a security camera. Perhaps you can me tell in which particular dimension you control this murder occurred."

Leon still said nothing. Then: "OK. It doesn't matter now. Yes, of course, I knew Mathew Agneau, poor bastard, and, yes, I was there. With Francis, in his Fubu disguise. It was an experiment, a game, but somehow a *real* mugger showed up. A complete screw-up. Poor Francis cried for a week!"

"*Our* Francis?" But it made sense. Gentle, childlike, gigantic Francis. He often went everywhere with Leon.

But another question crossed Tom's mind. If this started as "a game," was Eva also a player? It seemed a long shot but could she be part of one of Leon's multi-dimensional practical jokes?

"What do you mean by staged?" he asked finally, faking calm as best he could. "Everyone played a part?"

"Of course not!" Leon replied angrily. "What would be the point of that?" He snorted. "Oh, I see! You're worried about your new girlfriend Eva! I had forgotten—that's how you met her. But no. She seems a mean and sneaky bitch and I'd watch her if I were you, but I saw her getting well and truly mugged, just as I watched Matthew die."

"So what happened? What went wrong?"

"We had set up a simple experiment. We were trying to determine whether Agneau was a lamb *and* a lion. Would he come to the aid of a damsel in distress? Problem was the actors for our mugging skit got there too late. Real life trumped theater."

"This experiment—."

"Don't worry about it, Tom. Leave that to me. The science is too difficult and you just weren't *made* that way." Leon laughed. "If it makes you feel better, you can blame it all on *dad*."

Leon hung up.

39

Rachel said she had "important things to tell you" but wouldn't say what. Tom guessed she'd be trying to save old man Shivkovski again. He'd counter with the news that he and Eva were going to be married. When he reached O'Reilly's for their 2 p.m. appointment, she hadn't arrived.

His cell rang. "Rachel will not be coming," his mother said. "But please stay at O'Reilly's. Don't go home. Stephan will be there in thirty minutes."

Tom's mobster stepbrother was on the way; must be time to go to the mattresses. "Are you ready yet to tell me what's going on?"

"You will know in a few hours. Will has made some discoveries. He or I will get back to you. This has all gone on too long. Be nice to Stephan. He can help us. And he hasn't had the privileges you've enjoyed in life. The Shivkovskis will become even more unpredictable now."

"That's saying something." Tom would not confuse the issue by talking about the Times Square mugging but he needed to know something while he had his mother on the line. "Leon told me something on the phone this morning—."

"Hold on." His mother took or placed another call. Tom wondered how to frame the question. Was Mad Mike Daluskov crazy and brilliant enough to have modified the genes of his own son? The allegation had put a scare into Tom. His aggression, the so-called killer instinct—products of a petri dish? What about these small seizures, the bouts of apparent mental and emotional clarity? Perhaps they showed that his chemistry was out-of-whack and should be the subject of a manufacturers' recall.

What Leon alleged was possible in theory. Much predisposed human behavior was chemically based. This was why depression, anxiety and other emotional manifestations were often addressed by manipulating body chemistry through everything from Prozac to alcohol. If you knew which body chemicals affected certain moods, and if you knew which genes controlled the production and delivery of those chemicals, and if you knew how to modify those genes, you could theoretically modify an egg to produce a person who was more, or less, aggressive, introverted, passive, conformist or rebellious. Not to mention, judging by the study of heritable traits, smart, strong, determined.

"Leon claims dad germ-lined me," he told his mother when she came back on line.

"Leon is a sideshow, Tom. Mentally ill but peripheral. If he is dangerous at all, it is mostly because he hates you so much for bullying him as a child. No, don't deny it! And now he turns the tables on you in any way he can."

"Okay, I'll stipulate to the bullying. The question is, did I pick on Leon because I was born naturally mean or am I a genetically nasty Pinocchio carved by a Russian Geppetto named Mikhail?"

"Your father would have needed my egg to even attempt such a thing. Do you suppose I would have ever let him?"

This was true and Tom felt a surge of relief but rushed on to another urgent query: "Was there anything physically wrong with Dad in the last few days before—maybe a cold? "

Dr. Parviati was silent for a moment. "You remember that? Your memory never ceases to astound me. You're close. It was the flu, actually. He'd had it for several days and I could see it was getting him down."

His mother insisted again that he stay put and wait for Stephan. When she hung up, he called the lovely Gail Haggerty, M.E., and told her that Ray Franklin said Wally Anderson had a cold the day he died.

"Trust Ray not to know a cold from the flu."

Tom felt the hairs rise on the back of his neck. "Flu? How did you know Anderson had the flu?"

"Not from the body. One of the detectives found a receipt with Mr. Anderson's things and decided correctly that we might like to know. Anderson had been into a walk-in clinic the day before with a case of the wish-you-were-dead flu."

Tom's heart was doing a drum-roll.

"Oh, Tom," Gail said, suddenly mortified. "I'm so sorry. What an awful and inappropriate thing to say about Mr. Anderson. It just came out wrong. And I completely forgot about your father."

Tom sat stunned at O'Reilly's empty bar not by Gail's lame joke but by the bewildering coincidences. Two terribly violent suicides, several decades apart but connected, in a way, by the victims' involvement with the same loose scientific community.

And both men just happen to have caught the flu a number of days before they plunged into suicidal despair.

Tom's mind spun through the possibilities. He asked: "Is sudden depression or chemical imbalance ever a flu effect?"

"Not that I know of."

"What about a cold? Why does a buzzer go off in my brain whenever I put cold and genetics together?"

"Holy smoke, Daluskov, you've forgotten that? Pitiful! Cold viruses have been used as vectors in somatic genetic therapy."

"Right! I'd forgotten. The stripped down cold virus, right?" Tom's mind skipped back to Shivkovski's stories about vectors employing HIV cells. Somatic genetic therapy involved introducing new genes into the body in an effort to undo genetic damage or deficiencies or to enhance a person's state of health.

"Okay," said Haggerty, "the quick refresher course. Let's say the pancreas isn't producing the enzymes it's supposed to; you get hold somewhere else of the gene that designs and produces those enzymes, and you want to stick it into the ill person's pancreatic cells to replace the defective genes. But you can't just inject these genes into the body and expect them to survive the body's defenses, find their way to the right cells, bust through the cell membranes and manage to sneak on to the DNA. You need some sort of super versatile, commando Stealth fighter genetic delivery system to carry them in there. As it happens, nature provides one that has had hundreds of millions of years of practice at doing just that, right down to infiltrating and messing with cell DNA."

"Viruses," Tom said. "So viruses are sometimes used as these infiltration vehicles—or vectors, as they're called." Tom recalled that a few years back, corrective genes were sometimes encased in a weakened common cold virus. The adenovirus was injected; it found the proper cells and delivered the genes. But there could be problems and even deaths, especially when the patient was already seriously ill. "What about side-effects?" Tom asked.

"Mild in most cases. Inflammation and—" Gail Haggarty broke off.

"And what?"

"Well, now that you mention it," she said in a puzzled voice, "symptoms not of a cold, as you'd guess, but of the flu."

Two cases of severe flu symptoms, two suicides. The other common denominator in the deaths of Tom's father and of Wally

Anderson: Shivkovski. The master geneticist. The man who likely knew more about these methods than anyone alive. He had quarreled with Tom's dad in the 1970s. And 30 years later had felt irritated—and perhaps threatened—by the foolish Frankenfoods activist. All he would have had to do was introduce the vector. Tom remembered now that Wally's notebook had mentioned a "scarfaced whistleblowing GreenGene janitor," with whom he had gotten "falling-down drunk" one night trying to squeeze out information about "a new brand of supermice." Shivkovski's people had worked Wally, slipped him a Mickey Finn, injected him, and let the vector do the rest.

But what corrective DNA code could make a man kill himself?

Tom recalled that in his make-believe Gulag that night Shivkovski had spoken of dopamine. It was one of about 50 key chemicals involved in the complex electro-chemical operations of the brain. The length of the gene that instructed the body to utilize this chemical varied substantially in different people— which, in turn, affected in fundamental ways what kind of people they were. This made it one of many hundreds, if not thousands, of "personality genes" in our DNA.

People with the long D4DR gene—located on the short arm of Chromosome 11, if Tom recalled correctly—tended to have a diminished response to dopamine. Those with the shorter D4DR gene—they had only a few splices of a 48-letter repeat sequence in the code, rather than up to eleven—had brain receptors that captured dopamine more effectively. The latter tended to lack motivation and innovation—"being dopamined out," as the glib old scientist put it.

"The go-getters and, of course, the scientists," Shivkovski had said," have the long gene." To hear him tell it, the long D4DR gene on Chromosome 11 was about the greatest thing that ever happened to humankind. "The long-gene people seek novelty. are easily bored and get high on exploration and adventure."

"Have you checked yours out, Doctor?" Tom had asked him.

"Are you kidding," the old man had roared, laughing. "I don't have to. I can feel it in my blood. I'm not doped out. I am a seeker! The kind of guy with the big questions and the big heart who will get all the short D4DR slackers to the stars!"

Haggerty picked up the implications immediately. "I checked for puncture marks but the boy was pretty banged up." She paused. "This is weird stuff, Tom. Are you suggesting someone manipulated Anderson's genetic makeup?"

"Prozac, Paxil, most other anti-depressant medications, it's the serotonin levels, or uptake, that they modify, isn't it?"

"Roughly speaking, that's correct."

"Thanks, Gail. I'll get back to you." Tom hung up and began to think.

Shivkovski had gone on about at least a dozen neurotransmitters. But it was serotonin, practically a household word nowadays, that stuck in Tom's mind. Serotonin levels had become almost synonymous with happiness, or the lack of it. Sad and depressed people had been shown to suffer from serotonin deprivation. Short dark days depleted serotonin and led to the fall and winter blahs. Would-be dieters snacked compulsively not only because they lacked discipline but also because carbohydrates boosted serotonin—and a sense of well-being.

Shivkovski had actually talked about personality adjustment through genetic engineering. Serotonin levels alone could be genetically manipulated in scores of complex ways. Some genes directed the body's production of serotonin, others governed the sensitivity of serotonin receptors, still others decided which part of the brain would respond. Guessing the behavioral results was a bit like playing craps. "On the other hand, it's just the kind of challenge we long D4DR types were made for."

But what if careful adjustment wasn't your goal? What if you merely wanted to destroy a body's capacity to produce or use serotonin? Shivkovski already knew how to mess with brain chemistry. And what might a massive carpet bombing of a brain's serotonin systems produce? Might it not reduce a gutsy, committed young man like Wally Anderson to shattering self-doubt and suicide?

Eureka, the old-timers might say. Tom now believed that Shivkovski had deliberately caused the deaths of both Wally Anderson and his father—and that he'd known that Tom was certain to figure it out. But why kill Wally Anderson? Not, certainly, to conceal the long-abandoned Monkey House. By choosing this arcane and distinctively horrible means of murder, had Shivkovski been challenging him? Had he been saying: "Dear me, Tom, what took you so long to figure it out?"

O'Reilly's front door opened and a hawk-nosed man stuck his

head in. "There's a total babe double-parked out here. Rachel—says she needs to talk to Tom Daluskov.

Tom stepped out into the street, wondering why Rachel had come and how much she knew. No car. Instead, he sensed motion behind him.

Tom spun in a move he had practiced many thousands of times. A man lunged toward him. Hulking body, pulpy face. Unmistakably Fat Marco. The man Tom had punished for being rude to Rachel. Handgun in a pudgy hand. Tom's leg muscles exploded and his heel drove into Marco's shoulder. The weapon scudded along concrete. The big man staggered, then hopped on tiptoes, howling and clutching desperately at the agony surging through nerve, muscle, and ligament. The bone bulged out under his skin below the shoulder socket. Dislocated. "Welcome back to O'Reilly's, Marco," Tom said.

"Shut up and leave the gun there," said another voice. Tom turned and saw the older, raw-boned man who had announced Rachel's arrival pointing a .45 Magnum at his chest. "Okay, tough guy, into the alley or I blow your liver out."

They stopped behind a dumpster out of sight of the street. Marco's friend looked like he knew how to handle his gun and was willing to use it. Tom felt little fear, which had him thinking again about Leon's claim. A high fear threshold was not an attribute that would have easily survived through the thousands of millennia of evolution. Even the naturally brave felt fear but managed to push it at least partly aside. Marco was mewling and Tom realized that he wasn't enjoying the fat man's pain and subjugation as much as he once might have—although still more than could be considered healthy. Or genetically normal? Tom had had dislocations before. They stung.

The old man kept his distance. "Marco here has messed up again but you're still going to show him some respect,"

Tom smiled. "Did Marco tell you I'm an ADA? You going to pop a district attorney just to make your loser friend feel better about himself?

The gunman bent slightly forward a bit and squinted. "Yeah, you look familiar, like that guy on TV." He shot a disgusted glance at his friend but opted for bravado. "Yeah, sure, I know already. Marco told me. You're that Russian piece of shit who needs to be taught a lesson." He looked hard again at Marco, whose whole world had now become his torn rotator cuff. "What's that jacket you're wearing say?" he asked Tom.

"WHUPASS. It's a martial arts school."

"Take it off and throw it over towards Marco." Tom did what was asked. The man raised the gun towards Tom's face. "Marco, piss on his jacket. After that we'll get him down on his knees to say sorry and you can piss on him."

Tom could see that the wise guy was working to stir up the anger needed to overcome mounting anxiety and his own common sense. Marco had put him in a jam. He had assaulted an ADA. He would pay a price even if he walked away. The only other solution, pulling the trigger, was not very palatable either.

"He can't piss," Tom told the man with a friendly grin. "In fact, he's going to pass out any time now. Look, he's pale, he's trembling. Take him to the ER and get some pain killer into him. We can pick up where we left off some other time."

"Piss on it, Marco!" the gunman shouted, still trying for frenzy but feeling mostly frustration.

"I can't," Marco squeaked. "I can't unzip. I can't fucking move at all, Gino. It hurts too much."

Gino cussed and slapped his own forehead with his free hand.

"No big deal, Gino," Tom said. "I've seen your face anyway. Tough guy like you is bound to have mug shots. Take Marco to see the nurse. And then you both can take your medicine."

Gino took three swift steps and smacked Marco hard across the head with his free hand. "You fucking idiot." The big man howled in pain again when he moved to escape the blow. "OK, OK," Gino said, backing off. He was trying to calm himself—a good sign, as far as Tom was concerned, since the time for a peaceable resolution was running out.

Much about the broad crooked features of the man moving quietly up the alley behind Gino said he was his father's genetic son. Tom's half-brother Stephan had Mad Mike's deep-set eyes as well as the curious excited and expectant look of determination that Tom's mother once said seemed to signal that "Mikhail was either about to hit you or tell you something funny."

"OK," Gino continued, his weapon still raised. "The truth is I didn't know you were an ADA. This fat jerkoff told me you were threatening him. Extortion! And so as a friend I came here to try to scare you off."

"You've got the beginnings of reasonable doubt there, Gino. And I'm sure you have a good lawyer. You can call him as soon as you give me the gun."

"No way counselor. Me and Marco are going to get out of here. We can see what happens later."

Tom focused on Gino's craggy face but saw Stephan was close now. If Stephan grabbed the gun hand, Tom could help end this swiftly with no real damage being done. He was surprising himself again by feeling no need to hurt Gino a little or to hear the roar in his ears when his body attacked and struck the gunman down. A tinge of compassion crept into his voice.

"Listen, Gino," he said with a friendly open-handed gesture. "Your story only works if you turn the gun over as soon as you find out who I am. What do you say?"

Incipient submission lowered Gino gaze and loosened his facial muscles. The wise guy was thinking about being wise — maybe a plea to a misdemeanor. After all, it was Marco who had actually assaulted Tom and there were no independent witnesses. In a few more seconds, he would likely have turned the gun over. But he waited too long. Stephan took a final step and Tom saw what looked like an ice pick disappear into Gino's ear.

Blood arced over the alley and splattered Marco's shoes.

"Jesus Christ!" Marco screamed. "Are you a cop? What the fuck's going on here?"

"It is very confusing, no?" said the killer. He was as tall and wide as Marco but all muscle. Tom saw the faded tattoos of Cyrillic letters on the knuckles of the fist that encased the ice pick's bloody wooden handle. "Stephan, I presume," he said. From his courtroom encounters with Brighton Beach mobsters, Tom knew that these finger tattoos usually indicated a made man in the old Organizatsiya. His mind raced in search of a way to explain this to homicide and his DA colleagues but right now he was more worried about the fate of the whimpering Marco, whom Stephan was regarding with mounting impatience.

"Leave him alone," Tom said. Stephan raised a hand to indicate silence and Tom saw the receiver attached to his right ear. After a moment, Tom reached for his cell phone. "I'm making the 911 call."

"Please don't," Stephan said without a hint of menace. "Tomas, I plead with you. Please have the confidence in your mother. You must trust to me that it is still very confused."

Stephan paused again, listening through his earphone. He bent, picked up a candy wrapper, and used it to hold the business end of the ice pick. He wiped the handle carefully, using the closed palm and fingers of the dead man's hand. He dropped the weapon on the ground and pulled another from inside his jacket. It looked like a Glock and was fitted with a silencer. "As I said," he began quietly, "everything very now confused. This man who tried to kill you here should die with his friend but I will make exception if he is good boy."

Marco cringed. "We were just going to tune him up a little," he croaked. "Honest, please don't—"

Stephan kicked the ice pick and it spun to a halt at Marco's feet. "First I want you to put that in dumpster." He raised the gun barrel toward the injured man's head.

Marco grimaced as he slowly bent his knees to pick up the ice pick. He moaned sharply when it slipped from his fingers. He gripped the bloody handle more firmly the second time and managed to toss it on top of the mountain of plastic garbage bags.

The Russian scooped up Tom's WHUPASS jacket. "The rest is easy," he told Marco in a soothing tone. "You are in shock and best way is you stay warm. So I put this over your shoulders—to show that my comrade Tomas is a kind and forgiving man. You will walk back to the street and turn right. Do not look back. Keep walking past the bar for four blocks. If you follow these instructions, you can go to hospital, fix pain, eat the rigatoni with your good arm. If you don't, I will shoot your bowels and let die in your own shit."

There was no way Tom would allow Marco to be killed in cold blood but so far, so good. He would respect his mother's judgment and wishes, at least for the moment. Marco turned his back to them, like a lady waiting for help with her coat, and Stephan draped the WHUPASS jacket over the big man's shoulders.

Marco moved slowly up the alley, supporting his arm. As soon as he turned right on the sidewalk, Stephan took Tom's elbow. "This way. Quickly, please."

A minute later they were heading uptown in an Explorer with tinted windows. Thirty seconds after that, Tom heard a shot ring out from the next block, near O'Reilly's. Two more followed.

"What was that?" Tom asked the grim-faced Stephan.

The Russian waited a moment when a final shot sounded. "That is the second bunch of clowns who want your life tonight."

"What!" But Stephan waved him off, focusing again on his

earphone. He smiled and shook his head. "Amateurski!" He pulled off the earpiece and handed it to Tom. "You hear, Tomas. Is incredible!"

Tom pressed the device to his ear. At least two men were speaking. They were also evidently in a moving vehicle.

"He was wearing the jacket! WHUPASS!" said the first man.

"But he didn't look the same when we pulled up. This guy's fat! We weren't supposed to shoot him, I guess."

"This is *our* operation, no one else's. *We* make the decisions. We make the mistakes. But we'll get Daluskov. We'll just have to do it and tell them later. That will fulfill our obligation." There was a metallic clanging. "I've never understood why they didn't train us with good weapons."

"We're second-class. L is for losers, remember?" Now the second man tried calling for a third. "Gerry, come in, Gerry. You're late, Gerry. Proceed to second pickup spot." Obviously, Tom was listening in with the absent Gerry's earphone.

"Hey! There's Gerry." Tom heard the car door open. "They got him! And they got his earphone—." The signal went dead.

Tom said: "They sound like kids."

"Stupid but tough." Stephan spat out the window. "I saw the India man watching you. I saw his earphone. I pull him into the alley but he puts up a hell of a fight."

"You killed him?"

"No. Should have but didn't know then that they were trying to kill you."

Stephan was right, amateur hour. This could not be old man Shivkovski's work. Too—common seemed the right word.

"Where to now, Stephan?" Tom asked. "Brighton Beach?"

The big man chuckled grimly. "There are no secrets in Brighton Beach. Even your enemy Shivkovski might found out about us there."

"How do you know it's Shivkovski?"

"He is rival. You want his warm spot. He want yours. Is endgame!"

Give me a break, Tom thought to himself. Not another chess player.

40

Tom was surprised and touched when Sophia Parviati scrambled across the soiled motel meeting room carpet to wrap her spindly arms around him. She did not normally display her emotions. "I'm good, Mom," he said, holding her close but carefully. She regained her composure, stepped back, and embraced Stephan. "I thank you, with all my heart," she said. "That was too close." Her eyes were colder than Tom had ever seen them.

"The whole gang's here," Tom said as Will bounced a punch of friendly greeting off his shoulder bone. Eva slipped into the spot Dr. Parviati had vacated and gave him a quick kiss on the lips.

They were in a small meeting room at a Yonkers motel. It was to be the staging area for the rapid no-holds-barred strike on Shivkovski's clandestine operations they had decided upon via cellphone in the two hours since the incidents at O'Reilly's. "We'll make it short and exciting," Detective Ray Franklin said when they sat down at a conference table.

Tom had given up trying to keep Ray out of it. Eva also refused to be sidelined. Tom's stepfather Hank would stay behind with Tom's mother and get the word out if things went south. They all listened now as Will said he believed he knew where Shivkovski's "secret bunker" was.

GreenGene ran scores of research facilities around the world. It had seemed likely that Shivkovski would hide his covert ops within this structure or a subsidiary or with a low-profile supplier or contractor. Nothing had shown up. They could have spent months looking for an illicit test tube in the huge haystacks of legitimate research projects. Deciding instead to follow the money, the mother's milk of scientific experimentation, he had two of the country's best forensic accountants go through GreenGene's books and—when they showed up mysteriously in the mail—its tax returns as well.

They showed GreenGene to be a generous giver, with an eye on frontline biotech medical research and a fairer and better American education system. Its own high-profile GreenGene Foundation was clean, sending tens of thousands of the underprivileged young to school. The separate research grant program was also consistent. From modest beginnings, it had always provided only seed money, often matching those of other established known donors. The ventures might sink or swim after that but the GreenGene's grant program always moved on.

Except on one occasion. Humanity's Hope, Inc. had showed up for 10 straight years early on before disappearing altogether. More importantly, Will said, "HH" had received not only cash but also substantial chunks of the young GreenGene's stock. Worth pennies to begin with, it could potentially have generated tens of billions by now. Humanity's Hope's good works were extensive — the care and treatment of mentally and physically handicapped children and adults; full operation of seven orphanages across the country; outreach services for special needs kids in Asia, Africa and Eastern Europe; educational development camps for gifted kids. But the experts estimated that these operations were not great enough to burn halfway through the annual income that GreenGene's original gifts would likely be now generating had they been invested with even moderate competence.

HH's largest single undertaking was the Oneida Foundation for Child and Human Care and Development, a few hours' drive up the I-90 from where they now sat. From humble origins as the first HH orphanage two decades ago, it had become a massive facility that claimed to "address a broad range of emotional, education and health issues confronting young Americans who need a family's love, protection and preparation to thrive in the world."

Ray pitched in. "And we've got an ugly coincidence that makes this place an obvious first target. Remember Wally's two friends? The rich kids who disappeared after his Central Park number? They turned up dead three days ago in a car accident that nobody saw. Back road. A few miles from Oneida."

Tom turned to Will and his mom. "Oneida? That country picnic years back, when we were kids? Wasn't that Oneida?"

"Yeah," said Will. "The place with the child's tombstone. 'Here lies Billy Stricks' who went 'too far.' Remember? Maybe we're about to find out just how far that is."

They were two-thirds the way to Oneida when Stephan

dropped his bombshell. Something had happened that Tom was not going to like. "They did not tell you, no?" he asked. Tom was driving Stephan's Explorer with Eva beside him in the front seat. Will and Ray followed in their own vehicles.

"Tell me what, Stephan?"

"It's on television. There is little girl, seven years old. She is taken by man who says he lost kitty cat. Man ties noose around little girl's neck and ties other end round tree branch in Central Park. Let girl balance on chessboard—"

Tom felt a chill and again regretted diverting Ray from the Kitchen Sink killer case even for a day.

"But she's OK, Tom," Eva said hurriedly.

"Yes. Noose not real. Not danger knot. Not murder knot. Is slip knot."

Tom wondered why Stephan reckoned that he should be more upset than anyone else about this latest Kitchen Sink outrage. "And—?"

"All sorts of people saw the little girl teetering on the small chessboard," Eva said. "It stood on a small wobbly stool. She was crying so hard that they tried to calm her first before approaching. Bad plan. She slipped and the stool fell over. But the noose had been rigged with a slip knot. She didn't hang. Her feet hit the ground and she took a little spill. Not even a bruise. Not that she hadn't been tormented unforgivably."

So the Kitchen Sink killer had found a middle ground between murder and good deeds—terrorizing children. "And—"

"We figure it's not the serial killer, Tom," said Eva. "We think it's Leon."

"What's the link?"

"His hate for you. Whoever did this made the noose from a long white cloth belt from WHUPASS. It was embroidered with the name and logo, something every TV viewer was able to see over and over again before and after the little girl fell. That and Fat Marco shot dead in the WHUPASS jacket and your name's been all over every cable news broadcast in the world the last few hours. There just seems no way that Will was the target, not you."

"Your mother does not think it is the old man," Stephan added.

His mother was right on two counts, Tom thought. It had to be Leon and things truly were spinning out of control.

"If things get nasty, you let me go in first," he told Stephan.

"You've done enough already."

"You forget that we are both sons of Mad Mike Daluskov!" He massaged his tattooed knuckles. "We go in together. Like brothers!"

Carrie Hemingford's colonial bonnet was slightly askew when the posse arrived. Tom had called ahead. He was a New York Assistant District Attorney acting with family friends in a semiofficial capacity to investigate the deaths of Stephanie and Sean, the two young people killed in the car crash. "I'm sure you understand how this might give comfort to their mothers and fathers."

Carrie did indeed understand. She proceeded to name all the folks she knew who might be able to help. "We'll want to fill you in too Ms. Hemmingford," Tom said. "And we would like four rooms, please."

Carrie looked tense but determined when they arrived. When Detective Ray Franklin suggested that "a New York link to these events" had raised the possibility of "foul play," she set her heavy Yankee jaw and appeared ready to hike up her skirt and load her musket.

"I will help you any way I can. I must confess I feel I should have done more to find out what was troubling them."

"Any guesses?" Tom asked.

"They were very interested in the Institute—the big center we have up here for orphans and the mentally retarded and medical research and the like. The X-Farm some of our local yokels call it. Its real name is a bit of a mouthful: the Oneida Foundation for Child and Human Care and Development. Sean and Stephanie called it the Frankenfarm."

When eyebrows rose and the strange Russian with the tattooed knuckles flashed a thumbs-up, Carrie caught on immediately. "Oh! So there's an Institute connection! Then I absolutely must call Jason Hunter. He's their only neighbor and one of the few folks around here who is not beholden to the Foundation. I sent the two young people to see him."

"No time now I'm afraid, Carrie," said the large-framed man in his late 50s when the hostess offered him tea. Tom thought he looked familiar for some reason. Hunter got right to it. "This is where we are. Stephanie and Sean suspected something fishy was going on inside the Institute. I could have told them that fifteen years ago. They didn't tell me their full suspicions at first—just said the Institute might be testing these Frankenfoods, using humans instead of rats, or guinea pigs or dogs and cats. These foods might be rice or other grains that would have their genes adjusted to produce all sorts of additional nutrients. Get your meat and potatoes just from the potatoes, I guess. Nothing too new to a farmer like me but they were city kids, of course."

He addressed Tom and Will. "But when we saw the TV news about your adventure with the chimps, I'll tell you, their eyeballs just about popped out of their heads. It got them thinking about brand new possibilities. Me too. Especially when they told me that this GreenGene Corp. is the money behind both the monkeys and my next-door neighbor." He looked out into the clear black night.

Will spoke for first time. "Mr. Hunter, we should tell you up front that we are going into the Institute and we need whatever help you can offer to make this operation more successful than our last. But we're acting on our own, no authority or search warrant. In short, it will be illegal. We'll keep you out of it but if you're comfortable with that, we need your information."

Carrie Hemmingford gasped. The farmer touched her arm to calm her. "It has to be done, Carrie. The Institute people have crossed the line. I'm almost positive that they killed those two kids."

"Ohmygoodness!" Carrie's hands flew to her breast.

"You have proof?" Ray Franklin asked.

"I spent the last couple of days doing my own little investigation," Hunter said. "Dirty Larry up at the big gas station near the casino liked to look at Stephanie when the kids came in for that expensive coffee. Two days before the accident he noticed that a white Chevy van with tinted windows seemed to be tailing the kids' BMW. And Carrie here told me the day after the accident that she thought the kids might have been having some trouble with the car."

"Yes," Carrie said. She was pale now. "They were up and off before breakfast. When I went out to the shed I noticed their footprints and the tire marks in the dew where they'd parked on the grass. But there was also a long blotch where the dew had been wiped away and the grass was bent. It would have been near the back end of the parked car. I wondered if Sean had crawled under before they left to check on some problem."

"I got the answer to that question not an hour ago," Jason Hunter said. "From the man who owns the farm where the BMW went off the road. Mr. Daigneault—fine man, Carrie knows him. He and me worked it out that they died from the fire, not from the impact."

"Poor things," said Carrie, wiping at her tears.

"Mr. Daigneault was out behind his barn when it happened," Hunter continued. "Saw most of it from about two hundred yards. Two things bothered him. First, a van that was traveling about a quarter mile behind the BMW only slowed as it passed the burning wreck before speeding off. Didn't even stop."

"Must have been New Yorkers," said Ray.

"There was also a crash and burn puzzle," Hunter said. "Old Mr. Daigneault looked up from his work when he heard an explosion and it seems to him the car was on fire before it left the road and careened along the ditch. Not the other way around. The two of us went through it all again tonight and walked down and had another look at the scene. Tire marks, the impression in the earth when the BMW crashed and came to rest—they show that the fire came first and the crash afterwards. The car was in flames while it was still on the highway. It swerved back and forth then left the road."

"Sounds like a bomb or incendiary device," Tom said. "Remotely detonated from the trailing van?"

"The van was white and I had a good look at the road maybe 90 minutes ago. It's mostly washed away but there are still slight signs on the surface of the initial explosion." Hunter stood up. "I gave these Institute people the benefit of the doubt for two decades. I respected their rights. But they've killed two decent young people and I know they pretty well own the law enforcement in this town. So now they're going to see a different side of me."

He headed towards the back door, then stopped and looked back over his shoulder. "You folks coming?"

It was just past midnight.

41

September 11 2001

00:25 Hours

Jason Hunter led them up the steps to his front door. A low-pitched mumble at the far end of the darkened porch rose swiftly to an unearthly howl.

The farmer pulled the chain from a ceiling fixture. The light revealed old Dwight Hunter bundled up against the evening in a coat and a hunting cap. He stared out into the night, mouthing an incomprehensible incantation.

"Stroke," Jason said, stepping over to knuckle a tear from his father's face. "But he was in trouble even before. Won the Silver Star in the Big One. Combat maybe caught up with him. Saw other things too at the end: Belsen-Belsen. My mom dying and the Institute buying everyone out and building next to us really got to him." Jason nodded into the night toward Shivkovski's mammoth darkened installation. "But the crying, whimpering didn't start for a year or two after that. It's got worse the last six or seven. Lucky he can't speak; he'd be begging me to shoot him. I think about it."

Tom suspected that having a father who wanted to die was a good deal harder than having one who had gotten his wish.

Jason had phoned to tell his wife Chelsea they were coming. She waited in the cozy parlor with a wan smile on a heavily lined once-pretty face. Tom caught Eva's look of sympathy as the two women shook hands. How had this woman borne the strain of helping care for her father-in-law?

"Yes, I see what you mean, Jason," she told her husband. "They're an odd bunch but I do believe that you've finally found your army."

Hunter nodded and got right to his briefing. "Getting in won't be easy. This isn't the unguarded rusty-lock Monkey House. About a half of the 250 maintenance people are also trained security. So are the so-called 'farmers' who work the outer fields. They've got state of the art security right around the property — two 12-foot fence perimeters about 15 yards apart with a paved patrol road between them. Along with sensors and cameras, and God-knows what else — night vision capabilities, for sure. I've hollered about it. Mayor said they told him it was an insurance requirement. Several thousand children under care, had to make sure no one gets in or out and still allow some freedom of movement for kids inside and limiting staff numbers. Whatever, it would be difficult to even shoot our way in."

"No shooting!" Tom said sharply. "No firearms at all. Not with kids in there. We want a covert entry to establish leads for a legal search later by legitimate authorities."

"But let's not tiptoe through the daisies," Ray said. "We all have to be ready for felony charges. We all have to be ready to be hurt or to hurt someone else. We may have no other choice." The detective looked from face to face in the room. "Eyes wide open, everyone in?"

Everyone was in. "So where's this game plan, Jason?"

Jason walked over to a wall of bookcases and pulled down a large briefing chart. It was a map superimposed on an aerial photograph Jason said he had taken a year before from a Piper Cub flown by a Vietnam buddy.

Seen from the ground and from a distance on the closest roads, the Institute presented itself as a substantial but not spectacular series of scattered low-slung buildings on the sides of a gently sloping hill. The photo showed something far more immense — staggering, in fact. The old Leatherstocking-country-style brick buildings and white faux farmhouses and barns seen by passing traffic and from adjacent properties were strung along the outermost of eight concentric streets, seven of which lay in a shallow but mile-wide, man-made valley and were hidden by the circular ridge. The ridge, the highest point around, had been built with fill from the excavation of the valley.

This was about more than a few monkeys, Tom thought.

Jason had tinted the photograph with circular rings. The outer ring of the target was green and covered most of the open rolling fields, some cultivated, between the outer boundary fences and where the circular built-up area began. A very narrow yellow band separated the green ring from the broad orange band that overlaid all seven concentric roads on the sides of the depression, as well as the hundred or more buildings that lined them. The bull's eye at the center was red. Within it sat a massive squat octagonal building. It was invisible to the outside world yet its footprint was larger, Jason said, than that of the Metropolitan Museum in New York. Much more lay below the surface.

"How the heck do we get past the outside perimeter?" Tom asked him. "And across all that open space to the outbuildings and through the orange zone and into the center?"

"There's one good thing about a system that puts most of its eggs into a perimeter basket: it's a hard shell on the outside but easy going once you're in. These people are desperate to keep snoopers out but they want things as natural as possible inside. They have thousands of children in there and, believe me, they let them be children. We can hear that from here. The seven orange zone streets seem to operate on simple security principles. Do not leave your area; mind your own business; but otherwise feel free to do your own thing. Staffers are billeted beside or in assigned school buildings, which are completely self-sufficient, with their own dorms, kitchens, canteens, etc. They aren't supposed to talk to staffers or children from other schools or 'houses,' as they're called. Everyone wears IDs with computer chips so their movements can be monitored. They say this is to prevent contamination of study and research protocols."

"That will make it impossible for us to move through the orange zone undetected even if we breach the outer perimeter," Eva said with a frown. "How do you know all this? Not from air surveillance surely?"

"We were careful to make only one slow lazy pass pulling a banner for the country fair." Jason didn't answer the question.

Until now, Tom's mind had been rifling frantically through potential tactics for penetrating the outer perimeter: infiltration by delivery or garbage truck, a false fire alarm, maybe nighttime airdrop. How about hot air balloons! All were unpromising. But now he relaxed. Jason had been inside. Tom was sure of it. And he would also have figured out a way to bypass the prohibition on inter-sectional movement in the orange zone.

It also finally occurred to him where he'd seen Jason's face before, along with Dwight, the old man outside on the porch—the father and World War II veteran who had liberated Belsen-Belsen.

"Ia Drang Valley, right Jason?" Tom asked the farmer.

"Right. Who told you that?"

"Do you remember a bunch of vodka-and-strawberries picnickers with Russian accents? On your land. Way back—maybe thirty years ago? They were our parents. Will and I were there when you and your dad talked to my dad and the man who's behind the Institute."

Jason mined his memory but nothing came up.

"Billy Stricks?" Will asked. "The gravestone on a hill. Curious nature but he went too far?"

"Yes, Billy," Jason said as he considered this coincidence. He directed the laser to a point on the edge of the yellow target ring. "He died here."

"You've been there recently, right?"

"Affirmative."

"So when do we go in?" Tom asked him. "And how."

"Follow me."

0545

Mud-slick and chilled, Eva looked up at a million tons of rock suspended three inches above her face in the Hunter-Stricks cave. The dank air clogged her nostrils. The steady drip of water mocked her racing claustrophobic heart. Her fingers bled, her muscles trembled. As she wormed along on her back through a tomblike passageway between two cathedrals, she struggled to fight back panic.

If the past four hours were any indication, more such challenges lay ahead. More anticipation of sudden interment and lingering death, followed by the natural decay of her recently well-loved carcass. More clinging to rock faces while grasping beyond the light of her headlamp for the next invisible handhold and waiting for her fall into eternal darkness below.

"Stop whining!" she told herself. Her grandfather had it far tougher at Iwo Jima, as did his brother on the cliff face beyond Omaha Beach. Besides, people did this for fun! Can't be that bad.

To still her anxieties, Eva imagined the scene on the surface above her. The Hunter-Stricks cave system ran in a highly indirect series of connections from a point by a bridge on Jason Hunter's land under the perimeter and the green zone of the Institute to a camouflaged exit point just below the site where Billy Stricks had once been buried alive. That was in the yellow zone of the Oneida Foundation complex, only a short distance from the first ring of buildings. Eva closed her eyes and envisioned the clear night above with its last quarter moon and a dome of not rock but bright stars. The Foundation was deep in sleep, except for security, whose sensors and surveillance screens registered absolute normalcy.

Eva began clawing forward again. *We're coming*, she thought. *Shivkovski won't know what hit him.*

0625

Tom scrambled back down a 30-degree ridge, his feet and hands finding the toe and finger holds almost effortlessly. He and Will had just anchored a heavy rope to help the descent of Ray, Stephan and Eva. Jason had gone down first to help mark the bottom ledge, which wasn't very wide.

Tom was high on the cave and on the heights and menacing crevasses. He was in the zone again. His boots and hands seemed to have eyes. Ray, Stephan and Eva were doing well too, due in no little part to the equipment, direction, and caving rigging provided by Jason. The existence of the cave and the connection with Hunter were prolonging Tom's lifelong run of almost uninterrupted good fortune. The somber majesty of a natural yet alien world seemed to foreshadow what lay ahead. They would see and learn new things before this day was done.

Tom caught sight of Eva's flushed face in Jason's floodlight. He felt a surge of well-being even though Eva's unusual abilities further validated Ray's hunch. She was a woman with secrets. Thing was, Tom didn't care. He'd found a mate. She was a package to be explored and discovered over a lifetime, just as he was. She'd been rocked by his betrayal with Rachel. But she obviously believed there was more to him than his weaknesses.

"Listen up," Jason told them. They were in a large "room," maybe 40 feet high. It was divided in the middle by a pit almost 35 feet wide at its narrowest point. Jason had rigged a rope bridge across the gap. The sound of running water echoed up from very far below.

"We call it the Stricks River. We are now inside the Institute perimeter. It's a hundred and fifty feet down, with lots of ledges to bounce off on the way."

Eva cast an irritated glance towards Stephan who, still lashed to the others by a rope through his safety belt, was tugging the group this way and that as he examined the huge dome ceiling.

0630

Eva volunteered to cross the pit first. Heights didn't frighten her the way enclosed spaces did. The rope bridge bucked and swayed as she moved from rung to rung. She had to maneuver the beam from her Premiere Carbide headlamp down on the steps ahead and make sure she did not step into nothingness.

Now, from behind her came the ominous scraping of boots losing their grip. Then a crescendo of Russian curses, shouts of alarm, and a howl of terror and despair as Stephan went over the pit's edge into the void.

Eva hung desperately onto the bridge's guide ropes. Her brain filtered out every sound but the slick slithering of safety rope running out as gravity pulled the Russian deeper into the pit. She knew that Stephan had mishandled his gear and so she prepared for what would come next. Her hands were ripped free of the rope bridge and her body was wrenched out into thin air. It reminded her of her first dive off the 10-meter board. As she was falling, falling, falling to the center of the earth, away from light and life, Eva yelled: "Tom!"

Tom gritted his teeth and listened and hoped against hope that thanks to Jason Hunter's long, lonely preparations, the safety rope would halt her descent before she collided with the rock face or the bottom. When the rope ran out and tensed, he heard Eva shout.

He stood at the crevasse edge and yelled down into the

darkness. "Eva. Are you hurt? Stephan?"

Eva waited a moment but when she shouted back, her voice was strong. "I didn't hit the wall. Stephan's okay, too, from what I can see below me here."

The Russian was pulled up first. As he passed, he was too embarrassed to look Eva in the eye. Instead, he pointed grimly below. Hanging suspended in her safety harness, Eva maneuvered the light of her headlamp over a dozen dark, furry forms on a ledge below. It stopped at the small pink face of a chimpanzee, its features frozen in startled death, its arms spread wide and empty. Only a foot away was a small form. Mother and baby. They'd been pushed or thrown into the pit. These could be the chimps from the Monkey House. Shivkovski was burying the evidence.

Tom's voice—the voice that she loved—reached down from the glow of lights above. "We're going to pull you up now. Let us know if you're having problems. No bumps? Black eyes?"

"My toe is itching to connect with a certain Russian's hind parts—"

It was then that Eva saw the skeletons. They were on a long wide ledge not visible from above. The first appeared human. And tiny. And so did the next and the next. Eva counted the nine bodies in graduated states of decomposition before the 10th and the 11th corpses, which were more recently deceased and clearly showed that these were indeed the remains of infants and very young girls and boys. There were more, many, many more. The last she saw as she was pulled up was a girl with a red ribbon in her hair and flowers clasped beneath her folded hands.

"Eva?"

"I'm fine. Let's keep moving."

0815

They stood by a wooden ladder that would give them entry to the yellow zone. Eva had remained silent about the human remains but after the discovery of the chimp bodies at the pit, Jason had insisted on recon. The cave was clear. He had checked the trapdoor he had constructed to camouflage the cave opening into the yellow zone. It was secure too, with the slice of living sod that covered it from above still in place. They could proceed on Plan A.

"I think whoever's been coming in here from the Institute has been trying to hide their tracks from their own authorities. They obviously think the improvements I made are the work of the Foundation itself. I see some work's been done back there that means someone may have been going down into that pit for some reason."

"Whatever it was and whoever they are, they'd better stay out of my way," Will said. "They must have lured the chimps in here and slaughtered them in cold blood."

Eva said nothing about the children but thought that they probably didn't know the half of it yet.

0845

They entered Shivkovski's world of "child care and human development" through the opening in the earth that once gave up the corpse of young Billy Stricks. Where the Stricks' barn once stood, the Foundation had built a large storage and maintenance shed. It shielded their approach from the rest of the Institute.

Tom was surprised at the surge of noise as they slipped quickly aboveground. The raucous, cheerful voices of thousands of unseen children flowed toward them from behind a nearby structure. They followed Jason through the back door of the maintenance building. He had predicted the shed would be deserted at that hour, and it was. Within minutes, the six had been rendered "invisible" by bright yellow maintenance crew overalls liberated from the supplies inside.

This was Jason's secret weapon. This was how they would move freely throughout the yellow and orange zones while the rest of the community was restricted to a home section.

Jason's earlier incursion had established that men and women working in maintenance uniforms were meant to be seen and not heard. They did not speak to the children unless it was necessary and the children ignored them. Even eye contact was avoided. While teachers or supervisors might nod politely on occasion, they never engaged in conversation unless it was about a maintenance or security issue.

The yellow coats therefore moved not only unmanaged but almost invisibly. It was impractical to confine plumbers, computer techs, carpenters to a single area. The vast number of them worked in the evenings and overnight, which is why so many yellow coats were free. But there were always things that needed doing during the day. "Electricians have the run of the place," Jason said as he geared them up with belts and boxes of electrical tools. Stephan was handed a heavy spool of #12 wire.

Jason leaned against a red button on the wall and a large rolling metal garage door rumbled open. They stepped out into bright morning sunlight and a joyful roar of young voices. "What a racket!" Eva said. Tom glanced at her. Her grim face managed a tight smile.

Spread out before and below them, the Institute looked like a fifty-ring circus, comprising scores of buildings of all shapes and sizes, many with a large schoolyard packed with youngsters. The sounds of the youthful voices rose and fell like the waves of the sea. The ingenious architectural illusions were more obvious now. What looked like a small barn from a distance turned out to be a huge roadhouse gymnasium with fancy, expensive looking scoreboards. Judging by the signs, two rambling farmhouses were actually administration buildings, home to the "Finance" and "Human Resources" departments.

They had decided their assignments by lots. Tom wasn't leaving until he had penetrated the red zone and the mammoth main octagonal building. Stephan and Jason would go in with him. Will, Ray and Eva would form a second squad to concentrate on the outer levels. They would return through the cave to the Hunter farm. That way, if something happened to Tom's team, the second could withdraw, summon help and make immediate tactical use of the information they had collected.

Tom watched Eva stride off with Will and Ray. There weren't two other men on earth he trusted more to ensure her safety.

The last thing Eva expected to see was someone she recognized. They'd hardly reached the first mini-campus when a profile that Eva recognized immediately appeared. It was Francis, the hulking mentally challenged lab rat who had accompanied Leon to the ill-fated Times Square experimental mugging.

What threw her for an instant was his apparent maturity, his obvious grownup-ness as he addressed two rows of young students who also appeared to be either mentally challenged or afflicted by Down Syndrome. This was a very different Francis from the man Tom said had never progressed beyond the mental age of five or six. He stood confident and composed and, although Eva could not make out the words, he spoke in patient, gentle, even fatherly tones. His audience, for its part, listened with great attentiveness.

Eva did a quick 180 and steered Will into a turn as well. "Walk behind us, Ray," she said quietly. "There's someone in that schoolyard over there who could recognize Will and me."

"Who?" Will asked.

"Francis, your childhood friend. Leon's buddy. The man who was with Leon Shivkovski the night I was mugged and Matthew Agneau was stabbed."

"Ah!" said Ray sarcastically. "Another piece falls into place."

Ray no longer hid the fact that he doubted her story. She knew Tom had his questions too. But all would soon be revealed.

They detoured round the back of the school. Francis's voice, high-pitched despite the massive body, reached them for a moment.

"Your turn now," he said.

A chorus of young voices responded:

> My life is like the summer rose
> That opens to the morning sky,
> But ere the shades of evening close
> Is scattered on the ground — to die."

Eva was startled by the assurance and clarity of the recitation. And by its message.

"Richard Henry Wilde," Will said.

Eva didn't care who wrote it. So sad. So ominous. It made her think of the children in the cave.

0925

Tom, Jason and Stephan strode down a winding cinder path, watching hundreds of apparently normal children raising Cain before classes.

Tom double-checked to ensure that Jason was carrying the oversized yellow toolbox. It was crucial to their plan in its final amended form. The original goal of getting in and out of the Institute undetected was appealing but fundamentally flawed. No matter how perfectly the operation went, police, prosecutors and even the Feds might have difficulty using illegally gathered information to obtain search warrants. The whole case could collapse.

But if emergency responders, including the police, had to enter the Institute, they would be pretty well free to use any information they found once there. Tom and the others would provoke that emergency. When the time came, the firecrackers in Jason's toolbox would create the illusion of sustained explosions in a school housing thousands of children. Just in case, Jason had also brought an M-16 from his collection. He said it had been adapted to fire blanks. Police authorities from half the state, not to mention half the U.S. media, would descend upon the Institute if gunfire was heard. The ensuing invasion would lay bare Shivkovski's secrets.

They still hoped to make it out through the cave unobserved. If things went south in any other way before then, Jason's wife Chelsea would make a long list of telephone calls, the first to the local police. B&B busybody Carrie Hemingford was in charge of mobilizing the media. She knew the star reporter of a Syracuse TV news show and had the business card of a CNN news producer and former customer. Jason had already set up coverage by an NBC cameraman turned documentary maker whose career had begun during the Tet offensive. He had called him in New York before D-hour and asked him to head to Carrie's bed and breakfast with all his gear and lots of tape. "This guy will get the shots no matter how hot things get."

They had all laughed grimly when Chelsea joked about how Carrie might frame her calls: "We have this lovely orphanage up here with several thousand of the most adorable little children you've ever seen. And now there's a whole lot of automatic weapons fire going on over there that you may want to look into. As it happens, I have several rooms vacant. Special for you, a mere fifteen thousand a night."

0935

Tom, Jason and Stephan took one of the main sidewalks winding down the hill toward the red zone building. The schoolyards they passed as they crossed the first two concentric streets reverberated with typical playground anarchy. Elementary age behavior in the first two buildings—girls skipping, boys wrestling. Outside the second were the teens, complete with skateboards and slouches.

Class specialization set in as they passed smaller schools on the third and fourth terrace down. In the yard of a two-story building of Tuscan farmhouse design, 75 children, none older than 10, were busy with brushes and oil paint at their easels. *Van Gogh House*. Two teens, a girl and a boy, engaged a large block of marble-like material with hammers and chisels, revealing the partly formed and expertly rendered body of a voluptuous woman. Next door, at what was a replica of Monet's Giverny studio, judging by the colors, more K–12 artists were hard and happily at work.

"These kids are out of this world!" Jason growled, watching a group tear off rapid-fire pencil sketches. One girl, perhaps 8 or 9, saw Stephan stop in amazement. Tom watched her capture his features and crooked smile almost flawlessly with 20 or 30 swift motions of a tiny drawing arm. Every work Tom's eye took in— from simple sunflowers and still lifes in oils to watercolor portraits and nudes, and even a clever Picasso send-up featuring Bart and Homer Simpson—looked fit for a professional gallery. A lovely blond girl's near complete copy in oils of the Mona Lisa appeared ready to stand in at the Louvre.

The pathways and lanes spread out empty before them. Not

another maintenance man or security guard was in sight. The teachers sprinkled among the youthful masses, meantime, seemed to look past or right through any living being contained in a yellow wrapper. They moved on unobstructed.

Jason asked softly: "What's going on here, Tom?"

"Can't know yet." All this was clearly beyond the ordinary but the kids could simply be naturally gifted. After all, that's part of what the Foundation claimed to do—bring special children together to nurture their extraordinary aptitudes. "It looks strange when you see it all in one place," Tom continued, "but we know there are tens of thousands of kids in the country with super-high and entirely natural IQs."

Stephan sidled up. "This *not* like Super Race. Nazis start with Aryan genes, get young from mommas early, water and fertilize daily. The communists too. Fill empty vessel with fascist voodoo or commie mumbo-jumbo!" He spat on the path. "But these children have cooked up from scratch to recipes in Shivkovski's DNA pot!"

Tom desperately hoped not. Leon's taunts still nagged and he would feel a lot better if they could establish once and for all today that Shivkovski had *not* manipulated human genes. The schools made sense, after all. Shivkovski might merely be studying the end products of extraordinary genes rather than juggling them for special effects. For their part, parents would naturally want bright children to get the best education available in their particular field of potential genius.

Like music. The strains of Beethoven's Fifth drifted out from a large upstairs classroom. The children Tom could see were dwarfed by their instruments—and had apparently displeased their conductor, who now silenced them with an irritated clacking of a baton. The temporary silence revealed a contest in the courtyard of the mini-Schönbrunn-style building. Two lines of pre-teens waited their turn at a pair of dueling pianos. The long fingers of a young Chinese girl danced maniacally at the keyboard before a hushed audience. "That for virtuoso only," Stephan said, serious for once. "Liszt. Hungarian Rhapsody, two." She stopped, giggling, and an African-American boy whose feet didn't reach the pedals responded from the facing piano with an equally astounding performance as his teammates cheered. "Skippy," said Stephan with a knowing grin. "Thelonious Monk. Shivkovski baked in the Jazz gene."

0955

Eva, Ray and Will had seen no hard evidence yet of Shivkovski's genetic tampering but Will was alone among them in knowing for certain that it was here. His only question was how bad it would be.

Eva and Ray had moved ahead and stopped by a blacktop schoolyard. Will heard the urgent rhythms of basketball. "These kids are NBA size and as good as the Knicks!" Ray whispered as he caught up. They pretended to examine the anchor bolts of a towering set of field lights. The players weren't all "guys." No. 11 drove from the perimeter, took a dish from the point guard, and leapt high over a Shaq-size defender to tomahawk the ball through the hoop. She turned to reveal a lovely face that hinted of Arabian descent. She was a good three inches better than seven feet in height. She had purple eyes.

"Contacts maybe," Eva said. "Not evidence, yet. Means nothing, really."

"I'm glad you remain hopeful," Will said quietly.

1000

The closer Tom, Stephan and Jason got to the vast red zone center complex in the valley, the more utilitarian the architecture became. No more pretty themes and cute ideas, just boxy three-and-four-story buildings, some brick, some concrete with wood trim in pale institutional colors. Steel grills covered some first and second floor windows. The schoolyards shrunk, lost their play equipment and manicured looks. They were empty.

Through the windows, Tom saw room after room full of intensely concentrated high school age students. In one ground-level classroom, a teacher flashed a laser pointer from spot to spot on an exquisitely detailed 20-foot-high projection of a few twists in the DNA helix.

Tom stopped to read the scrawled instructions on a towering projection board in another large room:

ESSAYS DUE:
Monday: Can Smart Drugs cure dementia and let you buy IQ online or over the counter?
Tuesday: Is your mind worth uploading? (Oral presentation. Debate follows.)
Wednesday: Discuss hardware solutions for faster, better cognition and a bigger, foolproof human memory.
Thursday: Coding against indolence: identifying and rejigging the "laziness" genes.
Friday: Want to talk with the animals? Uplifting: should our furry friends join us in the trans-human (and post-human) future? Prepare to debate: pizza for top two finishers.
Saturday: Hardwiring culture: sketch genetic modification proposal for various fundamental and/or hate radicals, e.g., KKK, Nazis, Red Guards, Khmer Rouge, Taliban, your uncle or next door neighbor.
Sunday: Freedom: discussion (but watch what you say! Greenpeace is listening!)

Jason stopped and read from the board as well. "Guess this isn't precautionary principle week," Tom said. "If these kids are training to be scientists, forget about political correctness. There'd been no stopping them on experimentation."

If they're not products of dangerous genetic driving themselves, Tom thought, they're the genetically altered in training to do further genetic altering. Shivkovski's launchpad for exponential change.

Ray glanced back up the hill at the school where they had seen Francis. "Don't look now but we're being watched," he said. "A blonde man in a red uniform."

They moved on, toting their big yellow electric toolboxes, casually pointing at every power line, electric post, and circuit box they could see, trying hard to look like dedicated sparkies on an inspection tour. Outside *Babel House*, they gathered round a large newly installed in-ground transformer. Two hundred or so elementary and middle school students were making a racket inside but they couldn't see them through the windows.

"The blonde guard's moved to the green stucco building one level up" Eva said. "He's watching the kids on the outdoor gym set." They peeked, one after the other. Corn-color hair, brush cut, piercing blue eyes, square jaw, middle linebacker build.

"Right off an SS recruitment poster," said Ray.

Will dropped to his haunches beside the transformer. "I don't normally approve of stereotyping, detective, but it may be appropriate in this case. Because this guy comes in multiple copies. The one we saw first is still up there watching us. I've seen three others to the west and a couple to our east on the second level." He smiled at Ray, who whistled the riff for the Twilight Zone.

Eva remained grim. "Don't forget: Shivkovski said that cloning's for sissies." She walked on. "My guess is that by day's end these guys will be a footnote."

1020

Eva could not help but be stunned. They had expected surprises but to see the evidence in the flesh chilled her heart. Yet in one way she was also relieved. The discovery of apparently cloned security men provided a prima facie case and sealed the mission's success. The President's orders and the Executive Action Force mandate were to pursue all substantive possibilities of manipulation of the human genome to exhaustion. That, plus the tip about the Shivkovskis and her covert infiltration of the New York lab rat community through Tom, had led to this day.

It had come together far better than anyone had dreamed. Tom, Will, Ray, the taciturn soldier-farmer Jason, and that loose Russian canon Stephan, not to mention Tom's parents, had taken most of the risks and broken down all of the doors. This was huge and would get ever bigger. Eva would be decorated, secretly of course, but she didn't give a damn about that. What mattered now was that Tom would see why she had had to do her duty. Today would justify her deceit. And if he loved her as much as she loved him, he would forgive her and she would become his wife.

Now she needed to get into the red zone. The teams had taken a cursory look at perhaps one twentieth of the "houses" in the orange area but the real work was taking place inside the octagon. She felt they were being watched now. This and the team's new plan to raise the alarm by fireworks and to alert the networks through Carrie and Tom's parents had forced her to make a difficult decision. Like Tom, Will, and Ray before her, she was about to go rogue. Whatever else happened, Eva had orders to call in the tactical Executive Action Force before local law enforcement or, worse, the media, could access the Institute. The EAF was standing by at the recently closed US Air Force base nearby, disguised as an Airborne unit on an exercise. Arguably, given the team's whistle-blowing plan and the prima facie cloning evidence, she should make the call right now. But she did not want a lid put on the story. There had been too much secrecy already. She also believed that the EAF would detain Tom and her new friends on secret warrants. Hundreds of other "material witnesses" were being held at a new covert prison facility inside the U.S. Naval Base at Guantanamo Bay in Cuba. This would not happen if the country learned what was happening here. And by getting the truth out she could show Tom that she was more loyal to him and to the U.S. Constitution than she was to political needs and the national security interpretations of one president.

The risk to the thousands of children here only reinforced her reluctance to bring in the EAF troops. It would be reckless even if no casualties resulted, and criminal if even a single child died. In many ways, in fact, a rush to the rescue by the Oneida police and fire department seemed a safer idea. There was another imponderable, however. Some EAF commanders viewed the young people at the institute as de facto hostages and Eva felt unable to predict the Shivkovskis' potential for harming the children should he come under attack. So far the news was good. The clone guards were not armed. The orange area, where it appeared that most of the students lived, could be rapidly secured for an emergency evacuation. But there were also the images from the cave. Dead chimps. Dead infants. Not a good sign.

As they approached thirty 10 and 11 year olds dancing with the grace, skills and ease of Fred Astaire and Ginger Rogers Ray laughed. "Gershwin!" he said, apparently pleased. His face blanched when they got closer. As each pretty young girl spun out of a turn, head erect, the eyes—blues, browns, greens but also purples, grays, yellows, oranges, reds and golds—were a surprise. It was the faces that provided the real shocks. "Let's go!" Eva snapped. "What's the holdup? Never seen the humanoid look before?"

Will had taken note of Eva's new drill sergeant tones after they spotted the clones. Now she was in a rush to reach the red zone and Will had to slow her down. The guards had regarded them with little interest so far but if they stopped pretending and made a beeline for the main building, they might never get there.

He held the group up at another lamppost beside an outdoor assembly of perhaps 150 young children and pulled a screwdriver from his toolbox. "Slow down, folks," he said, removing the plate from an electrical box and peering at the wiring inside. "We're close. Let's not ruin it."

"This is more like it," said Ray. "The Tiger Woods look. Mixed race." Will reckoned this group had a vastly more important story to tell than superficial appearances. Yet looks counted. Evolution had made the distinction of faces one of the first lessons a human learned. At age four or five, kids already instinctively associated certain facial expressions with behavior not likely to favor their safety and well-being. In adults, the powerful primitive human response to the same facial signals could fire up fear, hatred, and cruelty.

The children were singing:

Sweet Land of Liberty
Let Freedom riiiing!

Ray approached the group and shook his head. "Shivkovski's polluting everything."

Eva snapped again. "Let's stick to business," she said curtly. "This is cosmetic stuff. There are far more important practical differences that you can't see, like the way Greeks, Italians and most Africans share an anti-malarial gene, while South Africa's Xhosa tribespeople and Swedes who look like the blonde bombshell up there don't." She stormed off.

Will screwed the plate back in and quickly caught up. He took Eva gently by her elbow and whispered: "Let's not mess things up just because we might have different agendas."

She gave him a sharp look of surprise. He smiled. "Maybe you're not the only one with deep dark secrets."

1045

"Look at this," Stephan shouted. "Shivkovskiworld has good South Bronx architecture!" The three rectangular warehouse style buildings were on the lowest ring road just outside the octagon's double perimeter fence. Ten-foot high walls topped with razor wire surrounded each lot. Their large dirt courtyards were jammed with sporting and athletic equipment, along with boxing rings and wrestling mats.

While structurally identical, the three were in vastly different states of repair. One looked like a war zone. It stood alone on the octagon side across the road from the other two. It had recently been on fire and, from the looks of it, probably not for the first time. Rubble and broken glass lay everywhere, although the sweeping up had begun. "At least someone loves it," Tom said, pointing to a square red flag flying crisply above the derelict's rooftop. Upon it were stenciled the letters SH.

"You want house proud?" said Jason. "Look at the one directly across the street." The trim on the identical building had been freshly painted in sleek blacks and silver-grays, and, while its facades and brick were chipped and dented, they looked like they had been power washed. It also flew the SH flag, whose meaning could be discerned from a large stenciled sign over the front door. "SPARTA HOUSE—Home of the Hoi Homoioi."

Tom knew that this was the name for the "similars," the elite class of Spartan warriors. It made sense. The institute was structured on the house system, like some schools, except that in this case the divisions were not random or by age or grade but based on gifts, aptitudes, training goals and, it now seemed clear, by genetic experiments.

He pretty well knew what flag the third building would be

flying. And, sure enough, there it was: a yellowing rag with a gigantic ratty L sewn sloppily on to it. L for Lacedaemon—one of the Hellenic names for Sparta. It was the same L that the young man tailing him at the World Trade Center had worn on his jacket. And he saw Stephan grinning now at the realization that this was the same L that had adorned the wannabe Spartans his stepbrother had outmuscled and outwitted at O'Reilly's and who had killed Fat Marco by mistake while trying to murder Tom. It looked like they were getting their heads handed to them here too.

"Seems like some sort of live-fire training camp," Jason said. Tom figured Shivkovski had arranged a state of perpetual war between the two Spartan houses, probably to test genetic concoctions against one another. The L team appeared to be busy preparing their Lacedaemon House for another attack by the clean and mean Sparta House inhabitants who had fought and won control of the contested building across the street. Figures scrambled around the courtyard erecting sandbag barriers. His eye followed a rappelling line rising from the yard to the rooftop—where he spotted something more worrying. One of the L team warriors was watching them through binoculars.

As they headed quickly for the octagon, Shivkovski provided Tom with one last laugh. Observed closely from the ground, the heavily damaged SH building across the street was revealed as the former property of yet another L Team. But the fighters of the former *Lenin House* had been driven off. It seemed perverse, even for Shivkovski. The old man had assigned some luckless young men to suffer regular whuppings in the name of the Russian communist whose dark genius for terror had inspired the perpetrators of Shivkovski's years in Gulag hell.

1050

The opportunity was too good for Eva to pass up. The no-contact, no-communications protocol might make sense for real maintenance personnel but seemed a bad idea for intruders collecting evidence. How could they learn what was happening if they didn't talk to the kids?

The pretty, freckled redhead sat on a whitewashed rock just a few feet from a three-girl hopscotch game. Her little face was in her hands. No supervisors around, no clones in sight. "Are you feeling all right?" Eva asked, squatting to eye level. "May I ask your name?"

The child's fingers parted. Her red-rimmed eyes were full of tears. She was pale. "It's my turn," she said and began quietly to sob.

A brunette, six or seven, rushed up with her skipping rope. "Yes?" Eva asked gently.

"You can take her now," the girl said softly. She pointed to her weeping companion, and looked away. "She can't play anymore. She doesn't work or is defective, or something like that. You can take her to, you know — to Betty and Sonia and Marylou."

The hopscotch game had stopped. Three sets of eyes locked on Eva. "I'll send someone back," she said, turning and walking on to join Ray and Will.

After a few seconds, they heard laughter behind them. "Wow!" said an excited young girl's voice. "*That's* never happened before!"

1055

The octagon's perimeter proved a soft target. Security was designed for control rather than defense. Shivkovski merely wanted everything and everybody to stay put in their assigned places.

"This is the third time I've seen this guy," Jason said, indicating the squarely built man with a blonde crew cut who sat on a high stool at a guard post beside the front gate. He was checking credentials and signing people in.

"Make that four," Tom said, pointing to a window in an adjacent building where an identical man was conversing with two child-size people who appeared to be in their 70s or 80s.

"It's worse than I thought," Jason's face was tight and angry. He looked up at the towering smokestack above the octagon and back at the guard. "I say we go right through this guy and see what the red zone's all about."

The security man and the miniature elders had left the window and no one was else was nearby. Tom led the way up the ramp, carrying a clipboard they'd brought along as a prop. "Hey," he shouted "We're going to need your help on this." He held the clipboard out to draw the big blonde's attention, checked the lobby behind him and, seeing it clear, knocked the man out cold. Stephan caught him before he hit the ground and dragged him into the guardhouse, where he was gagged, hog-tied, and deposited in a supply closet. They stood a "Wet Paint" notice outside the booth.

1101

They passed through the unlocked revolving door into a large hall. It was immediately clear that the main building had several entryways and, from its octagonal shape and this hall's configuration, Tom guessed that there were eight segregated sections, each with its own access point. They could only hope that this one would lead them to the heart of the matter. The odds weren't great but the fact that the hall was deserted might be a good sign. Perhaps this was a highly restricted area. The administration and technical departments and other offices necessary to keep an establishment of this magnitude and complexity up and running were likely less secure sections that allowed more traffic.

On each side of entrance hall were banks of elevators. A long wide corridor led off to the right. Tom moved ahead to peer through the 20-foot high tinted Plexiglas wall that blocked their progress toward the center of the building. What he saw buoyed his hopes. At the center of a high circular atrium was another broad corridor that descended in an extremely steep grade toward what Tom guessed from Jason's descriptions of the colossal excavation activities must be a major underground facility. Shivkovski had a fetish for the secret and the subterranean. This could be the jackpot.

"Must have run out of clones," Jason said, pointing to a numeric security pad next to the inch-thick Plexiglas door. Stephan jogged up from a nearby electrical room. He said it was unlocked. "Maybe I hide and see code when someone goes in."

Tom glanced back at the main entrance behind them. It was only a matter of time before they were discovered — if the alarm had not gone up already. "Good idea, Stephan," he said. "And see if there's something around that can break through that door. Jason and I will make a quick run up that corridor." He had noticed the red cross on the wall and a gurney part way up the hallway. If they were not back in 15 minutes and Stephan had obtained the code, he was to go in himself.

Tom looked at the small keypad again. He was about to suggest that Stephan grab any likely candidate who approached or passed through the door to scare a combination out of them. Remembering the ice pick, however, he decided that he and Jason might be more temperamentally suited to that task should it become necessary.

1112

The corridor was leading them in the direction of the smokestack. Tom and Jason passed through a pair of swinging doors into what was clearly an infirmary. The corridor was lined by ward after brightly lit ward, all crammed with modern equipment, along with an army of doctors, nurses and orderlies. And children. Hundreds of them, all ages and all sizes, reading, watching TV, noses in video games, and talking with their caregivers and with one another.

They shifted at a crossroads to a parallel, less crowded service hall at the rear of one rank of rooms. The further they went, the more somber the scenes through the doorways became. A small girl with sunflower pajamas slept fitfully; a boy, perhaps five, bald and emaciated, stared glumly off into space; a skeletal teen sat on the side of a bed, holding the hand of a small child whose chest heaved with sobs. Staff stood attentively over more and more beds in which children lay immobile and often intubated, updating conditions with digital clipboards. Tom hoped that these were children brought in from elsewhere for specialized treatment. If the Institute's own kids were ill in these numbers, they were witnessing a calamity.

The last five rooms were intensive care wards. Access was controlled by sealed sliding glass doors. Masked attendants floated between ranks of pumping, sucking, flashing, blinking and occasionally squealing equipment. Hundreds of small forms, many only infants or toddlers, lay in the serpentine clutches of high-tech life support.

"Don't want to think about it," Jason said as he slammed through yet another swinging door.

But Tom *had* to. The scale here was epidemic. Were these genetic experiments in progress — perhaps diseased kids brought to the Institute for a last chance? Or were these children who had been toyed with genetically and were now on the way down and out?

1118

Medical staff and even a man in maintenance yellow passed silently and, despite the odd hint of a nod or a slight smile, made no eye contact.

Traffic disappeared. They bore left at a fork. Through a heavy steel side fire door they entered a large chapel-like chamber. Two closed elaborately carved 15-foot-high wooden doors marked the main entrance to their right. The room was empty.

"This isn't Christian," Jason said. Not a surprise, Tom thought, given that Shivkovski hoped to put "God" out of work, whatever hat she or he happened to be wearing. But the old man was paying lip service to religion here. Tom could guess at the mocking Shivkovski rationale: the search for some greater authority must be honored because it was the stuff of human nature. "God" deserved recognition as a creation of Man.

The walls of the towering room were heavily adorned. Paintings, figures, inscriptions. Alongside a Roman Catholic image of the crucified Christ, Tom recognized one in the Greek Orthodox style. No one faith dominated. Buddha and Vishnu and icons that Tom recognized as Taoist and Shinto were accorded equal prominence. An inscription in Arabic was from the Koran. Moses was there. From the Abrahamic faiths to Zoroasterism, Shivkovski had given at least 30 of history's dominant religions their due.

Tom guessed that a small raised dais at the front was used for memorial services. Behind it was a floor-to-ceiling display in which two to three dozen video screens were encased by ornate frames. Each displayed the face of a different child or young person. A much larger screen, perhaps 16 feet wide, dominated at the center.

"They must put the picture of the kid they're about to bury in the middle," Jason said.

"Assembly-line stuff." Tom slumped into one of the pews and counted the children on the wall: Teresita, 6, Douglas, 14 . . . . The latest ceremony had apparently ended with a tribute to Agnes, a radiant eight or nine year old, who may have been part Polynesian, with a touch of African or South Asian alleles. "A Joy to All Her Friends," read a heading over the beautifully posed picture. Her uniform bore a familiar pattern, drawn from Starry Night by Van Gogh. Maybe she'd been an art student.

Tom reached under his thigh and peeled a relatively fresh glob of chewing gum from the bench. Two empty boxes of tissue lay upended on the floor. Agnes's friends had wept here only recently.

When Jason moved towards the center, the strains of Beethoven's Ode to Joy flooded the room. A sensor, Tom reckoned, designed for when folks wandered in for a private moment.

He stood and moved to the rear pews. They had touch-screen terminals that displayed the pictures from the wall. Tom supposed that if another frame was chosen, that child's image moved to the enlarged central frame of honor. The loved one's favorite music might be played, along with a video tribute.

Tom's hand moved towards a screen but he didn't have the stomach or the time for it right now.

Instead, he charged after Jason who was barreling down the center aisle in the direction of the smokestack. Tom tried to harden his heart.

"No Admission to Unauthorized Personnel." They went through the door knowing roughly what to expect.

The walls rose 50 feet to a peaked roof of glass and steel through which they could see a blue sky and the octagon's soaring smokestack. Three sides of the courtyard were solid concrete. On the fourth, built into a façade of red brick, rose five stacked rows of four stainless steel doors. Each shiny door was roughly three feet wide and two feet high and framed with black iron.

Under the wispy clouds of Upper New York State sky, they had found Shivkovski's ovens.

They stood speechless before the wall. Tom wondered for a moment whether he was really here.

In that instant a thundering cough erupted behind the brick. The crematoria roared and the floor below them began to vibrate. Seconds later, the first effluents from the combustion of the bodies of innocent children rose from the Institute's anti-pollution stack into the fresh countryside air.

"Boy! Has someone ever steered you guys wrong!"

A large smiling African-American man approached from behind a forklift-like vehicle apparently used to load and unload the compartments. He was easily the oldest person they'd seen today, with tufts of white in his mustache and a belly protruding from none-too-clean blue overalls. And the first to speak to them.

"No one can work on these units right now!" he said, waving vaguely at the brick wall and a tangle of filtering apparatuses and above the ovens. "Which weenie sent you in here this time of day? Hell! Cool-down don't even start till eight tonight. This takes a while, you know!"

Jason turned his back and walked slowly to the far side of the room, his eyes glued to the wall of doors.

"You must be talking about some other crew," Tom said. "We're here for a safety walk around. Checking outlets. That sort of thing."

"Hell yes!" said the man, winking. "Last thing we need round here is a fire!"

He quickly turned serious, however, "Upset, huh," he said with a concerned look, nodding towards Jason.

Tom turned to see Jason pound the far wall and then lean against it, hands splayed above his bowed head.

The worker shook his head. "You don't want be comin' roun' here unless you already settled it all inside. Know what I'm saying?"

Tom nodded.

"Take me. I got two kids who would be dead except for—well, you know, all the treatments. You must be the same, right—you know, family of beneficiaries? But it's still tough. You just kinda have to believe it's all worth it in the end." He kept his eyes on Jason. "It's hard today for me too. Did you ever see little Nelson? Physics? Crick House? No? Well, I worked on the plumbing there for a while. Nice, nice kid." He looked up at the wall. "But he's in the smoke today, God bless him."

In the smoke? Tom resisted the urge to strike out. And yet anyone could tell that this had once been a decent man.

"I'll give you fellas a moment." He departed with a friendly pat on Tom's shoulder. "Got work to do."

A door closed behind him. Tom joined Jason, whose eyes were red-rimmed but diamond hard. "Evil bastards! This is what my dad has sensed all these years. It's tortured him day after day." The big man covered his face with a large knobby hand and inhaled deeply. "It was in the air somehow, despite all the smokestack filters. Somehow he's always known it. The death camps all over again."

Tom felt cold and ready now. "Let's finish this," he said.

1145

Stephan smiled proudly when they slipped into the maintenance closet. Sitting against the wall, hands duct taped behind his back and legs spread wide, was a member of the cloned identikit security clan. The blond man looked happy to see them. Tom quickly saw why.

Stephan had opened a circuit breaker in an electrical panel, interrupting the flow of electricity, and had replaced the outgoing line with a length from his roll of wire. He had then stripped two feet of insulation from the free end of the wire and wrapped the neutral around the man's throat. The hot wire disappeared into the youth's half unzipped fly. "I did not do that part myself," Stephan said gleefully. "I make him tie tight around his youknowwhat! I tell him, if he not give us code we have barbecue!"

The clone guard looked up at Tom and Jason with wide eyes but seemed pleased rather than terrified.

"Are you bad boys?" he asked. His manner was child-like and completely out of sync with his manly physique. "Are you the bad boys from Sparta House or Lacedaemon House? We know you must be cruel sometimes because that is what you are learning to do." Another Shivkovskian joke, Tom now realized, expressed this time through the creation of a human being. This man was meant to make an intimidating first impression. That of the SS trooper or KGB Gulag guard, a perverse statement of Shivkovski's contempt for totalitarianism and for the conventional sameness in human nature, here signified by the clones. The punchline was the man's personality—that of a helpful child devoid of ill will. A sweet kid in storm trooper drag.

Tom interrupted Stephan before the Russian could speak: "Yes, we're the bad boys," he told the clone with a smile." Now tell us the code and stay here while we finish our game."

"Press K," the blonde clown said cheerfully. "Then punch in the date in numbers—year month day. Then put in my code, 31715."

1159

The others showed up as Tom punched the code in. This wasn't part of the plan but at least they were six again: Tom, Eva, Will, Ray, Jason and Stephan. The entry door slid open and their work boots clomped on the polished floors as they rushed towards the descending hallway. In a brightly lit cafeteria to their right, teenagers in baggy jeans sprawled on their chairs by a Coke machine. One gawky boy had his arm around the narrow shoulders of a coltish girl. As they turned to look at them, the gross enlargement of the backs and tops of their skulls became obvious.

"Maybe we should split up again," Tom said, stopping for a moment to consider deployments. "Someone should talk to these kids while we have the chance. And we need pictures of those heads."

"Not right now, I'm afraid," growled Stephan. "Look like Round Two with Spartans!"

Tom looked up. A group of Shivkovski's Spartans—from Lacedaemon House judging by the homemade "L" insignia stitched to their clothing, stood blocking the way to the descending corridor and showing no lack of cockiness despite their apparent history of defeat.

The tallest of the six declared in all seriousness: "On your knees, inferiors." It was a ludicrous situation but one that had to be taken very seriously. Cooked up in a test tube or not, these men had powerful builds and their scar tissue had been earned the hard way.

From the doorway of the canteen, a Nefertiti-like beauty with a large close-cropped skull shouted: "Take off, losers, or we'll call the real Spartans!"

"Up yours, Socrates!" replied one of the L squad. "One day I'll drag that geek into our cave and leave her for the rats."

"Like you did with the chimps?" Will asked.

"Don't about holy things," the leader said, surprised and indignant. "Do not question the ways of Lacedaemon."

Eva asked: "Is it holy to leave infants to die?"

What infants? Tom wondered. But there was no time to think about that because the fight was on.

Ray had been only partly right. While the battle was indeed exciting, it was far from short. Or easy. The wannabes had youth and real skills and lived up to the Spartan rep. They seemed to feed on pain and injury and the violence itself. Yet the danger they presented did not lack the inevitably eccentric Shivkovskian touch. In the day's latest bizarre twist, this was not to be a free-for-all. Instead, the L-team insisted on naming and squaring off with individual opponents.

That worked to Tom's and Will's advantage and they managed, although only with maximum effort and several setbacks, to eventually subdue their matches. So did Stephan, who was less fit than Tom but had the brutal knowing finish of an experienced killer. Eva clearly had training too but gave away too much size. Ray was simply getting too old for this kind of thing.

The game changer proved to be farmer–solider Jason. He'd simply lied about the M-16. No offense folks, he said later, but only a fool goes into the kill zone unarmed. The assault rifle was loaded with live rounds not blanks and he had brought plenty of clips.

The turning point came as Tom's opponent finally collapsed unconscious. Will was finishing his adversary off, though bleeding profusely from the mouth and nose. Stephan had a death grip on a semiconscious Spartan's throat. But Ray was down and in the fetal position, gasping. His opponent stood above him screaming" "Do you submit? Do you submit?" Tom saw him but raced instead to rescue Eva who lay trying to protect herself on her back while her beefy foe poised to strike her again.

Jason's first round dropped the man before Tom could get there. The farmer then shot his own match partner, whom he had put down with a length of metal wire conduit, as well as Ray's, Stephan's and Tom's opponents. When he moved to kill Will's downed Spartan, however, a bloodied Eva jumped up and blocked his way. "No Jason," she said, shoving hard against his thick shoulders. "We need this man alive!"

The gunfire set off a deafening siren and flashing alarm lights. Tom also heard a deep rumbling behind and spun into a sprint toward the descending corridor.

He glanced once over his shoulder to see if Jason was controlling his rage. Will's L-team opponent had risen on to wobbly legs and was swinging wildly at anyone coming near. With Eva and the others providing the distraction, Jason knocked him down with a vicious kick to the side of his knee.

Stephan, Tom also saw, was following close behind.

1204

A giant steel door to Shivkvoski's inner sanctum was dropping at the bottom of the corridor and was now barely two feet from the ground. Tom was about 7 yards away when he launched himself like a swimmer off the block, twisted to land on his side and flipped on to his back to skid along the waxed marble floor.

He turned his head to his right and nearer the ground to lower his profile. As he slid, he saw two things: Eva watching from faraway, hands raised to her bloody cheeks, eyes wide, mouth open; and, near behind him, the look of fear and recognition on his stepbrother's face.

1206

Stephan was still and quiet now. Crushed and cut nearly in half. It had been a terrible and hard death. Tom owed this man his life. He struggled briefly with a wave of guilt. It passed in a moment, supplanted by the thought that this man would both understand and applaud the need to battle on. Tom's breathing slowed and he opened his eyes.

The flash of artificial light was as bright and clear as the sun breaking through on an overcast day.

Tom turned and approached a wall of floor-to-ceiling plate glass. He had found Shivkovski's vast underworld. Its sky-like ceiling resembled the billowing roofs that float on pressurized air over huge sports stadiums. And the viewing room in which Tom now found himself was Shivkovski's version of the well-appointed luxury box—leather armchairs, a working desk, computer stations and even a mini-bar.

Now that all would be known, Tom wasn't sure he was really ready to see. But he allowed his eyes to fall slowly down onto the scene below. At first glance, it resembled an indoor trade show, the kind where building contractors or high-tech buyers wander a grid of walkways between hundreds of roofless display booths and information cubicles. But this was more permanent, a complete replica of a working town, with buildings that, like doll houses, had no roofs. Sidewalk benches, potted plants, a central public square, complete with bandstand, outdoor cafes and restaurants, stores with goods on their shelves and lineups at the cash, places where people—or what should have been people—seemed to be at work. Shivkovskiville.

As he looked more closely, Tom's hands and feet went cold, his jaw tightened, his lungs instinctively gulped for air. Neurons and glial cells, dopamine, serotonin, norepinephrine and the other neurotransmitters raged through his nervous system down into his guts. His legs begged him to cut and run. This was the old brain, the animal centers that spoke only the language of survival. It asserted itself in other ways, too, sucking blood from the rational neo-cortex and pushing the ancient emotions—fear, anger, sadness—to the front of the stage and sending his basic senses into overdrive.

The appalling smell of Stephan's blood and waste matter that he had somehow shut out just moments ago now suddenly overwhelmed him. His heart beat a panicky tattoo against the inside of his chest. His eyesight had never seemed sharper. His mind seemed to be firing randomly and in all quadrants at the same time, seeking manically to absorb, remember, interpret, and believe the information that his darting eyes were conveying. Which was nothing they had ever seen before and nothing he could have ever imagined.

Virtually no one here in the inner ring of Shivkovski's experimental Hell was normal. Certainly not in physical appearance, to which Tom was now reacting with physical revulsion. The range, scale and degree of human deformity, mutilation, and appalling metamorphosis both astounded and shook him. His alarmed, disbelieving, hungry eyes darted from one place and individual to another in an autonomic panic of their own, before lurching back for double and triple takes. The absurd line of a forehead, the displacement of a nose, faces unsymmetrical, eyes far removed from their usual configuration and distorted in shape, number and form. Profaned profiles. Warped and truncated appendages, skeletons and structures. Grotesquely deformed, outsized, superfluous—or entirely missing—human features. Strange skins and feathers and bodies that seemed to have neither. Fins, flippers, claws, beaks. This was nature defiled, debased, despoiled, desecrated.

Yet Shivkovski's people strolled the avenues, sat on benches with their noses (or what passed for them) buried in books, chatted amiably at store counters, dined in gregarious groups, kicked soccer balls, tossed Frisbees, sat pensively before computer screens, took cellphone calls atop their weaving bicycles.

Of the many sights, the distortions of the shape, structure and organs of the head were the most numerous and jarring. But the twisted limbs, stunted extremities and the bowed backs, less threatening somehow, and more *possible*, also broke Tom's heart. Some bodies were so misshapen he suspected they must be permanently attached to the small electric vehicles that sped them around Shivkovski's genetic underworld.

The observation deck was perhaps two hundred yards long.

Tom stumbled along it, his eyes captured by first one grotesquerie and then the next.

Near one end of the room, he spotted a hospital-like setting segregated by higher than normal walls. In three of the larger rooms, the walking genetically wounded were the caregivers of the genetically crippled and maimed. But he could see that the medical facility continued into the covered portion of the underground facility. Who knew how much more was concealed in the hidden places beyond the open towns, and on the floors that stairwells and elevators indicated might lie below?

There was just enough light for Tom to see into the first of the inner rooms. He bent his knees and pressed his face against the glass for a better angle.

It was a nursery.

And in the three glass-sealed cribs closest to him lay three infant beings, perhaps a month or two old by human measure, judging by their size.

Tom's heart seemed to stall then skip at what he saw. These children seemed physically robust but had reached only a primitive stage of fetal growth. They were throwbacks, in other words, to the earlier forms of life through which humans passed on the road of evolution. Yet viable! At least for a time. These were Shivkovski's false starts! Trial runs. Throwaways!

Tom slumped into a chair, stunned. Shivkovski had not only hacked into the human genome, he had held nothing back. Relentlessly, he had rolled the genetic dice again and again, shuffling code to see what might emerge and every once in a million throws might survive. Single-handedly, he had ended, fouled and polluted many hundreds of millions of years of Nature's, or God's, work. And by introducing alien DNA into the gene pool, he had begun to steal the "us" from the human race.

This thing had to be contained. The people below and all the kids outside were almost certainly products of "germ line" engineering. If they had their own children, their modified genes would pass on not only to their offspring but also to all their descendants. The changes they represented could become part and parcel of the human gene pool. The double-dome skull of a young man Tom now saw loitering beside an ersatz fast-food outlet could appear again and again and again for the next hundred — or thousand — generations.

And who could know the true extent and the exact nature of

the mutations Shivkovski had concocted? The flaws Tom now examined could be nothing next to the health, personality or intellectual benefits—or perversions—that lay beneath the surface.

Tom stood and picked up a four-foot steel-frame bench from the floor and threw it against the glass. It bounced right back at him. No one below seemed to notice.

1210

"Calm yourself, Tom! Please."

Tom whipped around and addressed himself to the built-in wall speakers that had conveyed Shivkovski's words. His own voice was surprising weak. "You really are a mad old man."

"I regret that you had to see this, Tom." Shivkovski's disembodied tone lacked its usual aplomb. "I did not expect you to get this far this fast."

"I could say the same about you." Tom's mind suggested a number of taunts and threats—what hole are you hiding in? I'm coming for you!—but they seemed not only more clichéd than usual but irrelevant. He sat himself down on a bench. Shivkovski's arrest would be almost meaningless after this. The damage was done and irreparable. And the colossal unforgivable failure to stop it from happening was in good part Tom's. If not for Wally Anderson, in fact, Tom would have been back at Center Street, playing the big-shot law enforcer and protector of the public good, using chess moves to pick on Leon, feeling sorry for the lab rats, snickering about science. Blind to even the concept of R-evolution while it ripped the guts out of the natural order of things and the nation's well-being practically in front of his eyes.

"I suppose it's fortunate that I am not nearby," Shivkovski said through the speaker. "Thank goodness for the wonders of global communication."

"Your security stinks," Tom said softly. They had brought the crime into the light, at least.

"Not my thing. We only really wished to protect our people and our privacy. Mine is not a military mind, I'm afraid. Your father was a far better soldier than I was. So are you, evidently."

Tom stood slowly again to survey Shivkovski's work. These people might be members of the human species but they were also alien. The rest of the six billion humans on earth shared a precise genetic formula evolved over eons from the first spark of life. In Tom's view, this was what comprised the human soul and the foundation of any hope humankind had of building a better world together.

"Do you realize what you've done, Doctor?"

"Somewhat less than I would have liked; yet somewhat more than Joe Six Pack at O'Reilly's might have guessed was possible." He waited. "I've done what man has always done, and always will. I have dreamed, explored, ventured, risked, learned, bettered myself, and all of us. You know, Tom, the reason there are always reckless people around is that, throughout evolution, they have often served both themselves *and* mankind extremely well."

"You've killed any chance humans had of getting our act together."

"Nonsense," the scientist replied calmly. "*Not* getting our act together much of the time *is* our act and always will be. Or, should I say, would have been? I have taken small steps, though some have occasionally been bold. But I am only the first of hundreds and thousands of scientists who will inevitably follow. You talk of nature, Tom, but this has always been in the cards, humans being human. In ten years, less probably, they'll be fiddling with the human genome in the backstreet labs of Burundi and Bangladesh." He laughed. "The Wallys of this world wail about the loss of species! But I am trying to broaden and enhance biodiversity! Why is it that GreenGene can invent a better tomato plant but I must do nothing to show there can be better humans?"

Tom's eye fell upon a clutch of people reclining in bizarre contortions before a large public television screen. A woman with an astoundingly large head was speaking, perhaps reading the latest Shivkovski-scripted news.

"And the ovens, Dr. Mengele?"

"Nonsense again! A crematorium, as morally neutral as the neighborhood funeral parlor. Your association is ridiculous. We honor those who leave us. There is purity in a passage conferred by fire, as many civilizations have known. We not only respect the individuals we have lost, we loved them. They simply could not survive." He went on more sternly. "It hurts me when you suggest that my people—and especially the non-viable—are treated with anything less than reverence. We took wrong turns at some points, and moved too quickly at other times, especially after rather spectacular early successes. But—"

"A wrong turn for you is a life of torture for them!"

"Don't be made a fool by your initial primal response. And it is a natural primitive physical reaction you are experiencing as you first look upon these people. They're different from you—ugly, in your eyes. They disturb and frighten you. But that's your problem, not theirs and not mine. Remember, Stephen Hawking is also unusual to look at. Many of my warm gentle companions here are as accomplished in their own fields as he is in physics."

Tom's eyes continued to roam over faces and forms. He was steadier now but still felt an urgent need to turn away.

"Have you noticed how happily these people live together? This is a wonderfully close and cooperative community. There is an overwhelming atmosphere of mutual respect."

"Makes me warm all over, Doc," said Tom, "but where's the respect in creating lives destined for the incinerator."

"We are all destined for the oven or some other last stop." Shivkovski's telephone or mike scraped against something metallic. "Existence here is no crueler than the run-of-the-mill life in Manhattan or Milwaukie. The process of evolution will be improved, speeded up, and ratcheted exponentially by technology. Man's technology. Our future will be boundless."

"Yes, Shivkovski's boundlessly obscene brave new world."

Shivkovski obviously had a video feed from the observation deck because he paused after Tom made a sweeping gesture over the scene below. The old man's voice softened. "Think clearly, Tom. You people worship nature and yet nothing could be more natural than this. Nature gambles, and its roll of the dice has always brought random mutation. And nature shocks. It has all but wiped out life on earth on occasion. Nature also knows that life merely rebounds in new ways and with incredible diversity. All that I am doing here is helping humankind aid in nature's work—by rolling the dice for ourselves."

Tom glanced toward the huge steel door blocking his exit. A delta of bright red rivulets and tributaries flowed from the pulpy midsection of Stephan's body towards a low point in the floor.

"I want to see the rest, Doc."

"I cannot allow that, Tom." He knew what Tom was looking

at because he spoke of Stephan's death. "I haven't seen a man killed by violence in 50 years. Who is that?"

"Stephan was apparently my half brother."

"What a pity. Yes, Mikhail's little mobster. In many ways, a chip off the old block. My condolences." More static on the line. "This has the feel of approaching climax, does it not, Tom? The tying of loose ends?" Shivkovski's voice strengthened. "I've made life as pleasant as possible for all these good people, and believe me I won't let them down now either. They are my lovable dead ends. My could-have, should-have, might-have-beens. They'll leave no lasting mark but they've served mankind well. They deserve to go gently into the night. With the dignity you quite properly insist they deserve."

"What do you mean?" Tom asked, although he had an awful suspicion already. Each time Shivkovski seemed to have reached the outer limits, he had always upped the ante.

"I will do the people and government of the United States a favor," Shivkovski said with a smile in his voice. "Spare them the hard choices by doing what I know is best for my people. I do not want them to be hated and persecuted simply for what they are. I know what that is like."

Shivkovski's obvious threat turned Tom back to the underworld town. Some inhabitants had finally noticed him. On a park bench, a woman holding a book with a misshapen hand raised her other limb and waved. He scanned the scene again. Every eye had a bright, intelligent, human glint.

"Be a man and face the music, Doctor. You are talking about mass murder—and you know what that's all about too."

Tom would try to stall. The M-16 fire would have set off a series of alarms, and help would be on the way. Perhaps Shivkovski lacked the means to implement his implied threat immediately.

"But before we go any further, Doc, I have a couple of final questions. Anyway, I think we've moved pretty well beyond the need for secrecy now." Tom took a seat.

"Ask away. There is no one with whom I would more happily converse."

"Did you kill Wally Anderson?" Tom asked. "Did you also arrange to kill his friends Stephanie and Sean?"

"I won't answer that question," Shivkovski replied sadly. "I would never have wished them harm and regard their passing as a tragedy. But I cannot say anything that might implicate someone I care very deeply about."

Leon, Tom thought. But he expected a more honest answer to his next query and, as he put it to the old man, he felt himself coming to the end of a long journey. "Did you kill my father?"

"No, my dear boy, I did not." Shivkovski sounded relieved. "And it is quite wonderful to have all of this out at last. No, I would not have harmed him for the world. I fed on his genius. Stubborn but in the most admirable and creative ways. Brave. A man of action from a time when the term was measured in hard currency."

"Please explain this, then. Why is there evidence that he was the object of somatic genetic treatment? Why was a cold virus used as a vector? Why did he kill himself in a self-hating frenzy, like Wally Anderson? Both showed similar side-effects in the days before their suicides—flu symptoms."

"It is simple and tragic. And very much in your father's character. He experimented on himself. Repeatedly. He had to be on the front lines, whether it was Stalingrad or in the lab. When I objected, he laughed it off, or threatened to kick me in the pants." Shivkovski chuckled. "Not a threat you take lightly from big Mike Daluskov—or from his son."

"Is that what your split was about?"

"I found his approach quite ludicrous. Like sending your best general on a bayonet charge. He hated my approach, too. Our tactics in science reflected our innately different personalities."

"So my father would have been against all this?"

"Absolutely—and I suppose that must please you. My view then, and now, was that we could not make sufficient progress unless we hurled ourselves into wholesale experimentation. To some extent, this would have to be hit and miss. There was simply no other way to get anywhere quickly enough. Remember, we had Stone Age computing power and none of the advantages of today. None of the sequencers, for example." His voice trailed off. "And we—I—found ways. Again and again."

Tom wondered whether Shivkovski was as impressed by his own brilliance as the world would be appalled by it.

"And my dad's experiment? That last time."

"Somatic treatment, as you say. Tremendously innovative, of course, and every bit as aggressive in its way as mine. He was attempting to rebalance serotonin uptake. He had his target gene, and his vector."

Shivkovski hesitated before continuing. "It was an early attempt at new treatment for depression. You may know that your lovely and profoundly gifted mother suffered from persistent dolor. I believe that her deep sadness is primarily a philosophical one, a remnant of her experiences before and during the war. However, she is innately capable of deep feeling whereas I, for example, am naturally shallow in this regard. So your father knew that in this and several other ways, genetics must play a role in his beloved wife's suffering."

"He looked for somatic treatments and something went wrong?"

"Neurotransmitters are tricky. You can't really tell which way things will go. Serotonin's many roles are not fully understood even today. It was compulsive to some extent, I believe. He loved your mother and adored and greatly enjoyed you, but on some days I think he felt he just had to get back to the front."

At least he had risked only his own life, Tom thought. "And Wally?"

"We have your father's notes, of course," Shivkovski continued, apparently reading his mind. "Scrupulous, as always. I would venture to guess that someone simply replicated the experiment these many years later on Mr. Anderson. Acting on SLC6A4, perhaps. It would be, of course, a cryptic message to you, and the act of a not entirely healthy mind."

This was Shivkovski's way of implicating Leon. Tom said nothing, however, given the precariousness of Shivkovski's own state of mind and of the current situation.

But he had one more question he had to ask. "How much does my mother know about all this?"

"Just about nothing, Tom, very little, although she will always suspect the worst of me. I think she also blames me indirectly for your father's death and his reckless approach to work." Shivkovski paused for a moment. "This is unfair. But your mother humbles me in several ways. Her goodness has actually made me wonder whether humankind might one day be reformed without being genetically remade, which you will understand gave me pause at one time or another about proceeding with my work. And while you do not fully realize this, she stood many rungs above your father and me as a scientist before her self-imposed inactivity. She is a genius, in fact, although one not so far widely recognized. "

"You say she gave you pause. So why didn't that hold you back?"

"Because goodness was not enough, Tom. It was also in your mother's nature to withdraw from difficulty and reality, to leave the field to those she saw as her opponents, to close her eyes I believe, and in a way to abandon her responsibilities. You may have some of her goodness in you Tom but it is the genetic inheritance of the rash and warlike but honorable Mad Mike Daluskov that has brought you here today to do what you think is right."

The trick now would be to find a way to get *Shivkovski* to do what was right. Tom looked down at the 3,000 or 4,000 living beings whose existence the old man had implied he was willing to end. One young woman was affected by two genetic atavisms that were not entirely unknown. Hair covered her entire face and arms and what Tom could see of her legs. From her tailbone, a stiff bone-like tail protruded for three or four inches. It was clearly discernible through her loose fitting green gown. Tom followed her smiling gaze to one of the many giant billboard-like television screens throughout the town.

"Big Brother is speaking," he said.

"Oh," replied Shivkovski. "Am I making an appearance? The first thing you must learn about TV is to be still. Talking corpse works best." He paused. "It's my daily message. Afterwards, they'll rest in their rooms, perhaps take a little something to buoy their spirits."

The Kool Aid, Tom thought. Time was running out. "Another question: was my germ line DNA messed with, in the gamete, or my mom's egg?"

"Your father would never have allowed it! It would have been worth my life even to suggest it. Remember the differences. I want to be the general. I send the others into battle. But your father would never dispatch another person into the front line of science, and especially not his own flesh and blood. And do you imagine your mother would ever let me near one of her eggs?"

Tom leapt to his feet. He had been inside the sanctum for 20 minutes and had not even reached for his video camera. He pulled it from his maintenance overalls and began a slow sweeping shot of the floor below.

"Please don't do that, Tom."

Tom ignored him. He saw people gathering in groups now, conversing. Many drifted towards large doorways at the far side of the open area.

"What's happening, Doctor?"

"I told you. They'll rest now. Please stop filming." For the first time Shivkovski sounded tired and defeated himself. "My security is poor but you must know I cannot let you leave with those videos. All other evidence of the existence of my people here is now being automatically destroyed, especially anything visual."

"Are you going to kill me by remote control," Tom asked as he shuffled alongside the glass barrier, stopping every few steps to focus on something of special note. "Your sloppy Spartan gunmen missed me back at O'Reilly's."

"Someone tried to shoot you?" Shivkovski's asked, his voice rising. He either didn't know or was an excellent actor. "Oh, Leon, what am I to do about you?"

"You, him—it doesn't really matter, Doctor. Let's talk about these people here."

"Do not underestimate my resolve to protect them, as well as the rest of my work. I have cared for and know each and every one of these individuals. They exemplify the best of human nature. But their lives will be unlivable in a world for which it has unfortunately turned out they have been misdesigned."

"I thought we are the ones who are misdesigned? Don't be insane. Don't add to your crimes."

"No, someone had to take the steps we have taken here," Shivkovski continued calmly. "And to serve the greater purpose. Many of these people are ill, borderline nonviable. But their lives have been as pleasant as I have been able to make them. I will not have them experience abandonment. They are both the beginning and end of their lines."

"You know damn well this country will help them lead dignified natural lives."

"You kid yourself, Tom. You will see when the fear takes hold. You will be shocked. And for what purpose will they live? To be used as prejudicial evidence. The crazies will call them creatures and exploit their strangeness. They'll start a witch hunt against science and cut mankind off from its rightful future."

"Don't harm them, Shivkovski."

"Do you know how many species have come and gone

through time? Hundreds of millions. That most likely includes several hominids like us that we do not know about. This will be nothing new."

Tom moved closer to the glass to film the last few dozen people now filtering through the exits. He shouted: "Don't."

Shivkovski yelled right back. "*Think, damn you!* The butcher bill today, if I may put it so crudely, will be nothing compared with the mass suffering and casualties ahead if we do not upgrade our species. The new world wars, the smug and righteous new persecutions, the new Holocausts. We have always and will always revert to form. We are sick and yet we are capable of healing ourselves. Through Wally Anderson's R-evolution."

Above him, Tom heard a motor engage and the grumbling again of heavy machinery. Behind the glass wall, a heavy slotted steel post descended slowly and locked into concrete foundation forms. A metal wall about five inches thick began sliding down the steel guide ways.

Tom raised the camera again and kept shooting. He dropped to his knees and lay on his side, focusing where he could, panning to catch the last of Shivkovski's mutant family gesturing politely to one another as they waited in a small traffic jam to leave the great room.

The steel walls slipped down into slots in the building structure. A loud grinding and squealing sounded through the glass. Tom guessed some sort of bolts had been engaged.

Shivkovski said. "I doubt you'll question my ability to disable you, or worse. You're like a rat in a trap."

"Don't do it, Doctor! Think about it. If they are as gentle and bright as you say, people will feel compassion for them, not hatred. They'll make your case."

"There are still the children outside."

"So you admit to modifying their genes too?"

"Yes, of course. And there are many, many more already out making their way in the world. For themselves and their descendants." The machinery was still roaring, but changing gears. "They will make my case. You do not need to humiliate these decent beings, as you call them. Promise to deposit the camera there in that bin to the right and I'll allow you out of here safely. You can return to your friends and join the many men with guns outside."

"No promises or deals, Doctor. I am your enemy."

"Maybe you are but you are also special to me, like it or not."

Tom doubted Shivkovski would kill him but he could not risk something more important than his life—the testimony he could give to the world of what he had seen.

From the behind the steel wall, Tom heard and felt a series of deep-throated explosions. Great whooshes. The floor below him shuddered. The wall and glass began radiating intense heat almost immediately.

Tom listened for screams but heard none.

"They have taken their medications," Shivkovski said quietly. "They will relax suddenly, totally, and almost instantly pass away. The staff will have exited. I suppose they will now be arrested, although they have done this work because our breakthroughs have saved their children and mothers and sisters and brothers and fathers."

Tom wanted to shout again at Shivkovski: "You didn't have to do this!" But he no longer had the heart. There was nothing to do now but escape.

"Goodbye, Tom—for now." The background buzz went dead. The heat was becoming unbearable. Tom called out for Shivkovski a number of times. No answer. He returned the camera to his pocket; it was already growing hot. Hidden there, he managed to eject and remove the memory disc. He waited a moment then made a great show of producing the camera and holding it above his head.

"You win, Doctor," he said before tossing the Sony into the bin.

He could barely breathe. He feared his clothing would burst into flames. His skin felt as if it was cooking. Beside Stephan's lower body, he crouched near the floor, seeking cooler air. He reached into his pocket, feeling the insulation of his pants and thinking he should toss the camera's memory disc away while he remained conscious. Surely, Shivkovski could not have been fooled by his cheap sleight of hand.

Just then, the door that had crushed poor Stephan rose a foot to let Tom out. Before he could retrieve his step-brother's body, it then closed on Shivkovski's secret inner sanctum for good.

The central atrium was empty, except for five fallen Lacedaemonians. No sign of the sixth.

Tom ran hard for the front door. He was almost there when Eva intercepted him and threw her arms around his neck. "You scared the hell out of me!" she said, burying her face in his chest. She had staunched the flow of blood from her nostrils with tissue paper. "My God, you're burning up! This way! Let's get some cold water on you."

"Where are the others?" Tom asked, resisting for a moment. The explosions continued to rumble underground. From outside he heard the chopping of helicopter blades.

"We helped evacuate the hospital wards and then Jason and Ray went back to the offices." Eva steered him into a washroom where he soaked his hands and arms in a sink of cold water. She used a pail to bucket more water over his head and suck the heat from his face, scalp, neck and back. Then she ran to find fire and rescue outside. Perhaps they could save some of the inhabitants. There obviously were other ways in and out of the inner sanctum.

Jason and Ray appeared in the atrium carrying a large box full of files, DVDs, CDs and ZIP disks. "Ray thinks we should get as many documents as we can," Jason said.

"Half the United States Army's here," Ray continued. He'd been on the losing end of the L team scrap but seemed otherwise okay. "We found a utility supply tunnel that leads to a delivery depot near the cave. We've loaded up a couple of the electric minivans they use for deliveries with this stuff."

"Good," Tom said. "You two go now." He handed the detective his video disk. "With your life, Ray. It's all on there. Everything I saw inside. It will be hard but please go back out through the cave. The government might seize the video and we need it out there. So make copies and send them to every news organization you can think of. "

"Funny," said Ray, "great minds think alike! Eva said the same and that we should keep the cave secret until we get it done." Eva had won Ray over—no small victory.

Through the high atrium windows, Tom could see scores of heavily armed men spilling down the lanes from the higher rings of the orange zone.

"We can make a good start on media over at Carrie

Hemingford's place," Jason said. "She'll be HQ for the networks, cable and wire services."

As they rushed off, Tom yelled after Jason: "Tell your dad it's over. And thank him."

Eva was waiting with Will at the front guardhouse. "The Army won't let the firefighters in yet," Will said calmly. However, Carrie had done her job. Three television news helicopters were jousting above them with a dozen unmarked Blackhawks.

Beyond the top ring of buildings, Tom saw the distinctive shapes of STOL aircraft descending, presumably with reinforcements. There must be a battalion on the ground already, he thought. How had they gotten here so fast and in such force? And who were they?

"What do you think, Will?" he asked his friend. "Do we demand our right to counsel and keep our mouths shut for a while?"

"I can be yours and you can be mine," Will replied quietly. "I believe Jason's M16 got lost for good in the crematorium." They watched the squads of men in battle dress securing the small school buildings, flushing terrified children out as they went, and moving them up the hill to safety in the fields beyond. "I doubt anyone will stand on niceties today."

A young Latino lieutenant and two privates strode down the path toward them. Aside from shoulder bar to indicate rank, the young man's black uniform bore neither insignia nor ID. "Mr. Thomas Daluskov, Mr. William Jefferson, Muzz Eva Martin?"

"You're talking to them," Will replied.

"We understand there are two additional males in your group, besides the casualty. Can you tell us their locations, please?"

The lieutenant was well informed. Tom glanced at Eva. She looked away but seemed willing at least to lead the soldier astray. "We've lost track of them," she said. "They're still inside this building, probably in the section east of here." She pointed them away from the hospital service tunnel.

"You will all follow me, please."

The lieutenant led the way up the path. Four soldiers brought up the rear.

The maelstrom still rumbled in the belly of the octagon. Shivkovski's makeshift nation had been invaded. Its citizens huddled in groups in the playgrounds and along the pathways. The phenoms were palming their basketballs and trying to hide the trauma they surely felt. Their home was going up in flames. Little girls held hands as the light from the murderous flames played on their damp cheeks. Other children clung to each other and wept. Tom saw a tear roll down Will's cheek as he watched one of Shivkovski's small creations tremble uncontrollably while a giant American soldier tried ineffectively to calm him. Most, mouths agape, simply watched Eva, Tom and Will climb the hill. They were sad, vulnerable, terrified. Their old world was dead. The new one aborning was unknown and likely full of peril. Trepidation did seem the natural human reaction. Tom felt it himself.

It was eight days before the inner sanctum cooled sufficiently for the EAF to safely enter and inspect the ashes. For that was all that was left.

Part Three

42

To the so-called Junk Generation crisis each day were added fresh reasons to panic over R-evolution. Wally Anderson's coinage, pronounced in English with a long "e" and spelled with either a hyphen or the italicized *R*, had become a commonplace on TV and computer screens and front pages around the world and in its scores of linguistic derivatives on the lips and tongues of billions. Mother Earth, once seemingly rock solid, was shifting beneath humanity's feet. Nothing seemed permanent and safe anymore. In the US in particular, the single largest island of prolonged safety and certitude in the world, the violent dislodgement of the foundations under "life as we know it" provoked heights of hysteria that were unmatched anywhere else. They reflected the privileges of sanctuary from the world's greatest woes the homeland had taken for granted for so many generations. The exceptionalism bestowed largely by happenstances of history and geography was showing cracks.

Not that the new threats were overstated. The latest information, for instance, was that thousands of Shivkovski's Junk Generation creations—the ones judged suitable for the production line—were out in the real world living among everyday Americans. Anonymous, secret cells, in more ways than one.

The short story was that, in its compulsive search for new frontiers, humankind had not only sailed to the edge of the world but had fallen off. Sad, Tom thought, but when you knew the history, inevitable and kind of funny too. The people were too frightened to laugh, however. One monologue about what his great-grandchildren might look like once R-evolution gained traction cost the leading late-night TV host his job.

News, or a facsimile thereof, was a profit leader again as cable TV and talk radio tossed every flammable rumor or factoid that came to hand onto the brushfires of fear sweeping the nation. R-evolution knocked crime, terrorism, the exhibitionism and/or parasitical media exploitation of the rich and famous, the presidential impeachment proceedings, and even the strangely hypnotic travails of a bored spoiled teenage star behaving like a bored spoiled teenager into the pre-commercial break 15-second roundups. Terms were coined to describe those individuals whose genetic makeup had been deliberately manipulated to effect physical and personality changes from the human norm. The most politically correct was *homo sapiens reformus*, which indicated a new genus of the species *homo sapiens sapiens*. "Man remade."

But it was "the Junk Generation" or JunkGen or JG, for short, that stuck, thanks at first to tabloid headline writers. The name had begun as an alliterative but generally meaningless reference to the scientific jargon for the apparently largely unused "junk DNA" in the human genome. It had gained weight later when word leaked from Oneida that Shivkovski's ability to control the previously unknown key role played by the junk genes in governing life lay at the center of his experimentation.

Whatever its provenance, Tom disliked the term. It would encourage the lazy-minded to file this mortal threat to human existence alongside gas-guzzlers and obesity, ills that beyond constant whining no one willing to do anything about. The term was nonetheless far less derogatory than other constructs that quickly came into use. These included "Dorfs," for *homo deformus*, and the very popular "Greaks, as in "genetic freaks" and "Nuke the Greaks."

The deaths of roughly 3,000 strange beings in Shivkovski's inner sanctum at the Oneida institute appalled but produced little grief. Some of Shivkovski's creations were recognizable from the telecasts of Tom's heavy censored video as sentient, intelligent, and fundamentally human but people often had difficulty caring about individuals whose skin colors, or languages, or diets differed only marginally from their own. Empathy for these strange looking things with different watchamacallit coursing through their veins was for practical purposes out of the question. It didn't help that the Greaks scared the heck out of people.

In fact, many felt that the danger would have been worse had the "dead ends" survived. Some of the straight-talking, right-thinking politicians to whom many Americans paid daily attention said so out loud and thereby comforted the fearful and the confused. The next step toward regaining the sense of safety of the pre-R-evolution world, it was implied in the usual code, should be to find and get rid of the rest—the ones who maybe looked like us but were obviously some other kind of creature altogether. This would be problematic, however, since the JG hordes were unlikely to congregate in one or two geographical locations where they could be sprinkled with bunker busters or neighborhood cluster bombs in the usual fashion. One enterprising congressman suggested, however that, since these "rat people" were genetically altered, science should develop a targeted poison not harmful to real humans that could be systematically added to the nation's water systems and force the vermin out from their holes and into the light to die.

Tom felt the true strength of trauma's grip on the nation was most evident in the sudden disappearance from broadcast of all but the most sanitized images from the Oneida catastrophe. The networks and cable channels instead built their JunkGen logos and graphic art around the less troubling images of children in the orange zone. Purple eyes; enlarged yet aesthetically inoffensive foreheads and skulls. A pretty little girl doll's mouth combined with a gnarled shoulder. These were doable, perhaps with images in the background of perfectly exceptional 100-percent natural American children to provide contrast and, of course, a billowing Stars and Stripes, under threat again in the new dark night but always there in the morning.

But if reality was judged unhealthy for viewers, wild speculation and any other conjecture or pronouncement, however outrageous, was fine, as long as it was likely to hold their attention. Experts and pundits, including the serious and knowledgeable, sparred endlessly on TV and talk radio. Anyone else capable of agitating millions in the time and space of a few sound bites seemed to get the same chance. Several became instant stars. Favorites often conflated the R-evolution question with other longstanding hot button ideological issues, with calls for the unshackling of capitalism from regulation while putting science in irons, as well as for producing JunkGen gardeners and day laborers on an industrial scale, including a few battalions to build and police a wall on the southern border. Both the imminence of the end of days and a new dawn for American world dominance were announced. The devout prayed, steeled their flocks for battle with the devil, and advertised Armageddon in the streets. If they could not get at all the JunkGen vermin right away, just about everyone wished to inflict maximum pain and punishment on those they perceived to be *really* responsible for the mess. Upon whose skin the fiery napalm gel should fall or for whom the water cure should be prescribed was a matter of a roaring debate unlikely to be settled soon. Folks would nonetheless stay tuned.

Eva reached for another slice of pizza. In the six weeks since Oneida, she had lost her raccoon look and her nose has been reset to good effect. "They love it when you dis them," she said, nodding toward the TV. Tom was on screen, standing on the courthouse steps and answering the question that no one tired of asking: how dangerous, really, were these JunkGen suspects? "No more dangerous, Harry, than the folks who sell crack in Queens or peddle swaps on Wall Street." Eva ruffled his hair. "Mean of you! Naming the other network's reporter in the middle of the bite!"

Tom was tired of feeding the media beast. He had cooperated fully at first in an attempt to get the story out half straight. Interminable calls, daily street ambushes, as well as regular DA office media briefings. But he had his old job back, with much greater responsibilities, and couldn't afford to waste the time.

The New York Bar was sitting on the cases for his and Will's disbarment, "given the extraordinary circumstances pertaining now and at the time of the complaint." It stunk to high heaven but it was clear that the normal rules had been at least temporarily suspended. Within a week of Oneida, Rubenstein had made Tom the head of the team putting together New York County's case against Shivkovski. The DA had been going down with the president's political ship but now Tom was his life jacket. "We busted them!" Rubenstein had crowed daily after Oneida. "By the time the United States cavalry arrived, a New York ADA and a NYPD detective were heading home with the evidence!"

On a practical level, Tom believed that the Feds should handle most of the case, perhaps including the multiple conspiracy to commit murder charges. It was too big, complex and jurisdictionally widespread for New York County to effectively handle. The local statutes, moreover, were vague and out of date where Shivkovski's genetic activities were concerned and the way forward legally murky. But he also worried about Washington's will and motivation. Anyone could tell that the secret Executive Action Force would have suppressed some of the truth from Oneida had it been given half a chance. Perhaps he and Will, with New York County's backing, could keep President Mason honest by setting an aggressive example and pushing him to make the federal investigation and prosecution full and transparent.

The heat was off Tom in other ways, however. Eva said she had "written off the one-night-stand episode." She believed she knew and trusted him "as well as I ever will any man on earth." She said she liked and admired Rachel and had known "deep inside" that he'd have to get her out of his system one way or the other before the two of them could move on.

Eva had also come clean on the full motivation behind her urgent demands to join the Shivkovski posse. Tom had renamed her "Spot" after Oneida but had warned that he might have to rebreak her nose unless she explained "the secret agent stuff." Yes, she said, she had indeed undertaken "quasi-intelligence secondments" overseas in the past and had worked with Defense and the FBI at home, as well as with State. But she said she had picked up the assignment by accident only two weeks before Oneida when she first checked on Shivkovski "with several agencies" in Washington. "They were interested in GreenGene and saw how conveniently well I was placed. I figured that backup couldn't hurt us and might actually be needed. It helped that these folks asked no questions and weren't worried about us crossing the line." When Tom had readily acknowledged that it had worked out for the best, she said: "That's whole story, except for a few wrinkles that I can't reveal right now but will tell you about soon. Just know that I will never lie to you again. From this day forward, Uncle Sam's on second fiddle."

Documents seized at the institute had lifted another great weight from Tom's shoulders—the one Leon had tried to dump there only days before the event. They showed conclusively that neither his father nor anyone else had tampered with Tom's genes. Instead, he had been the central figure of an entirely natural born "control group" against whom the first of the JunkGen children had been measured over time. "Daluskov One of Us!" announced *The New York World*. This was important to more than just his sense of well-being. It freed him to help lead the way in confronting the huge legal, moral and political issues that R-evolution and the emergence of the Junk Generation had raised for his country and humankind.

After Tom stopped taking their calls, the media went ahead without him. He figured in three more *Newsweek* cover stories and four in *Time* before the TV crews decamped from outside his apartment building. When things grew stale, news editors moved from the hagiographies to the inevitable next step: what's the *real* story on this guy? The incident at Manny's Café was exhumed and reexamined, as were the accusations of excessive force and extrajudicial execution. "Tonight, *Nightline* asks: Does Thomas Daluskov have a vigilante streak? Are we entrusting our hopes and the JunkGen case to someone prone to extralegal action and violence?"

When the same show wanted a fifth booking "to talk strictly about the issues," Tom steered them toward Will. "How about the both of you?" the producer asked.

Will and Tom had shared the media burden unequally at first. Will had appeared on half a dozen newsmagazine covers, five times with Tom and once with the entire crew—Tom and Ray Franklin and the doctored images of paparazzi snaps of Eva and Jason Hunter, who had otherwise managed not to be photographed or interviewed. But Tom had been featured alone on three covers each in *Newsweek* and *Time*. Treatment was more equal on the celebrity TV shows and in the entertainment and scandal weeklies. Both "heroic buddies" were needed to keep the fires burning under rumors of intense jealousy and a possible love triangle, with the ravishing and eminently photogenic Rachel supposedly in play.

Will, like Tom, was sometimes irritated by media demands but also showed considerable willingness to accommodate them. Tom knew it wasn't about ego per se and wondered whether Will had caught the political bug. It also felt a bit like a contest, maybe even a continuation in another form of their friendly if sometimes painful sparring since puberty. Shots via sound bites.

"TV needs you two to butt heads," Eva said. "Then their talking heads can argue about your argument." And Tom and Will had indeed taken up some opposing positions. Tom wanted an immediate crackdown on human genetic research, including jail time for culpable scientists. Will wanted to wait and see. His rationale sounded distinctively Shivkovskian: much of the good that humankind had achieved we owed to the quest for knowledge and to the proper application through experimentation of the know-how thus acquired.

On a one-hour *60 Minutes* special only a couple of days after Oneida, Will had possibly fired the first shot in what would certainly be a long, fierce, multi-front war over JG rights.

"I cannot believe that federal authorities have used physical coercion to force these individuals to provide blood and tissue samples. These people are the victims of a crime, not the perpetrators. Yet the ACLU does nothing. Ordinary Americans do or say nothing. And we know where that can lead. So I'm going to file an injunction in federal court tomorrow morning. We will put an end to it."

In response to the correspondent's question, Tom had disagreed. "I'd have to argue the other side on this one. But I'm glad Will is stepping forward. The survivors must have the best legal representation possible to protect their interests and rights. And especially in times of confusion and stress, we must always keep one eye on the Constitution."

When another interviewer pointed out that Will and Tom were hardly qualified to preach to anyone about abiding by the rule of law, given their actions at the Monkey House and the Oneida Institute, Tom muttered a sheepish defense about hypocrisy in defense of the common good sometimes being a virtue. Double standards notwithstanding, theirs were the voices that anxious Americans wanted to hear — at least judging by the TV ratings. Week after week, they were greeted as fresh yet wise, informed yet politically untainted, the first battle-tested heroes of the R-evolutionary War.

Now Tom switched on CNN to hear what President Mason would say in his latest nightly update. A banner at the bottom of the screen said anti-abortion, anti-JunkGen marchers had clashed with police outside Congress. Four hurt, ten arrested. Fear begat anger.

The President insisted again that there was no cause for panic. "The crimes unearthed at Oneida were horrendous but this was an isolated incident. Tragic but passing. An aberration that must not prejudice us against the science that has given Americans so many advances in medicine and technology."

Tom's eyes lingered on the screen after he turned it off. For the first time since the missing billions mess began, he was sure Mason was lying.

43

The tsunami of evidence seized at Oneida and elsewhere threatened to overwhelm Tom and the New York County DA office at large. Even the Feds were struggling. And they had vast resources to work with, including the new intelligence apparatus under Mason's shadowy Executive Action Force.

This seemed the reason why, in a perverse reversal of form, Washington was sharing. The FBI and Justice passed along every valuable nugget from their own evidentiary mother lode almost as soon as they uncovered it. The territorial Rubenstein, for his part, remained very much in character, feeding the Feds only tidbits well past their due dates.

Although compelling in other ways, the revelations had so far not answered Tom's most urgent question. "How big was Dad's part in all this?" he asked his mother the moment he first saw her after Oneida. "And what the hell was he thinking?"

Tom only partly believed her response—that she did not really know. "His inner motivation and his attempt at moral justification died with him, I suppose," she said. "I know only the general outlines of his scientific rationale." She had proceeded to rehash the worn Gulag theme. Shivkovski and his father as rebels and daring thinkers, the camps as a laboratory for observing every type of personality, perversion and pathology in extremis. A gift from the gods of science—the gods' joke was that the scientists had to dine on maggots too. Years of harsh reality and deep thought led to conclusions that later directed their scientific research and drove their breakthroughs. "They deduced that Pavel's mean streak was as much a genetic inheritance as his bald spot. Cruelty, courage, intelligence, creativity, imagination, wiles, wisdom, stupidity, artlessness, aggression, fearfulness, restraint, calm, anxiety, selfishness, generosity, cupidity, greed, asceticism, willfulness, intractability, obedience, docility, self-denial, pride, shame, cynicism, idealism, empathy, cold-heartedness, forbearance, stamina, fatalism and frailty—they were all genetically governed predispositions."

"Hardly ideal conditions for drawing general conclusions," Tom said.

"They realized that, of course. Genetic predispositions might bear fruit or might not, depending on admittedly complex environmental factors. Nevertheless, Yuri would begin life with good odds of becoming a funny guy while Leonid never had much hope of not growing into the morose pain in the ass he had turned out to be."

"That's how the old man put it?"

"Your father liked to dumb concepts down for Joe Six Pack and try them out on his buddies at O'Reilly's." She wasn't smiling and moved on. "From there, they got the idea that humankind and indeed human history were locked in a genetic prison. The prison walls were made high and impenetrable by the range of genetic instructions that govern or at least generally limit the range of human behavior and human thinking. This was the hard wiring evolved over hundreds of millennia of adaptation and evolution. Later they would call it the hardware of human existence. The software was environment, including culture, in the very broadest sense of the word, and a few other things."

"Not exactly a revolutionary viewpoint," Tom said. "Let's see if I've got it right. The genetic hardware would determine the general urges or range of likely reactions to a situation—fight or flight, for example, or war-war or talk-talk, as Winston Churchill put it. The environment would provide the stimulus and the variant factors. It would also provide past experience and norms, e.g., you grew up in Sparta or you grew up in Athens. Culture, even if partly the product of geography, etc., would determine whether you were taught to fight at the drop of a hat or to try to engage your assailant in Socratic debate. Of course, you could be genetically predisposed to a brawl, like the Spartan-at-heart Athenians who ultimately did Socrates in. Culture would also include your technology and the range of options open to you. For example, you got your ass kicked or suffered massive losses in your last war and were no longer so keen for a fight. Or you hadn't been very blooded in your history, were far more powerful than your rival neighbors, and had been stocking up on spearheads for the last decade. It was time to try them out."

"Something like that. The software generated the colorful varieties of behavior, outcomes and history individuals and groups produced but the root tendencies were genetic."

Tom now remembered how much his father had loved the story of how Charles Darwin from a distant and very different Britain had shared a genetically driven moment of disgust with a native of Terra del Fuego. Their hardwired neurological reaction and facial expressions were identical but not their cultural software. Darwin was disgusted because the South American had touched his meal; the South American was disgusted by what Darwin was eating.

"Your father and Shivkovski recognized the complexities, of course," his mother said, bowing her head slightly. "Depression, for example. He was interested due to my own difficulties but he also thought it a predisposition that might be evolutionarily adaptive. Those who managed not to succumb to it—Abraham Lincoln, for example—were often high achievers. Darwin himself wept endlessly whenever his wife went away on a trip and said his only unmiserable moments were when he was hard at work. Mikhail believed that these people got things done."

Hank had been there and had pitched in. "As I understand it, Mike reckoned tribalism, clan loyalty and the distrust and fear of the Other were all adaptive hardware. What steered the emotion and energy would be environmental, although you often get feedback, where the cultural expression reinforces the stimulus."

"Yes, your father called that the Nuremberg Loop. After the site of Adolf Hitler's orgiastic Nazi rallies. The role played by tribal hardwiring in Nazism and in war overall is not difficult to see, of course. The same primal adaptive urges that are the glue of warm, loving communities also fueled the great slaughters of history. With twists, of course: having fought the Germans, he knew their martial courage but also believed that powerful cultural collectivism and deep fear of recent societal disorder made them civic cowards—to the extent that scores of generals who recognized that the little man with the moustache was dooming their armies and country to destruction would rather watch Germany burn than risk the dishonor of removing him."

"As your mother has explained it," Hank said, "Mikhail also thought that, just as we are prefitted neurologically by evolution to seek out and learn a language, we are hardwired to seek and internalize patterns of understanding and belief in approaching the world and life, be they doctrine, dogma, ideology, myth or homespun philosophy. His Fill-in-the-Blanks Syndrome."

"Right. So we have to have beliefs, ergo beliefs exist, ergo sharing beliefs brings us together or sets groups apart in the same way that blood and skin color and appearance and language do." Tom remembered the tributes to world religions in the Oneida chapel. But the ferocity with which folks held to the creeds of Marx and Lenin and the Klan, not to mention the perfection of the Free Market, showed that true believers were not limited to the spiritual realm.

"That's where the Nuremburg Loop came in," said Hank. "A lot of this behavior was reinforced by another human proclivity that only helps to complicate matters. Playing with ourselves!"

Tom's mother smiled wanly. "Yes, your father and Sigurd believed that a lot of our culture and behavior is the product of a widespread animal habit of manipulating our hard wiring. Pushing our own buttons, so to speak. Apes groom one another, releasing a wash of pleasant, calming neurotransmitters in the brain. Horses alone in a pasture will snort loudly to release neurotransmitters that give them a neurochemical thrill without the presence of actual danger."

"We gossip, sing and dance and listen to music, consume huge amounts of drugs like caffeine and alcohol that affect our brains, engage in highly emotive rituals and experiences from religious ceremonies to football games, frighten ourselves and evoke every other kind of emotional and neurotransmitter response in movie houses and on TV, have non-reproductive sex over the Internet, eat far more than we need to survive and be healthy, give far more of our life to our wage masters than is necessary so we can buy far more than we will ever need. Because all these things rev up our brains and pump chemicals around and give us the feelings of safety, happiness, comfort, satisfaction, smugness, abandon, freedom from care and momentary euphoria that we have addicted ourselves to."

"So an oceanic moment during a religious ceremony or the buzz of a couple of drinks or the ah-hah feeling when the suspense novel plays out are all about us sticking a needle in our arm?"

"Per your Dad and Sigurd Shivkovski? Yes. The same thing the villagers sought when they buried their dead in a mass grave of seashells their people had been tending for hundreds of years. Or when Hank's tone-deaf relatives roar out Oh God, our help in ages past at church. Or when he does that Zen mediation he picked up in Japan. Or when the Roman emperors got their unruly citizens stoned on blood and gore and neurotransmitter explosions in the Coliseum."

"So the Nuremburg rallies not only expressed the hardwired

tribalism but were also addictive." Tom thought for a moment. "Problem is, this is all pretty ordinary stuff, given the emergence of evolutionary psychology. How do we get from here to the old coots totally messing up mankind's future?"

"They regarded mankind's future as already messed up— inevitably, by the default imposed by human nature. Their evidence was the past, from deep history to what they had lived through themselves. The rapid development of the software that expresses our hard wiring was pointing directly at disaster. Stalin and Hitler and Mao and even the Allies' comfort in annihilating civilians in the terror bombing campaigns left them little doubt that the nuclear age would destroy the human race."

"And this R-evolution thing won't?"

"Someone else was going to do it anyway. Nation states. Greedy capitalists. Why not get a head start? That's what I now suspect your father believed. Why not two men who understood and cared about humankind enough to try to make us better?"

"So my testosterone time bomb of a father was trying to make new people who would play nicely together? No wonder we've got a genomic train wreck!"

"You father understood himself. He wrestled with his inner gods and demons. I am sure he knew that he must avoid trying to impose his will on life through these experiments. He understood that the urge to dominate is hardware. He saw it expressed through the software of religion, state bureaucracies, and ideologies like capitalism and communism. He would not have wanted to play that game."

"Are you apologizing for him? Do you in any way support what he did or what Shivkovski has done?"

"I hate what they did and I hate what is being done. Our marriage died because of it, my son. Your father thought I would be satisfied as long as he left you, our child, out of it. But I could not condone what they talked about doing. Instead, like so many in Nazi Germany, I took the coward's route. I suppose I tried to pretend that it wouldn't happen—or, in the end, wasn't happening."

"Is that why he killed himself?"

Dr. Parviati fell silent again and Hank picked up the thread. "We just spoke about domination, Tom, and I'm sure you realize that the instinct to create terror in pursuit of domination is also deeply embedded in animal and human hardware. The witch burner, the Inquisitor, the Impaler, the imagination behind the invention of Hell, the high school bully, the airplanes dropping their bombs on weak countries, the bombers from weak countries threatening to blow up airplanes. Every good dictator or occupying force would smile knowingly at the dominant female chimp that Jane Goodall saw comfort the grieving mother after she had surreptitiously eaten the subordinate's baby.

"The ultimate stick or carrot message," said Tom. "Do what I want, obey me, accept my rule, love me, or I am capable at any moment of killing any one of you or your children. I guess the mother chimp was not to know but to strongly suspect that the dominant female was responsible. Heightens the terror for every mother in the group."

"Mao took it to a new level by having the people themselves torture, starve, and murder their neighbors. They became both the agents of terror and its psychological objects. They terrorized to escape terror and survive. He set quotas—10 per cent of the population, say. He had children terrorize children. He caused the deaths of 30, maybe 40 or 50 million people, and yet died peacefully in bed, still the ruler of China."

Tom's mother spoke softly. "I must admit my own responsibility in all this, my son. Your father knew that I loved him deeply. I was terribly needy in the early years after the war, drawn to his strength and perhaps even to his anger. After abiding with my wishes that you not be tampered with in the least, he needed to reestablish his dominance over me. He wanted me to agree to experimentation with the other eggs we had harvested. We had originally seen this as necessary if I was deliver a child at an advanced age." Her voice was so low now Tom could barely hear. "There were so many!"

"It seems Mike would never have used them without your mother's permission," Hank said. "Trying to obtain it, he terrorized her with the threat of the death of someone she loved — himself. The experiment gone bad that killed him was only the latest of dozens, each more wild and reckless that the last. All were aimed at forcing your mother to let him use her eggs."

"It is better that he died, Tom," his mother said softly, her head bowed. Then she looked her son in the eye. "If he had not, the terrible calamity we face now would actually be much worse."

44

Each day fresh facts—and surprises—emerged regarding the new national obsession of who was JunkGen and who was not.

The wannabe L Team Spartans, for instance, turned out to have been 100% natural-born Americans. "A control group like me," Tom told Eva as he read the daily evidence summary from Washington. He felt a stab of remorse at the deaths. They were also Shivkovski's victims, after all, including the one who had been spared due to Eva's intervention—and who had apparently later escaped in the confusion. "Their behavioral patterns were largely determined by environment and cultural influence," the summary said. "Aggressive sensory seekers, low startle response, predicted large body types may have been culled from the larger sample natural group of adoptive/orphaned/hijacked in vitro infants for the experiment. Raised according to deeply researched interpretation of ancient Spartan mores and education systems."

They were trained from age 12 "to disdain comfort, weakness and to honor strength, hardiness, stoicism, resistance to pain, self-reliance, courage and martial ruthlessness. Theft, scavenging, extortion were required daily to meet subsistence needs. Beyond this encouraged learning behavior, the L Team observed a ban on dangerous interference with the rest of the Institute population until late adolescence when they drifted out of control. Ultimately, the beatings and humiliation they endured in years of a constant losing struggle with the genetically modified rival 'Spartan' cohort pushed them over the edge."

Tom and the others were obviously fortunate not to have faced the synthetic hard men. The JunkGen Spartans, a.k.a. Similars, had always been "more than capable of killing" the L Team, according to Institute documents. But they had "maintained remarkable discipline for many years by limiting their victories to vicious but non-fatal thrashings." Now they were out there—in the wind, so to speak—20 to 30 soldiers whose full skills, capabilities, tools and intentions were unknown.

Just who had originally designed the experiment remained unclear. But documents showed that Leon had volunteered to help "straighten the L Team out" when the teenagers began to act out two to three years earlier. They were scrappy, however, and hard to pin down. Records indicated that no one beyond Leon knew that they had stumbled during their foraging on a way to get in and out of the Institute undetected, although they had managed to keep the existence of the Hunter–Stricks' Cave secret even from him. They began using their frequent illicit furloughs to explore the outside world. That explained the outbreak of moonlight barbecues involving thousands of dollars' worth of Oneida County prime livestock. It was Leon who had put an end to the nighttime raids.

"He knew they were on the loose," said Eva when she read the summary. "Do you think Leon sent them after you?"

"Too linear for Leon. If it wasn't Byzantine, it wasn't fun, but you'd need to find the worm hole to his other dimension to figure it all out. Those Rangers ticket stubs they found on the bodies? What was that all about? Maybe he just told them I was dissing the great Spartan way of life and left it up to them—kill him if you want or just beat him at Shots." He had recently told Eva about his childhood tormenting of the younger Shivkovski.

"You're probably right," she said. "And they gunned down the chimps on their own. Simply because they could. The animals weren't covered by whatever protocol protected the Institute's human subjects from serious harm at their hands. They could finally go all the way."

The infant corpses were also explained. The non-JunkGen L Team members, according to recent Institute records, "continue to hunger after ritual. Through it, they soothe their suffering from the Similars and try to endure. They clandestinely obtained a copy of unexpurgated Spartan history. Source, unknown." An overnight burglary at the Utopia Second-Hand Bookstore, Tom guessed. "They now taunt their Sparta House betters with claims that a strict hierarchical system is bound for collapse."

Fascination with all things Spartan also led to the theft of infant cadavers from the morgue. The L-Team had read of Spartan eugenics—the abandonment of the newborn weak on the cliffs to die. It comforted them to emulate this practice, even if only symbolically, in their secret cave.

"They were at the end of their ropes," Eva said as they read.

"Yeah," Tom said. "Just another bunch of poor harmless screwed up humans looking for something to believe in."

45

Gerald was pleased. The Boss's first visit. He was sitting there, right in the middle of the kitchen! And full of praise! "Good job, Gerald," he had said not a minute earlier. "There's no other way to put it. Good work!"

Gerald blushed. It was hard to think straight after such praise. Even a small compliment could push the Big A back into its cage for weeks at a time and this was much more than that.

"Nevertheless," — ooops, here it comes, Gerald thought, preparing for a kick in the gut — "we're still shooting for that final touch: perfection."

Gerald was starting to feel that the Boss sometimes asked for too much and returned too little. Gerald had just performed faultlessly on an exceptionally tricky job. That wasn't perfection? He got you high and then shot you down. What briefly seemed glorious unlimited approval then felt more like a passing, patronizing pat on the head. His dismay changed to curiosity, however, as the Boss savored his freshly steeped cup of tea — brewed from the best leaves, not some lousy bag. Gerald detected a very slight tremor in the Boss's hand. And the Boss seemed edgy, almost as if he was wrestling with the Big A himself!

"I have some extra special assignments for you," the Boss said. He put three envelopes down on the freshly ironed tablecloth. "They're numbered and dated. The dates are only targets. Give yourself leeway, a few days, even a few weeks on the last two. But the first must happen exactly as directed. It's a bit of a challenge!" He smiled malignantly and slid the envelope across the table. "What do you think?".

A challenge, Gerald thought disdainfully. You want a challenge? Try balancing a little girl on a chessboard in the bushes in Central Park with a cloth belt noose around her neck! But he picked up the envelope as the Boss continued: "A last hurrah, so to speak. Rounds things out nicely, don't you think?"

"It's funny," Gerald found himself saying once he'd read the note. This smiling was something new. In fact, it was only one of several new things in his life in the last month. He felt compelled to add, "and I'm beginning to enjoy funny things."

The Boss raised his eyebrows in his please-tell-someone-who-cares way. "Yes, Gerald, you're becoming a real all-around guy. Growing is the term they use, though in the case of most people it amounts to becoming an even bigger zero."

Gerald grinned again. Funny! His smile died quickly because the Boss's gaze had fallen upon the kitchen sink.

"Is all well, Gerald?" the Boss asked with false solicitude. "No aches or pains? Happy in your work?"

Gerald's chest tightened as the Big A rose up and took command. Yet somehow it seemed not as powerful as usual. Gerald was nodding at the Boss, demonstrating his compliance, submission, subservience, and utter dependability. But for the first time ever, he was also resenting it a tiny bit. And then he was suddenly wondering: why must I always debase myself in this way when I have never–NEVER EVER–done less than was asked and have often DONE MUCH MORE? And now suddenly words were blurting from his mouth, pretty much unbidden.

"Sometimes I wonder why I have to be the Kitchen Sink Killer. Isn't there another job for me? When I read the newspapers—"

"Then don't read the goddam newspapers!" With curled fingers, the Boss made two quotations marks in the air. "You are not the 'Kitchen Sink Killer.' That's a name dreamed up by a bloody newspaper editor It alliterates, it seeks to corral chaos, it projects the use of the mundane for works that are marketably horrible, it stacks conveniently in three decks of headline type."

The Boss's long elegant fingers were now pressed tips to tips, constructing a steeple of imperious patience. "Think clearly now, please. You and I know that it is all far, far more complex than that, don't we? Would the people you know out there be capable of understanding what is happening here? I mean, seriously!"

The Boss cast another sidelong glance at the sink, more narrow-eyed this time. He said with affection: "Dear Gerald, that is why you are so absolutely marvelous. Who else could do the job you do?"

Gerald felt an explosion of pride blow away all doubt. The Big A beat a retreat.

"Shit happens." The Boss was chuckling but his eyes were scanning rapidly over Gerald's teeming yet tidy tool shelves. "In life, you must have the good and the bad. But someone has to *make* it happen, right? And that's hard, demanding work, not for the lily-livered, or the weak-kneed, or the mediocre."

Gerald felt his childish resentment giving way to his sense of duty and respect. The Boss had a job to do too. Lots of people woke up in the morning with life's heavy boot on their chests. But you didn't hear them complaining. They didn't ask why it has to be this way? Or whine, "why me?"

"The dignity of hard work," the Boss was saying. "Serving the community. Getting your hands dirty. Doing something that someone has to do but most people won't. Attention to detail. Perseverance. Pride in a job well done afterwards. Small bits of all these things are what make up the whole of our existence. They're the meaning and our reward. That and the fact that we are privileged to understand part of the grand design and things that the multitudes will never guess at." He drained his tea. No comment on it whatsoever. Not even thank-you. But what could Gerald do? The Boss was the Boss and he was what he was.

Yet as he prepared got up to leave, a tick of some sort seized the right side of the Boss's face. "You'll be surprised by this new work," he said with a quaver as his fingers rose to his cheek. "It will please you, I think, especially the first job." Gerald's own hand froze on the door knob. He was stunned. The Boss looked faint and, for the first time that Gerald had ever seen, distraught.

"Don't feel oppressed," the Boss said, seeming to recover himself. "You lack a little confidence—that's just the way you're put together. But let me assure you that I greatly envy you a good number of your qualities. Especially your doggedness and your disdain and complete disregard for the extraneous. You just do it and it's fucking finished! Forgotten! Now if I had some of the advantages you have been given—." He stopped, turned and looked around the room. From floor to ceiling, shelves displayed the artifacts of brief intense moments that had touched—and had often ended—lives in every social and geographic corner of New York City. "Well, people wouldn't bitch so much about what we're doing if they truly knew the randomness of it all. In fact, half of them would slit their own throats."

The Boss tried but failed at a smile. Gerald struggled with a tumble of responses. Disdain, for one. To see the all-powerful and all-knowing Boss practically blub before his eyes was pathetic. And apprehension. If the Boss was losing it, what did that say about everything else?

And yet—and this was also new—this embryonic contempt was softened by a kind of sympathy. And relief. And . . . warmth. The Boss was showing him something here, giving out signals. And Gerald had been thinking lately that maybe he should have a friend. That thinking was turning to feeling now in the doorway and Gerald could see how it could soon become a need.

"Do I get to see you again soon, Boss?" he asked as casually as he could.

"Oh, you will see me soon, Gerald. Very definitely." Gerald jumped a bit as the Boss touched him on the shoulder. "You'll see me, big time!"

"I'd like that, Boss."

"You would, would you? A lot of people would find that strange." The Boss was gathering himself emotionally, it seemed. He set his narrow shoulders, as if trying to shake this episode off. "It's good that you understand that we all have our bosses. Even me." He examined his watch. "Of course my boss doesn't know that he's my boss and yours. It's just that he thinks he's a god so I decided to make him one. So you see, there really may be a pattern to all this unknowing we live with." Gerald watched closely. It seemed that his superior was now beginning to ramble.

"In any case . . . in any case, let us now—" the Boss screamed the final words—"TALK ABOUT THE GODDAM PLATE!"

Gerald froze. He'd forgotten! How could he have forgotten? He had known in advance that the Boss was coming—and yet! It was almost as if some subordinate within him had risen up and overruled his natural habit and will! Gerald tried to speak but his lips wouldn't move. After all, how could he possibly explain it?

"That fucking plate, Gerald!" the Boss bellowed, pointing to the awful evidence where it lay unwashed and unstowed by the kitchen sink. "What the hell has got into you? This has never, ever happened before! There was some sort of awful crap on it—roach eggs or rat shit, or something."

"Apple seeds." Gerald was surprised that he found a voice, but there was something reassuring in the Boss's demeanor that provided hope.

"Holy smoke! He eats the cores. What a guy! But it won t be good enough for us until you cop the seeds as well!"

The Boss was grinning at him! He was joshing! A joke!

"I know it's time for me to lie down and die when I see a dirty plate in Gerald's Martha Stewart kitchen," he continued.

"But I have to know that it's a onetime thing, Gerry. Or maybe you were just pulling my leg, right, trying out your new funny bone? It's not real backsliding, is it? Mid-life crisis?"

"No," was all Gerald could get out past his own gigantic smile.

"Good, because I'm counting on you. The next thing will be tough but I need you to come through for me on this. The script has to be perfect, whatever the distractions."

Gerald had never felt more sure of himself. "You can count on me, Boss," he said solemnly. An unfamiliar yet pleasurable physical sensation slipped into the hole where the Big A so often resided. This talking and horsing around had something going for it.

As the Boss was leaving, he turned and said: "On the last thing, the finishing touch we talked about, I leave that entirely in your hands."

"Be creative, right?"

"No, not just the how but the actual decision. Do it, or don't do it. It's entirely up to you. A lot of life is about free choice, you know. And next time you see me, don't call me Boss."

"Okay Bo—okay, but what should I call you then?"

"Leon," the Boss said as he went out the door. "Call me Leon."

46

Tom was on the phone with Rachel when Detective Ray Franklin arrived and plunked a filing carton on one of the overflowing desks. The two had barely talked since Oneida. Tom was working 24/7 on the JunkGen case, Ray on the Kitchen Sink Killer task force, of which he was now in charge. Despite some squealing from the media, his disciplinary charges were on hold, vigilantism being at least temporarily in vogue and the killer having kept busy throughout the JunkGen uproar.

Tom's more immediate concern was the tense, flat tone of Rachel's voice. She had called to say she was "mortified" that Tom's would-be assassins had used her name to lure him out of O'Reilly's. She had also asked: "Aren't you going to interrogate me about the institute and all the rest of it?" She had not laughed when he said she'd have to wait for his 4 am knock.

"Are you all right, Rachel?"

"I'm sorry that it had to come to this." Her voice remained unusually small. "Will dropped by last night for a very long talk. I'm trying to put it all in perspective. It's not easy. But I can promise you that I had no idea it had gone this far."

As he put down the phone, Tom noted that her mention of Will's privileged proximity, which would have tied his guts in knots not long ago, now evoked virtually no response at all. So much for constancy in human emotions.

Ray sat down next to Eva and pointed at the new carton. *Not more documents!* Tom's office was overwhelmed already, which was one reason, along with her liaison duties for the White House EAF, that Eva was helping out. The Feds continued to do the bulk of the work, including DNA examination on the remains of all those killed at Oneida. Until Will's injunction put a temporary stop to the process, Washington had also provided the genetic results from analysis of the DNA of the JunkGen survivors.

These children, teens and adults were now in "protective custody" at three U.S. counter-biological warfare bases that had been adapted to accommodate them. "Prisoners," Will contended. Their status and pretty much everything else about them remained shrouded in secrecy. Initial testing had shown that all of the individuals at the Oneida Foundation, including the adult teachers, nurses, doctors and researchers, had been genetically modified either before birth or in somatic treatments. The later interventions had likely been efforts to cure various diseases or prevent onset when hereditary risk was high. That had helped explain the silence and loyalty of the Foundation staff. Most owed their lives or the lives of their children or other family members to Shivkovski's research and to successful genetic treatment that was in many cases ongoing.

Ray got up and brought the box to Tom's desk. "Bingo," he said. "Jason found it in the cache he left in a neighbor's barn. It's got another set of your original papers—but don't worry, you're still an NBA." NBA was the new shorthand for natural-born American. "But there are surprises about some other people."

Tom reached for the box and began skimming. The first file established that Leon Shivkovski, weirdo par excellence, was a natural too. Not that surprising. It merely confirmed that old man Shivkovski loved his own genes too much to toss them into his mixer. But Tom winked at Eva anyway. "Still reckon he's part gunk from old test tubes."

Their chuckling lacked enthusiasm. These records represented the lives of real people. Many terabytes of data had established that Shivkovski had created perhaps tens of thousands of JunkGen Americans over the years. His convenient cover and tool? In vitro treatments at hundreds of fertility clinics across the nation. The parents had not known. Nor had their doctors, who had depended on reputable GreenGene medical lab franchises.

Initially, the covert nature of this program had limited experimentation. Genetic modifications were often modest. Shivkovski had tried to enhance IQ and cognitive ability, boost stature and athleticism, tweak character and personality and moderate predispositions to aggressiveness, introversion, fearlessness and risk-taking.

Frustration over these constraints may have driven him to go underground and to adopt the no-holds-barred hit-and-miss methodology he put to work at the Foundation. The approach proved cruel but efficient and greatly accelerated the learning process. Genetic manipulation formulated, honed, fine-tuned and perfected through the savage trial and error process could then be safely applied in the fertility clinics, where there was no room for glitches, never mind Shivkovski's "lovable dead ends." Quite the contrary. Customers were more than satisfied and business grew exponentially. So, obviously, had the Junk Generation.

Eva was now reading down the day's updated master list of possible or positively identified JunkGen individuals. It continued to expand despite the DNA testing ban as investigators plucked more details from the institute's voluminous and meticulously kept records. For example, Shivkovski's longitudinal follow-up procedures on JunkGen individuals over the decades included school transcripts, IQ and SAT tests, university records, medical data and even IRS files to which the old man had somehow gained access. The public record, including most media reports, was also part of each individual's file.

"Probably got the tax info with this guy's help," Eva said She held up a *Newsweek* cover featuring 2000's top computer hacker. The man's file showed he had been genetically targeted for "numeracy, introversion, sensation-seeking."

Although widely diversified in all other ways, Shivkovski's subjects had one attribute in common: none was average. An improbably large number were doctors or lawyers but they also included a kid who had knocked a rookie-record number of fastballs out National League ballparks.

"Grab some files and read," Eva said one evening when they brought work home. In the first couple of hours, he had perused the records on two female dot-com magnates; five convicted murderers—all second-degree you-looking-at-*me*? types—and several others felons, with fraud and insider trading dominating; decorated cops, male and female, and a fireman who died after emerging in flames with the last of three children he had rescued from a burning Chicago tenement; a pilot whose airliner tumbled into the North Atlantic, with only sounds of a violent struggle in the cockpit to hint at a cause; several musicians, including a top rapper and an astonishingly beautiful classical violinist who had successfully crossed over to country-rock; two Emmy-winning sitcom writers and a scattering of so-far unheralded poets, novelists and painters; as well as what seemed like a busload of prominent academics and activists.

Eva smiled. "Edith Greenwood—recognize the name?"

"You're kidding!" Tom said without looking up. "*The End of Philosophy*, right?" In the past week, Op-Ed pages across the country had been carrying author Greenwood's thesis that moral and political philosophy had been rendered irrelevant by R-evolution. As a foundation, she argued, philosophy required that the basic nature of man remain constant. Many great theories and ideas would now collapse upon shifting sands.

Still, four-fifths of the names in the JunkGen data banks were inconspicuous everyday Americans, though obviously the run of a very different genetic mill.

"There's more, "Ray said now, moving the box on to Tom's desk. "You'd better have a look at these today. Because I'm picking up chatter that says the Feds may shift their approach and make a grab for all our Oneida material. The detective seemed subdued to Tom, even a little apprehensive. "These records here, in this box, cover the Mom and Pop stuff at the beginning. You know, the lab rats. Your friends."

"You might say the Founders, right?" Eva asked Tom softly. She watched him closely.

"What's a founder?" Ray asked.

Tom reached in and grabbed a handful of folders from the box. He said: "In genetics, a Founder might be the first random mutation that survives and moves on into the mainstream, spreading over generations and starting a new branch."

He opened a file, read a bit, set it aside and opened the next. Given the potential repercussions, Tom felt uncomfortable intruding on the lives of these people, many of whom he liked and respected and had played with as a child.

Most of them, Tom now saw, had been modified. He flipped from one file to another but couldn't bring himself to say the names out loud. One renowned psychologist had used him as the go-between during a high school romance. Tom had protected another from the relentless needling of none other than Leon.

"On top of everything else," Tom said, "we've got a hell of a privacy issue here." He pointed to the lists and attachments beside Eva. Lily Cranbrook, Saul Goldstein, Max Poderski and, indeed, half the biotech CEOs in town and a bright array of stars on the faculties of Caltech and MIT were "Group B" JunkGen. Worse, they had already passed their rigged genes on to their children.

The room went quiet for a moment. Curious, Tom looked up. Ray had taken his feet off the desk. His facial muscles tightened. Eva watched them. "I kept these last two separate," Ray said, handing Tom a file. "It's Rachel's."

Tom read the handwriting on the tab: "Rachel Arianna. Group B, Prime SubGroup." He opened the folder. It was empty. He considered the eloquent void, feeling a little hollowed out himself. He didn't really need the details on what Shivkovski had hoped to achieve in manipulating the genes of Rachel Arianna. Merely knowing her said it all.

"We should put a lockdown on all these documents," Tom said quietly. "Until there are some policy decisions, these people need to be protected from the media." He was wondering how much of the happiness and the heartache he had experienced wanting this woman had been ordained by sick games in an old Russian's lab.

Ray held out the final folder. It was blue and thicker than the others.

"This one will blow your socks off," said Will Jefferson from the office doorway. Tom's best friend and the closest thing he had to a brother was smiling broadly. "Read it out loud, Tom. I'd like my new friend Eva to be in on this too. But, afterwards, we really do have to shut things down."

Tom was beginning to get the joke. The label on the folder read: "Group B–SubGroup Prime: William Jefferson." Scribbled beneath was: "Comparison partner in the natural control group— Thomas Daluskov." Tom tried to grin and began reading. The contents explained a lot. Painstaking alterations had been attempted on Will's DNA in germ line to produce "a man of transcendent superiority." Tom tried to mask the grief in his voice with a lousy joke. "Shivkovski struck out big-time on this one!" He now knew that two innocent people he cared about most would be punished for the rest of their lives. And Tom would have to help inflict the pain.

Will moved forward and handed Tom some papers. "Injunctions—just what you'd expect from an *inJunkGen* like me." Tom guessed they would contain motions to suppress the release of any personal information seized at Oneida or elsewhere that endangered the rights and privacy of so-called JunkGen individuals.

Will flicked a feint with his left and followed with a fake right. "Don't take it too hard, partner," he said gently. "I would have told you before, if I could." He turned on his heel. "And it's about time I taught you some constitutional law."

Tom kept his eyes on the file, shaken, pretending to read. When he looked up, Will, jury-rigged junk genes and all, was gone.

47

Eva and Tom came out of the Park at a jog and slowed to a cool-off walk on the last two blocks home. The media encampment was gone. The last stragglers had pulled up stakes from outside Tom's apartment building when the main JunkGen story had shifted to the Supreme Court.

Will and he weren't off the hook yet, however. They'd been invited, along with dozens of other seemingly more qualified experts and petitioners, to present arguments before a special Supreme Court session on the legal and constitutional issues raised by R-evolution. That neither had legal standing to warrant such an honor was tacit acknowledgement of their unique story. They had come to symbolize opposing sides of the Janus-faced R-evolutionary conundrum both biologically and in law.

The Court had pretty much thrown away its rulebook for the special hearings. *The World* called the session "the declaration of a state of Constitutional emergency." The crisis was not only weighing heavily on the creaking structure of American political stability — already strained by the Mason impeachment — it seemed to be spreading a virus of looming menace and calamity around the globe, like some medical pandemic or systemic financial failure. The Russians were suddenly acting out, threatening smaller former Soviet republic members with invasion over trumped up charges of aggression. With no explanation, India had quietly withdrawn its ambassador to Washington. And out of nowhere, magnitude 10 political and social upheaval in the deep impoverished recesses of western China seemed set to unleash chaos on that country's 1.3 billion people.

Barring doomsday, however, Will would be ready for his big day in the big court. He had been relentless and skillful in pitching his JunkGen rights argument on TV, radio, and the Internet. His basic message was, don't be afraid. Look at me! I'm warm, charming and JunkGen too! All will be well as long as Americans have faith in and abide by the Constitution. In support, Rachel had returned to doing Oprah, late night, and the news magazines. She had also wowed a congressional investigation with invocations of a brave but genetically free new world purged of the predispositions to depression, wife beating and overeating.

Not all the debate was polite. Some in Congress called for internment of all JunkGen suspects, mandatory national DNA testing and IDs, and preventive detention of all trained geneticists to head off an apocalyptic stampede by Shivkovski copycats. "Hunt them down before they multiply," read graffiti near one of several killings in Alabama and Texas blamed on mistaken JunkGen paranoia. "JunkGen are children of the devil," one of the nation's best-known Christian evangelist leaders had announced.

While the media had backed off, panic-stricken opponents of R-evolution, not to mention a small army of spin-doctors attached to the Democratic Party, never let Tom alone. They wanted him out there every day countering each and every one of Will's speeches and sound bites.

He had been doing what he could but this morning he and Eva were taking time off. And now as they came through the building's front door, he heard the thumping of a basketball on a landing several floors above them. That had to be Carlos! It was only as he charged up the stairway that he recalled that it was the country's new Public Enemy No. 1 who had dispatched the noble Carlos to the special school for the blind.

"Watch this, Tom," Carlos shouted when he heard Tom's familiar steps on the stairs. He did a crossover, spun and launched himself into a mock dunk jump.

"Wassup, Carlos?" Tom asked, while suddenly realizing for the first time that he wanted to be a father one day. "How was school? Still straight As, I hope."

"Well, Sir, I guess I'm just about unbeatable now—look at this!" Carlos deftly retrieved a soccer ball from his doorstep, flipped it up off his foot and began dribbling both balls, something slipping one between his legs and out the other side.

When Eva applauded, Carlos cradled the balls and, with some contortion, held his palm out for Five, which Eva promptly provided. They stood for a moment, smiling. Tom winked at Eva. "What a kid!" he said. "The world's best blind—"

Carlos interrupted, tilting his small face upwards in the direction of Eva's. "You're even prettier than I thought, Eva," he said. "But *every* girl and *every thing* is prettier than I ever guessed!"

The boy turned his huge bright dark brown eyes toward Tom and took him in.

Carlos could see.

The soaring of Tom's heart overwhelmed his incipient irritation. Wiseacre Shivkovski had thrown him another curve ball. He had made this young boy a pawn but in a way he knew it would be impossible for Tom not to welcome. To make things worse, Carlos threw his arms around Tom's neck, abandoning boyish machismo in favor of his obvious joy. "And you look just right, Tom—I mean, Sir," he said. He held Tom tighter. "Thank you, Sir. Thank you for making me see. Doctor Shivkovski said it was you who made it happen!"

Eva crouched down and put her arms around the boy. "You can see? You can see everything?" she asked.

"20–20," Carlos replied, and wiped a tear from his face before stepping back.

Eva quickly ferreted out the basic information. Another small town Upstate—thank goodness it had not be the Foundation! The school was actually a hospital with only a few patients. When Carlos asked about the futuristic Braille-like reading system he was supposed to learn, Dr. Shivkovski had said, "let's see if we can't do better than that." He told Carlos he lacked certain tissue and nerve connections. The doctors would give him needles to "see if we can make these things grow." First had come some light, and then the world!

Shivkovski's barter skills had been honed in the Gulag, of course, so Tom was not surprised to learn later from Angela Chavez that Carlos's good fortune came with a rider. She had been told that the gains made through the somatic genetic treatment might not last or could even reverse if he did not undergo follow-up treatment. "Maybe you can advise us, Tom," Angela said after fulsome expression of her thanks. "Dr. Shivkovski's lawyers are hinting that the treatment may depend on us helping 'other young people get the same wonderful help.'"

"And how are you supposed to do that?"

"'If the occasion arises,' is the way they put it, we might have to testify in court or even to Congress."

"I think Shivkovski will have other things on his mind for the next while, Angela." The old man continued to amaze. How could this mass murderer possibly imagine that he'd be permitted to pitch R-evolution to the House or Senate? "I suggest you do precisely what you think is best for Carlos. If the courts or the government need to hear from you later, I see nothing to fear in that." The fact, of course, was that Carlos would be a perfect advocate in the witness box or at a congressional microphone. Notwithstanding the evil inherent in Shivkovski's other experiments, the gift of sight to a wonderful young blind boy was clearly an absolute good.

48

Tom had been slow on the uptake all weekend. Eva had suggested twice that he take the Sunday evening flight to Washington with her even though his Supreme Court date was not until Tuesday. There were "people" she'd like him to see. Perhaps this was her segue into unveiling the remaining "wrinkles" in her story. Although curious, he was also busy preparing for the Court. And now Leon had contacted him, demanding what he called "a final match."

Leon wanted them to meet at 11 Monday morning at a West Side address that he would provide only a few minutes before by cellphone. "At this meeting I will answer all the questions your unr-evolutionized brain can frame." The voice was mocking as usual and Leon was apparently undaunted at the likely prospect that he would spend the rest of his life in prison. "After all," he told Tom on the phone," I understand from *The World* and the *Times* that we are both fully documented *naturals*, untainted by our *dads'* genetic deviltry. That sort of makes us brothers!"

Leon more repulsed than angered Tom now but the guy was dangerous and needed to be under lock and key. So when Eva once again asked him to join her on the Sunday evening flight to Washington, he asked whether it could wait until Monday night. She put her hands on her hips. "I see I need to spell it out for you, Daluskov. This is big. This is not only about little old you and me but also much, much larger things. And no, they cannot wait. We're going tonight."

"Consider me airborne." But that meant he could not meet with Leon. Tom could and perhaps should have planned to tip off the tactical squad so that they could grab Leon after he revealed the meeting place. But he still wanted take Leon down himself, albeit less now to inflict punishment personally than out of a feeling of responsibility for perhaps helping make Shivkovski Jr. into the sick maniac he had turned out to be. Plan B became simply to not show up. Let Leon twist and turn. He'd get in touch again and then he would start to pay for all he had done, including the terror he had imposed upon the little girl in Central Park. The fact was that Leon's own neck was in a noose rigged by his constant obsessive need to somehow cause Tom pain. It would be this hatred that would eventually kick the chair out from underneath his feet.

The mood in Washington was somber, even by the miserable standards of recent months. The President would address the nation at 8 Monday evening. Many felt that Mason might, as this morning's *World* had so delicately put it: "GO AWAY!!!"

The President's scattered and battered army of supporters now hoped he could somehow explain the massive misappropriations as a secret expense in a huge covert defense operation against the JunkGen threat. Unfortunately, the horrors of Oneida been not been uncovered by the United States government but by a Russian thug, two defrocked lawyers, a vacationing diplomat, a suspended New York cop, and a dairy farmer. Even if Uncle Sam had led the charge, the likely expenditures would remain a pittance beside the missing funds, now sometimes put at one trillion.

Tom glanced at the *Post* headlines and stayed quiet when their government driver delivered them not to the State Department on Monday morning but to the Pentagon. As they passed through security and strode rapidly down long hallways, Eva grew pale. When he touched her arm, Tom felt her trembling. "Give me a minute," she whispered. "This is hard. Just give me one more minute."

They also seemed to be attracting attention. Up ahead, a tall, black man in a naval uniform emerged from a doorway and stopped dead in his tracks when he saw them. A much smaller man in civilian clothing who followed did the same before the two turned on their heels and walked hurriedly away.

Tom feet stopped moving, and then he broke into a run. "Hey come back here!" he shouted. "Get the hell back here, Mathew!"

It was Mathew Agneau who stopped and, after a pause, turned and raised a half-hearted wave. This was followed by Eva's own half shout down the crowded corridor. "Matthew! Vic! Come meet Tom."

As the two men approached, Tom's mind scrambled to piece together a new narrative from the shrapnel of the old, because what had been a reality at the core of his many life changes during the past year or so had just been blown apart before his eyes. Here was Matthew Agneau, very much alive. Ergo, he had not been murdered with great gore and fanfare in a mugging beneath the NASDAQ ticker in Times Square.

Eva snapped out the introductions, her face taut and ivory white. "I am sure you recall Matthew, Tom. He is now with DND although his exact position is classified. And this is Commander Victor Brown, an old friend and one of those Navy SEALs I used to hang with. You will not have seen him before but he has been described to you as a large, violent man carrying an equally large carving knife and having a deep scar on his chin."

The scar was gone, of course, and like the knife and the blood and the mugging itself had been part of the artifice and street theater that day. "Should I try to deck you for Eva's black eye, Commander," Tom asked Matthew Agneau's 'murderer.' "Because I know at least that part was real."

Brown offered his hand and a smile. "You're welcome to give it a try, counselor," he said. "But I guess you know Eva well enough now to understand that she does nothing half way and is always ready to take one for the team." The commander seemed unhappy about the way that had come out and he added: "Allow me to say how much we appreciate all you've done and, on a personal level especially, for making our close friend and comrade here so happy."

"Yes, thank you for everything, Tom," Matthew Agneau said as Tom shook the officer's hand. "I apologize for the deception but I'm sure you realize that it was all for the good of our country." He glanced uneasily at Eva's discomfort and caught Brown's eye. "Meantime, I'm sure you have a lot to talk about, and the two of us have a meeting."

"Come here please, Tom," said Eva quietly as they walked away. She led him into an empty conference room and sat in the chair beside him. He felt surprised but was also, surprisingly, relieved. It would be good—for him *and* for Eva—to have it all laid out. Her obvious distress when they'd entered the building had troubled him deeply. It was the first time he had seen her deathly afraid. He covered her hand with his. "You must know how much I love you," she said, finally meeting his eyes." He said: "I do, and we're good, but let's have the whole story now, wrinkles and all. What's the rest, besides Matt Agneau not being dead?"

"Matthew was on our team," she said. "He came to us about the Shivkovskis quite a bit before the staged mugging. We recruited him."

"You were his handler?"

"He responds well to women."

"It seems I do too." Tom smiled. He wondered why he wasn't angry. This obviously meant that their meeting and even the relationship were pre-planned. But he wouldn't ask whether the quick hop into bed was part of the op. Given the stakes, it would be a naïve question and unnecessarily cruel.

"It did start as a job." Eva remained flustered. "I admit that. But that changed for me. Very quickly."

"Was I a target, then?" It was the operation that now fascinated him. After all, it seemed to have been an extraordinary success.

"We saw you as a kind of vector. The Shivkovskis were the targets but when Matthew told us you had such a close but volatile relationship with them, we began to think of you as one of those stripped out virus cells that can penetrate the body's defenses. A rogue missile, given your reputation, which needed some guiding to help us find out what the Shivkovskis were up to. The powerful emotions you stir in both father and son were another potential asset. Matthew said they both seemed to need you in some way. Given the right situation, your natural aggression, your job, and your concern and curiosity over your father's death would steer you right up their stern, so to speak."

"That's it? You knew nothing about Oneida? What about Wally Anderson—a secret agent on weed?"

"We knew nothing about Oneida. And Wally was just a lucky break, for us at least. We knew from Matthew's suspicions that Shivkovski might be playing with the genome. Not a whole lot more than that. But we believed that he would carry out any serious experimentation offshore, probably in India. We just wanted you banging on the cage and messing with the Shivkovskis' heads. We were hoping that would shake new leads and information loose."

"Why a mugging? A hot babe like you! If you needed to connect, why not just pick me up on the subway?"

"The mugging was originally planned just as Leon described it. As an experiment. We hijacked it. Another lucky break. The funny part is that Matthew's JunkGen programming backfired on Shivkovski. He's actually what Shivkovski apparently tried to design him to be—a wonderful man, kind, considerate, deeply law-abiding, loyal to his country, dutiful. In short, a potential whistle-blower. Apparently, a tendency to support the established order has been long recognized as a genetically inheritable quality."

"How much did Mathew know about R-evolution? He's not an insider, obviously."

"That's right. Matthew wasn't told about his JunkGen status—not the way, say, Rachel was." Eva spoke the name without pause or inflection. "He'd been adopted by parents who received financial help from Shivkovski. That's all he knew until a lab rat friend who often preyed on Matt's generosity began spilling information whenever in his cups. When this fellow claimed that Mathew's DNA had been seeded with 'nice-guy genes,' Matthew called the FBI. Things grew from there."

Exploded from there was more like it, Tom thought. A covert department under the White House! The small secret army they had all seen at Oneida? That seemed a whole lot to rest on the slight altruistic shoulders of Matthew Agneau. "You hijacked the show in Times Square?"

"His boozy friend tipped Mathew off. He didn't know the whole story but because Leon used him to hire the actors he had the script. Even though Matthew's character had been tested and re-tested for years, Leon wanted to have some fun. He arranged for Matthew to be in Times Square one evening and to witness a staged mugging. They'd see if Matthew would step in and do his duty as John Q. Citizen. Leon wanted to put Matt's better instincts and his survival instinct up against each other."

"Who came up with the twist?" Tom was smiling at her.

"We wanted to extricate Matthew for more tests and deeper interrogation without tipping the Shivkovskis off." She returned his smile. "And, yes, based on Matthew's information and insights to the Shivkovskis' world, I had identified you as a vector. The mugging would be a chance to pour fuel on your fiery attitude toward the Shivkovskis. We'd get the clues to you when it was time. Leon the secret evil genius behind it; you the prosecutor in love with take-downs. Magic combination, from our point of view. Wally Anderson's death was tragic but also a huge unexpected bonus for the investigation."

"Why me, not Will?"

"First, I'll answer a question you still haven't asked. Sleeping with you was not in the script. It was to be avoided, in fact, but when the time arrived, it just came so naturally to me. Just as it has even since then, and always will."

Tom smiled. He was inclined on a practical level to believe otherwise but the newer mellower him was ready to consider the matter irrelevant, given all that had happened since.

When Tom said nothing, Eva continued: "Will was never seriously considered. He seemed protective of Shivkovski at the time—and perhaps we now know why. He was much less a risk taker. More stable, if you like. You had the short fuse and packed a far greater potential explosive charge. You also had the legal firepower and resources of the DA's office and could be put on the mugging and, through later good fortune, on Wally's GreenGene break-in as well. We made these assignments happen. Langley liked that you were clearly capable on occasion of being a law unto yourself. Know the difference between the FBI and the CIA driving tests? They both ask candidates if they would run a red light at 4 a.m. when no traffic was around. FBI rejects the ones that would; CIA rejects the ones that wouldn't."

"How did Matthew end up undead?" Tom thought for an instant and answered his own question. "Fleet Week!" he said. "The Navy was in town and they have that joint civil disaster operation every year with the city." He remembered Ray complaining that Agneau had been pronounced dead and taken away by Navy paramedics operating an ambulance as part of Fleet Week civil emergency exercises. They had not followed proper homicide procedures, had not waited at the scene for the ME, as was required, and did not know that a police officer, preferably one from the scene, should be present at the autopsy, which was supposedly conducted in a ship-board morgue. Like the death, the post-mortem had obviously been faked.

"Ketchup and rubber knives, okay," Tom said. "but half the Sixth Fleet? Seems a huge effort. You sure you didn't know about Oneida or of anything on that scale? I'm wondering whether we could have saved three thousand lives."

"I think not, Tom," Eva said sadly. "Luck and Leon's timing helped. It happened to be Fleet Week so it was easy to use a SEAL team to pose as the ambulance crew. We had only short notice and skimpy intel on the Shivkovskis at the time. In fact, until almost the end, the Shivkovski operation was a fishing trip, even though we caught Moby Dick. And I'm afraid we are in a kind of war here, Tom. Casualties are a given." She smiled at Tom and took his hand in hers. "But at least one good thing has come out of it."

"I agree. You and me."

She moved his hand and held his palm against her abdomen. "You and me and our daughter or son."

Tom hadn't seen that coming, either, and the Pentagon seemed a strange place to be feeling the way he used to feel to when Rachel touched him or he saw his mother emerge from a dark period and begin to laugh. They managed a clumsy kiss on the conference room chairs. Tom's cell rang but he ignored it. Eva wore a look of silly happiness and she let him hold her for a minute before looking at her watch.

"Wish we could savor the moment but there's more to do. It's fortunate in a way that we ran into Matt and the commander like that because we would be running behind if we had seen them, as scheduled, after I told you the rest of the story."

"So everything's on the table? No more wrinkles to iron out?"

"Not everything exactly," Eva said, "but the rest of it has nothing to do with me." She stood up. "We have to get going. You've got a very important meeting at 1100 hours."

On the way to the White House, Tom decided to switch off his surprise button and just go with the flow. He guessed he was about to connect with someone on the EAF staff. Eva was on her own phone as they moved through the capital and he saw on his Blackberry that Leon had texted him the address for their West Side meeting, along with a phone number to call when he got to the front door. He dialed. The man who answered seemed to be expecting him, addressed him by name, gave him a room number, and said he would "buzz him in." When Tom wanted to speak to Leon, the man said he was not available and asked where Tom was. The minion had sounded irritated when told he was in Washington and needed to set up a new appointment. "I will pass the message on, Mr. Daluskov, but I doubt the Boss will be available after today." He then hung up.

Tom figured it was just as well he hadn't sent an arrest team to the meeting address. Leon might not have been there after all. Another lame opening gambit. But Tom was sure to hear from him soon. And then he'd devise a final reckoning, featuring a surprise appearance by Mathew Agneau. Tom smiled, imaging the look on Leon's face. They would see who felt like the guinea pig then.

49

Gerald arrived at the West Side address on time and on task. It was 10:30 a.m. The key fit perfectly and after ascending the rear stairway, he knocked on the door of the assigned apartment. It opened immediately. The Boss, who now wished to be called Leon, stood there for a moment, saying nothing. He looked upset, however, which sent a spike of anxiety through Gerald's body.

Leon turned and took a seat in an antique maple rocking chair.

"Proceed," he said in a tight voice.

Gerald felt his eyes widen. He was surprised again. He looked around. No one else here. He thought for a moment, focusing on the back of the Boss's smallish close-cropped head. A warm syrupy feeling began to flood through him, overwhelming the Big A. So, he thought, with awe and a certain flush of pride, the dispensation of good and evil *really is* indiscriminate.

Gerald moved around to face the Boss. He gripped Leon's eyeglasses with a finger and thumb, exactly as his instructions stipulated, and ripped them off. His hands grasped the back and sides of the rocking chair. He leaned over and shouted "you're a fucking monster, Leon!" several times into Leon's wide-eyed face. He slapped the Boss hard with the tips of his fingers, leaving an angry red spot on Leon's cheek.

The files he'd been told to bring were in a white WHUPASS kit bag the Boss had provided, along with two bamboo sticks. Gerald opened a folder, fingered the typewritten top page and shouted again.

"It says here, Leon, that you made a clone of Rachel way back in 1987!" Gerald had needed to rehearse this part exhaustively because the Boss had told him that the accusation was untrue—he had indeed "captured" some of this Rachel's DNA but only recently and for "research purposes" alone. So this demanded real acting, which Gerald intended to deliver. "She'd be a teenager today," he screamed. "Where is she? What are you doing to her, you pervert?"

"There are two answers to that question," the Boss replied in a strained voice. "The first is: everything *I* want. And everything *she* wants too. And believe me, Tom, she's indefatigable—just like her namesake. Have to pass her around; she's simply too much work."

This really wasn't good enough, Gerald thought. If the Boss was hoping to battle the Big A, he'd have to do a better job. His performance sucked. The words were defiant but his voice was shaky. He looked like he was going to cry.

As directed, Gerald now used the file folder to smack Leon robustly about the head. He stepped to one side and bounced a hard punch off the small bump that was Leon's shoulder muscle. Not too hard but hard enough to see the Boss wince.

"Tell you what," Gerald said with the inflection he'd copied from the TV appearances by Thomas Daluskov that he had recorded, "you keep giving answers and I'll keep delivering shots. Until I hear the right response." The Boss said he need not worry about the voice itself, which indeed was very similar to that of the famous ADA. There were parts of Gerald's face that looked like Daluskov too.

"The second answer is that there is no clone." The Boss was barely audible. "It's all an invention, part of our little game of life as chess. No clone, no abuse, no affront to the Her Holiness Rachel, no excuse for you to come here to assault and torture me. No more Mr. Superhero."

"Don't count on it." Gerald hit the Boss again, a little harder. Leon's small hand flew to his shoulder. This wasn't part of the script. But had not the Boss told him to be creative? "Who's going to care what I do to you?" Gerald–Daluskov asked. "It can never be as painful as what you deserve."

Gerald flinched inwardly, anticipating the Boss's instant correction. But Leon seemed startled, confused. So Gerald hit him again.

"You're not supposed . . . ."

"Give it a rest, Leon," he said, casually landing another shot. He'd heard Daluskov use the phrase to reporters on several occasions. All this TV watching had introduced him to another side of the Boss. Mad scientist and the country's No. 2 most wanted fugitive. The Shivkovskis had pushed Gerald down into the No. 3 spot. But while the elder Shivkovski was accorded a certain grudging status by the media, Gerald noticed that the Kitchen Sink Killer rated a far more respectful tone than did the Boss.

These apparent dents in Leon's omnipotence had come at a

bad time. Leon had revealed that Gerald would undergo some "changes" in the coming months, once a few more assignments were complete. The Big A would recede. He'd feel "more relaxed about himself," and less "obsessive." The words hurt Gerald deeply. He had always done such a good job. Never once had he failed the Boss or flubbed an assignment. And now, because of a single unwashed dinner plate, he was to be gutted of the natural instincts and values that made him what he was. If he was so wonderful before, so perfect at what he did—and that is what Leon had always told him—why change him now? That was the problem with the Boss. No real appreciation. Or consideration. Only a few insincere words once in a while. No effort to make Gerald feel good about himself. Or, really, to help him keep the Big A at bay.

Gerald stared long and hard at the Boss, who was rubbing his shoulder and rocking gently in the chair. He thought: no wonder so many people hate him.

"Gerald," the Boss began tremulously, beginning to get up out of the chair. "Change of plans. We won't go through . . ."

Gerald pushed the smaller man gently back into the rocker. In your dreams! he thought. The Boss knew darn well that once under way, no project was to be stopped—even if that cost Gerald his life! Fail-safe precautions were for fuck-ups. Those were the Boss's own words.

What's more, on this occasion Gerald had been granted power and responsibility he'd never possessed before. These had been bestowed upon him explicitly by the Boss. Gerald recalled the exact words "I want to leave that entirely in your hands" and "do it, don't do it, it's entirely up to you."

"Ger . . . ."

Gerald gave the Boss a couple of hard smacks across the wrists and chest with the bamboo fighting sticks to shut him up, then cast his eye about the room, seeking inspiration. Time was running short.

"So you think you've played me, do you, Leon?" He used the Daluskov voice as he crossed to a small table by the window. He would ad lib now to trim the script for length. "But I'll have the final move and the last laugh. We'll save the taxpayers of New York County a few bucks and take some of the strain off of the garbage disposal system. Just like I did at Manny's Café."

The Boss was silent now but feverishly waving Gerald off and mouthing the words "no Gerald, no, I'm calling it off." What had gotten into him today? Gerald wondered. The Boss was falling apart at the seams.

Gerald lifted the beautiful 15-pound chessboard above his head. The Boss watched, appalled, before briefly becoming his old self. The haughty curl returned to his lips. He whispered disdainfully, "You fool." Gerald hesitated an instant, the Big A ballooning within him at this open disapproval. But there were the old slights to think about, too, and this plan to destroy his nature, maybe even turn him into one of those JunkGen freaks everyone was so upset about. More important, and, in fact, the only important thing, was the job at hand.

"Checkmate," Gerald screamed as he brought the chessboard down on Leon's skull.

When the Boss slumped forward and fell to the floor, Gerald turned him on to his back and messed him up a bit more with the Arnis fighting sticks, making sure they were properly bloodied.

Checking his watch, he also checked for a pulse. None. Whadyaknow! Gerald thought. For the first time today, the Boss had got something right.

The rest was quick and easy. A deliberately sloppy attempt to wipe away fingerprints with tissue from a nearby box. The glasses and several parts of the chair left purposely untouched. A bloody thumb impression on the bottom of the Kleenex box.

Gerald sat and waited for 30 seconds. The phone rang, and he picked it up, ready to buzz Tom Daluskov in.

"Hello."

"May I speak to Leon, please?"

Gerald glanced at the crumpled Leon. "He's unable to come to the phone, Mr. Daluskov, but he is expecting you. Apartment 904. Please come straight up and join him at the chessboard. The apartment door will be open. I'll buzz you in now."

"Problem is, I'm not downstairs. I need to speak to him. I still want our meeting, same conditions, but I'll be out of town for a week." Daluskov paused. "Who am I speaking to?"

"An employee, Sir. He can't come to the phone right now. Can I tell him where you are?"

"Washington. An emergency visit."

Gerald very nearly gagged, nauseated by the gross incompetence of the planning for this day. Bile seeped into his voice when he told Daluskov: "I will pass the message on but I strongly doubt the Boss will be available." He was eyeing his fallen hero with contempt when he then hung up the phone. If this was what you could expect from those who lacked the Big A, he had no wish in the world to join them. If the Boss's "farce" was to work, Tom Daluskov needed to come upon the murder scene at 11 a.m. just after Gerald slipped out the back way and just before the police arrived. Instead, he was hours away in the nation's capital where he likely have several big shots available to provide an iron-clad alibi.

So why had he taken this sloppy, incompetent, ungrateful man so seriously all these years? "Switch me off!" he hissed quietly at the crumpled form on the floor. "You dare to suggest you would switch me off!" Well, that wouldn't be happening now, he thought as he stepped over the body on the way to the door. Whatever else lay in store, it would be the Big A all the way.

50

"Please sit." President John Mason pointed to a large sofa, grabbed a folding chair left over from a recent meeting, and positioned himself directly in front of Tom. Broadcast paraphernalia littered the Oval Office in preparation for the national address scheduled for 8 pm EST. Rolled up in Mason's hand was a sheaf of papers. A red ball pen protruded from the presidential shirt pocket.

"You've got a nice head of political steam going, Tom," Mason said, "but Al Rubenstein and Mayor Santini tell me you're going to let it go to waste." Mason looked and sounded more assured in person than in his recent television appearances. Perhaps something had changed. "Allow me to say that I consider it criminal at this point in America's history for someone with your current standing and view not to hold his nose and get involved in the political process."

Tom opted for silence and a Fifth Amendment smile until Mason's phone rang and the President returned to take the call at his desk. Tom doubted that Mason needed him to run for any office, whether it be dogcatcher or Manhattan DA. More likely, the summons was connected with the special session of the Supreme Court before which Tom and Will were to appear the next day.

Having waved most of its normal procedures in recognition of extraordinary times, the court had been working for several weeks to establish a solid legal and constitutional context within which to consider the JunkGen crisis. This effort was viewed by many as the last best chance to return reason and order to the nation's search for r-evolutionary solutions. But the hearings themselves had become unruly and often veered wildly from matters of law. The risk was that the judiciary would be no more successful in steadying the ship of state than the executive and legislative branches had been. And outside waited the mob.

Up to a million demonstrators were encamped in the capital region—"everyone from Star Trek Nation to Sharpshooters for Christ," quipped one local columnist. So were 30,000 troops, although some feared that would not be enough. Clashes between hardliners had become more frequent and serious.

Will and Tom were not expected to add substantially to the technical debate. Instead, their appearances would stand as closing arguments. "These two men symbolize all that is difficult and painful about this decision," declared *The World* this morning. "It is a choice between two life-long friends, one white and one black, one N.B.A., for Natural Born American, the other a symbol of all that could potentially be good and right about the Junk Generation."

"Regarding tomorrow's Supreme Court arguments," Mason began briskly when he returned. "I want to confirm that you're 'No' to genetic manipulation of the human genome, beyond therapeutic use and disease control. No to JunkGen rights, particularly the right to reproduce? No, no, and no, right down the line?"

"Yes, sir. No right down the line. And I should add that I will also call for the tracking and shutting down of any Oneida-type manipulation out there that we—or should I say, I?—don't know about yet." Had not Eva said that "a lot more" was going on?

"Tom, the country owes you and Eva and Will, Ray, Jason and, of course, Stephan, a tremendous debt. Your parents, as well, and everyone else who helped out. We had no idea how far Shivkovski had gone."

This is getting us nowhere, Tom thought, so he decided to play prosecutor. "I find it hard to believe, Mr. President, that the huge secret security apparatus you've built up didn't know more and couldn't have moved faster."

Mason turned toward the garden just as the sun moved from behind a bank of clouds and light flooded through the south-facing windows. "A beautiful day," he said quietly, "and yet here we are embarking on a frightening and epic long struggle." When he turned back again to Tom, he said: "Good question, Tom, and I'm pleased to say that the time has now arrived when I can finally answer it. We didn't go into Oneida earlier for two reasons. One, we really did underestimate Shivkovski's science and ambitions. Two, and more importantly, we knew that once his story was out, the rest would inevitably follow."

"The rest?"

"Yes, the country will learn the rest tonight." Mason tossed what Tom supposed was the working draft of his speech onto another nearby chair. "I don't want the country, the court, or people like you, who can make a difference, to make a final decision in these matters without all of the facts and full understanding of what is at stake. It's one reason I've asked you here today. After my speech tonight, you'll be one of the few public figures Americans will remain disposed to trust. And, like it or not, my friend, you are now a public figure. Elected by events, recruited by the times and, if I have my way, pressed into duty by his president."

Mason returned to his desk and began what Tom reckoned must be a preview of his 7 p.m. performance. "As you know, Tom, scientific breakthroughs often come in bunches. Solutions to the same challenge can be authored by different people in different places and in different ways all pretty much at the same time. Often, an earlier discovery has made a slew of subsequent breakthroughs virtually inevitable. Scientists all over have sent different boats floating down the same river toward the same Niagara Falls ever since the discovery of DNA. Just as $E=mc^2$ led to the Bomb, the DNA breakthrough made what Wally Anderson called R-evolution certain to happen one day."

Get to the point, Mr. President, Tom thought.

Mason paused and Tom could see that he found it difficult to finally spit the last bit — the long suppressed truth of the matter — out. Then: "The five to twenty thousand genetically modified humans that Shivkovski can be held responsible for are not, repeat *not*, the only specimens of *homo sapiens reformus* on this good planet. Frankly, they were a huge surprise. We never expected that corporate genetic adventurism would move in that direction. Attempts to remake human nature, which, after all, is what drives us to buy things we don't need, seemed highly unlikely from big business."

"Shivkovski is not about the bottom line, perhaps unfortunately," Tom mumbled, trying to take it in — another JunkGen model out there? "Thinks he's a visionary."

"Yes. There are always so many visions out there and so many different motivations at work." He scribbled another note. "The first signs came from India. We were tipped off by one of the thousands of South Asians who have become such a presence in American science and technology. Did you know that there are science colleges in India with standards that match Caltech's and MIT's?"

Tom said he'd learned from the evidence that Shivkovski certainly did.

"We knew all about the back-street cloning. Profit stuff. Straight need and greed. Radical Hindu nationalists became involved. The vision thing again—on the dark side. Tribalism, India-Pakistan. They came at it with aims different from Shivkovski's. Religious aims, culturally attuned to stubborn concepts of reincarnation and the caste system. Should not the offspring of Brahmins be genetically enhanced and those of Untouchables, particularly in a time of political ferment, be genetically shaped to accept and suit their predestined stations in life?"

"How far have they gone?"

"We don't really know yet. Not as far as Shivkovski, we hope. We have strong allies within the Indian government who are determined to close experimentation down."

"Big country."

"Yes. And when you learn that, in southern states with populations in the hundreds of millions, a huge black market exists through which high-tech quacks are guaranteeing a male child, you wonder what may actually be going on in those test tubes." Mason paused. "That's what first got us looking hard at this problem. We recognized the implications immediately. I signed a finding authorizing a full court press by the CIA around the world to find out everything we could. We brought other agencies into the act too. Your fiancée, Eva Martin, was a star in that regard."

Tom considered this a moment. "China?"

The President nodded. "State sponsorship or direct state involvement in genetic manipulation makes the problem strategic and far more grave. Nations, governments, political thinkers have a heavier touch than your average capitalist. China can get things done quickly and in a big way when it sets its mind to it. It remains a centrally run command society and is preparing in every way for the day when it will compete directly with us on the world stage."

Tom filled in a short silence: "They'll do things a democracy won't or can't do."

"I understand that Bill Lee introduced you to kung-fu," Mason said grimly. "When he returned to Shanghai after working with Shivkovski and your father, he taught his Chinese counterparts new moves of a different kind, based on the theory that Shivkovski developed with your father." Bill Lee! Tom thought. That meant the Chinese program was at least 25 years old. "What route the Chinese took from there, we don't know — yet."

Mason picked up a twisted paper clip. "The problem is that once you know how, you can try to manipulate human nature in almost unlimited ways. And each success opens up new possibilities."

Mason said the first signals emerged from Chinese crime statistics. CIA analysts noticed dramatic spikes in spousal homicides in several of the poorest Chinese provinces. "Husbands killing their wives." Mason said. "We're talking increases of six, seven hundred per cent, year on year. When we finally uncovered the Chinese genetic experimentation program, it was all explained. Hardline party and PLA factions had launched a massive genetic experimentation drive in have-not regions. Thousands and then tens of thousands of impoverished women were artificially inseminated without their knowledge in state clinics under the cover of the one-child-per-family program."

"Going for the male child, as in India?"

"Yes, they were told they were being injected vaginally with hormones to make them more fertile and likely to conceive a son. That's how the genetically modified eggs were implanted. Wives and husbands were instructed to step up sex in the month after the so-called treatment. Next thing mom's pregnant, the baby's a boy. Even in back-country China, the best advertising is word of mouth. Business booms at the clinics; a few years later, there's massive new state funding for special schools and gifted children. But unintended consequences as well. Domestic husband-on-wife murder rates rose sharply. The program forgot about trying to at least roughly match the physical typologies of the supposed fathers. When their children showed physical characteristics dramatically different from their own or their families, a lot of the husbands thought they'd been cuckolded."

"How far did they go, say, by a Shivkovski benchmark?"

"Not as far, at first. Going for higher IQ mostly. But this same faction and some hardliners in the military later accepted what we're now calling R-evolution as part of their asymmetrical warfare doctrine. Right now, they know they can't bridge the huge strategic gap in our respective weapons systems in the short term. So their war gamers cook up ways to make our main strength — technology — a weakness. Can't touch the Seventh Fleet?

Forget it! Knock out the Internet instead. Cripple the banking, television, communications systems, power grids, water supply — in short, the economy, and our day-to-day comforts. Long-range, however, they're betting that genetic engineering will be what puts them over the top in the battle for global pre-eminence."

Mason paused and considered his tormented paper clip for an instant. "It's not Chinese national policy yet, but it hasn't been shut down, either. We don't know the full details or the extent but it's safe to say that a branch of Chinese science now under the control of forces inimical to the United States and the world's democracies is trying to create a whole new tier of innate human abilities far superior to, and dangerously different from, those that have been shaped by natural processes since man rose up in Africa."

Tom thought that this part must be straight from his speech.

"Bill Lee gave us the outline," the President said, passing the information through a network that Eva had run out of the Beijing embassy. His "other country," the United States, had to be prepared, as did the rest of humankind. "He had wanted to help China regain its footings and its dignity but also hoped for political reform. Instead, he saw that the genetic enhancement program was spinning out of control and in the hands of hardline totalitarians. He feared for the survival not only of free, open, diverse societies, but also of the kind of human traits they're designed to celebrate."

"Did we get him out?"

"No. He disappeared."

Mason seemed to be waiting for some kind of response — a preliminary one-man test poll of possible reactions to tonight's revelations — but Tom was momentarily silenced by the immensity of the challenge the President had described. Shivkovski's operations had been limited to some extent by space, resources, security considerations, and his own concept of the better man but a R-evolutionary China could pose far greater threats. It contained vast areas and huge populations over which government could exert total control in absolute secrecy. Things had improved dramatically in recent years but government excesses in the service of ideology and radical goals had at times in the past approached the worst humankind had committed anywhere. Backsliding now with a r-evolutionary twist would have a cataclysmic impact. China's twenty million live births a year left room for experimentation on a frightening scale.

"We have to stop them," Tom said. "There's no other choice." When Mason showed no sign of standing on ceremony, he continued. "Expose their R-evolution programs, impose sanctions. Go to the UN. Use force, if necessary."

"We're looking at all those options, of course, and more. We've run all the scenarios over and over again—even war with the People's Republic. But that would inevitably lead to nuclear exchanges. We'd win the best of seven series, or whatever it turned out to be, but the prize would be a world in ashes, including many of our own cities, and most of the rest of mankind awaiting slow death on the next hot wind or extinction in nuclear winter."

"Do nothing and we sign the death warrant for the human species anyway." Tom heard his voice rise. "We will not survive a free-for-all in genomic sciences. After a few generations, there'll be nothing much left of what we are today."

Mason watched him closely and for an instant Tom thought the President might say, "but there will at least be something." Instead, Mason straightened the blotter on the Oval Office desk and spoke in a more upbeat tone. "This is how I'm explaining our thinking and the actions we have taken. A war to stop R-evolution is a war that we just can't win. Abroad, the cure could be worse than the disease. And the victories would likely be temporary in any case. Even at home, eliminating R-evolution or even strict regulation would be problematic and almost certainly unsustainable. Very soon, the technology will become too advanced and widespread to suppress. Now, in principle, there is nothing wrong with using diplomacy and sanctions to try to put a lid on things—say, through an international treaty. But that strategy has a fatal defect. While we talk-talk, to cite Churchill— we can't build-build our own program. The Chinese and everyone else will leave us in their dust."

"What are you proposing?" Tom's tone was now devoid of deference. "Another race to the moon? A competition to see who can grow the Earth's first home-made alien?"

"Tom, imagine that the Soviets or Hitler had developed the atomic bomb before us—would we have been out organizing a nuclear ban treaty or would we have pulled out all the stops and caught up?" Mason didn't wait for an answer. "Although we have often abused or played politics with the responsibility, the fact remains that we Americans are the premier guardians of a democratic way of life on this planet. We, with our democratic allies, cannot afford to be second best in any crucial area of human endeavor. There have been close calls before, 1939–42, in particular, and there will be close calls again."

Tom was starting to see that this was a moot point but he asked anyway: "So is the United States going to get into the R-evolution game itself?"

Mason's brushed several bent paper clips off his desk and into his hand. "As I will be telling the rest of the country tonight, we're already in it." He dumped the paper clips into a trash can. "We have been for some time. That's what this thing tonight and all the other press conferences and the impeachment circus have, are, and will continue to be all about." He gestured toward a TV camera waiting on a dolly. "All the noise. All the smoke and mirrors. Every penny, every billion. All invested in so-called R-evolution. And there will be trillions more."

Tom was speechless.

"The United States has embarked on large secret undertaking to investigate and effect changes in the human genome. Call it a new Manhattan Project, if you like, because the media certainly will. Just as Franklin Roosevelt secretly built the first atomic bomb, we gathered top minds and set them to work to produce the first of what the boys in the lab have dubbed GIAs—Genetically Improved Americans. And we have succeeded."

"Good politics," Tom said dryly. "Now you can tell an anxious people, 'See, we've got some, too.' "

"That would be an ungenerous interpretation of our motives," the President said with a smile. "It also presupposes that I will run for re-election, which, given these circumstances, I will certainly not. No, like many presidents before me, I was forced to do what's the toughest part of this job—make a likely unpopular decision that will have a tremendous long-term effect on all Americans, on behalf of all Americans. I had to do it alone, and without the crystal ball. Strange, I know, but again I refer to Roosevelt, the Democrat. From the start, he knew we belonged in the fight against the Nazis and in the defense of liberal democracy; ninety per cent of Americans opposed him. But with great help from the Japanese, he got us to do the right but hard thing both for us and the rest of the world. He was right. This time? Who knows? But it's on me."

Scenes from Shivkovski's JunkGen menagerie flashed in Tom's mind. He doubted that a government effort would produce fewer mistakes. "What's the monster count, if I may ask, Mr. President?"

"Low. We've been cautious, although we have had one tremendous breakthrough, a universal systemic one. Mindboggling, but we cannot let our competitors know. Please do not mention it in any account of our discussion today." Competitors, Tom thought, not enemies. He guessed this breakthrough would involve accelerated maturation. The military would dominate a government effort and it would want its prototypes up and running as soon as possible, especially if the Chinese and possibly others had had a head start.

"How many, sir."

"Can't say."

"So Shivkovski will join you. He'll be, what? Pardoned?"

"We need him. More importantly, we need his science. His federal plea bargain was arranged after he turned over all of his central records—the entire experimental history from day one. Invaluable! Our people tell me he's come at this thing from an entirely different direction."

"Shivkovski is a mass murderer."

"He's doing life, Tom; it's a small step down. He'd probably never live long enough for us to execute him, in any case. And by helping his adoptive country, he will at least make some restitution for his crime."

"I'll fight this, and so will most Americans."

"No surprise there. This really is too big to leave to the traditional political parties or to professional politicians. No one really trusts us, of course, but they have no real choice and no other voices to listen to." The President touched his jawbone as he referred to an apparent sore spot. "Believe me, every special interest group and every kind of nut case you can imagine will have something to say about it, even within my own party. There are free market zealots, if you can believe it, who want R-evolution *deregulated*, top to bottom. Let the consumer decide! They worship this idea. Shivkovski was right—it's 'fill in the blanks.' We have to believe in something, with the result that we'll believe almost anything—and damn the evidence and the end results."

"You're not running for a second term, sir?" Tom asked

hopefully. The country needed someone else in this office. To repair the damage.

"But I'll be a player, believe you me." The President stood up and came back to the folding chair. The warmth of Mason's smile surprised Tom. Didn't this man know what kind of fight he was in for?

"This is where you and Will Jefferson come in. You can fill a vacuum. You're intelligent, honest men of character. You have the strength of your convictions. These are not attributes easily adapted to political life. But you're also young, good-looking, charismatic, articulate and famous — things that count in politics. We in this country constantly make crucial decisions with real flesh-and-bone repercussions not based on facts but on fantasy, myth and carefully crafted disinformation. You two offer us a special opportunity. And one that's needed in a special time."

"You're happy that I am going to attack your position before the court? Is Will getting the heads up too?"

"He was in this morning. You two will guarantee that the real issues are addressed. I had no other choice but to get the R-evolutionary ball rolling. But now everyone will have to take responsibility for where we go from here. Although I believe that it should not or cannot be done, the option to stop it somehow and restore things to the way they were will be included in the debate. Ten, twenty years from now, no one will be able to say that the other side of the argument — your side — was never brought forward."

"Will and I are wet behind the ears."

"That's show biz — which reminds me —"

Mason glanced at his watch, a sign Tom took to mean that it was time to leave.

"Good luck, Mr. President."

"And to you, Tom. We'll speak again."

Mason called out when Tom was halfway to the door: "We're writing the first chapter of Volume Two of Human History here," he said, without looking up. "If Volume One is any guide, it won't all be pretty."

51

Tom pounded up the Mall in a swift sunrise run, occasionally dodging wind-blown debris. The President's speech last night had unleashed brief but terrible rioting. Eleven dead, hundreds injured; tear gas, rubber bullets, and reports of live rounds confirmed by gunshot wounds at nearby hospitals. Some protesters had brought their children and four were crushed in stampedes. The police and the Pentagon claimed force had prevented even worse mayhem.

Now that the first roar of anger had past, Tom's mind was clear, like the Washington sky that had been washed clean by overnight rains. No one challenged him and a few of the hundreds of troopers securing the Mall and many federal government zones greeted him by name or shouted encouragement, like he was preparing for a big game. "Kick some butt today, Mr. Daluskov, sir!" They were mostly kids and dazed like everyone else.

Tom slowed to a walk at the steps to the portico of the Supreme Court Building. He stood for a moment, recalling his first visit, an educational holiday with his mom and dad, probably the year before his father died.

Tom remembered standing in front of the Court's huge front doors, his father crouched before him, watching his son's face as he spoke. His mother, a little behind, had one hand on Tom's shoulder. She would usually augment and annotate her husband's lecture later, always with the instruction to "think about it and talk to your dad and me again when you have more questions."

Mike Daluskov had spoken at length about the decorative bronze panels in the 17-foot-high doors and the reliefs that adorned the building. "They tell the story of the law," he said, "but they are really about us, men and women, trying through the ages to understand what we are and how to make the best of it."

"All of this," his father had told him, "all the laws, all the religions, all of our cultures and our civilizations are mere expressions of the behaviors and personalities that evolution has served up for us." He had ruffled his son's hair. "The birds have their nests and the ants their hills. And we've got our pyramids and the United States Supreme Court."

If Tom remembered correctly, they had adjourned for ice

cream.

This time, almost three decades later, Tom headed towards some bacon and eggs. In just a few hours, he would be back.

The Court's accommodations to the R-evolution crisis included much longer times for oral arguments. Hundreds of millions around the world would watch on live TV, another first. The Justices needed to be seen to be trying to get it right—even though their final decision would be viewed by a large segment of a deeply divided nation as horribly wrong.

The justices must also be mindful that the last case of similar weight had marked the Court's darkest hour. In Dred Scott, 1857, the majority had legally upheld the concept of slavery. The decision argued that at the time of the Constitution's writing, African-Americans had been considered "a subordinate and inferior class of beings" who were "unfit to associate with the white race" and had "no rights which the white man was bound to respect." That view, the Court ruled, must continue to guide the interpretation of the law and "no change in public opinion . . . should induce the court to give to the words of the Constitution a more liberal construction."

Now, whatever else happened, the justices were certain to project respect for all humans, whatever their race or origins. "The law can still be an ass," a Harvard law professor who had coached Tom for a couple of hours the previous week told him, "but the Court can no longer act in an overtly cruel or evil manner."

The justices had already heard from the best and the brightest, as well as from the loudest and most impassioned. Every conceivable aspect of the legal debate had been covered. The justices had spent an entire weekend in a crash course on genetic engineering and the theories of evolution and human behavior.

Today's finale, the "Tom and Jefferson Show," as *The World* was calling it, would appeal more to hearts than minds.

"A sly maneuver," declared one of the networks' talking heads. "For public consumption the Court is pretending to consider the science and the social and political issues rather than only the law. Then again, maybe it isn't pretending. The perverse logic of Dred Scott was followed by the cataclysmic bloodshed of the Civil War. Ignoring the political implications of this decision won't be any easier. Problem is, they are far more complex and unpredictable."

Tom checked his watch. It was 9:59 a.m. On cue, the gavel sounded and the Marshall's stentorian voice echoed through the chamber. "The Honorable, the Chief Justice and the Associate Justices of the Supreme Court of the United States. Oyez! Oyez! Oyez! All persons having business before the Honorable, the Supreme Court of the United States, are admonished to draw near and give their attention, for the Court is now sitting. God save the United States and this Honorable Court!"

Tom watched the nine enter from behind the towering red drapes, the Chief Justice and two senior associate justices through the center entrance, and the more junior associates though two entryways to the left and the right. Their long raised mahogany table was wing-shaped so that they could more easily see and hear one another. The order in which they sat on each side of the Chief Justice reflected their seniority on the Court. Not that it mattered much, Tom thought. It was one man or woman, one vote.

Tom wasn't greatly concerned by the wide and oft-discussed ideological sweep of the Court. Judging by questions and comments so far, the issue would be decided by a single swing vote. That would be cast by the recently appointed Chief Justice, Howard McMaster. McMaster had a sure hand for fashioning compromise and often unanimity on key decisions. But he was also ready to stand alone. Appointed by Mason, the first African-American Chief Justice had first come to the law after two Marine Corps tours, three wounds and a Silver Star in Vietnam. He combined a love of order and moderation in human affairs with first-hand knowledge of some of the extremes.

Will would open. He would be interrupted repeatedly by the justices. In what might sometimes resemble a free-for-all, they would use their queries and observations to clarify issues and to undermine opposing views and bolster their own. So far it had been a little like the nation's best minds thinking aloud on the foremost issue of the day—or perhaps of the age.

Watching and waiting, Tom could not help wondering how Shivkovski would size up the court. The old man had once contended that most of history's great legal cases were little more than genetic crapshoots.

Judges were people, and people, said Shivkovski, were born

with either liberal or conservative tendencies, based largely on their share of highly heritable traits. Authoritarian, traditionalist temperaments, and people whose genetically written brain chemical "loop" patterns rewarded order and adherence to the rules with chemical hits of contentment and pleasure were more prone to be conservative. Highly social or individualistic personalities, or folks who got high on change, or those rewarded with a warm, fuzzy feeling inside when they helped other people, might be more disposed to the policies of a Franklin Roosevelt.

Looking up, Tom saw Will watching him from across the way. The look on his face—eager, friendly—quickly widened into a grin of complicity. They had never expected to spar in quite this way or at quite this exalted a level. Yet in some ways, it felt like another day at WHUPASS, with gloves freshly laced and license to do combat.

The moment passed. Their smiles faded and they looked away. This wasn't sport. There would be consequences and casualties, and even the chance in the end of terrible catastrophe.

His lectern adjusted, Will got straight to the point.

His argument was carved in stone on the architrave of the Supreme Court building: "Equal Justice Under the Law." He asked the Justices to rule that all members of the so-called Junk Generation, a.k.a. *homo sapiens reformus*, "that is, American citizens like me, whose DNA may have undergone some manipulation before birth," qualify for equal protection under the Fourteenth Amendment of the United States Constitution.

"Those who argue against my right to be different genetically," he said in opening, "should remember that we rigorously defend in our laws the rights of people to be vastly different on the cultural level. All beliefs, including those that are mutually obnoxious to contending segments of society, have protection under the Constitution."

"Yes, yes, Mr. Jefferson," snapped Associate Justice Sarah Cronin. "We get that part, believe me, sir." If the Court had heard or read it before, it would demand something new. And the country's top constitutionalists had been tramping back and forth over this particular legal territory all week.

"Now," Cronin continued, "what about the government's responsibility and right to protect the welfare and safety of its citizens? Eminent experts contend that by passing on your manipulated genes through procreation, the Junk Generation will contaminate the human gene pool. With unknowable consequences. Do we allow that? And let's remember that almost three thousand lives have been extinguished in a horrible act—"

"Of attempted genocide, Your Honor?" Will was pushing it. You did not cut off a Supreme Court justice. But Cronin was a brilliant mind, who in addition to a long human rights record that included 1960s voter registration campaigns in her native South, greatly valued vigorous discussion. She was the least likely of the nine to rap his knuckles. Besides, Tom thought, this was do or die for Will Jefferson's constituency and clients.

"That act," Will continued, "was committed by a man with DNA from the pristine, pre-JunkGen gene pool—untouched by human hands, as it were. He is an immigrant, Russian, possibly a Jew but, who knows, perhaps Orthodox Christian. Do we now remove the rights of immigrants, deport all Russians and deny all those whose parents were born in the Russian Christian Orthodox or Jewish faiths their right to reproduce?"

Will paused and caught the eye of another one of his probable supporters, a onetime American Civil Liberties Union president who sat to Cronin's left in more ways than one. "If we have to decide which of us Americans—the so-called natural-born humans, or the first Junk Generation—are capable of the worst crimes, I'd say *homo sapiens reformus* has got a lot of catching up to do. Limit the evidence to our own country, if you wish. Native Americans and my own ancestors might wonder whether the real threat to the continuing welfare, safety and survival of the species isn't the natural gene set itself."

"Are you saying you're better than us?" asked Justice Ronald Matthews. He sounded indignant but that was probably theatrics, Tom thought. Maxwell Matthews wanted all things decided by the divine oracular wisdom of the marketplace. That made him Will's most solid vote.

"I'm saying," Will replied, "that there is no 'you' and 'us' in this matter. Only we the people. But if freedom were to be allocated only to members of those species that, from past performance, posed no threat to the general welfare, all humans would be under lock and key from birth."

The next question, from Raymond Clements, seemed to surprise the Justice who asked it as much as it did Will. "But at least we're a known quantity, are we not?" Clements, ACLU all the way, boasted a simple lifelong mantra: individual freedoms above, beyond and before all else. Yet his observation couldn't help Will. Tom reckoned that Clements' gut had spoken up in dissent. He was scared of R-evolution, and by showing his fear and appearing ready to abandon his hallowed position, he would make a powerful impression on his fellow jurists.

"Respectfully, sir," Will replied, unfazed and smiling warmly at his erstwhile ally, "crack babies are an unknown quantity too. Not a single JunkGen individual has been convicted of a crime in the United States. Yet we already know that crack babies may have a greater propensity that babies not afflicted in that way for anti-social behavior and criminal and violent acts. Even if this was proven, would or could we limit their rights?"

Will would use reason to guide Clements back to his natural position. "We also know," he continued quietly," that the children of alcoholics, manic-depressives and abusive adults are often unlike children raised in a healthier environment. They face special challenges, pose special problems, and can even present a special threat to social order. Indeed, most children are not like other children. They're bigger, smaller, quieter or more fiercely aggressive, bright and not so smart. Do we determine that they should not play, go to school, grow up, vote, pay taxes, share a full ration of our fresh air or be considered equal in every way to every other citizen? Do we tell people who we can likely reliably predict will be lousy parents not to have children? The schoolyard bully with a two-digit IQ who smacks his girlfriends around, does time for robbery, and will never read a book? No. He can sire six children he'll barely support without fear of the federal courts."

It was Felipe Gonzales' turn. "You're dodging the issue, Mr. Jefferson," he said firmly. Rumor had it that the scars on the former union lawyer's large knuckles had not been earned drafting injunctions. Tom was counting on his vote. Gonzales would suspect that free marketers like Matthews saw R-evolution as a route to cheap, skilled JunkGen labor.

"You're asking us to accept not just you and your JunkGen sisters and brothers," Gonzales said, "but an entire process. This permanent, irreversible process will change many things in the world forever. And in ways we cannot foresee."

"So did agriculture," replied Will, playing the patient man of reason soothing the hysterics. "So did the inventions of writing and of currency." Will went down a list, looking from justice to justice as he did. "And before that, speech, tools and cooking with fire, which some believe let us concentrate nutrients in our diets so that our brains grew much larger and could work harder at devising the new, injudicious and dangerous concepts that other animal species were fortunate to have been spared. Many, no doubt, warned that only disaster could follow the abandonment of human sacrifice. Civilization might have collapsed with the demise of the divine right of kings." Will flashed a smile at the most junior jurist, David Rubin, a cherubic neo-conservative. "In the view of some, I suspect, this in fact remains an open question."

Having got his laugh, Will continued. "The English, American and French revolutions set in motion unprecedented *processes* that we can say were out of control in their time. What about the industrial revolution, a *process* whose immense social upheavals is at work on hundreds of millions of lives even as we speak? Railroads, electricity, highways, air travel, movies, television, the computer. I give you the Pill, gentlemen and ladies. Did it change 'nature?' Did it not set off a *process* that promised unpredictable consequences and whose massive social consequences are still not fully known? Of course it did!"

Will's voice softened. "Times change. We adapt and move forward—usually to a better future. The one constant is our Constitution and the inalienable and perpetual rights it guarantees. One day, quite literally, we'll take them with us to the stars."

"Do I detect a note of defiance, here, Sir?" asked Charles Mansfield. "Do you say that the Court *should not* stop this manifestly evil undertaking, or do you say that it *cannot*?" Associate Justice Mansfield favored the tone and affect of a big tent preacher. He was the Court's most conservative vote on issues pertaining to civil rights or any other kind of privilege that was not dispensed directly by the hand or in the book of his god. He was anti-abortion, anti-divorce, anti-ERA and very much anti the theory of evolution, despite the dramatic additional evidence R-evolution now seemed to have offered.

"Mr. Justice," Will said, bowing slightly under Mansfield's stare. "I am here to plead my position under the great American Constitution that God has provided to help us solve this argument."

Tom smiled to himself. Justice Mansfield had served up a sucker ball for the radical, uppity, black Greak he saw before him, hoping Will would lose his cool and discredit himself and his race, or races. But Will was on his game. He wasn't swinging and while it wouldn't help in the Court, it could disarm a few fence-sitters out in TV land.

"And may I add, your Honors, that I do not believe that all this—this R-evolution—would be happening if the Lord did not intend us to take this next step . . . ."

A tactical lie. Tom knew Will held no such belief. But the suggestion of God's hidden hand would open potential philosophical escape hatches for Creationists and the religious. Probably hurt him with the Court, however. Will pulled up quickly when he noted the Chief Justice's scowl.

"Some practical considerations," he continued in a more business-like tone. "Starting with this problem: It is far more feasible legally to ban the so-called 'process' than it is to limit the rights of the people the process produces. The second is, in fact, impossible under the Constitution."

"I see, I see," said the bulky, gray-haired figure near the far right end of the table. Pensive so far, Justice Henry Jamieson appeared suddenly excited. Jamieson accorded the Constitution almost mystical powers. Given sufficient attention and thought, he believed, it would always deliver an answer to the nation's problems.

"You are offering the solution, are you not, Sir?" he said now. "As always, it lies in a strict observance of our laws. The members of the Junk Generation and all those people who have been produced under the United States government's GIA program are given full protection under the Constitution. But we—or, more probably, the Congress, through new law—will ban all further genetic experimentation of the R-evolution kind in the interests of public safety and welfare. Shut it down. For good."

The loud Georgia drawl of an equally agitated Justice Wallace Crowe interrupted. "Yes," he said, turning to address his fellow jurists, "and, as I understand it, the impact of the few JunkGen and other *homo sapiens reformus* on the human gene pool will be minimal. Through intermarriage, changes will be quickly dispersed. In fact, the more and wider and faster *homo sapiens reformus* reproduces, the better!"

Crowe, who never hid his belief that the Court had a role to play in righting history's and society's wrongs, desperately wanted for the court a way out that was both humane and honorable.

Justice David Rubin pitched in, addressing not Will but the eight colleagues to his left. The Court was going intramural again. "One moment, please. We have not yet decided whether these creatures are suited to equal treatment. I, for one, am not convinced."

"Let's discuss equal treatment." Will spoke in a loud, calm voice, drawing the focus back to his lectern. "Take me, for example," he continued more softly after an instant of quiet. "Perhaps one ten-thousandth of my DNA has been altered. Does that make me 1/10,000th less human than any of you? And if you are prepared to say it does, am I to be accorded no human rights whatsoever? Or am I merely limited to 9,999 ten-thousands of those that are the birthright of my neighbor?"

No response, so Will went on: "We confront a key problem here. At what point does the law decide that a sentient living being descended through natural evolution from man, and adapted genetically by man's own intervention, is not human? Is it merely a matter of being different—or changed by man's design? If that's the case, I'd be doubly condemned today. Some of your largely white ancestors undoubtedly manipulated the genes of some of my African ancestors through forced breeding of slaves. Justice Rubin, I understand, is Jewish. Many Jews have taken great care through genetic screening over the years to prevent marriages between individuals who display a genetic disposition to a disease prevalent in their community. Is that a manipulation of love's and nature's ways? One has only to run down the list of pejoratives used in every culture in the world to describe the offspring of mixed-race relationships to see that there's an inherent tendency in the human personality to feel that people who mix their genes outside the tribe are less than human. And let's not kid ourselves. It was not long ago that this view translated into diminished rights for people in many parts of the world, including the United States."

"The Court is called upon to make such distinctions and draw such lines all the time," said Justice Cronin.

"Seldom on matters of this magnitude, import and difficulty," Will said. "And this problem will not go away. No matter how hard the government may try to suppress human genetic manipulation, experimentation will continue to expand, apace with advances in technology. It will be a nightmare for regulatory and police agencies—particularly in our democracy. And yet a small and not particularly complex challenge compared with the problem of deciding, as the Court must do now, who is human and who is not. The likelihood, I submit, is that the courts and government will end up trying to manage the process, with not much success."

"And what do you suggest, Sir?" asked Matthews in an obvious prompt. What Justice Matthews was hoping now, Tom guessed, was that Will would advocate the opening of the legal way for a more or less laissez-faire style of R-evolution. Matthews was known to grow teary-eyed at the noble concepts underlying the empty calories and sacred obsolescence cycles of American consumer culture.

"First," Will replied, folding his large, lethal hands on the lectern, "you must guarantee equal justice under the law for all evolutionary, or R-evolutionary, genetic descendants of *homo sapiens sapiens*. We are crossing an historic threshold here and so we must make clear that some things will never change. First among them is the Fourteenth Amendment. Your decision will show future generations how to protect fundamental human values during the jarring and often frightening change ahead. Your decision will echo down through the ages."

"That would be a sweeping gesture," Cronin declared. "We don't know what kind of folks we'll be dealing with."

"It will ensure a legal balance of the common good and the great gift of individuality," Will said. "Over the next decades and generations, this Court will hear similar cases over and over again, all centering on the rights of humans who've benefited from—or suffered at—the hands of technology. I would suggest that if you can't bring yourselves now to grant the first generation of *homo sapiens reformus* this basic right, it will be more difficult for future Courts to safeguard the rights of any of your grandchildren's great-grandchildren who may not be sufficiently enhanced genetically."

Ouch! Tom thought. Not a wise tactic to hold people's great-great-grandchildren to ransom. Of course, Will had made his point: deny equal justice now and the concept was structurally weakened.

"Pardon the digression, Mr. Jefferson," Justice Clements said, "but are you saying that the genetic revolution not only will go ahead but also that it should?"

"Yes, Mr. Justice," Will replied. "We can't stop it. And we shouldn't. We can't turn our backs on our future. That has never been the American way. This is just another frontier, and beyond it lie many, many more. One day, we will genetically engineer plants and animals to colonize nearby asteroids and faraway planets, easing the demands on and the damage to Earth. One day, *homo sapiens reformus* will be adapted into many forms for space exploration and settlement—to exist in different temperatures, atmospheres, and gravity."

Eyes widening, Justice Mansfield roared: "Little green men? You mean our own home-made little green men?" He looked up and down the table. "Where does human dignity go, if that happens? He is threatening the destruction of Man, who is made in God's image."

Tom's Will-watching antennae were twitching. If they were sparring right now, he'd be giving himself extra room, expecting something hard, fast and different to come his way. When he looked up from his doodling, he could see that Will had been waiting for this question.

Politely and with a touch of indulgence in his voice, Will waved off the little green men and Justice Mansfield along with them. "Deep space travel and colonization are probably centuries away," he explained, appearing surprised and perhaps a little amused at the justice's alarm. Having attempted to soothe Mansfield, Will turned to the big kids in the class. One by one his eyes engaged each of the remaining eight justices. Here it comes, Tom thought, as Will continued: "And we won't even start wrestling with genes and space issues until long after we've solved our problems here on Earth."

Right, Tom thought, now he moves on to the small matter of repairing the world's woes. All in a day's work, no doubt for R-evolution and the Junk Generation. It occurred to him again that Will might run for public office. In fact, to protect himself and "his people," he likely had no other choice.

"We elect governments to work for the common good," Will said with just a hint of a deep-breath beginning. "Those governments must ensure that science serves our country's basic democratic principles."

Here it comes, Tom reckoned. Equal justice today, the Fourteenth Amendment forever, making the world constitutionally safe for our grandchildren's grandchildren—these were all abstract notions to the great audience out there. They were confused, scared and angry. The gut issue was: how can you make us feel better? Where's the upside? What can you, or R-evolution, do for us?

"There must be regulation and standards, of course," Will told the justices, as if he was giving away all the ground they had asked for. "Something along the lines of the FDA procedures for pharmaceuticals, perhaps."

Tom expected a challenge from Matthews but Laissez-Faire Max failed to rise to the market's defense.

"It is essential to our future as a people and a nation that R-evolution be woven into the American way of life in a manner wholly compatible with liberal democracy and individual rights."

Tom imagined tight Jeffersonian head-and-shoulders shots on TV screens round the world at this moment. "We must never forget that our goal is to provide benefit and happiness equally to all of the people all of the time. Parents must have the final say on certain kinds of genetic enhancements in their children. That will celebrate individual rights and freedom of choice and guarantee continued diversity. But a certain minimum package of genetic improvements for such things as intelligence and general health should be, at least, as compulsory as public education and vaccination.

"Here comes Big Brother," declared Justice Rubin.

"Who pays?" asked Matthews, looking shocked.

"I'm afraid," Will said softly, adopting his best bedside manner for the terrible news, "that with R-evolution, we'll require a certain level of guaranteed public health care in this country."

Justice Matthews seemed dumbfounded for a moment. Will had shown such promise! "Why not let people buy the genetic products they want?" he asked. "Let the market decide what's good and what's not."

"Because the best and most valuable genetic treatments will follow the money straight to the rich. The grandchildren of the wealthy already start life on third base. Many get unlimited innings and strikeouts for decades on end without paying a significant price. Is it really necessary that, along with the best schools, they have genetically enhanced IQs as well?"

"Are you advocating social engineering?" Justice Rubin appeared slightly unhinged. "Is that the hidden agenda in your proposed R-evolution?"

Will never had a chance for this justice's vote, Tom knew, but he was playing to a different gallery in any case. All the men and women out there who had never been entirely satisfied with the raw genetic deal the old kind of evolution—and their natural parents—had saddled them with. And all the moms and dads to be, wanting the best for their future families. Not a constituency you could lightly ignore.

Will continued: "Outside of the law, one thing is evident to all of us: All men are *not* created equal. And I'm not talking about trust-fund babies. The awful inequities and the painful injustices of genetic inheritance are complex but undeniable. Some people are plainly born with far less chance of success or even happiness in life than others. One example. Decades of scientific testing have shown that the undeniable differences in inherited intelligence lead to social inequality. In crucial areas, from rates of poverty, welfare, illegitimacy, imprisonment and divorce, to educational achievement, employment, career success and, of course, income, IQ is an excellent predictor, even among members of the same family brought up in an identical environment."

Perhaps recalling their own lofty IQ scores, the justices listened without comment.

"Height, physical appearance, personality, timber of voice, athleticism and countless other attributes, talents and gifts provide certain people an advantage in life. Just as other genetic deadweight will weigh upon the shoulders of others until the day they die. Genetically, some start the ball game on third base with no one out, the NL hitting champ at the plate, and the umpire on their payroll. Others are asked to play with a broken bat and no glove."

"Are you advocating a universal right to genetic nose jobs," Justice Jamieson asked, "because, if you are, I call first in line."

Will ignored the crack. "Just as we have debated affirmative action in the admission policies of universities," he said, "we will soon begin to argue over the use of genetic enhancements to redress historical wrongdoings and current inequalities in our society. So why not start today? What if I propose, for the sake of argument, that we begin a formal program of genetic enhancement for the offspring of the poorest twenty per cent of Americans? Or, to heal the suppurating wounds of our nation's past wrongs, for the future children of impoverished native and African Americans? Give the next generation of obviously disadvantaged people a bit of a break? Would that be so awful?"

For the first time, the Chief Justice spoke: "To be clear, you are suggesting that genetic manipulation be a wholesale, largely mandatory, government-run and publicly-financed universal practice?"

"We inoculate against meningitis and polio," Will replied, sounding more like a politician than a lawyer. "Why would we not act against low IQ? Why would we insist that vast numbers of future Americans suffer over what is, after all, quite literally a roll of the genetic dice?"

Good question, Tom thought as the light came on signaling that Will's time was up. And it was up to him to answer it.

52

Two hands on the lectern, Tom looked up at the nine justices. They had their heads together in three separate clusters and seemed agitated — twisted in or half out of their seats, speaking in low voices but gesticulating excitedly. Like kids acting up before the teacher arrived.

Little clear thinking on R-evolution was likely for many years. The nation was in shock, the folks on the bench included. Their robes might hang straight and their eyes burn with wisdom but their thoughts and emotions had been doused in a flood of neurotransmitters from overloaded synapses and leaky brain mains.

The good news was that they were trained to try to ignore emotions, including those posing as rational concepts. More important, they'd cling to the security blanket provided by the U.S. Constitution and many centuries of Anglo-Saxon common law that had been forged and refined to protect human beings from each other and themselves. Things would work out — provided these nine very human human beings agreed to use these tools to override their emotions. Every emotion, that is, but caution. Caution would be good — caution that led to an imposed moratorium, for example. That would be a start, because Tom was beginning to see these hearings as a temporary blocking maneuver, a bid to buy time to regroup for the many more furious further assaults that would be needed to truly defeat R-evolution.

But he guessed, as had Will, that most of the justices were at sea on the matter, almost as ready to follow the people as they were to lead. Noses to the wind, they would have recognized how beautifully Will had played with public sentiment and some pretty fundamental human instincts. Like denial. He had made R-evolution an opportunity, not a problem. A golden child of can-do American optimism. And, as a special one-time bonus, all on the taxpayers' dime, we'll make all your children smart, beautiful and perhaps perpetually happy.

The thought returned Tom to his notes and some recent doodling. On one page was a sketch that had emerged during Will's oral argument. Tom's mind had turned to Eva. What he'd drawn, however, was not the woman but a small child. It occurred to Tom that this might one day be his daughter and that at least in part this case was now about her.

Will had opened the door with his sly Pollyanna pitch. Sure, the grandkids might have perfect teeth and straight As. But they might also live in a twisted R-evolutionary nightmare of genetic monstrosities and predatory new life forms. Tom needed to stiffen the Court's resolve. Restore a proper level of anxiety in both the justices and the national audience. Instill what he believed was the only reasonable reaction to these events—icy, clarifying dread.

The light came on.

"The Big Fix," Tom began. "We're always on the lookout for a Big Fix. And there's always someone around to offer one up. This time round it's R-evolution. But the Big Fix always turns into a bad joke, a trick played on humanity by God, or nature, or fate, or by humankind itself It always starts as the perfect answer but ends up getting out of hand. Next thing you know, there are tens of millions dead in gulags and Great Leaps Forward and Final Solutions. We the people end up decimated or desecrated or, in the case of R-evolution, just plain gone. The Big Fix, so bright and shiny in abstract, becomes the Big Mistake, paid for in blood and bone. And here we are again. The leaders brilliant, the ideas large. Time for another Big Fix. Time to sign the death warrant for the human species."

"Quite an opening, Mr. Daluskov," Justice Clements said sharply. Tom knew the justices would resent the histrionics but he needed to score points fast and early. "You're over the top, Sir," Clements said with a tired voice. "Your allusion to the Holocaust is a cheap and disrespectful exaggeration."

"Once I elaborate, Mr. Justice, you'll see that's not the case." Tom gave silent thanks for Clements' remark. Now he'd make headway with almost any reasonable comparison between the potential outcomes of R-evolution and the Twentieth Century catastrophes inflicted by the Marxist-Leninists and the Nazis.

Clements the libertarian was riled. "You suggest that all the great ambitions and new ideas and aspirations have turned out badly. You suggest, in effect, that there's no such thing as human progress, or no beneficial results from humankind's natural impulse to reform. But the exercise in which you and I are now involved, and the institution that makes it possible, and the form of government of which it is part, and the historical process of remakes, fixes and fine-tuning from which it springs—all these things prove you wrong. You live in and thrive in the soft feather bed of all of the big fixes that Western Civilization has fought and suffered for over thousands of years."

"True, your Honor, at least, so far. But R-evolution puts it all in mortal danger." Tom considered mentioning that while fixes like democracy and equality before the law had indeed evolved over millennia of trial and error, that very process that been defined and governed by the complex urges and boundaries of universal human nature. Which was precisely what R-evolution would slice, dice and toss into the trash. Too esoteric, he decided. These folks needed to see red. "And so I argue that the Court must rescue America and our way of life from a death that will be as ugly as it is certain. Rule One of genetic engineering—don't start—has been broken. So we must battle to our last breath to implement Rule Two, which is, nip it in the bud."

Justice Charles Mansfield offered a hand to someone he saw as a conservative ally: "You want restrictions on JunkGen and GIA rights? How do you square this with the Fourteenth Amendment?"

"We're not arresting our JunkGen sisters and brothers or demanding that they not speak their minds, vote, move or assemble freely. Their liberties, as understood under the Fourteenth Amendment, are not in question. We recognize them as faultless victims. Their germ line DNA has been altered without their consent in an unethical, immoral and illegal way. They are the innocent bearers of a genetic affliction that can be passed on to the rest of humanity and to all subsequent generations in only one way—reproduction."

Justice Rubin joined the search for a Constitutional end-run. "You're calling this quarantine?" He sounded hopeful.

"Yes, in effect, you're Honor. On reproduction. One that can never be lifted. It is constitutional, wise and no more objectionable than stopping someone who's carrying the Ebola virus from attending a rock concert. All governments have the right, responsibility and, indeed, the duty to use police powers to promote the health, safety and welfare of the American people."

"You say disease; they say blessing." Justice Matthews reminded Tom. "Who decides these people are, as you imply, infected with anything dangerous to our people."

"We elect lawmakers and engage experts for that kind of

work," Tom replied. "I'm confident that our governments will eventually ban all further manipulation of the human genome except for strictly therapeutic medical purposes. The Court must order a halt to the federal government's GIA program. *Homo sapiens reformus* and the events at Oneida, New York, as well as the brief involvement of the United States government in the manipulation of the human genome, will become a brief but instructive episode in our social and legal history. The wrong turn almost but not quite taken. Instead, we'll make the right choices and we'll fight to implement them. We will use our genetic technology to improve our lives as natural humans, not to remove ourselves and our children from our own future by creating some half-baked, home-made alien invasion."

"Grandstanding again, Counselor?" Justice Cronin asked. "God save the Species? Isn't that the simplistic, absolutist position?"

"No, your honor, we have a long hard fight in front of us." Tom felt loose but it was time to turn up the intensity. "The Court's stand and the government's must be firm and unambiguous for that very reason. Genetic research must be regulated. It will stick to its proper business — disease prevention and the improvement of overall physical health. The hammer is felony law, including sufficiently coercive penalties. The way to stop R-evolution, the pollution of our gene pool and the sabotage of human nature is to draw a line and stop scientists from crossing it. We must monitor and hold the people with the relevant know-how accountable. Before you're unleashed on your community with three tons of car or truck, you need a driver's license. A scientist, whose power and ability to harm us is exponentially greater, should expect the same regulation."

"No wiggle room, Mr. Daluskov?" Matthews again, with his mind on the possibilities for venture capital. "What if we want smarty-pants grandchildren? You know, kids born bright like you and Mr. Jefferson? What's wrong with a reasonably priced and widely available genetic intelligence booster?"

"Too risky, Sir. We'd make mistakes. Dozens, then hundreds, then thousands. Each slip could foist gigantic problems on posterity. Here's an illustration from something familiar. We've always had people with small and completely natural genetic glitches living among us. They're not merely indistinguishable superficially from the mainstream but often extremely personable and popular. But they lack empathy, or the respect for family, friend, clan, society, law, morality, culture that comes naturally to most of us. In short, part of what is innately good, with a capital G, about human beings has been removed or subverted in them through a genetic defect. Their talent and taste for cruelty make them wonderful bad guys in scary movies and outstanding serial killers."

"Psychopaths," said Matthews.

"Yes. Each time we nudged the genetic code the wrong way in some R-evolutionary lab somewhere, we could introduce new maladaptive behaviors into the human menu—behaviors whose full implications might not become clear for years, decades or even generations." Tom had worried that someone would point out that marginal psychopaths could make not only good salesmen but successful politicians but the justices passed.

"Mr. Daluskov," Justice Jamieson said, leaning forward on his elbows as he spoke. "The United States does not exist in a vacuum, Counselor. The President has warned that if we allow other nations to pull ahead of us in this particular branch of science, our survival and that of the freedom we represent and defend may be imperiled."

"So we make our stand now—at home and abroad. We must use our military superiority, if need be, to help bring an end to R-evolution everywhere on the planet." This was far beyond the hearing's scope, but it seemed no holds would be barred today. Mason had said he wanted a full debate, although Tom suspected the President might be tossing a shoe at his TV screen right about now.

"War with China? Probably nuclear?" The fine bass of Chief Justice McMaster rose from behind the mahogany table. "Unleash a pestilence to combat a plague?"

The Chief Justice followed that with what seemed at first a damaging question. "Isn't it possible, Mr. Daluskov, that we're already too late and Pandora's Box is open? Technology has taken on a life of its own—even a self-sustaining evolutionary track. Is it not possible that Science rules the world now, not us? That knowledge is no longer our servant, and we, instead, are its slaves?"

This was a break, Tom decided. McMaster's voice had the power to move both the Court and the public at large. And he had now cut to the heart of the issue.

Survival.

The right of self-defense was inscribed in language older than the spoken word. Too primal, too fundamental to require a panel on the Court's giant bronze doors. It was, You or Me, and Us or Them.

"What you say is true, Mr. Chief Justice. We are in a battle for our survival. Give Science its way and humankind will expire. It's as simple as that. But it is not too late. We have a choice, and this is a war that we can win."

Tom paused. He wanted the Bench and the millions watching or those who would see and hear accounts of the appearance later to pay attention now. They needed to understand that the going would get tough not only on the world stage but here at home too.

"At this moment, though not forever," he continued, "science can defeat us only through the acts and agency of our fellow humans. Science has no military force, no policemen, no coercive apparatus of its own. But we have the legal means to herd the men and women of Science to the common will for the common good. As a sovereign nation, with approval of Congress, we may also bend or defeat or destroy the states that threaten our right to survive." He bowed slightly to acknowledge the gravity of McMaster's warning—that the cure must not be worse than the disease. "We've face stark choices before. We chose between the dissolution of the Union and civil war, for instance. We could have let the Confederacy go, let slavery spread and persist on this continent. But where and what would we all be now?"

"There you go again, son," snapped Justice Crowe. "With you, it's always my way or Judgment Day. Drop the scare tactics, Counselor. All sorts of calamities were supposed to follow *in vitro* fertilization too. Or are you too young and green to remember that? Behave yourself! Help us find the middle way."

"I will remind you, Sir, that R-evolution has spread so rapidly precisely because the *in vitro* process has been massively abused on at least three of the world's continents."

Before the white light signaled five minutes and counting, Tom needed another crack at John Mason's Genetically Improved Americans program.

"President Mason has tried to find this middle way, of course. He says we'll show the world that Americans can build a bigger, better, star-spangled Junk Generation faster than anyone else. For a desperate fallback position and a recipe for suicide, it is nicely packaged and easily spun. But there is no surer route to mankind's demise. And any so-called middle way will have the same result. The world will be sucked into the Hobbesian Trap from which, eventually will creep only the curious surviving creatures who will definitely not be us."

The allusion to Thomas Hobbes had occurred to Tom only now. The English philosopher had argued more than 350 years before that war often became inevitable not because one nation was compelled to attack the other out of old-fashioned aggression but because it feared the growing strength of its rival and decided to strike before it was overwhelmed itself. An early example had been the Peloponnesian War, a couple of millennia ago, brought on by anxieties in Sparta over the growth of the power of Athens. Adolf Hitler had later been obsessed with the rapidly growing power of Stalin's Russia. "Without a total worldwide ban on R-evolution," Tom said, "every nation, and countless sub- and trans-national interests—your garden variety religious, ideological and tribal terrorists, for example—will worry that the other guy is pulling ahead. Governments may talk the Middle Way at the U.N., etc.—but will keep the pedal to the metal on their scientific accelerators. They'll lie and cheat because deep in their fearful, eminently human hearts they'll be sure, often correctly, that the other side has secret programs too."

Tom needed to implant a picture in the mind of his audience that would roil its guts and influence its thinking. The AP wirephoto of a naked Kim Phuc, 9, running in agony as napalm seared her flesh changed the way everyday Americans thought of the Vietnam War. But these justices and everyday Americans had been spared—or deprived of—the most troubling of the stills and videos from the Oneida Foundation. Even the mild, cosmeticized visuals that had been everywhere for a week or two were no longer seen. R-evolution was becoming a fuzzy intellectual concept when what Tom needed was for the impending horror to penetrate and capture the most primitive regions of the collective American psyche.

"Let me outline what will happen if this Court fires the starter pistol and we allow the Great Genetic Race to go ahead. Human DNA will be edited, trimmed, expanded, reordered, jumbled, tumbled and reshuffled in first thousands and then thousands of millions of ways. You and I don't know what great scientific theoretical breakthroughs Sigurd Shivkovski put to work in his genetic crucible. But we do understand the underlying strategy. It's the strategy that all nations and all players will have to apply in the Genetic Race if they wish to keep apace: Try anything. Try everything. Do anything and do everything. Never, never stop to consider the risks of your work. Go for it! Get some!"

Tom raised his eyes to the lens of a camera positioned almost directly behind the Chief Justice. He and his widening team of volunteer supporters, both Republican and Democrats, had tipped off the major news departments that this cue was coming. Tom had provided them with fresh video of the horrors of Oreida, though still not the worst of it. He hoped a few would be shamed into showing the new shots now as he spoke — or, at the very least, the sanitized yet profoundly disturbing material they had stopped broadcasting.

"I ask the Court to recall the people we found that day in the Foundation's underground world. See their faces, remember the forms that emerged as their genes, perverted by R-evolutionary processes, were, using the scientific term, *expressed*, in flesh and blood. And believe me, you have seen only the most palatable of the abominations. Dante and Michelangelo would kick themselves for their somewhat unimaginative visions of Hell. The decisions of this court in the matters before it today will also be *expressed*. In flesh and in blood. For the rest of human history."

Justice Rubin appeared affronted, his cheeks rosier than usual. "This isn't tabloid television here, Mr. Daluskov. Stop playing to the cameras." He nodded over his shoulder towards the lens peeping through the red curtains. "Forget the ghastly images and the grisly predictions. We're here to consider issues of law and the Constitution. Stick to that. It's what got us here and it has served us well."

"Not always, Mr. Justice," Tom snapped back. "If that were true, Dred Scott would have been decided correctly and the cemeteries for the dead of our bloodiest war might be empty fields today." These men and women needed reminding that they'd better get it right. "Speaking of images, I forgot to mention a final injunction under the Shivkovski strategy that participants in the Great Genetic Race will find it necessary to adopt: keep the mills running twenty-four/seven but dispose of all substandard product."

Sneaking a look, Tom saw that McMaster had taken that one

in. The Chief Justice knew firsthand what people were capable of. "Do we know what the Chinese R-evolution is doing?" Tom asked. "And what we may have to do in response? Do *we* know what *we're* doing, even now? Our President has assured us that we are respecting the integrity of human nature in the so-called GIA program. What exactly does that mean? And now the United States of America has engaged the special services of Sigurd Shivkovski! For what? Quality control? Will he be VP in charge of ethics? Recycling? The search for new energy sources? It does not bode well."

Tom let that sink in. Trusting your own government, never mind someone else's, was always a challenge. He wasn't surprised when the justices apparently felt it wise to make no response.

"We will begin the Great Genetic Race determined to do the right thing. But we will end up creating strains of human behavior and abilities that we now think we would never consider. We will do things that are beyond our comprehension now. First in the name of national security, then in the name of national survival. Eventually, R-evolution, which is quite simply the weapon of our own mass destruction, will become self-sustaining and progress to a point where we—or whatever quaint parts of *we* are left by then—will not be able to control or even understand it. Our creations or the creations of our creations will run us. We will eventually be discarded and our niche genetic strain discontinued. And if we are not, we will certainly wish we were."

Justice Gonzales was leaning forward, two hands spread on the table, looking up and down at the faces on the bench. The scowl showed he thought Tom was getting too much leeway. "Let's hope you're as reliable a prognosticator as your 17th Century guru, Thomas Hobbes, Mr. Daluskov," Gonzales bellowed. Tom recognized a kindred spirit, though not a shared opinion. Gonzales had won many arguments and probably flattened a few men in his years as a labor warrior and now wanted to land one on Tom.

"Wasn't Hobbes the guy who said that if men were ever given individual rights and the freedom to rule themselves, life would become solitary, poor, nasty, brutish, and short? A strange expert to cite in an American courtroom."

The justice pulled himself up in his seat. "Let me pose the glass-half-full question. Let's say none of the disasters you predict come about. Quite the opposite. R-evolution proceeds and huge benefits, both sublime and ridiculous, quickly accrue. Everything from much more plentiful and affordable food and basic necessities for billions of the world's poor to those pre-natal nose jobs Justice Jamieson was so clearly in need of." He jabbed his thick stubby index finger in Tom's direction. "The naysayer bears responsibility for the product of his position, too, Mr. Daluskov. You call for total bans. You call for tight policing. But you also know that heavy regulation will inevitably slow or stop research and experimentation. Do you think our grandchildren's grandchildren will thank us for preventing cures for AIDs, heart disease, cancer? Is that what you'd like to be famous for?"

"Good point," said Justice Cronin. "And let's not romanticize human nature. Natural evolution has dumped a lot of useless baggage on us. Our feather-trigger stress reactions worked fine when we were hunting mastodons and running from saber-tooth tigers but they blow out our arteries and wear out our tickers in the modern work place. We treat millions upon millions for the chemical imbalances that lead to depression. We already know that the long variation of the 5-HTT gene makes people more emotionally resilient and less vulnerable to chronic depression. So if we can touch up our genetic makeup to eliminate these problems from the gene pool, why not?"

Valid points, Tom knew, and highly dangerous, because they made a sort of benign, gradualist R-evolution look not only possible but also inviting. "It's true that we're not always happy with what we are," he replied, "but these behaviors, like all behaviors, have survived because the people who displayed them survived. Not only endured but thrived and often triumphed. Abraham Lincoln suffered from depression. It was part of what made him perhaps the greatest American ever. Whatever the downsides, these attributes benefited the individual, the group and the gene pool. They provided a so-called selective advantage. At worst, they were neutral."

Tom locked eyes for an instant with Cronin's pale blues. He liked the woman. He liked them all, and he was sure that concern over one example or another of evolution's perceived excess baggage was as present in their hearts and in their families as it was in everyone else's. "Introversion or shyness has as many benefits for the species as extroversion, obviously," he said, "or the two propensities wouldn't be around and so universally common anymore. If everybody felt comfortable and even eager to stand up and give her opinion on every subject, the world would be an unbearably noisy place. And who would do the real thinking? The guy who's not the life of the party may also be the one who leads the charge up the hill. And if she's not happy in social situations, stressed by some chemical glitch that unleashed unnecessary adrenaline, maybe she'll stay home and compose Ode to Joy or come up with the Theory of Relativity."

"I'm sure Justice Cronin was referring to the hard cases," offered the ever gallant Justice Crowe, "not run-of-the-mill neurotics like you and me."

"Hard cases, Sir?" Tom replied. "Okay, let's suppose we had had the technology in the late Nineteenth Century. You'd have needed an army of geneticists to sort out Winston Churchill. Predisposed to depression, an alcoholic, the cantankerous loner whose flagrant risk-taking cost many thousands of British soldiers their lives in World War One. A racist. But if his genes had been fine-tuned and his evolutionary baggage removed, Normandy might remain a western province of the Third Reich today."

"On the other hand," said Rubin, "what if we isolated the Hitler Genes and got rid of them? And you haven't addressed the question yet, Mr. Daluskov—what about the great cures and benefits that your proposed ban might steal from our grandchildren?"

Tom nodded to Rubin. "I agree that it is only right that the Court consider intergenerational justice in this matter. It will be other men and women of the future who will have to live with the results of our decisions. Will there be no cure for cancer if we regulate genetic research? On the contrary, I say it will arrive faster. With strict limits set on R-evolution research, science can concentrate its full talents and investment on disease, rather than dissipating its resources on trying, first, to build a better Man and, next, to clean up after its mistakes."

Rubin had mentioned Hitler. Better him than me, Tom thought, but it provided an opening. "What if, as is likely, we create new and different monsters along the way to finally producing our new Hilter-gene-free, emotionally balanced JunkGen models. What if the folks with the fine complexions and cute noses turn out to be the monsters themselves? What if an adjustment for higher risk-taking produces fearlessness? Or less emotional sensitivity and low blood pressure generates a lack of feeling for others? Or greater athleticism turns into a killer instinct without an off switch? How do our great grandchildren deal with such a scourge, perhaps bred to hide, fight and multiply? What will or can they do about other modified humans they find they don't need, want or like? Incarceration? Sterilization? Extermination? And what, in turn, will that do to their own 'humanity' and values?"

Tom paused. It was time to go for broke. "And what if, in genetically rounding mankind's rough edges, we remove some of the feelings that give life its joy and its essence?"

"Such as?" Cronin sounded interested.

"Love for our children, let's say." Tom glanced down at the child in his pencil sketch. "A feeling that flows deeply through every culture. A feeling so deep and universal that my friend and colleague Mr. Jefferson has appealed to it today in support of his arguments to this Court." This was a reminder of the figurative open door.

"As an evolutionary factor, or baggage, if you like, these oceanic feelings have an obvious practical use. They are evolution's way of urging us to reproduce and care for our young. But that function does not diminish in the slightest the pure unrivaled pleasures and satisfactions these drives bestow on generation after generation of human beings. They make it a privilege to be human. They're perhaps our greatest reward."

Bingo! Tom thought, surveying the faces along the table. The Chief Justice looked sour; but the others appeared stunned. "Give R-evolution a few years," he continued, "and perhaps some GIA cabinet secretary will decide that a little less parental affection might be a good thing for society as a whole. After all, institutions run well by suitably programmed JunkGen staff, government or private, can cook, do laundry and get the kids to bed far more efficiently than Mom and Dad. Mom in fact may be very happy not to have to endure the long discomfort, inconvenience and the pain of bearing society's children to begin with. That's if Mom's and Dad's genes haven't already been tweaked to take the edge off of parental anxiety, which the experts may decide is excessive and counterproductive. Or JG toddlers are instinctively kicking Mom in the shins every time she attempts one of those sweaty yucky unwelcome embraces. Let the state do it. Or the KidsrUs Corp. Free up time for adults; reduce stress levels; increase economic productivity."

Tom now decided that there might be too many *ifs* in this direction. It was too Orwellian. So he would 'however' himself onto a new track and toward a fact of life that people related to far more easily — Murphy's Law..

"But it's more likely to occur by accident. We're tweaking genes to build a neater teen when, oops, something gets erased, or a tiny stretch of code is changed, or A causes B to bump into C at the sub-molecular level. A few genes become inoperable. Turns out they're the ones that build and operate the biochemical switch that tells other sub-systems to flood our feelings with joy and well-being when we look at the daughters and sons we love."

"The death of love?" Justice Cronin, whose face seemed an expression of the words she spoke, asked softly.

"Who knows?" Tom continued a little harshly. "Maybe it's the genetic flip side to the death of hate. And who cares? Love may be seen in retrospect to have been just more evolutionary baggage that was delaying our liftoff to the stars."

Tom reconsidered the sarcasm; better to play it straight. "Nobody can predict the precise consequences of R-evolution. What we can predict is change. Accelerating change. Change that will magnify exponentially through the rest of time. If allowed, *homo sapiens reformus* itself will beget ever more and different varieties, powered by its own vaulting super-human skills. These sub-species, in turn, will feed upon and generate ever more advanced biotechnology. Reverse engineering of the brain — first ours, then theirs — will be just a matter of time. We'll figure out how the current model works, replicate and go from there. We will have the experimental melding of computers, robotics and nanotechnology into our — or, by then, *their* — frail flesh. And, along the way, as a side-effect, perhaps little noticed, it is likely to be, as the old song said, *Bye-bye love, bye-bye happiness*. At least in the forms we know them now."

The white light came on. In five minutes, the red would warn him to complete his last sentence.

It was Justice Matthews's turn to lapse into sarcasm. "Let's hear the bad news, Mr. Daluskov."

Tom could have warned Matthews that genetic manipulation might weaken the human hunger for status, with disastrous effects on SUV sales and the consumer economy in general. But no time. "I was just getting there, Sir. I was about to say that I doubt we'll get that far. We'll destroy ourselves first. We face a conundrum of a particularly human kind. We know we need fixing. And, technologically, we're learning how to go about it. But if we try to fix ourselves through R-evolution, it's precisely those things that need fixing that will do us in."

"Always a catch, huh, Mr. Daluskov?" Justice Jamieson said. "So what do we do? Pour a stiff whiskey and get out the Doors album?"

"Soldier on, Sir," Tom said with a collaborative smile. "We've had the means of our total destruction in hand for sixty years now. We've dodged some bullets but we've managed to improve our cultures fast enough to keep from destroying ourselves. Finally, after many thousands of years of history, we've begun to understand ourselves. That understanding — that growing knowledge of our huge complex range of strengths and weaknesses — is what can save us. But add the whole slew of new incalculables that R-evolution would bring? In this world where the big money is still spent on new and better ways of destruction? We'd be asking for it."

"Be more precise," Rubin demanded.

"In a new R-evolutionized world," Tom replied, "where would we find the common ground? I am talking about the conventions of behavior that help us at crucial times to peer through our distrust and anxieties, and recognize one another as human. The diversity of new JunkGen people and the novelty of their personalities, behaviors and appearances would soon outstrip our admittedly limited ability to accommodate The Other psychologically. We'd have different societies genetically hyping the predispositions they value–and that others distrust, dislike, fear or hate. Even within national populations, there'll be a heightening of differences."

"Examples?" The Chief Justice seemed impatient.

"Libertarians and perhaps free-marketers would want genetic codes skewed to produce risk-taking, adventurous, independent-minded and even rebellious individuals. Others in our society — the labor movement, for instance, or organized religions, or social conservatives — would want to adjust the genome and brain chemistry in ways that would produce stronger collegial, collaborative instincts and obedience, even though others might rightly fear that that could intensify the herd and tribal drives that have powered history's cycles of mass bloodletting. Who's going to decide? Will we retool the government's Genetically

Improved Americans program every time a new party occupies the White House or controls Congress?"

"Think we're not up to it, Mr. Daluskov?" Justice Clements asked, with a hint of insult in his voice.

"Our society is a living organism, I believe, your honor. It has at least as many conflicting and irrational impulses as your everyday human being. The concept of Equality Under the Law has survived these challenges but it's been twisted, soiled and at times trampled into the dust. In our weaker moments, when we've been afraid, angry, in shock or just feeling mean, we've stomped all over it. R-evolution will test, tear and ultimately shred our commitment to freedom."

The Justice waited.

"Consider how a single, man-made issue—slavery and institutionalized legal racism against African-Americans—has strained and drained our society. For two hundred years now. Multiply that by first one big r-evolutionary problem, and three smaller ones, and the dozens and scores of big and small issues that will follow!" Tom paused and surveyed the Bench. "The social and political implications will grow exponentially. And when I say social unrest, I'm talking the early days only. What will we call the conflicts when engineered humans eventually become another or several other species entirely?"

Jamieson asked: "Timeline?'

"Closer to fifty years than one hundred." Tom addressed the wider court. "We've finally found a scientific tool that is simply too dangerous to use. We cannot introduce new divisions into the human community, particularly ones far more substantial than the superficial distinctions we've had such a problem overcoming throughout human history. A house divided against itself cannot stand. It's the job of the law to protect us from ourselves. To ensure that what's good and true can survive and prosper, despite our flaws, I ask you to let it do its work."

McMaster, glancing at the stopwatch he always laid before him on the table, interjected:

"But your argument, in its essence, predicts that this issue will never be fully resolved. You say that we are divided innately to some extent between the conservatives—who cling to the traditional and say don't fix what ain't broke or at least don't make things worse—and those who seek and long for change. It's not a solution to the problem you're seeking. It's victory."

"Yes, and the Court will decide which side will win."

"In Round One, you mean, Counselor, don't you. Who will win Round One?"

"In important bouts, Mr. Chief Justice, I've always gone for the first round knockout."

The red light came on.

As Tom turned away, he was surprised to hear the Chief Justice speak.

"I believe that we all in this courtroom understand the scope of the dilemma that faces the United States," he began. Tom didn't need to look at McMaster's face to know the man was scared. The question was what that would mean to the case.

"We are told that R-evolution must be stopped," the chief justice continued in a voice he might have used to steel his men under fire. "And we are told that it is unstoppable. Even the initial attempts to impose a moratorium would involve the pursuit, detention and infringement of the rights of reproduction of thousands of individual Americans and their offspring." McMaster had at least decided that the Junk Generation was American. "And this is only the beginning."

The remaining eight justices — men and women, short, fat, lean and tall, representing a rainbow of mixed and muddled philosophies and political instincts, some kindly, polite, generous, others nasty, cruel, neurotic, with their varying degrees of intelligence, diligence and honesty, and certainly not all happy, or even capable of happiness — listened quietly to their colleague. Their faces were uniformly glum.

The Chief Justice continued: "We are told that genetic manipulation of the human genome must be strictly regulated by law. To make those laws is not our responsibility but we can be reasonably sure that if they are crafted and adopted by the other branches of government, we will very quickly be called upon to consider and interpret them in the light of our Constitution. One day, we may be asked which types, even brands, of *homo sapiens reformus* should be produced by whom, for whom and for what purposes.

McMaster cruised through a few possibilities. Smarter, taller, more articulate? What about miniaturization, he asked, perhaps for military purposes? Could *homo sapiens reformus* be fitted out for specific commercial or industrial purposes, or even use in the home? Would a minimum of self-identity and self-assertion be required? How great a genetic predilection towards obedience, loyalty and self-abnegation could be allowed before you had armies of genetically skilled craftspeople willing to work for what the Chief Justice described as "the kind of room and board laid on for the chickens in an industrial poultry plant."

"How would you prevent hidden time-bombs or horrible moral crimes? Mankind, the original model, is capable of rationalizing the most terrible acts in support of the concept *du jour* of the common good." For example, McMaster suggested, America's public and private pension funds would be demonstrably better off if more people remained healthy throughout their working lives but did the next generation the service of dropping dead soon after retirement. If this happened peacefully, suddenly and quickly, with minimal demands on the health industry, all the better.

Jamieson jumped in. "Nature had a similar idea," said the Justice with a nose that only evolution would claim credit for. "My aching bones tell me that once you reproduce and raise your young, Nature's through with you."

Mansfield remained concerned about little green men. "If some R-evolution is allowed to proceed, do you insist on a minimum retention of human characteristics? And if so, which ones?"

"Most characteristics are double-edged," Gonzales offered, "with aspects that can both repel and attract, depending sometimes on who's considering them. We're different in our natures and experience and environments and so we differ in what we value and condemn in human behavior. Didn't someone argue this week that the propensity to vote Republican or Democrat may be in our genes long before we have a trust fund, or get to know our lunch-bucket parents?"

As he returned to his seat, Tom wondered whether the entire Court would get in a last word. They all wanted it on record that they have been handed an impossible task.

Cronin: "And who decides how many neat nuts, and libertarians, and folks like Beethoven who never cleaned his chamber pot, it takes to make a workable society?"

The unspoken and, Tom noted, probably unanimous answer from the justices was *not us nine, we hope.*

McMaster decided to wrap things up. "On the other hand," he said, reaching for his stopwatch and perhaps some restoration of confidence and calm, "these are in many ways mere extensions of questions we have posed to ourselves over what the President last night called the first volume of human history. It's not always nice, easy or pleasant to look at. But we accept it, quite simply, as life. To live is to choose."

Yes, Tom thought as the nine rose to go do their duty, to choose, and along with everyone else, to live with the consequences.

53

Will called Tom just before midnight. "I'm wired," he said. "How about you?" Twenty minutes later they were running in their sweats down the National Mall. It was deserted except for the cops and soldiers enforcing the off-limits ban. They slowed each time they approached a new checkpoint or patrol but every one waved them through. One young guardsman even saluted.

"The perks of fame," said Will.

"Or infamy," laughed Tom. "I've had a few salutes of the single finger kind."

They jogged West from the Capitol side by side until just past the Reflecting Pool when Will began a sprint up the steps of the Lincoln Memorial. He stopped half way and turned and waited, silhouetted against the vast illuminated structure. Will held out his hand as Tom approached. "Good job," he said.

Tom shook Will's hand and threw an arm over his shoulders. "No better than you, as usual," he said. "I'm glad you called. We've got to get things back the way they were."

"It's way past that, I'm afraid. No turning back." Will nodded toward the great marble man inside. "Still, I reckoned you, me and Abe could chill a little tonight. Old times' sake. "

"Okay, but lose the end-of-the-world nonsense. Whichever way the Court goes, we'll still be down at WHUPASS together whenever we can."

Tom meant it. What was said in court stayed in court. Come hell or high water, they would die best friends.

"We'll see." Will moved up the steps.

"What's your call?" Tom asked as he followed him up.

"The decision? Oh, the Court will bail. Decide not to decide and throw it back to Congress and the president."

Tom agreed. The justices would mull the matter for a week, deliver something but cop out on the key issue and kick the can down the road. Let the politicians do the dirty work. The Court could look at it all again when new laws were challenged and new cases filed.

"What do you say we forget the case tonight," Will asked. "I want to clear the decks on some personal stuff."

"What's to clear?"

"Rachel."

Tom tried to conceal surprise and discomfort with a joke. "We're just good friends," he said.

"Be honest. Abe's watching." Will continued the climb toward the brooding Lincoln. Tom followed and joined him at the foot of the sculpture, where they stood silently for a minute contemplating the man who saved the Union and, in America at least, perhaps the concept in practice of equality under the law. Tom waited. Will obviously needed to get something off his chest.

Will turned to look out over the Mall. "It is a very strange feeling but from the inside looking out I don't really know for sure that I'm black." He smiled. "I mean, *really* black, beyond the pigmentation, the manly black face and form, the natural cool, the rap, the air time."

Tom laughed. "Well, friend, I can tell you that from the outside looking in you are definitely an African-American. And you know better than me that for most practical purposes that makes you one. What's it got to do with Rachel?"

"I'm leading to that. She and I share the curious experience of having long known that we truly are JG, Greaks, whatever you want to call us. That's very different from not knowing who your birth parents are. Those people never question their commonality with the rest of the human race. If they are disposed to do so, they can even believe they're created in God's image. But Rachel and I know that some of what we are was first dreamed up on a bad day in a labor camp by two men who probably despised humankind. Each time we do or feel something, it may be to some extent a product of their hatred and ill will."

"Maybe you're better off. Ever heard of Konrad Lorenz?"

"Sure. Eminent Austrian anthropologist, German soldier, Soviet POW camp survivor."

"Seen some of the dark side, certainly." Tom quoted: "'I've found the link between apes and civilized men. It's us!' I'm surprised you didn't use it in court today." Tom turned to consider Lincoln and give Will some space. He continued: "So clear the decks, Will! Are you trying to tell me in your fumbling way that being JunkGen brought you and Rachel together?"

"Okay, I'll tell you but you can't let Rachel know. She would kill me for doing this."

Tom hesitated, not sure that he really wanted to know. "Why does this sounds like we're all back in high school?"

Will shook his head "Because you two never left 9th grade! You've been a jealous jerk for decades now. And the whole time I've also been serving as a one-man audience for Rachel's highly accurate portrayal of a self-hating teenage drama queen."

Tom realized with shame that he had never once apologized to Will for the many times the green monster had threatened their friendship over the years. "You're completely right Will. I have been a total assh . . . "

"Shut up for a minute and listen because I need out of this." Will lowered his voice, as if someone, possibly the nation's 16th President, might overhear. "The short story is this: Rachel loves you, Rachel has always loved you, Rachel will always love you."

Despite himself, Tom felt his head spin.

"When I say forever, I mean it. She's been dumping her garbage about you on me ever since we hit puberty. Along with the absolute need for you never to know and for her never to do anything about it. So you're unloading on me on one side and she's her crying on my other shoulder about her desperate needs and the pains of self-imposed abstinence. You have no idea, pal! She once told me that your mere presence threw off her menstrual cycle! Like I wanted to know! The result is, I now suffer from battered-friend syndrome." Will paused and smiled slyly. "Of course, I did strike back once in a while. Remember those three bruised ribs I *accidentally* gave you back in '99? You were really acting up that year. But the fact is, given all the crap you've laid on me over the years, I should have broken every bone in your body by now."

Will stopped and pointed at Tom. "You should see the goofy smile on your face!" But his laughter seemed cold, perhaps pained. Tom wondered whether Will had also suffered the agonies of unrequited obsession.

"I'm sorry, Will, but are you—?"

"*In love* with her? Took you long enough to ask but the answer is no!" Will paused to look up at the Lincoln in Georgia rock who as a man had struggled with demons. "But I do love her, of course. I love her because she is my sister and one of the saddest women in the world."

"Your sister?" Tom mumbled dully. His stupidity seemed have known no depths. What hadn't he guessed it after Oneida? Given Rachel's and Will's JunkGen roots, R-evolution had made it a distinct possibility. The thought of Rachel locked into a secret world of sadness also mortified him. Another woman he should have helped but hadn't.

Yet it was Will who was sorry. "I've always wanted to tell you," he said, leaning back against the cool marble next to Tom. "We both felt for you but we were trapped in the JunkGen lie." His face took on that rare look of anger Tom had first seen at Oneida. "Your dad's partly responsible for this, you know. He and Shivkovski and our so-called parents. Those perverse bastards! It somehow fit their scientific conceit not to let us look like the siblings we are."

"Why did she keep it secret?" Tom asked him. "If we wanted each other, why not let it happen?"

Will moved toward the inscription of the Gettysburg Address. "Remember that time at the Oneida picnic when she went off on us? 'A mass of insecurities and contradictions, and so on?'"

"The 'bubbling borsch of incoherent bio-chemical reactions' — sure, who could forget?"

"There's been a powerful mix of nurture and nature in Rachel's choices. The good things in her nature played a role—her integrity, sensitivity, intellect. Also the fierce stubbornness. But on the nurture or environmental side, you have one overwhelming and almost unbelievable fact. *She always knew everything*. Her own parents drummed every detail of her genetic makeup and the experimental targets and risks into her right from the get-go. She knew she was a lab rat way back at the Oneida picnic when I was still happy, stupid, and supposedly an all-natural, all-American boy."

Will stopped for a moment and looked down the Mall toward the Capitol building. This decision would have been part of the protocol devised by the Shivkovski–Daluskov tandem. Tom knew they would have told one or more of the subjects simply to see how they would behave, and then compare that response with the behaviors of their JunkGen contemporaries who were kept in the dark. Calculated cruelty against children. No wonder Will had been so upset to see the new Junk Generations suffering at Oneida. "How did you find out?" he asked quietly.

"That nasty prick, Leon, of course." Will's trademark world's-my-oyster grin was back. "It was like hearing about sex on a street corner for the first time. He saw some documents somehow and whispered in my ear in the schoolyard. No small animals to torture that day, I suppose."

"Before your—"

"Yes, I learned part of it before Mom and Dad died. I went straight to the lab after Leon told me. My mother was calm and reassuring, as usual. Dr. Sensible. She said they'd attempted only minor improvements—very carefully. Probably wouldn't take, and she claimed a huge chunk of me was still *them*! Along with significant bits of Rachel's mom and dad, of course. And the really good part was that I remained 98 per cent chimpanzee!"

Will seemed pleased at the memory. Tom asked: "Not a major childhood trauma?"

"Come on," he replied evenly. "You've had more of that to deal with than me." He laughed again. "My old man took a different tack. He rubbed his bald head and laughed, 'You want this? You *really* want this?' Then he was rubbing the head and that big belly of his at the same time. 'Want this, too?' They were both lying, of course, but I've always known they loved me. It was Rachel who provided the real full story after they died. We spent many teenage hours going over our data, trying to decipher the genetic fine-tuning. Rachel always claimed that her test tube had been dirty, which opened the promise of sizzling sex.'

"She could laugh about it?"

Will's smile thinned. "You know Rachel. It's theater. To conceal an almost pathological self-hate. Old man Shivkovski went so far as to tell her at puberty that she might find herself obsessively attracted to a single male."

A science prodigy, Rachel would have known that genetically predisposed preferences to certain pheromones were often what created instant and lasting attractions between men and women.

"So she's like me." Will continued. "When she feels or thinks a certain way, she can never be sure whether the experience is natural to most people or something perverse and peculiar to oneself. She seldom gets through a day without feeling used and manipulated. She doesn't trust her deepest feelings. She tells me she disgusts herself." He turned to Tom. "There's a part of Rachel that wants to be out there with the anti-JunkGen mob waving torches and shouting 'Kill the beasts!' "

"You know that we finally got together?"

"It was a once in a lifetime thing," Will said quietly. "She was briefly more afraid of the R-evolution story coming out—and hurting you—than what it would do to her deep inside. Or to you and Eva." He gave Tom a thumbs up. "A fabulous woman, by the way. You've lucked out again. And rest assured: Rachel could never have been with you. It would have torn her apart every day. She is also terrified of reproducing. Will never pass on her McGenes, as she calls them. 'I'm not a missing link,' she tells me, 'just a false start.'"

"Shooting star, more like it." Tom wondered at yet another of Rachel's skills—the ability to so completely hide her vulnerability. "What about you? How do you handle it?"

"Me?" The Jefferson grin again. "I've got the keep-on-keeping-on gene. Just keeping on going keeps me going on "

"Yeah, I've noticed." He pushed Will playfully off balance. "So what happens now?"

"Like always—I kick your butt."

"Think Abe approves of Shots?" Tom said, looking back towards the Great Man.

"No way we do shots," Will chuckled, bending to take off his shoes. "My bones can't handle that stuff anymore. But I'm happy to whup your ass in some sparring." Standing with his socks in one hand, he clipped Tom lightly across the ear with the other. "Three points."

"Half speed," Tom said, bending to remove his own footwear. He pulled his shirt over his head.

They bowed, touched imaginary gloves, and before their marble audience of one, began trading light kicks and punches. Their taunts and the sound of bare feet smacking on cold stone mingled in the warm night air. Tom feasted on a flood of old memories of happy faraway times. "Point," Will called as he scored on Tom's forehead with a backfist. Tom wondered whether the unspoken tensions over Rachel and the JunkGen secrets that had often made their matches so intense were finally gone now. He felt closer to Will than he had since they were children.

One-one. Then 2-1 for Tom, a tie again, advantage Will, and 3-3.

Will stepped back and lowered his fists. "Call it a draw?" This was another first.

"Works for me," said Tom.

For a moment Tom thought his friend was going to give him a hug. Another first. Instead, Will bowed low and held it there—a nod to the past and Bill Lee. Their way to reaffirm and honor their mutual respect and friendship.

Tom wanted to hold his bow longer than Will's, as a mark of

apology and remorse for the many wrongs he had done his friend over Rachel. And he wanted Will to know that he believed him to be the better man. So he faked Will out, raising his head slightly and bowed low again. He remained there, waiting for the retort he knew must be coming.

When it didn't, he looked up and saw the top of Will's head explode and his body drop, arms splayed, in a mist of blood and flesh.

Tom would remember every instant of the ensuing moments for the rest of his life. Will's death came soon afterwards and the doctors doubted that he could have ever regained consciousness. But Tom's strong impression was that Will had whispered to him during the awful seconds when he held his dying friend in his arms and had said: "I trust you to do what's best."

54

The world had been made strange by Will's death. So this is us, Tom thought, as he considered the ranting and the rage and, despite passing moments of grace and dignity, the delirium underlying much public thinking and discourse, however slick the code or clever the camouflage. Forget DNA, forget nurture. Behold the end product. Our true ugly nature stripped bare.

Tom guessed that this was how his father and Shivkovski had felt in the Gulag. They had seen the primitive regions of the brain take charge, overrunning the fragile sunlit new territories that had recently made us able to perform the tricks of modern societies. The ancient us leapt from its dark hole within and on to our backs. There it steered us where it willed, shutting out the light of reason with brutal overpowering paws.

The strangeness was accentuated by his grieving—and it must indeed be grief that had taken hold of him upon Will's death although he could not remember experiencing it before, even after his father died. It had an almost physical weight that dragged on his will when he rose in the morning and bore down on his spirit when he lay back to sleep. It was leaden, cold and rocklike and an anchor on even his joy in private moments with Eva. The only answer was to accept and adapt, of course, and as the days went by he recognized that its constant presence would become a permanent and one day familiar part of him and his life.

If this was new, so was the suspicion that he knew less about himself than he thought. Tom was far less shaken by the behavior of the world around him than by what he'd done on the night Will died. He had been overwhelmed by panic for the first time in his life. Fear had once been a mere adjunct to the adrenalin that powered him forward. He'd been shot in the face at Manny's, for instance, but had felt the physical effects only later. In the moment itself his mind had never stopped roaring *go, go, go!*

He heard nothing like that on the Lincoln Memorial steps. What rose instead inside him was a terror from beyond and before language.

Tom had skittered down the steps like a cockroach exposed to light. He'd made gasping, guttural sounds. He had crawled back to Will, of course, but it been much harder than anything he had ever done. He had taken Will's shattered head into his lap—and had felt the first harrowing grief. But the fear persisted. He had seen and recognized the gunman from 50 feet, the last of the wannabe Spartans, the one Eva had saved from execution by Jason at Oneida. Come to finish his combat with Will. The L man had aimed his old rifle straight at Tom's cowardly head. Tom heard no *go, go, go.* Instead, it had taken all of his conscious resources not to plea for his life, or to flee or, worse, to pull Will's body over his own for protection.

The Secret Service settled the matter with a fuselage. They had bungled a presidential assignment to keep the premier JunkGen debate protagonists safe but they saved Tom from running. More surprises followed. Tom had never wept when his father died but, when the Secret Service agents reached him, he was sobbing over Will as he held him in his arms like a baby.

This was not what would have happened in the past—that Tom was sure of. It would not have been *oh no, I've lost Will and they're trying to get me!* but *they got Will and now I'm going to get them!* Even there on the steps, part of him had asked: is this stranger me?

Mimicking the mental loops into which shock victims are often locked, the communal American mind—i.e., the networks, cable, print and the Internet—relived Will Jefferson's murder endlessly. Flashbacks, 24/7. There was no waking up.

It didn't help that a security contractor had captured it all on his video camera. The replays were relentless, although the assassination, as it came to be described, graduated to the upper echelon of national traumas when all outlets abruptly stopped showing the moment of death.

The few minutes of Hi-8, artfully edited, worked at all levels. The arrival of two good and famous men caught in a struggle over the meaning of liberty. A setting dominated by the effigy of the slain secular saint of American freedom. The joshing and the obvious deep affection between the two men, who also happen to look, at least to many women, like they should be carved in marble themselves. The controlled violence and striking athleticism of the sparring. Honorable combat bound by rules that reflected respect for civility and the common good. The long deep bows afterwards. Once the death scene was removed, the clip often ended with this noble image frozen on the screen.

The narrative seemed to say that, yes, these are soul-trying times but if we keep our heads and remember the values we aspire to, we have a chance to get it right. Of course, the expletive of the rifle shot that followed (and was now deleted) argued for more likely outcomes.

The killing provided a brief respite from tribal passions. The Mall began filling almost the moment Will's death became known. Police and the military decided it wise not to resist what seemed a natural and national instinct to come. Not everyone thought that a good idea. Pundits, paid hacks, and well-coiffed maniacs warned that JunkGen hordes were descending upon the capital to seize control of the government from patriotic, right-thinking 'Real Americans." In three days more than a million people had gathered and more were on the way by road, rail and air. A slim majority of the mourners—and of the supporters of Will's R-evolutionary stand—were African Americans. Whatever Will's precise genetic provenance, they knew that he had been their brother, having taken breath in America while Black. But the mourners were from all racial, ethnic, and cultural backgrounds. Most simply supported Will's constitutional beliefs. Even some who differed had come. "We can't conduct our affairs this way," one told the cameras.

The guard's video lied. From the particular camera distance and angle, Tom's terror and flight at the moment of Will's death looked somehow professional and smartly executed. He was also shown returning to Will's side almost instantly. Tom knew that his fear had made the delay seem longer. The camera did not capture his trembling. It made it appear, instead, that he had been staring down the shooter.

Word got out that Tom had wept, although the camera was too far off to catch it. "We're at quasi-war so the visuals would have hurt you among men," an exceptionally nasty but amusing friend and big-time political strategist told Tom. "Just don't do it again." The man had never given up on his insistence that Tom and Will run for public office and had supposedly called to express his condolences. "Because without the image, you're a winner. Women love a man who'll spring a leak at the appropriate moment. And a lot of men are into this macho homo buddy stuff—

it's all over the movies."

On the other hand, many R-evolution opponents were angry that he mourned Will the Greak's death at all. Some of Will's supporters said Tom had benefited from the murder and cable news was happy to pass on the "suspicions" of fringe groups that Tom had planned the whole thing himself. After all, they said, the anti R-evolution faction had the most to gain and Daluskov had demonstrated a willingness to do just about anything to get what he wanted. Then again, it could all be a slick trick by JunkGen conspirators to gain sympathy and tilt opinion on the Court.

As the talking heads dueled, Will's death was folded into the nation's low-grade nervous breakdown. No easy catharsis or relief was in sight. There was no small dusky nation with strange ways and a bad reputation to bomb into smithereens. (China, though a R-evolutionary culprit, was thought perhaps too big a mouthful.), Americans would content themselves for a while with continued wariness of other creeds, races, communities, and ideologies overseas, and become increasingly twitchy about subspecies sleeper cells within their own borders. "Your father believed tribalism provides primeval animal comfort and an addictive neurotransmitter wash in times like these," Tom's mother told him. Folks would be flocking for protection from whatever dog whistling rabble rouser made them feel safe.

That made compromise and a return to clear thinking unlikely for the time being. In this state, many people could not bear to listen to another point of view, never mind consider one dispassionately. To do so would be to forsake the psychic safety and comfort that one's kind and clan provide. To do so would spark a neurotransmitter event and the clutch of dread in the gut first felt eons ago by some freethinker threatened by his fellow wanderers with expulsion from the campfire and a lonely death out in the cold and the dark. And Tom himself, now finally fully acquainted with raw irresistible physical fear, could see why moral courage might take a long time to flower.

Will had been an atheist. Tom knew he would not want a funeral. He had often joked about more absurd burial rituals mankind had come up with. So when his best friend's last will and testament specified "cremation a.s.a.p." and "more of a wake than a memorial service," Tom was not surprised.

This could not be said of the public at large and of Tom's R-evolutionary antagonists in particular. Will's most fanatic followers could not believe that he had named their enemy his executor. This was no anachronism, rendered invalid by Oneida. The document had been recently renotarized with Will's annotation, "All as before." It made sense. Tom was by far his closest friend. Will had established no relationships deeper than the sexual with any of the scores of women in his life, apparently yet to find one with whom he felt he could share his secret and his burdens. There was his sister Rachel, of course, but Will would have known not to burden her. She was devastated and had sought refuge in the guest room at Tom's mother's apartment. Tom called repeatedly from Washington but Rachel could not come to the phone.

Tom's mother, grieving herself, had little to say. So Tom bounced ideas for a memorial gathering off Hank, who was steady and accessible as always. Given Will's preferences, a private get-together at WHUPASS was agreed upon in consultation with Will's closer lab rat friends. A celebration of his life, with some student demonstrations, cake and ice cream for the kids, refreshments for the adults. Will had allowed for "a moment to remember good times," but no formal religious pronouncements. Neighborhood religious leaders that WHUPASS had worked closely with over the years, a priest, two rabbis, an imam, a couple of ministers, and Taoist, Buddhist, Sikh, and Hindu community leaders would be invited. If they wished, they could join anyone else who wanted to say a few words. Will would have liked everyone to be comfortable, especially the young students, whatever their beliefs.

They wouldn't get off that easily, however. Except for the president, Will and Tom were momentarily the most prominent figures in the United States. Will's supporters considered his death a national tragedy and demanded a public ceremony to honor that fact. They saw the minimalist apolitical memorial Tom announced as a plot to diminish the impact of Will's passing on the R-evolution debate. Tom would have liked to grant their wishes and clear himself of the appearance of conflict of interest but that meant ignoring his friend's explicit request.

In the end, it was the President who rode to Tom's rescue. Mason had called Tom the night of the shooting at the hospital where they had brought Will's body. He telephoned again the next day. He said he wanted to respect Will's wishes by consulting Tom on a few things. The Secret Service had obviously retrieved the will. They agreed on a private cremation as soon as an autopsy was complete. Mason had ordered that the procedure be conducted by a broad team of doctors that included two JunkGen pathologists. He welcomed Tom's suggestion that Will's longtime friend Gail Haggerty be one of the examiners.

Only minutes after Tom announced plans for the private WHUPASS memorial, Mason was on the phone again. "We need to do three things," he said. "Honor Will, achieve some closure for the country and his supporters, and get this debate off the streets and back where it can be settled by the courts and through the ballot box." Tom could guess what was coming next. A million and a half highly agitated, directionless people were now camped out in Washington, mostly in and around the Mall. Their obvious distress reflected a potential for unrest throughout the country. Mason believed that a remembrance ceremony in the Mall and on the steps of the Lincoln Memorial would achieve the catharsis necessary to steady the nation. "It can be done with you or without you. I believe Will would understand. He would want to continue his service for peace and unity in the country.

It would also inevitably generate political sympathy for Mason's—and Will's—position on R-evolution but Tom saw that it was the right thing to do and, more importantly, that, knowing the circumstances, Will would feel the same way.

"My respect for you grows, Tom," Mason said before ending the call. "I think that Americans who believe that Will might have become our first African-American president are entirely right. Please don't forget what kind of responsibility that belief lays upon you. You were his best friend and you share all of his talents and his finest attributes. We expect much of you as well."

The feelings loose in the land and savvy television choreography had pretty well guaranteed that the Washington ceremony would be moving. It lacked the sad silliness of the WHUPASS gathering two days earlier. No seven-year-old girls and boys performing their martial arts forms with child-like intensity and gap-toothed joy. No hilarious reminiscences by Carlos and other students of the things Will and Tom had done and said when one had scored heavily or knocked the other on to his keister. No cake and ice cream to assuage the tears.

But solemnity was what Washington needed. And the raft of famous speakers who spoke so eloquently of Will's love of democracy and dedication to civility did much to soothe and guide the emotions of people on the Mall and across the country. There were appeals to political factions as well, of course. But they were muted for the most part and respectful of the occasion.

Tom was surprised that there were so few boos when he approached the rostrum to conclude the ceremony. The ritual, secular though it was, had obviously done its job. Those who mourned Will had begun their passage into a world without him.

Tom was brief. He evoked another time when uncertainty, rampant emotion and national divisions had beset the country and anger and fear had threatened to crush all hope. It took only two minutes or so to read aloud the approximately 270 words of Will's favorite composition in the English language, which began, "Four score and seven years ago our fathers brought forth on this continent a new nation, conceived in Liberty—"

There was subdued but prolonged applause when he finished. Sign of a mood shift, Tom hoped, and acceptance of the suggestion that now was a time for reflection. He thanked all for coming and left the stage. The crowds went home.

The President called a few hours later. Mason noted that because Lincoln's words could be interpreted either way in the R-evolution debate they had achieved a welcome neutrality.

"I think Will would be most concerned with giving Lincoln's 'better angels of our nature' a boost," Tom replied.

"Yes, I believe he would. And I strongly believe that was precisely what you did."

Tom was on the phone most days with Hank. Rachel remained in the guest room and spoke only with Tom's mother. Hank thought they should be left alone to decide "when they should rejoin the living." He was clearly worried, however. So was Tom. His mother lived always at risk of slipping into clinical depression.

Hank was more sure-footed when it came to Tom's afflictions. Tom had confessed to his paralyzing terror the night Will died. "Damn it, Hank, I fell apart! What the heck's happening to me?" Hank's told him to get over it. "Welcome to the real world, son."

Tom was simply getting older and maybe smarter too. Smart people realize they won't live forever, especially when the bullets are flying. Youthful fearlessness wears thin. Tom had Eva now and was looking forward to a long, happy future. "It softens you a little. Dead men are unsuccessful as parents." He spoke of a cumulative effect. "You don't get braver, in my experience. It gets harder, not easier. You've had the near thing a couple of times now. Gradually wears the defenses down."

Hank told him he had been right to hit the ground at the first shot, right to go back to see what he could do for Will, right even to cradle his head, which shielded Will from a second head shot. He was also right not to have charged the gunman. At Manny's, Hank said, Tom had been close enough to save himself and others. On the Memorial steps, it could have achieved nothing beyond suicide. The fact was that he would be dead had the Spartan's wretched old L-Team Garand not jammed.

To this point, Hank had sounded like Hank. Wisdom unrolling whole and unvarnished from long, rich experience. But now his stepfather paused and Tom could sense him choosing his words.

"You've had a free ride for a long time now, Tom. You were born with a low survival response. From what we hear of your dad at Stalingrad, you come by it honestly. The history of war is full of exceptional men whose acts of courage simply astounded the mass of worthy but ordinary soldiers. You don't—or didn't—scare easily. Now, with age, I guess, and repetitive stress, you may be losing some of that edge. You're feeling the fear we regular folks have to live with. You're just going to have to work harder for your courage, the way we mere mortals have always done."

The throwaway line that came next was meant to sound off-hand: "But it could be a one-off thing, son. You may be back to your old self before you know it."

Tom thought back on it when this turned out to be true.

At first Tom discussed none of this with Eva. More evidence of creeping cowardice? Yet within a week of talking to Hank, the burden simply lifted away. He told her the whole humiliating story but could also honestly say that he was sure it would not happen again. As Hank had predicted, he was feeling his own old self.

Eva listened but beyond observing that only liars claimed invulnerability to fear she commented alone on Tom statement that Will's revelations and death had humbled him.

"Humble's good. You've got room to spare for humble."

And the truth was that Tom felt better about himself and his fellow man than he had in years. Things had come too easily for him for too long and he had been spoiled in a way. He could dish it out but didn't know how to take it. Now he was chastened. He understood other people much better than he ever had before. And he knew now how much he and they had in common.

55

Far from abating, the pleas and demands that Tom get into politics mounted by the week. He sometimes called Hank several times a day with updates and for advice. He could also feel his resistance weakening. To begin with, he actually listened to some of the callers now and recently had been rude to almost none. Was it their reasoning? The calls to "duty?" Or had his meltdown on the Memorial steps signaled a more general breakdown of his once steely will? Whatever the reason, his *no!* didn't pack the wallop it once had.

The arguments seldom varied. If Tom wanted his R-evolutionary positions upheld in law, he had to get down and dirty in the trenches. And after that he'd have to get up and over the top to help lead the political charge. Ironically, given his recent self-doubts, the cleverest lobbyists tended to question his courage.

The good news was that his mother and Rachel were doing better. Today they had left the apartment for the first time since Will's death.

"That's a breakthrough," Hank said. "They've gone for a chick flick and an early dinner. It was Rachel I was most worried about."

"Why's that?"

"Your mother is plenty scarred but also plenty tough. She knows how to find a hole to hide in and heal. Rachel is brittle. She said a few things that alarmed me."

"Same here." Rachel had been eerily calm during Tom's only conversation with her since Will died. And her wit had been dark. "I'm a bad joke that's been too long in the telling," she said at one point. "I need a punch line fast."

"She seems a lot better now," Hank told him." She wants to see you when you get back to New York."

"We'll be there on the weekend. Meantime, I think I better shut this political speculation down. It's out of control." The more outsized the proposals—that Tom run for the U.S. Senate, for instance, rather than the congressional seats once suggested for him and Will—the more excited the political classes seemed to get and the higher his ratings climbed in the polls.

"I'm not surprised," Hank replied when Tom told him that a secret covey of high-ranking Democrats even wanted him to seek the party's presidential nomination. "We've had an unprecedented confluence of black swan events. And any party that goes into this election pretending the world has not been turned upside down is going to lose. The candidate must be new — right out of the box, in fact — and marketable as 'right for the times.' "

"It's ridiculous! I'm not qualified."

"That's certainly not true but even if it was it didn't stop a lot of men who didn't have your smarts or integrity from winning the White House. In a perverse way, it might even help. One key qualification of your Dem supporters is their belief that you will do what they think should be done, rather than what a qualified professional politician might. And you have the only qualification that is indispensable. You can be elected."

"So they claim." The Dems had told Tom that if the R-evolution crisis rolled on — and there was no reason to believe that it wouldn't — their current batch of potential nominees could not win against even a mediocre Republican opponent. John Mason wouldn't seek re-election but his polls had improved dramatically after revelation of the Genetically Improved Americans program. He had proved he wasn't a thief. He had acted in good conscience. The team he would bequest to a Republican candidate at least knew the JunkGen and R-evolutionary file. Younger and better educated Democrats believed that none of their current contenders had the skill set the next president would need. The sad fact was their dunce-like ignorance in even the genetic basics was already grist for the late night comedy mills.

"Mason's looking responsible, decisive, even noble," Hank said. "If he anoints the right person, the Democrats could be sunk. The Dem strategists have to change that dynamic. Your job is to decide how you can do what you think needs to be done."

"Mason's nominee would go full speed ahead on R-evolution. A disaster."

"What does Eva say?"

"Things like, 'if you go to war, you better lead from the front.' 'Know any better candidates?' 'Who would *you* trust?' 'Who would *Will* trust?' 'Have you seen their line-ups!' But she's biased." Tom smiled to himself. "The way I see it, I can use my passing fame, notoriety, etcetera, to influence public opinion from outside the sandbox."

Hank was dismissive. "Influence won't do it. You need power. And there'll be no second chances. Emotion decides elections. There's runaway fear out there and you can ride it right into the White House."

"It's a dirty game."

"That why it's so often left to scumbags. But there are many decent people who hate the smell but hack it anyway to fight for their principles. Come on, son! You're at least as mean as they are and twice as tough! Stopping R-evolution will take brains, balls, and the opportunity. Step up!"

Tom had considered other approaches. "I could throw my hat in and seek the nomination—but only to influence policy. If I ran up votes in the primaries, I could influence the final pick and help head off backsliding on R-evolution."

"That's chickenshit and you know it." Hank seemed to be running low on patience. "The party platform goes into the bottom drawer on Inauguration Day. The Dems would still lose and even if they won, you'd end up one adviser among scores, begging for a few seconds of time from a man who would never understand R-evolution or what to do about it. If you ran and won, you'd have four years, with a Democratic Congress, a strong mandate and no desire for a second term. You could shut R-evolution down in that single term period because that's as close to untrammeled power as you'll get in a democracy."

"Untrammeled power?"

"That's what it will take, as will soon become obvious to you. You really have no choice! I say you not only run, you do *whatever* you have to do to win and fix this thing. The nice guys, the good guys wimped out when the game got dirty, as you put it, in Russia and in Germany in the Thirties. They must be held partly to blame for what happened later. It's even more important now because there will be no going back."

Tom found Hank's vehemence unusual and impressive. It stirred some juices deep inside, which at least showed he still had some juices left.

"Okay, partner," he told his stepfather. "You make good points as usual. And since I'm not a nice guy or a complete chickenshit yet, I'll sleep on it."

56

Eva reached for Rachel the moment she saw the gaunt, drawn face at Tom's Washington hotel room door. Rachel allowed herself to be held. "You're very kind, Eva," she said. Her eyes sought and found Tom's. She looked hunted and—Tom kicked himself for even thinking it—human. Beauty laid low.

They all sat down. "I suddenly wanted to see you," Rachel said.

"You're always welcome." Eva reached out again and took her hand.

"Always," Tom said. But he did not touch her. His betrayal of Eva was on all of their minds.

Eva asked if she should order up a drink or some food. "I have a meeting in about half an hour," she lied, eyeing her watch. "So I can't join you." She smiled, as if she couldn't imagine a reason in the world why the two of them should not be left alone.

Rachel said nothing. Will's death had drained her of some quickness and poise.

Eva touched Rachel's hand again. "I hope you don't mind me asking this, Rachel, but I'll feel better once we know how you feel. Tom and I are about to get married. Our original plans were to do the deed very quietly a week from Saturday. We'd like to postpone it if you feel it's too soon after Will's—"

"Absolutely not!" Rachel's smile was manufactured but firm. "Congratulations!" To Tom: "Will would have hated the idea of you putting your happiness on hold." She sounded sincere. "He adored you, Tom. Like a brother."

Tom would wonder later whether Eva's next comment was necessary or wise. She laid a palm on her belly and said: "Thank you, Rachel. We're in a bit of a hurry. For an old-fashioned reason."

There were congratulations again but this time Tom saw the pain in Rachel's eyes. "The rest of the debate notwithstanding, Tom, I wish the very best for all three of you. You are greatly blessed to be able to create a new human life in the old-fashioned way."

Eva gave Rachel a hug and was out the door.

Rachel changed her mind about a drink. They fished a carafe

of California white from the mini-bar and sat by the window, looking out at the Capitol and the Supreme Court building.

"Are you going to be okay?" Tom asked gently. He still had not touched her.

She watched him for a moment, with that face that still seemed able to still his heart. "Do you wonder how I feel?" she asked finally, "knowing now what I am? Whether I feel grief, for instance, in the same way you and Eva do?"

"I know you hurt every bit as much as any of us — probably more. You, Will and my parents have been the people I have felt closest to all my life until Eva. That will never change."

"I believe you. You've always been more capable of kindness than people give you credit for." The old sideway glance of irony flashed for a moment but then was gone.

Tom had wondered whether he would still feel the volcanic rush in her presence. But it was no longer there. More change. Since Oneida, he told Eva just the night before, he felt as if he had left a winding country road with sharp, unexpected turns and was now cruising on a wide open highway.

Rachel read his mind, it seemed. "I've never seen you this relaxed," she said. "I credit Eva."

Only the second part, about Eva, seemed insincere.

"Strange thing is I haven't worked out or sparred in weeks," he said. "It's as if I'm losing a physical need."

"Maybe it's an after-kill effect," Rachel said a little sharply. "Satiation." She smiled tightly. "You feel like we JunkGen freaks are as good as dead — or should I say, extinct."

"I don't think that way," he replied evenly, "and you know it. It's a bigger question than what you or I feel about each other." He touched her glass with his.

"Well, if you're female side's emerging, make sure your Democratic handlers don't find out."

"I'm not in that game yet," he said briskly. And if I do join, he thought, I won't be handled.

Rachel served up the knowing smile. "Don't rule it out," she said after a moment. She looked out at official Washington. "The only thing that made Will more excited about fighting the political battle himself was going up against you. Shots all over again." She shook her head. "Will talked about me, did he?"

Tom wondered how to reply, but Will was gone now and Rachel deserved the truth. "He told me everything, I think. I am so ashamed about how I've behaved towards you two all these years. All I can think to say is that I will always want to be your friend — and that, whatever else Shivkovski and my father have done, in you they have produced a work of art."

"Too bad they didn't make me happy about it." Rachel put down her glass, leaned across the table, and kissed him on the forehead. "But both you and Will have always been so sweet." She stood. "Do you have an aspirin around here somewhere?"

When Tom went to check the medicine cabinet in the bathroom, Rachel poured the Roofies into his glass of wine and stirred it in with her finger.

Tom lay in a doze on the couch, an opened newspaper across his midriff, as if he'd slipped into an afternoon nap.

Rachel was sure he'd never learn about the injection.

She wrapped the syringe in the towel she had brought and buried it deep in her bag. She kissed Tom again on the cheek and gently on the mouth. She locked the door behind her.

Her part was over. She had never done anything to harm Tom. And now she would be out of his life forever. In many ways, this last injection would help him greatly. And when all was said and done, there were far worse fates than not knowing.

57

The New York World

September 11, 2003

She was the woman who had everything: brains, beauty, billions.

Rachel Arianna, scientist, biotech heiress, entrepreneur and a fringe player in the JG crisis, was found dead yesterday in her 15-room Eastside apartment.

Foul play wasn't immediately ruled out but *The World* has learned that Dr. Arianna likely committed suicide.

Homicide sources said she was found hanged from a roof rafter by a rope-like plastic device she often used in the popular Columbia University guest lectures that briefly made her the Carl Sagan of the universe known as molecular biology.

Ironically, the 20-foot prop was meant to represent a stretch of the twisting ladder-like chemical structure of DNA, often called the Book of Life.

Though famous in her own right and a certified first-batch *homo sapiens reformus*, Arianna was not a central player in JunkGen politics.

She was a so-called "lab rat," however, one of the once close-knit Manhattan community of overachieving children whose émigré scientist parents secretly laid the groundwork for the covert R-evolution explosion of the Eighties and Nineties— and the epochal revelations that followed.

The World's Frankenbrat sources said yesterday she was "extremely close" to star New York Assistant A.D.A. Tom Daluskov, who, rumor has it, is soon to become a presidential hopeful. She was also the friend of Daluskov pal and JunkGen superstar Will Jefferson, assassinated by a JunkGen terrorist immediately after an historic appearance before the United States Supreme Court. ("Given recent events," one catty Republican put it yesterday, "knowing Daluskov is like having a death wish.")

With a stratospheric JunkGen IQ, Dr. Arianna breezed through Harvard and M.I.T. and straight into the lab. But her breakthroughs in plant genetics, while significant, were arcane and uncontroversial. "Even Greenpeace ignored her," a genetic ethicist noted yesterday.

"Rachel was not always comfortable in her own skin," said another Columbia colleague. "It was a tough, almost schizophrenic role to play. She was once featured on the covers of Vogue and the American Journal of Science in the same month, yet you got the sense that she found even such notable accomplishments not entirely real."

Dr. Arianna's annual guest lecture at Columbia had become a tradition. It inevitably sizzled with her undeniable sex appeal. In her last appearance, one sophomore recalled yesterday, Dr. Arianna said that she chose to speak to the first-year class because "it was the best place in New York to spot genetic mutants."

She continued her distinguished research career long after large holdings inherited from her late parents' biotech ventures made her a bona fide billionaire.

Despite her outward vivacity, one colleague said yesterday, the scientist had been despondent for some time "for purely personal reasons." He doubted that "the large JunkGen issues" played a role in her death, but she was "crushed" by the death of her friend Will Jefferson and "deeply saddened" by what R-evolution had done to people she had known and loved since childhood.

Dr. Arianna never married and left no children.

Tom called the ME's office from Los Angeles and asked for Dr. Gail Haggerty.

"I'm so sorry for you, Tom," the medical examiner said when she came to the phone. "And I can't get over Will. It seemed to the rest of us that you two were joined at the hip. And now Rachel I don't know how you can handle it."

"Thanks, Gail. Anything I should know about Rachel?"

She lowered her voice. "No sign of the flu, if that's what you mean. From what the guys at homicide told me, she seems to have prepared in a very composed manner. No indication of frantic despondency, like Wally Anderson—or your father. I presume you know that she did not die from hanging. In fact, that thing around her neck never tightened at all."

"Yes, Ray told me. He said death was due to an overdose of chemicals whose names I've forgotten, washed down with champagne."

"You can be sure she didn't suffer. She would have been unconscious before the chair tumbled away. Her body was actually suspended in some kind of safety belt and from airplane wire intertwined with the plastic DNA strand. Took a lot of staging, determination. It was a statement. Sad and clever theater. As if we're all in a way condemned and strung up by our DNA."

"Rachel more than most, unfortunately," he said. He meant tragically, but saying it might shake loose more pain than he was prepared to deal with today. "Sounds like she delivered her punch line."

The ME hesitated before continuing. "The Feds took the body, you know that?"

"She left written instructions. The discretion assigned to the U.S. Surgeon General."

"Eva Martin came with them, to make sure respect was shown."

"She didn't tell me." This act of decency was entirely in character.

"Perhaps I shouldn't have gone into details, given Eva's condition."

"What details?"

"Rachel was in the first trimester. Pregnant."

Tom was reintroduced to one of his newest acquaintances, the deep cavern for remorse that had long remained hidden and empty in his chest. The child had almost certainly been his and had been murdered by a mother who hated her McGenes and who did not want it to come into the kind of world its father was trying to shape. "How did Eva react?"

"We had a little cry together. She's very sweet, especially for a White House superspy, or whatever the heck she is."

"She's pregnant herself."

"Yes, she told me. And newly married."

So much for secrets, Tom thought.

"Are you really a conservative, Tom?" Gail said. "If you are, I'm not sure I can vote for you."

"I'm not running for anything."

"That's not what they say in *The Leader*," she replied. "Pretty well a done deal, right?"

When he didn't respond, Gail went on. "Don't close your mind. It may be my work, but now that I know we can change people a little, I can't see why we should stay the way we are."

"You would if you saw what I did at Oneida, Gail."

"Maybe. But if you do this you have a big responsibility. I don't know what they do during sex but you can tell that most people make their political decisions with their eyes shut tight. If you want to guide us through this, you've got to keep yours and your mind wide open."

"Oh yeah, I know all about you open-eyed ME types," Tom said, inserting the transcontinental needle. "Nothing gets to you. Eat pizza while doing autopsies. Lick your fingers too."

"I see you're mouth's fully recovered."

Tom laughed and touched his scarred cheek.

Gail asked: "You're going to be good to Eva, are you?"

"Nothing's more certain."

"Finally growing up, huh?"

"Fast."

As he hung up the phone it felt more like growing old.

58

The decisions he faced and thoughts of Rachel and Will often kept Tom from sleep. One night he called Ray Franklin and found him working late. Thirty minutes later, in his jogging togs, Tom dropped into a chair at the Kitchen Sink Killer task force center. The place was empty except for his longtime friend and ride-along buddy, who was considering a map of the five boroughs on a computer screen.

"The red arrows mark the killings, right?' Tom asked. "What about the others?"

"The white arrows are the Good Samaritan acts. When he helps the old lady across the street or carries Mom's groceries. Problem is, we know we've got lots of copycats. Kids, other numbnuts trying to scare people. Grabbed one the other day on Canal Street. He squeegeed a woman's windshield, and says, 'No charge but I'll be over tonight to fix your kitchen sink.' The blue arrows are solid possible sightings of the suspect."

What do the math whizzes say?

"Nothing I can understand. But they're running up the electricity bill looking for patterns."

Ray clicked, and five yellow question marks appeared on the screen. "We've got the psychologists looking at these yellow questions. We're pretty sure that these are all him. Yellow is sort of where his good side meets his bad side. Every once in a while he does something that's neither here nor there. You know? Kind, but threatening at the same time."

The arrows were scattered throughout the city, with heavy clusters in Queens and Brooklyn. Reflecting the pattern of the last few months, Manhattan now showed the densest concentration. Ray clicked his mouse button and the blue and red arrows disappeared. They were replaced by several dozen fairly widely scattered whites, although there was a heavy band right across the island from 72nd Street down to about 30th.

Tom stood up and spent a few minutes scanning the old-style New York City map on the wall. It was also peppered with red and white pins. No scheme revealed itself. But he noticed that there was no activity at all east of the Van Wyck Expressway in Queens. Not a single incident outside what appeared to be an arbitrary border. "I wouldn't be surprised if this guy is using a map himself," he said over his shoulder. "Maybe the map is not as big as this one. Maybe it doesn't cover anything east of the Van Wyck or south of Flushing Avenue in Brooklyn."

He heard Ray click on his mouse. "I think you're right. But so what?" They stared again for a moment at their respective New Yorks. Tom sat down. "There has to be something more," he said. "This guy is playing games. And games need patterns. We need to figure out what dimension he's operating in, if I may quote my longtime acquaintance and now fugitive looney-toon, Leon Shivkovski."

Ray clicked and looked, clicked again and examined the redrawn screen once more. "You can see the clusters," he said. "But we know that already. Now all the action's in Manhattan."

"What about the time element?" Tom said. "Can we look at the chronology?"

"There a list, somewhere here."

"May I?" Tom asked, reaching for the mouse.

"Go ahead. Take this seat."

Tom clicked on a box labeled Date and clicked on a day a few weeks earlier. The map was redrawn. He clicked on a red arrow in Long Island City. A pizza delivery man had been savaged with a brick. At first it seemed like a robbery. Later, two witnesses turned up saying a suspect they'd seen in the area looked like the Kitchen Sink Killer composite on TV.

Tom clicked on another date. A white arrow appeared near Shea Stadium. Ray said a man matching the composite had rescued two ten-year-olds being shaken down for pocket money. He'd made his point to the ersatz tough guys with a baseball bat, which he'd given to the kids. It had been autographed in 2000 by Mark McGuire and was worth more than a few bucks.

Tom clicked on three more dates. "So far they're in a wide lateral belt. You've got north–south and east–west axes. These sites were picked off a map. More precisely, off a grid." *Click.*

"Whoops," said Ray. "This doesn't fit. Too far apart. Corner store owner near the Battery, throat cut with a lawn mower blade—the mulching variety. We know because he left it behind. But Kitchen Sink suspect was IDed." The previous incident, a white arrow, had occurred far away in Queens. Mourners in St. Michael's Cemetery, touched by the help and care provided to elderly mourners by a youngish man at the internment of an 80-

year old retired dock worker, were stunned to recognize him later from the composites now all over the tabloids and the TV news.

"No, it would still fit. If you impose a certain sized grid over the NYC map, the Battery would fit as the southwest, or lower left, corner."

"Okay, so maybe he uses a map. Big deal. He's probably throwing darts at it. That means we can't get there from here."

"Let's try something else." Tom took the mouse and began clicking at boxes. "This is a hell of a program," he said at one point. After five minutes of fiddling, he hit the enter key, and arrows began popping up all over the map. "I'll slow things down," he said, opening another box, and fine-tuning the settings some more. "I've set it up so that it'll display the incidents from beginning to end at a steady pace. A day at a time. So if there's nothing on that day, nothing will happen. When there's a burst of activity, we'll see that represented. He reached for the mouse. "Maybe we'll see something else."

One by one the white, blue and red arrows began to appear.

"It's a bit like popping corn backwards," observed Ray. "Scattered pops at the beginning followed by a bunch."

The action did seem to be laid out over an almost square section of city, with a north–south axis. The incidents seemed to start in two parallel bands across the top and bottom of the square. The next ones moved down from the top and up from the bottom toward the middle. Then incidents began happening quite literally all over the square, but with spacing that suggested a grid. Once, however, there was a flurry of activity, two whites, two blues and two reds in the lower West 30s. Then, a yellow question mark, the first of five, appeared in Queens.

"Hold on," Ray said, about 30 seconds later. "You see how the square overlay seems to move to another part of the city every time the yellow question mark shows up? Look at it now. The square covers a smaller geographical area and has shifted to the middle of Queens . . . and there! The next question mark, and the square is suddenly over Manhattan."

They were both watching intently now, leaning on their elbows. "Look, the north-south axis is gone. He's using a Manhattan map now, aligned to the city's own street grid."

"Makes it easier for him too," Ray said dryly. "More land to shoot at this way. If the grid's north-south, half his darts end up in the Hudson."

Tom reached for the mouse and froze the display. "Okay, so we know that after every yellow question mark, the square grid moves to cover another section of the city and sometimes changes size." Tom had the computer display the first Manhattan grid incident pattern again at a slower pace. "In this first grid, you've got no incidents above 86th and none below 35th." A yellow question mark appeared. "Now the grid slides south. We still get action in Midtown and the Garment District but nothing above 72nd."Tom clicked on pause." There's something very familiar here but I still can't find the handle."

Ray said: "Like all the previous square sections, everything starts across the top and the bottom. Then the incidents move toward the middle before busting out all over."

Tom clicked and the chronological display resumed. After a few seconds, he said "What's this? This is different"

The killer's operational square had shifted again, further downtown. But the first arrows in this new grid were all white — almost a dozen of them. In the other grids, especially in Manhattan, the white and red arrows had tended to alternate, although the reds would begin to predominate as time went on.

"For some reason, all he did for ten straight days were good deeds," said Ray. "You missed that, being otherwise occupied."

After the ten white arrows had flicked off in the upper half of the new square, the red indicators, signifying seven killings over seven days, appeared in a grim rhythm below them on the map.

"That's different too," Ray said. "Never happened before." He glanced at Tom when he got no reaction. "What's wrong?"

Tom had turned pale. He clicked on a settings box. The blue arrows disappeared, the white arrows turned blue, and the red became white. Tom's right hand moved right to the screen. He held his thumb and two fingers together, as if he was holding something, and traced several motions in the lower half of the grid, starting near the bottom on the square. He made three or four straight motions. He made a diagonal line. He made an L.

"I'm white," he said quietly. "Because I always win."

"White?" Ray said. "Yes, you're white but what does that — wait, you mean white, like in chess?"

"That maniac Leon? My god! He's been running this thing from the very beginning. This is his chess game in multiple dimensions. The chess games we've been playing for years. He started using our moves to create murder in the streets of New

York. He has some JunkGen murderer or murderers out there expressing our moves in real life mayhem and petty favors." Tom slammed the table top, then looked away and shook his head slowly. "Forty-six lives."

"Forty-seven," Ray said, watching Tom closely.

"I'm astounded. There's at least purpose in his father's madness. But Leon is from a fucking other world." He looked at Ray and tapped a finger sharply against the screen. "And he wanted me to find out because he hasn't really hid it in this last grid. He took a series of 10 moves I sent him for a blind opening game and used them to set the venues for these killings. My chess piece moves to a certain point on the board and he has a killing in the corresponding square on the grid! And this homicidal maniac has the gall to use *his* moves for good works!"

"You sure?"

"God," said Tom, running his hand through his hair. "I wish to hell I wasn't!" He grabbed the mouse and clicked back through the earlier grids. "I can see it all clearly now. When it started, he ordered a killing only when I took one of his pieces. If he took mine, he set up a good deed, I suppose. But he began tying even my opening moves to this separate world he thinks he's running." He clicked back to the final screen, with its seven white arrows. "At least we've got a chance to stop these killings now. I'm betting Leon has only the one killer slash do-gooder. Keeps it intimate. We can head him off because I remember the last three moves." He leaned towards the screen. "We've got to flood Little Italy with plainclothes. Everybody we've got."

"Sorry, Tom," Ray said quietly. "I'm afraid Little Italy's already on the board. White arrow. Tonight. Waitress. It's not punched in yet."

Ray picked up the phone. Tom calculated the next sector likely to be hit. "Tell them SoHo and the East Village," he said. Ray relayed the information. The killer's disguises were a problem but they at least finally had a small area to concentrate on. Tom was mumbling to himself. "Match and series to you, Leon," Ray heard him say. When Tom turned to the detective, his face cast the unfamiliar look of defeat. "Guess I should have let him win a few games," he said softly, "but I just didn't have it in me."

59

It was Ray who found the corpse. Leon the Terrible, now as rotten in death as he had been in life.

The detective had applied shoe leather and a veteran's hunch to a task at which brighter men with more resources had failed. A relieved Tom had headed back to Washington when the Kitchen Sink killer did not strike in the East Village or SoHo or anywhere else in New York City. Leon's murderous multidimensional chess game seemed to be on hold.

Tom was betting that the EAF, in charge of coddling papa Shivkovski and keeping him productive, would have an idea where the son was hiding. To find out, he'd use whatever pull he had at the White House. Ray lacked similar friends in high places but had all Leon's offices and home searched again and put one of his top techs on the phone logs. Tom's call from Washington the month before to cancel their meeting had been forwarded to a landline number at what had probably been Leon's secret rendezvous site. Ray soon had an address on the West Side and decided, on a hunch, to check it out alone. Anyway, for Ray Franklin these days, a search warrant was only a speed-dial away.

No one answered his knock but the door was unlocked.

Though discolored, Leon's upper lip still wore the trademark curl. Perhaps death in this dimension had not lived up to his expectations.

The killer had placed a chessboard on a small table in front of the body. His right hand had been positioned to rest beside his toppled king. This was meant to signify the victim's surrender, of course, but was obviously just one part of a crude setup to implicate Tom in Leon's death.

Another chessboard, apparently made of jade, lay on the floor. From the look of Leon's skull, it had been used to deliver the final blow. It would no doubt be linked to the Kitchen Sink serial killings. Under a nearby chair, Ray saw two bloodied bamboo Arnis sticks—from WHUPASS, no doubt. They had likely been used in the brutal beating Leon had obviously suffered. The shoulder of the victim's shirt had been torn away in excuse-me-please-note-this-evidence fashion. The tear exposed heavy bruising on the flesh that would probably be found consistent with the game of "shots" with which Tom had tormented the young Shivkovski as a child.

Why precisely Leon was dead Ray did not know but Tom was clearly intended to be collateral damage. There would be other physical evidence to implicate him, Ray presumed—blood, hair, possibly even fingerprints. This was the JunkGen era, after all, and this kind of thing could be copied, faked, or manufactured from scratch. The fussy touches and the attention to props and script showed this to be the Kitchen Sink Killer's work. But who had crafted the skit and scheduled the premiere as a one-night stand? It could only be the self-appointed maestro, Leon Shivkovski. He was the only person on earth who hated Tom enough. He had either risked a severe beating that had spun out of control or had actually scripted and played out his own death scene in a final all-out attempt to lay some shots on his lifelong nemesis.

Unfortunately for Leon, however, Tom had been unable to fit the set-up into his busy schedule. The detective was willing to bet that the canvassing of neighbors would produce reports of a nasty disturbance on the day and at the precise hour when Tom was supposed to meet Leon here two weeks ago. The body's ripeness seemed to fit the time frame. But in the final moments, when hallucinations of Tom's downfall or disgrace may have lightened Leon's death throes, Tom had been chatting with the President of the United States. It involved name-dropping but was a pretty good alibi anyway.

Ray figured that Leon probably recognized that the frame-up had little prospect of success but expected, probably correctly, that the awful smell from his insane self-scripted swan song performance would stick to the presidential candidate. 'Maybe Daluskov didn't kill this guy,' people would think, 'but what about what happened at Manny's Café?' And, 'they say he never stopped beating this little guy up when they were kids.' And, 'whenever Daluskov's involved, things just get too weird."

Even Tom's great work on the Kitchen Sink killings was bound to generate blowback. Tom's reputation for win-column brilliance would be further boosted when Ray gave him public credit for the breakthrough but the details would also create an indelible image in the public mind of Tom unwittingly moving the chess pieces year after year in ways that condemned 47 people to die.

Whatever else happened, Ray intended minimize that damage. He called in his task force to secure the crime site. After all, Leon's death was a Kitchen Sink case—the 48th homicide—even if the victim happened to be one of the conspirators himself. The only difference between this and the other killings was that Leon, not Tom, had chosen the location. Ray's team would take full charge of every piece of the evidence. They—or, more accurately, Kitchen Sink Killer task force chief Ray Franklin—would decide how to interpret it all, as well as what to do next.

Ray left the moment his squad had sealed the apartment off. He'd confiscated Leon's cellphone and two hours later he was at the front door of a second-story Brooklyn apartment. Alone again. He would vet all additional evidence he found before bringing in his team. That way he could try to defuse any additional booby traps Leon had left behind.

The resemblance was subtle overall but pronounced in parts. So when the Kitchen Sink guy opened his front door, Ray couldn't help thinking about all those missing eggs Tom said his mother always worried about.

"The Boss told me it might be you," the man said with a smile. "He even showed me your picture." He was wearing sweat pants and an exercise hoodie and looked to be freshly showered. He ignored Ray's handgun, which was leveled at his head, turned and headed back to the apartment's small kitchen. The witnesses had been right about the walk and the bow legs.

"The Boss?" Ray asked, following with his gun still raised. "You mean Leon, don't you?" He knew he should cuff this guy but he also needed to hear what the killer might say before the mood turned sour. Ray stepped back two paces when Gerald moved to put a cap on a large jug of something he'd apparently just finished pouring into the sink. "So the Boss let you call him Leon too, huh?" The man appeared impressed. "I'm Gerald, by the way, Detective," he said. "but you probably already know that."

By now Ray had decided that Tom's enemies would have a field day with Gerald, even though he was less the Daluskov lookalike Ray had feared he might be than someone with a clear family resemblance. The obvious question would be, how similar are their inner lives and secret compulsions?

"You know the script, Gerald," Ray asked playfully," so what's next? What are the Boss's instructions?" Killings numbers 9 and 10 of the latest series, set by the chess code for this assignment, had still not been carried out.

"Leon wanted to switch me off."

"Wanted to do what?" Ray already knew the answer. He had read about it in a logbook Leon used to track his murderous interdimensional game. Gerald was referring to the long-established ability of geneticists to "switch" genes—and their effects—"on" and "off" by chemical means. Injection, probably, of things called vectors. "But that would be good news, wouldn't it, Gerald? No more Big A for you."

"But no more satisfaction either."

Quite the complex guy! On the way to "recovery," the shrinks might say, now that he "understood" his problems. Ray understood him and his problems too, thanks to Leon's logbook.

Gerald had been genetically "looped." The chemical rewards to make him feel safe, content and "happy" weren't available to him until his brain also knew that he had carried out his assignment. Call him obsessive-compulsive. A passion for precision was also coded in his genes. He didn't *feel* right unless he used the tools Leon dictated precisely as instructed and at the times and places designated in Leon's coded signals. When he did, he got a pleasant neurotransmitter rush. His empathy genes, inconvenient to his work, had been bleached out. The bizarre good deeds were just another job well done for Gerald the killer, equal in value to a nicely performed asphyxiation, especially when he was allowed an extra hit of serotonin for creativity. Under different direction, he might be the model employee or the perfect son.

"So, Gerald," Ray asked in a masterful voice, "did you finish those last two assignments before the Boss switched you off?" The detective's eyes wandered over the half dozen heavily annotated maps of the five boroughs. Like the task force, Gerald had color coded the murders and the good deeds. The homemade shelves heaved under scores of tools and artifacts from the killings, wiped down but no doubt crawling with forensic and DNA evidence. Everything was arranged neatly. The disguises, beards, wigs, etc., would all be here as well. And so, Ray thought, the Kitchen Sink Serial Murder case was coming to an end. All he needed now was to tie it up in a big red bow.

"No, I haven't done those last two," Gerald replied, bowing his head in apparent shame. That face! "But it's the Boss's fault! He was awfully sloppy in the end. A real mess the last time I saw him. I lost confidence in him." He spoke this last bit very softly, as if Leon might still be listening somewhere. "I'll switch myself off and I'll do it my own way. I'm now allowed to be creative."

"Like you were with the Boss?"

"Yes, like that. Just like that. The Bo . . . Leon told me I could 'go with the flow' as long as I 'checked all the boxes.'"

"And his death was the last box to be checked?"

Gerald's large Daluskov-like eyes widened. "No! That was me, my decision. He told me clearly that it was up to me. So it didn't count when he changed his mind. No! The last box was to be sure to leave lots of fingerprints. Not like all the other assignments. And I did that."

Maybe Tom and this guy really did share the same prints! "What do you know of Tom Daluskov?" Ray asked.

"Once long ago, Leon said that Tom Daluskov thought he was god and so we would make him one for a while. He didn't tell me how. He said nothing more about him but I often saw Mr. Daluskov on the news." Gerald was completely relaxed, leaning back casually against the kitchen counter, his hands in his hoody pockets, as if they were cold. "I think making Mr. Daluskov a god was only a small part of the Boss's and my main work, which was to help dispense random fate and so-called good and evil, etcetera. Before this last job, the Boss laughed and said that Tom Daluskov was going to get *some good news and some bad news*. He told me to buzz Tom Daluskov up when he arrived and leave by the back door. Outside somewhere I was to make a 911 call about hearing screaming and a beating. But Mr. Tom Daluskov wasn't on the next block as he was supposed to be. He was in Washington, DC. What can I say? Unbelievable, but the Boss messed up. I still see Tom Daluskov on the news all the time."

Gerald looked at Ray for a while, apparently awaiting another question. When none came immediately, he turned, leaned over the sink, and flipped a black light switch. "There, that's done." he said, glancing up at the wall clock and addressing Ray again. "There are ten units in this building. Don't forget the basement. You'll find the complete list of 42 residents behind you there, pinned to the door. Most are at work or school. You have thirty minutes to clear the place."

"Bomb?"

"The Boss insisted. Again, quite frankly, I wasn't impressed. But he told me precisely what I was to say—to you, or to Tom Daluskov. And it is this: 'You know these Shivkovskis; they're fond of pyrotechnics."

"Let's go, Gerald," Ray said, raising his weapon.

"I took the first two injections," Gerald said, not moving. "Supposed to be five. Haven't had a decent idea or a clear head since. How do you people deal with all the confusion? But I do have a remote control in my pocket here and my thumb is on the button that can detonate the explosives."

Ray raised his weapon again but hesitated. He should shoot or try to subdue Gerald right now, haul him outside and clear the building. But if he failed, he'd kill a lot of innocent people, along with himself. He speed-dialed the bomb squad.

"Did the Boss ever tell you who you look like?" Ray asked.

"Bits and pieces, he called me. He gave me the Beatles CD. The Boss was always joking." Gerald looked stern as Ray raised the phone to his ear. "I'd rather you didn't do that, Ray. It will only make things worse. Just get the people out of the building. Simple!"

Ray spoke quickly into his phone before pressing the mouthpiece against his chest. "Fire and bomb squad, Gerald," he said, almost whispering. "Don't get upset. I've got procedures too, you know."

"You're right. See? Just one of Leon's stupid injections and already I'm a whiner like him." He suddenly brightened and looked a little excited. "So, you've got your job, and I've got mine." He winked at Ray. "It's weak, I admit. But best I can do on short notice." He popped something into his mouth—a pill or a candy. He made a circus-like *ta-daaaaaah*, and opened his hands like a ringmaster. No remote control! "Ray!" he shouted. "Keep your eyes on the kitchen sink!"

After a big but brief grin, Gerald spun around and plunged his face deep into the liquid he had poured from the large container.

Ray watched for a moment, then turned away.

"Guess it was acid," Ray told Eva a few hours later. "And the pill must have been poison. I must be going soft. The guy's a mass killer but I still sort of hope he died instantly after that stuff started eating away his face."

"At least no one else was hurt."

"A small miracle. The propane tanks he'd prepped everywhere blew the fire all over the neighborhood. Place went up like a Roman candle. Homicide and the ME aren't too pleased that I didn't get the body out."

"What did you tell them?"

"The truth. Priorities. Clear the building, save life and limb. Worry about the dead and evidence later."

"Nothing left at all? Can you tell me about his face?"

"Just teeth and bones. I don't know how Leon did it, or old Shivkovski. Probably Leon, though. Playing in his own little lab while the grownups were working in theirs. But he's got bits and pieces in there, like the Beatles song. Will, minus the pigmentation. Rachel, and maybe one or two other lab rat types I've seen over the years."

"And Tom?"

"That's what jumps out at you from behind everything else. Cheekbones, shape of the forehead, and the eyes. Body shape, too. Not as big, perhaps, but this guy was powerful." Ray wouldn't make Eva ask. "I didn't mention it to anyone. Don't plan to, either. Not important to the case."

"It's your call, Ray. And Tom?"

"Why distract him?" Ray said. "We can fill him in later."

Epilogue

60

Washington, DC
February 11, 2003

The surroundings were more suited to a boilermakers' convention than a rendezvous between the two leading contenders for the Democratic presidential nomination. Tom and his security had been wandering the bowels of this Washington office complex for 10 minutes now, following a handwritten map.

Tom knew Senator Andrew Walker was planning a surprise. Walker, once a shoe-in for the Democratic nomination, had slipped disastrously in primaries after New Hampshire. He and Tom were now head to head in both the delegate count and the polls. They both knew that only an early accommodation could reignite the party's slim chance of victory in November and, with it, their flagging campaign to first halt and then reverse R-evolution. It was time to at least start thinking about a deal.

So when Tom sailed through the "Maintenance Chief, D Section" door he was expecting an intimate Democratic tete a tete. What and who actually awaited him inside stopped him in his tracks. He was momentarily speechless until the GOP luminary squatted on a paint-stained work stool rose and held out his hand.

"Mr. President," Tom said. Though he appeared more gaunt and fatigued than the last time they had met, John Mason's handshake remained strong. "Pardon my surprise. But when the Republican incumbent gains entry to the Democratic back room, I'm really start feeling like the rookie in the room."

Tom turned to Senator Andy Walker, who, less surprisingly, was also present. "Tom!" roared Walker, who had never remembered a name he wouldn't bellow or met a hard he wouldn't shake. Tom respected and liked the older man but the affection could hardly be mutual. If Walker was on his political death bed today, it was because Tom had put him there.

The President pointed to an empty chair. "Why don't we three sit down," he said, "and talk a few things out for the good of America." Mason looked grim. "This is beyond party politics, Tom, and I have but a small role here."

The President's beaten-down demeanor belied the fact that his rehabilitation, at least with the voters, was complete. Once American history's biggest bunco suspect and an almost sure bet to be impeached, he was now widely seen as a wise if anguished statesman and a reluctant and thoughtful warrior in the R-evolutionary wars. His pledge to work for full and open debate on all R-evolution issues and calls for reason from all sides had, however, created deep fear and loathing in important corners of his own party.

Republicans could at least be happy that the stock of the leading Democratic presidential contender had waned as the outgoing Mason's had waxed. With the President insisting on the high ground in the debate, Walker had had little choice other than to take the low road. The cost had been high and his image of decency had been perhaps irreparably tarnished. He had likely lost many of the independent voters who would decide the result in November.

Walker had adopted a down and dirty style in his battle with Tom as well. The attacks had hurt and had probably kept the senior senator's nomination hopes alive. They targeted Daluskov's "dark side," the man who "cherry picks the laws he'll obey" and boasts "fists of death." The fingerprints identical to Tom's found all over the Leon Shivkovski murder scene were easily explained but still added to what *The World* called Tom's Freakiness Factor. "When Daluskov's involved, we enter the Twilight Zone—and stock up on body bags."

And thus the Democratic deadlock, which was looking increasingly fatal. Lifelong public servant of reasonable integrity Andrew Walker looked safe, dependable, presidential but had soiled himself during his campaign and was clearly a technological dinosaur in the new R-evolutionary age. Confidence in Tom's skills and strengths in this area was obvious in the polls. His numbers jumped whenever R-evolutionary news broke or JunkGen alarm rose. Yet they did not entirely cancel out the fears that he was in some ways unpredictable, extreme, and dangerous.

"I can beat you, Tom," Walker told him now, still with the never-quit grin. "But this race is hurting the party. We need to sort out the policy differences right here and now. We can't go to the people with our own folks at one another's throats."

Tom glanced at Mason. *The party? Our own folks?* How could a Republican president be here playing inside baseball with the

Dems? Tom needed to brush these two off with a fast ball. "Before we go any further, Mr. President and Senator Walker, I'll make one thing clear. I will not compromise on the issue of R-evolution. Not even if it costs me the nomination or the presidency. It has to be stopped here in the United States and everywhere else in the world."

Strangely, although he was not yet ready to say so, this actually overstated his current feelings. The gradual shifts in Tom's temperament had continued in recent months. They had been accompanied by several of the most intense episodes of lucidity and serenity he had ever experienced. The experiences had been almost spiritual compared with those of his younger years and the aftereffects had persisted for far longer. Even as he drafted or toughened up his hardline speeches, he'd had to fend off a strange drift toward compromise and conciliation.

It was President Mason, not Walker, who responded to Tom's condition. "The early years of Abraham Lincoln's presidency have always fascinated me," he said, folding his hands on the work table. "We can learn from Abe today. A man trying to lead a country that was split by the most bitter hatreds in a time when the basest human passions ruled. At the center of things was an issue of fundamental right and wrong, Good and Evil, if you will. But Lincoln recognized that to act rashly or stubbornly to resolve this matter without also preserving all that was good about the nation would be an abdication of his responsibility as President to all the people of his and of future generations."

Walker picked up the lesson. "The nation had to survive We must keep our options open. The Emancipation Declaration came only midway through the war. In a time of flux and unprecedented instability, you cannot maintain a rigid position, Tom. You have to bend a little and thereby help the nation find the flexibility needed to survive. This country has to continue to work together as a democracy if we're to have any hope of protecting the human values we all feel are threatened."

Tom thought he could guess part of what was coming. Walker had lost too much ground to present a credible Democratic challenge. Alone, that is. Many of Tom's Democratic and independent votes — younger, hardline, counter-r-evolutionists — would stay home if Walker won the nomination. But that might change if Tom was on the ticket. So perhaps Walker was about to accept some of Tom's policy positions if Tom would accept the vice-presidential slot.

That would still leave Mason's presence a mystery. Why was he here? Why was he helping remake Democratic strategy in a way that might hurt his own party's presidential chances? Tom suspected it must have something to do with Mason's secret agenda. Perhaps Walker might not be as anti-R-evolution as he pretended to be. If that were true and Walker got the nomination and won the presidency, some of Mason's preferred policies on R-evolution would survive.

Tom asked Mason. "Maybe you and the Senator can tell me what exactly you feel Mr. Lincoln would do in our current circumstances?" He winked at both men. "And which of us should play Honest Abe?"

Walker smiled, glanced at Mason, and got the go-ahead. "First," the senator boomed, apparently from their pre-agreed script, "Abe would issue an executive order for the immediate suspension of all and any experimentation in, or genetic engineering of, the human genome by the private sector and unauthorized government agencies. He would sequester and centralize all private and research documentation, records, and materials relevant to the human genome, including eggs, sperm, gametes, and so on, and declare the federal government the sole guardian of such information and the sole legal agent of the American people for genomic research."

"Huge property issues," Tom said for argument's sake, adding repercussions he believed were inevitable in any counter-r-evolution assault. "You'd be in the courts forever, and accused of killing people by bringing medical research to a grinding halt."

"Not if you did it correctly," Walker continued. "The point is to move quickly and decisively. You use the element of surprise to gain total physical control of all ongoing research — "

"And private sector production?" Tom asked. "Do you believe there are other Shivkovskis out there?"

The President finally spoke up for himself. "Our best guess is, not yet. But it won't be long."

Walker said: "It can work. Take GreenGene, for example. You take legal control of its facilities, do an inventory and then their scientists can resume all legitimate research in as little as a few weeks — with regulators on site."

Tom was surprised. He looked at Mason: "Mr. President, word of this gets out and you'll never eat lunch on Wall Street again. Your party will lose most of its funding."

Walker said: "It was the President who approached me, Tom, with a view to approaching you. As you know, his party's two most likely nominees are ready even after the recent disasters to leave what happens in genomic research to the marketplace. President Mason, it is my understanding, believes that the market, while efficient in certain matters, is far from infallible and exhibits the moral sensibility of a shark. We don't let private companies build a better nuclear bomb or freely produce and market bio-war technology. So why would we be so foolish as to allow the future of the human species to be sorted out by the vagaries of the profit motive?"

Again Mason said nothing. Just the meaningful nod. But it had the ring of truth. Mason was known to be a Republican maverick on the subject of regulation in the financial industry, for instance, having been discouraged from reimposing stronger rules and enforcement on runaway risky behavior only by the Republican political considerations. Tom began to suspect that the President did not want his own words to be on the record. Just then, however, Mason said: "We'll work out restitution later."

Mason looked at Walker. This time it was the old warrior's turn to nod.

Mason now had a much greater surprise. He continued. "Actually, restitution will very likely come under your watch as president, Tom. When the time comes, you'll have to move quickly. The plan will involve virtually all the agencies of the Federal government, including domestic deployments of the armed forces. It may be necessary to impose martial law, mostly locally — if only for as long as needed to take physical possession of the human genomic resources."

The three men grew silent for a moment as the blockbuster implications of Mason's statement sunk in. When Walker spoke, it was with more gravity than he usually displayed: "The lawyers and legislators will have to work out the details. The intent, however, would be to put all research, regulation and experimentation involving the human genome under the exclusive and total control of the federal government. And it will indeed go on in the courts for years." Now Walker smiled and turned the twinkle back on. "That is, well into your second term."

There was no denying it now. The Republican president and Tom's primary Democratic rival were offering him their support, covert and otherwise, for the Democratic nomination for the presidency! Tom's physical response was more nuanced than at moments of triumph in the past. Some clenching of fist and molars but more oceanic and his mind remained clear, alert to the fact that his counterparts in this horse trading had not yet named their price. Walker was surrendering the ambitions of a lifetime. And Mason appeared not only to be betraying his party but to be backing off significantly from his pro-R-evolution policies. What did they want in return? He was almost certain it would be too much.

Still, Tom felt obliged to acknowledge Mason's gesture. "What you gentlemen suggest would be a move in the right direction. But, as I've said, you should support me, openly or otherwise, only if you accept that, if elected, I will put an end to the Genetically Improved Americans program and R-evolution in general."

The President would speak for himself now. His tone was patient and respectful even though Tom was in most senses of the word an upstart. "Senator Walker and I will accept that this may be your ultimate decision—one day in the future. What we ask is that you take some time to study the situation and to consider all the alternatives and all the possible outcomes of your decisions. It is dangerous to say no or never without a period of serious prolonged examination of the options. For America to end R-evolution now could have devastating unintended consequences. Some of these imponderables might put not only the United States but the whole concept of free, untrammeled democratic culture for mankind at risk."

"So we churn out only Junk Generations that love democracy?"

"I mean that we must understand that, as the old world ends—and it is definitely ending—the United States and its people must learn how to survive, prosper and, one hopes, continue to lead in the new world now being born."

Walker leaned forward and placed a hand gently on Tom's forearm. The older man's pale blue eyes appeared watery. "We believe that you have the stuff to be a new Honest Abe in this crisis. To guide us through what will, I'm afraid, be a terrible ordeal. You'll need patience, which I believe you have been gaining, and the wit to handle the complexities of the situation. Most important, I think you have the heart to help show

Americans what is right for them too."

"And last but not least, I'm possibly electable." Tom was polite but firm to put things in perspective.

"This is true!" Walker slumped back into his chair. "Not an endearing quality from where I sit, but indispensable." His pain passed, however, and he continued. "But that's not why this is happening. President Mason and I have discussed it at length and we both agree: I'm just not tough enough for this challenge. Lincoln could exercise good judgment and compassion only because he was tough enough to endure the losses and slaughter and ignominy and hatred to battle on and to win the war."

Mason interjected: "He had the killer instinct. So do you This will be a war—with new fronts and guerrilla attacks opening up daily on all sides. We need the reflexes of the young, plus the flexibility. You understand the genetics revolution and, what's more important, the American people feel confident in your knowledge. They'd worry that either of the honorable Republican nominees would be in over his head, not to mention open to manipulation by his staff, party handlers, and corporate America. As far as your own principles go, what you feel and believe is already out there. There's the Oneida incident and your heroism saving those New York policemen. Now all you have to do is have the courage and character to think about changing your mind.'

Walker stood up and seemed ready to speak but sat down and was silent again. He looked at Mason for a moment, then exhaled deeply. "Before the Ohio primary," the Senator now said, "I will withdraw my name from the list of candidates for the Democratic Party presidential nomination. I will ask my supporters to throw their wholehearted support behind a united effort to make you the next president of the United States."

"Won't that look like the fix is in?" Tom asked. He might be mellowing but he was not enthused about winning without a fight.

"I don't think so, son," said Walker. "On my part, it will be seen as an act of statesmanship or, more likely, realism."

"Say yes to us, Tom," Mason declared solemnly, "and you will be the next President of the United States."

"Let's say I say 'yes' to delaying my final decision on ending R-evolution if and when I reach the White House. What do I get from you?"

Mason did not respond, cuing Walker instead. "Andy?"

Walker was also hesitant to put the offer into words. Secret attempts by the select few to settle the American people's business were nothing new but Tom could see why the senator might waver. There had never been a back room deal anywhere near as big, broad or important as this one — at least, not that they knew about.

"My clear understanding from President Mason is this," the Senator said finally. "At the most appropriate and opportune time before Election Day, the incumbent President will withdraw his support for his own Republican Party candidate and publicly back you. From that point on, he will campaign openly and vigorously for your election. It will be a matter of personal conscience. He will encourage Republicans on this historic occasion and as needed in the future to vote according to their consciences too."

"And what precisely does he expect in return?" This was largely a rhetorical question. Mason knew that there was no way that Tom, once elected, could be bound to a particular course of action. In deciding to betray his party, Tom could see, the President had found himself in a position familiar to every American. His political choices had been narrowed by the party machines, special interests, Big Business, Big Labor, Big Money, Big Media, down to two men. He was "voting" for Tom because he couldn't live with a free-market R-evolution. He was also fearful of the deals his Republican front-runner had made on the right. For one thing, some evangelical Christians and social conservatives seemed to believe that the new Republican president would institute forced genetic treatment to "fix" homosexuals and try to R-evolutionize the predisposition out of the gene pool altogether. Atheism and non-Judeo-Christian predispositions might come next.

"I want you to learn the M word, Tom," Mason said. "M for moratorium. We simply want you to change your stand from the absolute, this immediate, total, scorched-earth war on R-evolution and damn-the-costs approach, to a moratorium. This is no great sacrifice or even necessarily a change. In its effect, a moratorium that never ends remains your ban. You enforce it ruthlessly but you adopt a show-me position. A moratorium can easily be explained as a cautious way of respecting popular concerns over forever losing R-evolution's potential benefits. You will be asking the American people for their trust, something they are desperate to give to someone and which I firmly believe they will be grateful to give to you. All this will bring you new votes. And it will have the important tactical effect of giving the private sector hope. That way, your first strike on their R-evolutionary infrastructure will catch them off guard and be more effective."

Mason also obviously hoped that a moratorium would force Tom to reflect upon and perhaps revise his policy. He would have shut down private-sector R-evolution anyway as part of an all-out, multi-front attack. Once all the scientific resources and information were in government hands and the White House was more or less in full control of America's version of R-evolution, Mason was likely guessing that Tom would reconsider all options. Due diligence.

"So why don't *you* roll up the private sector R-evolution. Mr. President? Right now. You have nothing to lose personally and you'd also have the advantage of surprise."

"Because it might not stick. It would lessen the chances that you will become president. My Republic successor would then certainly reverse my action." He glanced at Walker, including him in. "We've decided we want you, Tom. The next eight years will be crucial."

Tom had one last question. In the past month or so, he had stopped demanding that Mason reveal full details on the Genetically Improved American program. It had come as a gut decision, perhaps part of his gradual drift toward compromise but also on the advice of campaign advisers who warned him that Americans did not like national security secrets discussed publicly. But now he would like to know what he was getting into.

"Just how ugly is this GIA baby, Mr. President?" he asked sharply. "What are the numbers? How far have you gone in terms of manipulation?"

"You're not president yet, Tom." Mason replied evenly. "Besides, I don't think you should really want to know right now. That way, you can avoid pinning yourself down on future actions and you can walk into the White House with all your options open. You'll decide what to do when you see the whole picture."

"You're hoping I will change my mind." Tom stood up and thought for a moment. "I don't have to tell you this but I will say it anyway, given the circumstances. That is very unlikely to happen, Mr. President. Nigh impossible, in fact. Please understand that. I will make no commitments at all in return for your support or"—turning to Andy Walker—"for your withdrawal, Senator. In some ways, I don't think we should even be here. It is underhanded and even undemocratic."

Mason stood too, followed by Walker. "We have not asked nor do we expect quid pro quo for our support, Tom. And there has been nothing undemocratic in our decision to advise you at this time of our backing. Quite the opposite. Andy and I have made our own personal democratic choice and have explained to you that, in fact, you are the *only* acceptable choice available to us."

"We are acting in what we believe to be the best interests of the people," Walker said. "And, in my case, at least, my decision will cease to be a secret in only a day or two."

"I will keep my own decision private for now," said the President. "But I want you to feel free to announce my support for you from the moment we leave this room. If you do so, I will not deny it. As a politician, however, I would advise you to keep your powder dry and trust my own sense of timing. It's a purely tactical decision, not an effort to be underhanded. For my part, meanwhile, I will neither say nor do anything to deceive the American people about my feelings regarding unregulated free market manipulation of the human genome. People can tell I've never liked the smell of it. I have made this thinking clear to you and suggested a course of action."

"To me, right! But not to your own party's candidates. You certainly haven't suggested a lightning takeover of private sector R-evolutionary operations to the potential Republican nominees."

"No, I certainly have not. They worship at the feet of their benefactors on Wall Street. To reveal this possibility to them would tie any future government's hands in dealing with what I feel to be the single greatest threat posed by R-evolution. I will never lose a minute of sleep over putting the best interests of the country, our people, and indeed all of humankind before the partisan ambitions of a segment of the Republican Party." He held out his hand. "So, what do you say?"

Tom thought of Rachel and of Will's dying words and his responsibility to them. His hand gripped Mason's and then Walker's. "Done," he said.

61

New York
January 19, 2005

It was raining from grim low-slung clouds. A good day to sit by the fire and, in Sophia Parviati's case, to shed a few tears. She didn't weep often. It was largely self-indulgence, she believed. Once that was understood, however, the act was rather useful in placating despair. It also allowed Hank to offer comfort and they both derived benefit from that. He now stoked the flames in the fireplace while she dabbed at her eyes with a handkerchief.

In her other hand was a large envelope, the contents of which they were about to read for the last time. Sophia removed the papers inside. The top item was a short note written more than four decades ago by Dr. Sigurd Shivkovski to Dr. Anthony Arianna, Rachel Arianna's father, who, along with her mother and both William Jefferson's parents, had died in the same airplane disaster before the two children were fully grown.

Dated several months before Rachel and Tom were born, it said:

Dear Anthony:
   You and Mike should be proud. There can be no greater gift, I think, than the guarantee of true love in our lifetime. I believe your daughter and Mike's son will have more chance than most to find that gift. We will have to see. This is science, of course. The pheromones their respective genes express will make them mutually attractive and, at the very least, put them on the same wavelength, so to speak. She will respond to his and he to hers. How far this will determine their actions remains to be seen. It may go smoothly right from the start. Or there may be obstacles of various sorts that will make the case interesting. Personality will play a role, no doubt. As will their different control statuses. If current plans proceed, Rachel will be informed of her status, but Mike's boy Tom will not. Let's see where that takes them, and us.

Dr. Parviati set the letter aside and opened a battered folder underneath.

The flap read: Case Number: 0000013 Subject: Thomas Daluskov.

Inside were yellowing laboratory sheets and 27 numbered pages of scientific notes, all in the scrawl of Dr. Mikhail Daluskov. Affixed to them was a letter in the studied hand Mike used when he had something important he wished to convey to the woman he loved.

It was written two days after Tom was born.

My dearest Sophia:
What joy we share tonight!
I am awake beside you, savoring our miracle. You are asleep. Our baby is at your breast. Mother well, child healthy.
All done, except my confession.
Throughout all our efforts in vitro, a terrible question has dogged me. Why leave the greatest hope of our two lives entirely to chance? Why submit to the rolling of the dice in a game that's already fixed? Fixed by human limitations in favor of unhappiness and failure? We have seen the results, you and I. We know we cannot save our lovely son from the world outside. But it turns out that we can save him from some of the enemies that always lurk within us. This is because—and I must finally tell you now— Shivkovski and I have taken your work and on the springboard of your genius have made the quantum leap.
So I have succumbed both to my concerns and to temptation. I have altered the DNA within the gamete of our child. Do not worry, my love! Our methods are revolutionary. And they work! So well, in fact, that it is frightening!
I have applied only proven measures. Some enhancements for health and size, athleticism and a reasonable attempt to keep the plentiful "ugly" genes in the Daluskov family at bay. (Ha! So yes, I've aimed high!). Cognitive skills? Well, you will see! And we've coded for focus, perseverance and, most of all, clarity of mind. There are changes at sites that relate to emotional life and personality. Tom won't be part of the herd—neither a Soviet clone nor a glassy-eyed American consumer. More a free-ranging cowboy never afraid to be alone on the steppe. Altruistic but undeluded. A generous heart guided by a great bullshit detector.

Most other amendments are subtle but will be welcome additions to the gene pool.

Our son will be strong and willful with a keen sense of independence. He is our son, is he not? Sensation-seeking or risk-taking may be pronounced, along with a somewhat higher than normal tolerance for pain, and greater than usual comfort with danger and violence.

While these attributes can be immensely useful, difficulties may result. They also become less valuable with age. More important, I worry about the long-term cardiovascular effects. For that reason, we've coded for the chemical switch mechanism. It can be initiated at an early age to take the edge off the assertiveness if that interferes overly with social behavior and judgment. Several vectors should be injected before and after his 40th birthday. This will require planning. He cannot be aware of what has been happening. Some personality change will ensue, a moderation of temperament and attitudes but little that cannot be explained by advancing maturity and the ongoing instruction of life.

I have only a few minor concerns. To demonstrate in some small way my deep remorse for the suffering my own appetites have caused you, my love, I have tried to shape our son in a way that ensures he will have no taste for and little reaction to the ingestion of alcohol. The switching to be undertaken in his late third and early fourth decades may be tricky as a result. The switches will not turn him into a besotted regular of O'Reilly's but may reduce the induced neutrality of his reaction to drink. In short, he may come to enjoy a beer once in a while for more than just the taste. Alcohol may also in small ways inhibit the effectiveness and even the permanence of the switch to moderate aggression and risk-taking. (Strangely, I suspect that excessive anaerobic metabolism could also pose the same problem, but we can discuss the details and look together for possible fixes.)

No one must know what I have done for Thomas. Especially our beautiful son. And no one will. I have meticulously doctored, and double- and triple-doctored all records. All files except the one you hold now clearly show that Thomas was an in vitro child but the subject of no experimentation whatsoever. He is shown, in fact, as a control subject, a case with unaltered DNA, against whom the data of children whose genetic code has been modified can be compared. We can't be too careful. You never know when

*the next generation of Brown Shirts or Red Guards will march
around the corner.*

*I feel in perfect harmony with Nature, if the creative and
adventurous impulses of the human spirit are to be considered
part of its essence. And I feel blessed that our son is a product of
both our intelligence and our love. Because it was your intuition
and your hard work and your deep and courageous dedication that
unveiled the great secrets of the so-called junk sequences of DNA.
You saw that far from being useless, the junk genes were in many
ways calling the shots! Without your unwillingness to baah with
the rest of the scientific sheep, Shivkovski and I would be back at
the starting line. Abandon your fear and your tendency towards
shame! Be proud, my darling! You are a giant on whose shoulders
a new and better version of mankind will one day stand!*

*Nonetheless, I hereby swear on my life that I will use none of
your other eggs in a similar way again (at least not without your
full and express approval).*

*Our species has no choice but to better itself on its own. What
we've wrought with what Nature has given us — or perhaps what
Nature has condemned us to do and be — is simply not good
enough.*

This is our son.
Let's hope we have made him well.
We will adore him either way.

All my love,
Your Mikhail

Sophia handed the envelope and papers to Hank, who
squatted as he put them in the fire. "I have deceived him all of his
life," she said. "And now, I commit these final betrayals."

Rachel's injection of the final switching vector, achieved by
drugging Tom in a Washington hotel room, had only completed
the job that Dr. Sophia Parviati had begun herself several years
before. Believing no better chance was likely to present itself, she
had injected the penultimate switching vector into her son's IV as
he recovered in hospital from the Monkey House knockout gas.

This biochemical operation would activate genes that would,
in effect, even out Tom's personality through neurotransmitter
levels and thus reduce the stress on his cardiovascular system.
Tom had been in full battle mode for far too long. It was a

dangerous state, and one with which she was overly familiar from two generations of male Daluskovs. The genetic switch worked only gradually, of course, and had not stopped her son from leading the charge at the Oneida Foundation.

"Each time I lied to him outright," she said now, "it broke my heart."

"You've protected him, my darling," Hank said, crouching by the fire. "We protect the ones we love. You've given him the priceless gift of belonging. He has had his share of difficulties — witnessing his father's suicide for one — but neither that nor Mikhail's work can change the fact that he is as good a man as you could have asked for." Hank stood and smiled at his wife. "The country cannot do better, in my opinion."

"And Eva? Does she not deserve to know?" She straightened a stray strand of gray hair and wiped again at a tear. "I must deceive my grandchild as well? I don't know if I can bear it."

Neither spoke for a moment before Sophia Parviati said: "Poor Rachel. She hated giving Tom that last injection, knowing how the two of them had been manipulated. Tortured, really."

"Mike and Rachel's mom and dad didn't plan it that way. They imagined that their two children would hit puberty, respond to each other's pheromones, and fall promptly and irrevocably in love. Everyone, including the benevolent scheming parents, would live happily ever afterwards."

Hank flipped the half-burnt envelope with a poker. It flared once more. "Rachel's dad thought he had the right measure. He had done so much work for the fragrance industry on pheromone classification and genotypes, testing for strength of effect."

"Tom was much too susceptible."

"And Rachel too darn smart and stubborn." He paused. "Yes, I suppose 'tortured' does apply. But Rachel would not have injected Tom if she didn't believe it was for his own good."

"That's true but let's be honest. How can we predict the behavioral results of the final two adjustments? And those potential glitches with the on and off switching that his father feared. Mikhail and I never found the fix for that. Then my depression after the suicide. I simply have never been able to return to that kind of work again."

"The switching will protect Tom's health, a prophylactic."

"With what other effects? This we do not know."

Hank sipped his whiskey, so she continued: "I've noticed

changes, a slow general drift since the first injection. Tom's been more — compliant, perhaps. He's lost that look!"

"*That look*, as you put it, used to scare the devil out of you!" Hank laughed gently. "We're talking maturity. The final injection followed the Oneida incident. A trauma like that can change the way we look at life forever." Hank rattled ice cubes around in his empty glass. "Besides, there's no denying that the ages of man often mirror the neurochemical changes we undergo as we grow older."

"And politics? I never would have dreamed it! The last time he was here, I could see his positions already beginning to shift. Even on this R-evolution." Her eyes widened, and she shook her head, as if she needed to clear her mind. "My goodness, my son is the next president of the United States!"

"My condolences, ma'am," Hank said with a teasing grin. "He's shifting because he's thinking. He's a thinking man and the challenges are complex. No American expects he will do everything exactly as he promised." Hank wandered to the window. "He's what's needed. A perfect fit for a crucial time." He turned his back on the gloomy rainclouds and the Park. "Even the fact that he is a Founder, without knowing, is an almost incalculable asset under the circumstances. And an exquisite irony, as all will eventually appreciate."

"You believe it will come out?"

"Oh, it has to eventually! It's small miracle that it hasn't already. All anyone needed to do was a DNA test! But everyone loved Mike's planted control group story. And Tom's stand against his JunkGen brother Will. Folks wanted their hero to be a Natural Born American. Anyway, the outing, as long as it's not too soon, will prove a good thing. People will say, 'Guess what? Our great president — the man who has led us so brilliantly through the great tests of this new age — has a few touched-up genes.'"

"You are getting ahead of yourself, Hank. And wishing things upon my son I'd rather he avoid."

"None of us can avoid living with what we are."

Hank checked his watch. Time for them to sleep. He moved towards his wife and offered her his arm. She took it, holding tight, and slowly lifted herself to her feet.

"Yes," she said, "tomorrow is a big day."

62

Washington, D.C.
January 20, 2005

Tom kept it short and crisp. He had reworked the speech himself, rejecting a lot of his wordsmiths' nicest turns. Early drafts had evoked high urgency and stark choices. They cut too near the truth. Things were worse than the people knew and more complicated than they seemed. Decisions were harder to make once you saw the whole picture and had the power, the duty and the final say.

And so he was giving himself some room. Yes, he declared as he opened his inaugural address, he was a one hundred per cent Natural Born American. But he was also the President of one hundred per cent of the people, natural born or not. Yes. R-evolution would stop, and the Genetically Improved American program too. But the term "ban" had been replaced by "moratorium" in the campaign's last weeks.

"Give yourself time," John Mason kept advising. "Think before you act." And there was plenty to think about. The moles, for instance. Rogue Chinese intelligence operatives had planted them more than 20 years ago all over the United States. Bill Lee's handiwork. "Human time bombs" of every race and ethnicity. Outwardly normal folks who didn't even know they were JunkGen. A single injection or even a pill dropped into their pop at a baseball game would switch on hidden "attributes."

What these were, no one knew. Chances were good, however, that they fit the actions required by asymmetrical warfare, from harassment sabotage to wholesale destruction. The degree of the threat would vary with the mole's current circumstances. A young technician in a key post at the CIA? An engineer at a nuclear installation? Or at one of the depots for our vast stores of biological and chemical weapons?

At the White House briefing, Tom's first thought had been: do we have some of our own? Self-defense, which he had used to such great effect before the Supreme Court, could be brought to bear on both sides of the R-evolution argument. You couldn't nuke Beijing each time the lights went out or the phones went dead, but your own moles could tamper with their flood dams.

Then there was the debate over demands for a DNA ID system, with its compulsory tests and cards for every single citizen and resident. Conservatives, net of libertarians, were adamantly in favor. So were the Chief of Staff and Defense. Tom would have gone for it once. The price of freedom. Now, surprising even himself, he was no longer so sure.

He was no longer certain about a lot of things. Partly John Mason's doing. Mason had played him. He'd known Tom's positions must soften once he knew all the facts. Literally looked Life, as it had become, in the face. Now Tom had seen thousands of the GIAs, from the babies in the incubators at barracks for rapid-maturation infants, to young men and women ready to go. Teens, bright-eyed and beautiful. They had stood before him in the flesh, as eager and happy as any natural American kid and, reputedly, more focused and able. What did you do with them?

Tom was intrigued but not seduced. Let's see the screw-ups, he told his hand-picked executive-branch special teams, who were purloined not only from the FBI, the CIA, and the whole alphabet of military and government intelligence, but spiked with academics, hard-ass NYPD cops, take-no-prisoners journalists, and every other savvy shit-disturbing element Tom's trusted advisors could recruit. Find the GIA graveyards, they were told. The ovens. His own science team, with dependable Lab-Rat skeptics on board, warned of problems. GIA psychology, for example. GIAs could be smiley-faced and have three good tricks each but also harbor Nazi predilections or other scary monsters deep in their psychic basements. The program's rapid maturation mechanism was in early beta stage. These kids might burn brilliantly for a time then quickly go out. Or worse, have a glitch at some point and suddenly veer off in new directions, unguided missiles with uncertain payloads and unknown destinations.

Still, evolution of the old fashioned variety had often proceeded through mistakes that turned out in the long run not to be mistakes at all.

His scientists were exploring synergies between Shivkovski's theories and methodologies and the U.S. government's, along with the bits US intelligence had been able to steal from the Chinese.

Shivkovski! Not dead yet, unfortunately, and still at work in his "detention quarters," supposedly on cancer research. He had the temerity to get a letter to Tom. Mind gaming, as usual. "Tom, please know that I forgive you. You could not have known that your years of bullying would push poor Leon so far. It is simply part of who you are, innately, and, in other circumstances and with other people, perhaps one of your good or at least useful attributes. And look at you now! You have become our President!"

At one time Tom would have blown a gasket. But he was more open these days to—what? Other people? Other ideas? The answer seemed to be, just about everything. When he thought about it, he had to accept that he had indeed given Leon a very hard ride over the years—and that a lot of that riding had come to him naturally. He had always been eager to punish Leon—and he had *enjoyed* inflicting the pain. If he had laid off at some point or walked away more often, Leon, problem though he already was, might not have gone over the edge.

As he sometimes did these days, Tom felt the soft swelling of an unfamiliar ache begin deep in his chest as he began the last few minutes of his inaugural speech. It seemed the mark of a new way of feeling and of being. Anxiety, he reckoned—what Leon's tortured homicide puppet had called "the Big A." He was putting on a little weight, too. Getting old. Feeling the stress of the new job. The new world.

Not that these changes were complete yet or carved in stone. His stepfather claimed Tom had slipped into regression a couple of times while the two had been talking policy and enjoying their single malt on recent evenings. Scotch was a taste Tom had suddenly acquired after a lifetime of an occasional buzzless two beers during Rangers' games. "Maybe you should go back to Bud, my boy," Hank had said, watching him closely. But it could not be the alcohol because he also often felt the flush of his in-your-face old self during late night weightlifting. Tom would have preferred a run or some sparring but the anaerobic workouts often had to do (for security reasons) when he needed to blow off steam.

"The harder, meaner me wasn't all bad," he told Hank. "How the hell do you think we got the presidency in the first place?" The options that occurred to him on these occasions were indeed out there but he believed they deserved consideration even though—*and perhaps because*—his best-and-brightest transition team was unlikely to ever raise them.

"Why not a first strike?" Tom had said one evening as Hank and he sipped Glennfiddich. "Why not take out every other R-evolutionary program in one devastating series of surprise surgical tactical nuclear attacks?" Half amused, he'd dialed back a bit as he watched Hank's eyes grow big. Okay, they'd forget Russia (whose program sucked anyway and could still hit back hard.) And India (whose program of genetically reinforcing the caste system was pitiably self-destructive). But China posed a real threat, even though the huge JG operation in the West had become a colossal headache. While rivals and enemies gloated over America's stumbling start in the R-evolution race, Tom had said, they had foolishly forgotten its overwhelming (and, in fact, grossly underestimated) military superiority. "We know exactly where China's R-evolutionary plant, infrastructure and assets are. And believe me, Hank, we can reduce the whole shebang to a crisp tomorrow if I give the word."

"You're channeling Mad Mike," Hank had said, "—and Shivkovski." But Tom was back in the zone for the moment, body still, mind whirling. The PRC would be looking us in the eye one instant and stunned, shattered and flat on its back the next. Would it get up off the mat? You had to wonder. No opponent could hope to win a full nuclear exchange with the United States and, while it would have been deprived of its R-evolutionary capacity, China would still have everything else to lose. Washington could pitch its action as tragic but necessary, aimed not at any individual country or people but at removing an existential threat to all humankind. Tom might propose an international treaty limit or ban on R-evolution, with United Nations policing (backed by America's big nuclear stick). This would be hypocrisy, of course, since Tom would have bought time through nuclear pre-emption of the foreign threat to deal with R-evolution at home in his own way and to America's advantage. But big power hypocrisy well within historical norms.

Tom also guessed that a lot of Chinese, including much of the country's leadership, were likely not enamoured of R-evolution. They'd recognize the conundrum at its core. From the farthest valleys of Papua New Guinea to the penthouses of the Upper East Side, all of the religions (including China's), all philosophies large and small (including Confucianism, Marxism-Leninism and Maoism), all of the world's arts and cultures (including those of the oldest still up-and-running major civilization), and all the different ways the Earth's people chose to live and to eat, make music and love, raise a child and bury their dead were the end product—the *expressions*—of one thing: human nature. Alter human nature, destroy its great immutable wholeness and consistency, create first a hundred, then thousands, and eventually millions of new and different versions, and all of this would first become irrelevant, then extinct, then finally forgotten—including simply what it meant to feel, act and be Chinese.

Tom had brought the first strike option up only one other time. (He'd not yet told Hank that he sometimes visualized a first strike with the mnemonic help of a provisional target map of PRC JunkGen facilities drawn up by President Mason's EAF and the transition look he had also been given of the high-altitude video of tests of secret scale-able new one- to ten-kilometer kill rad us, low-radiation tactical nukes.) Hank was sipping his whiskey solo while Tom used some free weights at his New York apartment. "Stop hallucinating," his stepfather had said, seeming better prepared for the topic on this occasion. "You know darned well that the PLA would prefer a world in cinders to letting a first strike pass unanswered."

Hank had still seemed a little jumpy a couple of days later but Tom had put the idea aside for now. And that was where he, the country and the world stood on inauguration day—rocks and hard places no matter which way you turned. To head off the catastrophe of countless new humanoid lifeforms, you had to risk the blowback likely from stubborn version 1.0.

In fact, getting new Junk Generations up and running safely on the planet while version 1.0 was still hanging around could prove problematic. Talk about survival of the fittest! Shivkovski's sweet brainy dead ends for example would quite likely have been stalked, chased down, corralled, concentrated, cleansed or exterminated or eaten alive in some other new or time-tested way eventually, since the current reigning apex predator had proven itself over the millennia to be both ill-disposed to and murderously efficient in removing any threats to its existence, whether real, imagined, or cleverly concocted. Designing JG models that might survive alongside the premier edition of humankind would be a R-evolutionary engineering nightmare. Too kind or civilized, for example, would be risky since v 1.0 was often fearful and paranoid and saw offence as the best defense (not to mention weakness sometimes as an invitation.) It was hard to accommodate survival and problem-solving skills, a killer touch and a winning streak that all went back several million years.

Build too aggressive on the other hand and your JG products would end up the panting victors in a wasteland (although to do so they would probably need to be fitted out with some tactical nukes and/or equivalents of their own.) Finally, if you tried too hard to match the design that evolution had turned out, you'd end up with a version 1.1 or 1.2 and what, really, would be the point of that, given all the work and trouble?

It made Tom wish again that that everyone had left well enough alone. Just continued to work with what we had. After all, version 1.0 societies and nations and even international communities had whipped themselves into decent and, in some cases, rather admirable shape in many parts of the world (although what was "decent" and "admirable" were subjective and often disputed concepts even before R-evolution and would possibly soon be defunct.)

The problem was, of course, that things had already gone too far.

Yes, Tom had lots to think about, including family now, which was also something new. Eva was demanding full DNA sequencing for their firstborn to detect potential long-term health risks. Tom figured that the optics would be bad, given the current court injunction against involuntary DNA testing. But he adored his darling Sophia and so maybe they would go ahead and see what exactly was cooking in the little angel's chromosomes.

This was all back story for now, of course, and none of it part of his inaugural address, which was going very well, Tom thought, despite the subtle shifts in political direction.

It helped that he had a cheering section of invited friends to cue the applause. Young all-seeing Carlos Chavez was the most rambunctious, although Billy Franklin and his WHUPASS co-manager and fiancée Mary weren't far behind. Ray Franklin was here, of course, as well as Jason and Chelsea Hunter. Father Dwight sat calmly beside them, his dementia in regression due to an experimental genetic treatment spun off from the discoveries achieved through Shivkovski's malevolent methods at Oneida. Francis Boyd, no longer the "mentally challenged" giant he had quite naturally been born to be, looked on with a serious smile, although he had told Tom he found his new, unnaturally provided cognitive skills to be unaccompanied by a corresponding enhancement of enjoyment in life. Towering Jeremy Nelson, soon to be a chef in training in the White House kitchen and often rising today to join the applause, had also benefitted from the great scientific leaps forward at Oneida. Tom had tried repeatedly to find the man who had saved his life at Manny's Cafe's with the blow of a 40-ounce beer bottle across a gunman's wrist but it was Shivkovski who had tracked Nelson down and devised a somatic gene cure for his addictions. Newly re-elected Allen Rubenstein represented Tom's former New York County DA colleagues. Tom's long-ago fling, Dr. Gail Haggerty, was there on behalf of the New York ME. Carrie Hemmingford proudly waved a tiny flag for America and the Utopia B & B.

There was no one to stand for the long dead Billy Stricks. He was famous, however, and, thanks to frequent allusions to them in Tom's election campaign speeches, the words on his tombstone were now widely known.

Tom met the sad loving eyes of his mother now as he turned from the crowd before him back to Eva. His wife stepped forward with a smile and handed him their daughter. The touch and feel of the small yielding body and the tiny hand that gripped his neck wiped the Big A away. When he turned back again with little Sophia in his arms, a great throaty roar rose from the crowd. Old brain stuff. She was cute and curly headed and born in the USA. But today it was being a Natural that made her a hero.

It was the first time, Tom believed, that a baby had played a part in the inauguration of an American president. He'd been foolish to fear that it would be anything less than a triumph.

For now, at least, President Thomas Daluskov could do what he liked.

The people needed him and trusted him and wanted him to lead the way.

Author's Note

The author has only a layman's imperfect grasp of genetics. Despite efforts to keep things at least a little bit real, *Junk Generation* is riddled with simplifications, exaggerations (and, perhaps, howling errors.) All of which may make a scientist's hair stand on end or even fall out. Corrections are welcome, apologies offered. But this is not a textbook. It is a "what-if" entertainment originally aimed at the average 14-year-old (the age of my wickedly bright son and sounding board Dylan at the time of its conception.) Where necessary, current scientific beliefs have been stretched or overturned to meet the demands of speculative fiction. New discoveries are presented fictionally as secret Shivkovski findings (e.g., the work of Associate Professor of Surgery Hansell Stedman on a genetic mutation that may be part of the "missing link" (p. 59). The fact remains, however, that genetic science is riding off at blinding speed in all directions and may one day pitch us over a cliff. So, along with a few smiles (or grimaces) at its adolescent concoctions (e.g., Wally's severed head over Central Park), the book aims to provoke some thought on a question that humankind will almost certainly have to answer in the foreseeable future (unless we find another clever way to end our history first).

Hedging aside, the author did read widely before and during the writing. The following fine books in particular have much to offer lay readers who want to delve more deeply and authoritatively into a fascinating subject.

Richard Vokey (2011)

The Selfish Gene
by Richard Dawkins

The Blank Slate: The Modern Denial of Human Nature
by Steven Pinker

Genome: The Autobiography of a Species in 23 Chapters
by Matt Ridley (cited on Page 17)

On Deep History and the Brain
By Daniel Lord Smail

DNA: The Secret of Life
By James D. Watson
(*Co-discoverer of DNA*)

www.ingramcontent.com/pod-product-compliance
Lightning Source LLC
Chambersburg PA
CBHW020833030726
47496CB00001B/219